LET THERE BE
VVAR

BOOK 1: IN THE BEGINNING

SAMANTHA EKLUND

LET THERE BE
WAR

BOOK 1: IN THE BEGINNING

SAMANTHA EKLUND

GOLDEN MASQUERADE BOOKS

Know thy enemy.

PROLOGUE

The ram's head plunged into the cold stream with a splash, sinking several feet before floating back to the surface. As it bobbed along the water, a trail of crimson followed. The foul substance flowed out from where the head had been severed from the body, coloring the river red as it traveled downstream. It soon came to a thundering waterfall and plummeted downward with the raging water.

On the bank, a single figure stood and watched the head disappear over the precipice. He smiled to himself grimly, pleased that the imbeciles who worked for him had actually carried out his wishes. Now that it was all in motion, it was time to solidify things. As he turned to go, he saw a foe standing across the stream. He hissed lowly, angered by the presence. Although unsurprised that his plan had been discovered, it was too late to stop it. Gloatingly, he smirked at his enemy.

"You're too late. These pathetic sheep are going to fall; again."

"The Good Shepherd knows your will."

"*The good shepherd,*" he scoffed. "The very one that wiped them from the earth not so long ago? They've turned from him again; I'm doing him a favor. For what other reason hasn't he stopped me? I think your shepherd has lost interest in these pitiful creatures."

"You insult them, yet I know your motivation stems from jealousy."

The exquisite man glowered in silence, clenching his jaw.

"Cease your plot, fallen one. This is your only warning."

"Then be gone; your pleas are falling on deaf ears."

Suddenly alone again, the man glanced around anxiously. Looking back at the blood tainting the stream, he allowed himself a small smile. Much had been tried before, but nothing like this. This time, the war would be won.

CHAPTER ONE

"Only three hours to go!" I cheered.

"I know!" Melanie squealed back at me, jumping up and down excitedly.

I laughed as I applied another layer of mascara, using my reflection in the enormous wall mirror. "Before we head out, we should post a picture and show that loser ex-boyfriend of yours what he's missing out on," I laughed.

"Oh, definitely!" my best friend replied. "I hope that scumbag has the worst New Year's Eve ever. I heard that he's going to Vicki's tonight."

"Lame!" I proclaimed, throwing down my mascara bottle and picking up my phone. "Come here," I called. "Let's take this picture!"

Melanie hurried over to me, clinking over the tile floor in her stilettos. "Smile!" she ordered as she threw her arms around me and tickled me.

I laughed as I held my phone at arm's length, making both goofy and alluring faces as my camera clicked away. Moments later, we scrolled through the pictures and searched for the best one.

"That one!" Melanie insisted, pointing to one that illuminated her silky black hair gloriously.

"Of course," I laughed, also noticing that my bright blue eyes looked even bluer than normal. Blue eyes were envied by so many people, but I never liked having them. When I bothered wearing eyeliner I felt like my eyes were so light that there was no barrier between me and others, as if they could see into my soul. It was a stupid feeling, but one of my hundreds of insecurities.

"Are you complaining about your eyes again?"

I looked up from my phone, not realizing how long I had been staring at the picture. "Yeah, my bad," I chuckled. "You know every single one of my lovely insecurities."

"Know them and think they're all absurd. You are absolutely gorgeous, so I don't want to hear about any of your imagined flaws. I would kill for your eyes and olive skin! Although, dying your hair dark red is a bit out there," she laughed, pulling up a chunk of my curled hair. "But look at you in those leather leggings, you hot lady! Now, come on, let's get down to the party! I bet there are tons of guys down there dying to make your night," she said with a wink.

"Ha!" I objected, dashing for my clutch purse as she dragged me out the door.

We hurriedly made our way to the New Year's Eve bash that was being held in the hotel. It was the hottest place to be this year, flaunting quite a VIP guest list. Mel had insisted that we go, even though I didn't really want to. My mother was a top executive at one of New York's fashion magazines, so she was easily able to get us tickets. I unconsciously sighed as I realized I would probably have to see her at the party.

"Here we are!" Melanie squawked as our elevator stopped. "Remember to be social!" she whispered to me as we emerged and stepped into the party.

A short time later, I was down a few drinks and having a miserable time. Mel had run off to the dance floor with a couple guys, but I had chosen to stay at the bar. I had thought it would be easy to spot her shimmering gold mini skirt, but apparently that was a popular choice this year.

My head was starting to hurt from all the sparkling in the room. I usually tried to be fashionable for Melanie and my mom, but it just wasn't me. As I looked down insecurely at the ridiculous leather pants that I was wearing, someone stepped in front of my light. I looked up, surprised to see my mother standing there.

"Hello Adeline," she swooned.

I grimaced as she called me by my middle name, but was happy that she hadn't used my first name.

"You look marvelous darling," she praised, gracefully wrapping me in an elaborate hug.

I rolled my eyes as I endured the embrace, then tried to smile as she pulled away.

"Hey," I replied, trying to ignore the twenty-something-year-old guys that stood at her side. Turning my attention to her wasn't much better, as she was dressed like a teenager. Although she easily pulled off the look, it was absurd to me. Wasn't she fifty-something?

"How are you enjoying the party?" she asked, eyeing me with disapproval.

"Just fine," I replied, scowling as I saw her look. "What's wrong with you?"

"Why aren't you dancing? You look like a dream; go find someone to dance with."

I looked at the dance floor and saw the mass of moving people, all sweaty and rubbing against each other. A deep frown covered my face without me realizing it, making my mother look around in alarm.

"Stop it," she hissed, stepping closer to me and gently

placing her hand on my arm. Quietly so that only I could hear, she asked, "Why don't you ever fit in? You're just like your deadbeat father."

"He's not a deadbeat!" I disputed, ripping my arm away. Perhaps I'd had too many drinks, but I didn't care if I caused a scene. "Maybe you're the deadbeat!" I yelled, drawing many looks our way. "Look at you; you look ridiculous! You think you have friends here, but they're all fake!"

My poor mother looked as though she was going to die of embarrassment. With as much dignity as she could, she put her nose in the air, twirled on her heel, and stormed away from me with her guys following. I silently watched her leave, wondering if I should go try to apologize. Deciding against it, I turned back to the bar.

"Another martini please," I murmured.

"Are you sure?"

I looked up at the bartender. Either I hadn't noticed him earlier or he had just started, but wow was he a sight. Tall, dark, and definitely handsome.

"I uh…" I stammered.

He smiled charmingly at me as he said, "I noticed you had a slight argument with that woman a moment ago. Perhaps you would like something a bit stronger than a martini?"

"Like what?" I laughed skeptically.

"Have you ever had fireball?"

"No," I admitted. "I'm not sure I could handle it."

"I'm sure you can," he grinned with a wink.

As he turned to grab a glass, my jaw dropped open and I spun towards the dance floor. I had to find Mel! I dashed to the mass of moving people, grimacing as I shoved my way through the crowd. Finding her was next to impossible, and I ended up back at the bar a few moments later, defeated.

"Were you trying to run away?" the bartender joked. "If so, you didn't do a very good job."

"Ha," I laughed nervously. "No, I was trying to find my friend. She's dancing I think, but I couldn't find her."

"She'll come find you before midnight, right?"

"I hope so," I replied, truly hoping she wouldn't run off with some stranger.

"In the meantime," he grinned, sliding a shot glass towards me. "Fireballs away."

I looked at the glass, then back up at him. He was looking at me expectantly, with those big dark eyes of his. His dangerous lips were pulled back into a half grin, revealing glimmering white teeth and sharp canines. As I stared in wonder at him, he leaned down onto the bar, resting on his forearms. Bulging biceps flexed as he did so, accentuated by his tight black shirt.

"I'm sorry, what?" I asked, shaking my head to clear it. Was this stranger putting a spell on me or what? *Get yourself together!* I ordered myself in my thoughts.

"You were about to have the drink that I made for you," he said smoothly. "Here, I'll have one first," he offered, picking up the glass. He put it to his mouth and tipped his head back, pouring the burning liquid down his throat. I marveled as he did so, for he didn't slam it down like so many people did. He simply poured it down his throat and let the liquid burn as it slowly slid down. I wasn't positive, but he seemed to enjoy it.

"Okay," I said quietly, starting to understand him. As

charming as he was, he was a weirdo just like everyone else here. "Actually," I said sweetly, picking up my coat off the bar. "I'm going to go dance; I'll catch you later."

"Enjoy your New Year's!" he called as I walked away, seeming to be upset that I had left him.

"Sorry buddy, that's life," I muttered to myself. Hopefully I would be able to find Mel, since I had just given up my comfortable spot at the bar.

I searched for a while, finally finding her around 11:48.

"There you are!" I exclaimed when I found her lounging with a guy's arm around her shoulder.

"Addie! My bestie!" she bellowed when she saw me. "Oh I missed you!" She jumped up and threw her arms around me, smelling heavily of alcohol. I wondered how many drinks she'd had. "I saw your mom. She said you were at the bar. I tried to find you but you weren't there anymore. I even went back to our room to look for you, but you weren't there. Then I came back," she paused to hiccup, "and met Ivan. Say hi Ivan!"

She turned to the guy sitting on the plush couch. "'Sup," he said coolly.

I felt my jaw clench, for I was hardly in the mood to watch my best friend hook up with yet another scumbag who was just going to use her.

"Hey let's go outside and get some air," I suggested. "We can see the ball drop better from out there."

"Yeah!" Mel agreed. "Come on Ivan!"

"Nah, I have to get back. See you around Molly."

I glared at him for calling Mel by the wrong name, wanting to punch his lights out. Ignoring me, he then stood and walked across the way, where I saw him sit down with a girl. She immediately pulled him close and kissed him, making me realize it was probably his girlfriend. I happily took my friend outside, glad to have gotten her away from that loser.

We walked outside into the snowy weather, which seemed to sober Mel up a little.

"Wow!" she blurted as we eyed Times Square. "It's magnificent out here!"

"It sure is," I agreed, also marveling at the sights. There were people absolutely everywhere, there was music blasting, and lights dancing across all the jumbo screens in the street. I stared open-mouthed at all the sights, thrilled to have finally made it here.

"As much as you hate your mom, you have to thank her for getting us tickets to the party and putting us up in that hotel," Mel said.

"Absolutely," I agreed, laughing with sudden giddiness. After all these years of dreaming, here I was in New York for New Year's Eve!

We walked, or rather nudged, our way through the crowds, collecting party hats and goofy glasses along the way. By the time we had worked our way to the front of the fenced-off area, our hands were full of cheap memorabilia. We stopped at the metal barriers, standing in the street. High above us, we saw the ball waiting to slide down the building and light up at exactly midnight. I looked at Mel, who was making eyes with one of the armed guards watching the streets.

"Stop it," I said nudging her uncomfortably.

"What? It's New Year's Eve!" she laughed merrily. "Fine, then you hold me," she giggled, throwing her arms around my neck. I laughed merrily too, making sure to actually hold onto her since she was drunk.

She turned and stood beside me, keeping her arm around my shoulder. For a few moments we stood in silence, both staring up at the sky. Although we were looking at the ball, we were both reflecting on our past year.

"What's your resolution for this year?" Mel asked seriously, resting her head on my shoulder.

"I'm not sure yet."

"Well you only have... three minutes," she chuckled, looking at her diamond-studded watch.

"What's yours?" I asked her.

"Nothing."

"It can't be nothing," I objected, looking at her. "What is it?"

"Don't laugh at me."

"I would never laugh at you Mel."

"I want to find the one. Mr. Right."

"Uhm... that's not really a resolution."

"I told you not to laugh at me!"

"I'm not laughing at you! I'm just saying it's not something you can control. Resolutions are supposed to be changes you make."

"Well maybe I will change to find him. Maybe I'll party less. I've never found a keeper at a party."

I blinked quickly a few times, stunned by her words. My heart soared with joy for her, and I suddenly hugged her tightly. "I would love to see you do that."

"Ohhh, hello," she swooned in reply, nodding at someone to our right. "Maybe he's Mr. Right. I'd definitely take his application, if you know what I mean."

"Shush," I chuckled as I looked over at the person. To my dismay, it was the bartender. I looked away as quickly as I could, but apparently he had already spotted me.

"Hey!" he called as he waved and walked over to us. "What are the odds we'd meet up again?"

"You know him?" Mel mused as she pinched my arm and stood up straight.

"He's a weirdo," I whispered, batting her arm down as she raised it.

She just lifted the other arm, offering her hand to him. "Hello, I am her best friend, Melanie. You can call me Mel."

"Pleasure to meet you Mel," he said, flashing a charming smile at her.

I spotted those sharp canines again, making my heart skip a beat. As strange as he seemed, he also seemed mysterious and maybe dangerous. What girl could turn away from a man like that?

"And I'm sorry," he said, directing his piercing eyes at my vulnerable ones. "I didn't catch your name."

"I didn't give it," I replied coldly.

"You can call her Deli!" Mel laughed out loud.

Unable to help myself, I laughed too, failing to find her stupid nickname for me anything but funny. I guess it was my fault, since I didn't let her call me by my first name, and I didn't like my middle name, or its typical shortened version of Adele.

In response to Nick's confused look, Mel laughed, "Did I mention that I'm nicer than her?"

"I'm sure," the man laughed. "Well if you care, my name is Nick."

"It's nice to meet you Nick," Mel smiled sweetly.

Suddenly everyone started cheering. The three of us looked up at the jumbo screen, seeing that the minute countdown had begun.

"This is it!" Mel cheered, gripping my arms and hopping up and down.

"I know!" I squealed in reply, also jumping up and down. For years I had dreamed of coming to New York for New Year's Eve, and this year it had finally happened. "I can't believe I'm here," I said, gazing up at all the wonders before me.

Nick looked sideways at me, studying my face. Letting my guard down a little, I smiled at him.

"How about a kiss at midnight?" he asked, totally catching me off guard.

"What?" I scoffed. "A striking bartender like you has nobody else to kiss on New Year's Eve?"

"There might be a few candidates, sure; but I found the one I want to share the moment with."

I smiled in disbelief and looked away as my cheeks flushed red. A moment later I looked back up at Mel, then Nick. "How about right after? I want to share the moment with my best friend."

"Of course," he nodded with gleaming eyes.

We all three turned towards the ball. In that moment, I was on top of the world. To my left was my absolute best friend in the entire world, and on the right was a gorgeous stranger who was waiting for a kiss from me. Around me were thousands of happy people, and we were all gathered in Times Square for the same reason: to ring in a new year. As the clock counted down and the massive metal ball descended down the building, we all started counting out loud.

"Ten! Nine! Eight! Seven! Six! Five! Four!" My heart was pounding. The ball was about to light up! "Three! Two! One!"

Suddenly, everything went black.

CHAPTER TWO

Thousands of people began to yell, "Happy New Year!" but abruptly stopped short as all the lights went out. We barely had time to react before a horrendous screech filled the air. Below us, the ground suddenly started to rumble. We cowered down as screams erupted in the pitch black, echoing across the streets.

"Mel!" I hollered, making sure she was there.

"Yeah!"

"Are you okay?"

"I'm fine," she said quickly. "Are you?"

"Yeah, I'm all right."

"Ladies!" Nick called as I felt a strong hand gripping my arm. "Are you both okay?"

"We're fine," Mel replied in a shaky voice. "What happened?"

"No idea," he said.

"All the people probably blew the grid," a voice nearby said.

I felt Nick's hand pull me closer, and knew he did the same to Mel as I felt myself bump into her. I could sense that he was standing right in front of us. He leaned forward so that he was between both of our ears and whispered a warning. "Whatever the reason, people are going to panic if it doesn't come back on soon. We need to get out of the street."

"My phone won't work," someone nearby said.

Murmurs went throughout the crowd, and I heard a lot of movement. Everyone was checking their phones.

"Mine won't work either," someone else said.

"Neither will mine."

"What is going on?" a shrill voice screeched.

Hearing the panic in that person's voice suddenly set everyone on edge. I looked around in the darkness, noticing that not only was electricity off, but so were all phone and camera lights. No car headlights could be seen either. Recalling that our hotel had rustic braziers out front of it, I turned to what I thought was that direction. To my horror, I couldn't see any firelight. A hardcore chill ran down my spine as I realized all light sources had been extinguished. What on earth could do that?

"We need to move," I urgently whispered in a trembling voice.

I guess I said it too loudly though, because suddenly the person beside us scrambled to get away. He viciously fought past us, then it sounded like he climbed over the metal barrier. We heard running footsteps, then a dull thump and a cry.

"Watch it!" someone shouted.

There was a brief scuffle, then more commotion. Among the sounds, I swear I heard… growling? Then suddenly, two gunshots rang out. Several people screamed bloody murder, then all hell broke loose. People began panicking and running in every direction, having no clue where they were going. I felt Nick pull Mel and me down the street. Behind us, I heard more gunfire break out. As we ran, I felt something light hit my face. I viciously clawed at it, realizing that it probably meant me no harm.

It disintegrated easily under my touch and seemed to be falling from the sky. Had a volcano erupted or something?

Nick was pulling us to the right. Did he know where he was going? I put my hands out in front of me, sensing that we were close to something. I was correct; my hands soon came in contact with a stone wall.

"I'm trying to find a door to get us inside," he whispered harshly. "Hold on to me; do NOT let go of me. Understand?"

"Yes," we both replied instantly, nodding our heads vehemently even though nobody could see us.

We both clutched onto the back of his jacket with one hand, holding onto each other with the other. I could hear Mel crying, trying to stifle her tears.

"It's okay Mel," I assured her, also trying not to cry. "We'll be all right."

"Okay," she agreed, and from knowing her so well I knew that she was nodding again.

"You're allowed to be scared," I added as hot tears streamed down my face. "It's a freaky situation."

"Are you scared?"

"Of course I am!" I nervously laughed.

"You don't show it very well."

"I'm making an effort not to."

"Okay," she said again. I heard her sniffle one last time and wipe her tears on her shoulder.

"I think I found a door," Nick said urgently. "We'll be inside soon; don't worry."

"Good," Mel sighed. "This is so weird."

As soon as she said that, we suddenly heard a low-pitched clamor in the streets. It was a combination of growling and snarling, mixed with screams. My mind went to movies I had seen where wolves stalked prey and then ripped it apart. First the growling, then the snarling as they drew closer, then the screams and… was that the sound of flesh tearing?

"Holy shit!" I blurted out before I could stop myself.

Suddenly the ground rumbled below us again. I think we had forgotten about the first time because we were so freaked out about the lights going out. But this time, we felt the rumble as if it were the only thing in existence. It shook us violently, throwing us from our feet. I smacked the ground hard, hitting my head. I tried to sit up, but dizziness engulfed me. As I fought to regain my bearing, I heard the snarling grow closer.

"Mel!" I bellowed. "Mel, where are you?" I heard a weak whimper and crawled towards it. In a quieter voice I asked, "Is that you?"

"Yeah," she said weakly. "Where's Nick?"

"I don't know," I answered. "All I care about right now is you. Can you move?"

"Yeah."

"Get up, and hurry. Something is moving towards us and I gave away our position when I called out for you."

She clambered to her feet, swaying slightly after doing so. "Are you okay?" she asked as we hooked an arm around each other.

"I'm fine. Let's get to that building."

We took a step forward, then the ground shook again. We fell to the asphalt once more, both getting hurt. I landed on my wrist wrong, eliciting a yelp from my lungs. Mel groaned as well, but I didn't know what was wrong with her. As we regained our wits, suddenly a red glow shot into the sky. We could instantly see all around us, although I wish we hadn't.

The streets were littered with bodies. I guess not all deaths are clean, but there sure was a lot of blood on the bodies. As grisly as it was, it wasn't my main concern. I scanned the street for the thing producing the snarling, but didn't see anything. Maybe I had just been hearing things. My eyes went skyward, to the source of the light. The glow was a good ways from us; judging by where the buildings were, I could tell that it was north of us. A volcano seemed to suddenly be a legit concern, so I rushed to Mel and helped her off the ground. I spun around, spotting Nick coming towards us.

"Can you two walk?" he hurriedly asked.

"No," Mel groaned. "I think I twisted my ankle."

"Take her there," Nick said, nodding towards the door he had found.

"Now that we can see, why don't we go back to the hotel, where all our belongings are?" I objected.

"We might not have time," he huffed, picking up Mel and taking her to the door.

I dashed in front of him and opened the door, following him as he went inside. It was really dark in there, but I could tell that it was some sort of store. Nick didn't put Mel down by the door, but went deeper into the building. Finally he stopped, putting her down on an elevated surface that felt really soft. I groped around in the dark, picking up a piece of whatever he had placed her on.

"Come outside with me," he said, not giving me time to respond before he hurried back towards the door.

When we got back on the street, I looked down at my hand. I held a tiny little tiger. I chuckled as I looked at the sign above the door, noticing it for the first time.

"A toy store?" I scoffed.

"It's better than nothing," Nick replied. "Come on, hurry."

He took off at a jog, heading towards the epicenter of where the gunfire had begun. I cringed as we ran by bodies, disgusted by the senseless violence. Did all these people really have to get killed? Nick stopped a few moments later, kneeling down by one of the dead security guards. I recognized him as the one Mel had been flirting with.

"What are you doing?" I asked.

"Keep your voice down," he whispered.

I nervously looked around, jumping when Nick shoved something in my arms.

"A rifle?" I protested.

"Shhh!" he whispered, slapping a hand over my mouth. "We have no idea what's going on or what state of mind other people are in. Judging by the number of dead bodies in the streets, I'd wager the state is not a good one. I will say this one more time: keep your voice down. Yes, it's a rifle. We need to be armed just in case."

"In case what?" I prodded.

He didn't answer me, but looted a couple more things off the security officer. Waving me over, he shoved more items at me.

"Sling the gun over your shoulder. Get his utility belt and put it on. Take his vest, helmet, and baton too. Take all the gear you can."

I wanted to ask questions, but I hurriedly did as he

said. The glowing red light in the distance was growing brighter and then dimming, worrying me that it would soon be gone. If that happened, we wouldn't be able to find our way back to Mel. When I was done, I looked up and saw Nick dashing back towards me. He had found two more dead guards; donning the gear of one of them and carrying the other's, presumably for Mel.

"Let's head back," he said, to which I agreed and started jogging back to the toy store.

As we passed by a group of bodies, I could swear I heard one of them groan. I halted in my tracks, turning to look at them. Sure enough, a woman groaned and slowly rolled her eyes in my direction.

"She's alive!" I proclaimed in a whisper, excitedly looking at Nick. "We should help her."

"No, we don't have time," he answered.

"We have to help her!"

"No, we don't have time!" he reiterated. "Do you want to see your friend again or not?"

I looked past him at our destination, then back down at the woman. "Of course I want to see her again," I replied, "but I couldn't live with myself if I just let this person die."

"So you'll let your friend die instead?"

"She's not *that* hurt."

"If we don't get back to her tonight but someone else does, we have no idea what might happen to her."

I clenched my jaw and looked back down at the woman. Decidedly, I looked back at Nick. "I'm helping this woman. You're welcome to leave."

He grit his teeth and covered his mouth in annoyance,

pacing away a couple steps. I stared at him in disgust, wondering what was wrong with him.

"What's your deal anyway?" I hissed. "You don't even know us. Why do you want to help us and not this lady?"

He glared at me for a moment, then cussed below his breath and stepped towards the woman. He handed the extra gear to me, then squatted down and picked up the stranger.

"Hurry up," he advised as we moved towards the store.

I started to jog that direction, but hesitantly looked back at him. Since he was wearing all that gear and carrying the lady, he couldn't move very quickly.

"Don't worry about me," he said, noticing my hesitation. "Get to your friend."

I nodded, then turned and dashed to the store. Once inside, I dropped the extra gear by the door and slowly made my way to the back. I stumbled and tripped over several things, but Mel's voice guided me to her spot.

"Where'd you go?" she asked, grimacing from the pain in her ankle.

"Out to the street. We took some protective gear off a couple security guards."

"They just gave it to you?"

"They uh… they won't be missing it."

"Oh," she said solemnly. "How bad is it out there?"

"Pretty quiet at the moment; we didn't see any other people. But there are a lot of bodies out there. It's freaky Mel… there's a lot of blood. Thankfully, we found someone who was still alive. Nick is carrying her back here."

"He's quite the hero, isn't he?"

"Something like that," I said with a frown. "Listen

Mel, I know he's being nice to us now, but we need to be careful around him. We just met him. We can't rely on him to keep us safe. We'll spend the night here, but then I say we ditch him. What do you think?"

"I think," she said, finding my hand with hers, "that you usually have good ideas. But I can't walk right now."

"All we have to do is get back to our hotel. It's not even a block from here. We'll get there in no time in the daylight."

"Okay," she agreed. "Whatever you say. Too bad though; he's hot."

I rolled my eyes, kissing her forehead. "Get some rest Mel; I'll be on the lookout for us."

"Thanks Addie," she replied groggily. I felt her hand relax, and I knew she was drifting into sleep.

I stood and walked back to the front of the store, which was easier to find with the glow outside. I looked out at the street, seeing Nick carrying the woman. He was about fifty paces away when the red glow started to flicker.

"Oh no," I murmured, anxiously stepping towards him.

"Don't!" he cautioned. "Stay where you are. It won't do us any good to both be lost. Stay there and use your voice to guide me back if the light goes out."

A moment later, the glow dimmed and then disappeared. Anxiously, I called out to Nick.

"I'm here," he called back.

"I think you're almost here," I said, not sure of what to say. Filling the silence with pointless words was better than nothing, right? "Just keep walking straight in the direction you have been. You'll be here soon. Thank you for going back into the streets for us… thank you for taking me with you. Thank you for looking after us tonight. It's really nice of you."

I heard his footsteps right in front of me, so I put my hand out and felt his arm. "The doorway is right here," I said, guiding him through it. Since there wasn't another stuffed-animal display bin to lay her down on, Nick put the woman down on the floor nearby the display that Mel was resting on. I knelt down beside her and tenderly put my hand on her arm.

"Hi there," I said softly. "I know you can't see me, but we wanted to help you."

"Thank you," the woman wheezed.

"What hurts?"

"Everything," the woman replied. "I think... I think something bit me. I'm so weak. Please don't leave me."

"I won't; of course I won't. Get some rest. In the morning we'll get you some help."

The woman weakly thanked me again, then fell asleep. With her taken care of, I stumbled over to Mel. It seemed like she was sleeping soundly, so I sat back down next to the woman. I heard slight movement beside me and felt body heat radiating my way, telling me that Nick was beside me. He didn't say anything, so I didn't feel the need to either. After sitting in the pitch black for quite some time and fighting the urge to sleep, I heard him speak.

"Get some rest. I barred the door so that no one can get in. I didn't see this place in the daylight, but I'm fairly certain the whole front of it is glass windows. Since it's pitch-black outside I don't think anyone will notice. We should be safe tonight."

"Okay," was all I said, oddly not wanting to thank him

again. I had said it earlier; surely that was enough. I didn't want to be too nice to him since Mel and I were leaving him in the morning.

"I'll find us some blankets," he said, standing.

"I'll help," I added, also standing.

"I think there were some on the opposite wall," he said. "May I?"

"Uh, sure," I answered, uncertain as to what he was asking.

I felt his hand on my arm, then I felt it work its way to my hand. He locked his fingers with mine, closing his warm hand over my own. I fought the urge to recoil; he was probably just being nice. He carefully led us to the wall, where we found a whole bounty of blankets. We carried as many as we could back to the two sleeping people. As well as I could, I draped a few blankets over Mel. It seemed like the power was definitely off, but it wasn't that cold in the building.

"Give it some time," Nick said when I brought it up to him. "The power went out a short time ago; in a couple hours it'll be really cold in here."

"Yeah, I suppose," I answered. As I pondered where to sleep, I asked if he would stay by the woman if I stayed by Mel.

"The woman sounded like she was injured pretty badly. Why don't you sleep on one side of her and I'll sleep on the other side? She'll stay warmer that way."

I agreed, so we laid down our blankets on each side of her. As I snuggled myself tightly under several blankets, I wondered what the morning would hold. What in the world had happened tonight? Would the power be back tomorrow? Would our phones work? Was there a volcano waiting for us? My heart thudded from all these questions, and I lay awake for hours pondering them.

I could hear everyone around me breathing as they slept, and I was secretly grateful that they had all survived. Without realizing it, I gripped the tiny cross necklace that hid under my blouse. I barely knew Nick or the woman, but I was glad they still had their lives.

CHAPTER THREE

Sunlight hit my eyelids, waking me from a deep slumber. As I returned to consciousness, I recalled the night's events. They came to me in groggy pieces, seeming like a nightmare. Surely they had been just that—a nightmare—not real life. But when I rolled over and saw that cartoon-character blankets were draped over me, I knew it hadn't been a dream. I jerked further awake as I recalled my plan to ditch Nick. Looking around, I saw that both his blanket and the woman's were empty. Hastily, I jumped up and looked for Mel. To my relief, she was awake and looked surprisingly well.

"Gee thanks," she replied when I said that. "You were expecting me to look like hell? Like that would ever happen," she said, bobbing her head back and forth at me.

"You know what I meant!" I laughed. "Now the question is: can you walk?"

"I'm not sure. Help me off of here."

She scooted to the edge of the display, dangling her legs over the edge. From there, her toes just barely touched the ground. I eagerly draped her arm around my shoulders, excited to see if she could stand. Gingerly, she stood up.

"I think… I think it still really hurts," she said disappointedly.

"No matter; I'll just help you over to our hotel. It's close by."

As we hobbled towards the door, I noticed that colorful

33

and oversized confetti pieces littered the floor. I stared at them in realization; the things that had been falling on us last night had been the famous confetti that they shoot into the sky at midnight.

"Hey," I said.

"What?" Mel asked, following my gaze to the confetti.

"Happy New Year."

She laughed dryly, then said, "And the same to you, my fair lady."

I smiled back at her, then continued towards the door. Suddenly there was noise behind us. We turned and saw Nick walk from the employee part of the store into the main area where we were. He was looking down when he came in, wringing his hands or something. I awkwardly looked at Mel, trying to mouth to her not to say anything or make any noise. We stood as still as statues, but when he saw our empty blankets he looked around in alarm. Upon spotting us, he threw something on the ground and walked towards us.

"Where are you going?" he asked.

"We were—" Mel started, but I cut her off.

"Nowhere. We were just seeing if Mel could walk."

"By the looks of it, I'm guessing not," he observed.

I pursed my lips for a moment, then realized the woman wasn't with him. "Where is the woman we helped?" I asked.

He said nothing, but came over to us and put Mel's other arm around him. Together we helped her to a plastic table-and-chair set, which almost seemed made for adults, but not really. Once there, Nick gestured at the woman's blanket. It was soaked in blood.

"She didn't make it through the night," he said.

Mel grimaced and put her hand over her mouth, while I stared at the blood in silence.

After gulping, I asked, "Where is her body?"

"I wrapped it in a blanket and took it outside."

"Are you sure she was dead?" I asked, stepping towards the back of the store.

"Yes," he insisted, stepping in front of me and placing his hands on my shoulder. "Trust me; I know how to read a pulse. She was gone. We did all we could for her."

I said nothing, but sadly drifted my eyes towards the floor. As I did so, I noticed that his hands were stained red with blood. Alarmed, I jerked myself away from him.

"Why are your hands covered in blood?" I exclaimed.

"Did you not see the blankets?" he quipped, raising an eyebrow at me as he gestured towards the blanket. "She bled out and I moved her body. Why do you keep throwing not-so-subtle accusations at me?"

"Because something is off about you!"

I watched sadness cross his face, and suddenly I felt bad.

"I'm sorry," I offered, but he backed away and put his hand up.

"No, I wouldn't want to make you uncomfortable. Let's just go our separate ways. If you and Mel want to go back to your hotel, since I assume that's where you were headed a minute ago, please let me help you get there. There's something weird going on here, and I don't feel right leaving you alone out there."

I thought about what he said, then nodded. "I know there's something weird going on, but have you seen something else this morning that makes you say that?"

He sighed heavily, glancing at Mel and then back at me.

"Yes, I saw something."

"What was it?" I breathed, almost afraid to ask.

"The woman. When I took her outside, I examined her wounds. She had heavy bruising from being trampled, but that's not what killed her."

"What did?" Mel gingerly asked.

"Odd wounds… they looked like bite marks."

"She said she thought something bit her," I noted.

"Something sure did. It was bad. It wasn't just a bite. The flesh was ripped away and the wounds had a nasty infection around them."

"Good grief!" Mel wheezed. "What in the world would do that?"

"Maybe just stray dogs; I don't know," Nick replied. Looking back at me he said, "But with knowing that something like that could be roaming the streets, let me help you get Mel to your hotel. She can't run if anything attacks you."

"Yes!" she cried, leaping from her chair and standing on her good ankle. "Please help us!"

I locked eyes with my best friend, knowing that I needed this man's help to get her back to our hotel safely. I knew he was telling the truth about the woman's wounds, for I could vividly recall the sounds I had heard in the street last night. "Okay," I agreed, turning back to him and nodding. "Your help would be welcome."

He offered me a small smile, then strode to where his gear sat on the floor. "Last night I grabbed enough gear for all of us; I highly recommend putting it on."

A short time and some effort later, we were all geared up and ready to go. I hadn't been very close to the windows that morning, but I hadn't recalled seeing anyone walk by since the sun had come up.

"Did you see anybody when you went outside?" I asked Nick.

"No," he shook his head as he secured the last part of his gear and then walked towards the front door. "I'm going to unbar this, then I'll step outside and check our surroundings. If it looks clear, I'll signal you guys over."

"Were you in the military or something?" I chuckled to myself.

"Aye, you could say that."

"I knew it!" Mel cheered. "Military guys are always hot," she said with a wink at him.

I elbowed her as he grinned and worked on opening the door. Once it was open, he signaled to us, then stepped outside. We watched him creep by the windows, stealthily working his way down the sidewalk.

"Why did you say that?" I chastised her as we waited inside the store.

"Why not?" she laughed.

"Because it's not true! And military guys are not always hot. Do you remember Doug from high school? He went into the marines and he was hideous."

"Wait, are you trying to say Nick isn't hot?" she snorted. "Because I know you're definitely not trying to say that."

"He has his… charms," I admitted. "But I don't trust him."

"Well you need to chill out, because he has proven pretty trustworthy so far. He kept us safe all night, and now he's helping us get back to our hotel even after you called him weird!"

"Yeah…" I admitted. "But still."

"Whatever," Mel shrugged. "I have no problem with you disliking him. Maybe I'll get me some of that."

"Shut up," I giggled.

We waited a few minutes in silence, then finally saw him appear on the other side of the windows. He was moving pretty quickly; nowhere near as carefully as he had been when he left.

"Maybe it's all clear," Mel said hopefully.

"I don't think so," I said in a strained voice. My muscles were tensing up in fear. Something was wrong, I just knew it.

Suddenly someone else raced past the windows, towards Nick. Mel and I shrieked in warning just as he got to the door. He spun around and faced the person, but it clobbered him. We screamed as we heard him cry out in pain and watched him crumble to the ground. The lower half of the wall wasn't windows, so we couldn't see what was happening. Suddenly Nick's hands appeared in the doorway, gripping the frame with all his might. I dashed towards him, shrieking his name.

"Nick! Nick!"

"Go!" he bellowed. "Run!"

"We can't leave you—"

"GO!!!" he bellowed.

With that I spun around and raced back towards Mel. Hastily I picked up one of the rifles, threw Mel's arm around me, and then helped her hobble to the back of the store. We fumbled around in the darkness a bit, but eventually found the back door. I cracked it open and tried to look for other attackers, but it was hard to see anything without opening the door further.

"Okay Mel," I whispered. "Stay with me. I will help you all I can, but if I see anything, I need to be able to shoot at it."

"Have you ever fired a gun before?" she panted.

"Yeah."

"You have?"

"A while back. Are you with me or what?"

"Of course I am. Let's go."

We carefully went out the door, ardently looking around us all the while. Everything was covered in a fresh layer of snow, in which I didn't think I saw any tracks, indicating that so far nobody had come this way. I soon realized that the exit had taken us out the other side of the U-shaped plaza, meaning we'd have to go all the way around in order to head back towards our hotel. Movement in the corner of my eye made me jerk my head to right. Seeing nothing, I suddenly felt like a weak rabbit that was about to get pounced on by a wolf.

"Inside!" I spat harshly. "We're going back inside!"

I tried to fight the panic that was suddenly taking over me, but it was already having its effect. My pulse was racing and adrenaline was pumping through my veins. I couldn't hear anything except my pounding heart, and all I could see was the door. We made it back inside in record time, after which I locked the door.

"Why are we back in here?" Mel whimpered, looking towards the front of the store with fear.

"Because we're going out the front."

"What?" she despaired in a whisper. "Did you not just see what happened up there?"

"If we go out the back, it'll take us four times as long

to get to our hotel. If bad people or looters are out there, I don't think our chances are very high of making it that way. Let me check out the front. If that person is still there, I'll point the gun at him and tell him to leave."

"You're going to shoot someone?"

"If I have to."

"You really think you can?" she asked with a raised eyebrow.

"Mel," I said seriously, cupping my hands around her face and looking intently into her eyes. "I am trying to save my best friend's life. For that, I am prepared to do anything."

"Okay then, Captain America," she grinned.

I smiled and kissed her forehead. "Always making jokes," I mused.

"Well someone has to. I don't want to die unhappy."

"Don't talk about dying," I scolded.

"Okay, okay," she obliged, putting her hands up in surrender.

"Now I'm going to go check out the front. I'll get the other gun and bring it back to you. That way if anything happens to me, you can defend yourself and try to get to the hotel without me."

With that, I carefully emerged from the back of the store. I scanned the store for an intruder, but didn't see anything. My absurd shoes—party heels—made way too much noise, so I slipped them off. Why had I even put them on this morning? As quietly as I could, I crossed the store to where we had slept. There I found our blankets, still the way we had left them. Nearby I found the rifle I was looking for. It was half hidden under a display, making me wonder how it had gotten there and why we hadn't taken it before when all three of us had tried to exit. I dismissed the thought, snagged the gun, then hurried back to Mel.

When I handed her the gun, she had no clue what she was doing. After making a joke about typical New Yorkers, I showed her how to properly hold and use it. "If you have to fire it," I cautioned, "expect kick. Make sure it's snug against your shoulder, or it will hurt like hell."

Once I was sure she knew the basics, I returned to the front of the store. Warily, I crept towards the front door. All seemed quiet on the street, but I was afraid of what I might see outside the door. Would Nick's decimated body be laying there? Would his assailant be nearby, waiting to attack the rest of us? I found myself holding my breath as I approached the door, making me gasp when I finally exhaled. I paused, taking a moment to breathe and calm myself.

"Chill out," I whispered to myself. "You have no idea what is going on; all you can do is stay levelheaded and try to get back to the hotel. Keep breathing, and try to stay calm."

Moments later, I took a deep breath and decided to keep moving. I slowly inched towards the door, eventually making it there. On the sidewalk, to my surprise, there was no body. Nick's body wasn't there, nor was the body of the person who attacked him. I gulped, trying to decide what that meant. Had the person killed him and dragged him away? There sure was a lot of blood on the sidewalk; that much I could say.

Realizing I had been looking down too long, I swept my eyes to the street. No movement. I scanned left and right, noticing that there was a clothing store right next door.

Since Mel and I both needed decent shoes, especially in this fresh snow, I slowly made my way over to it. As I went, I continued scanning the street. I didn't see any other people, but I did notice that the snow had buried the bodies that littered the street. Every so often, though, there was a hole in the snow, covered by a smear of blood. It seemed like someone had come by and uncovered bodies, then hauled them away. Maybe, just maybe, the city or FEMA was already here cleaning up the mess. Desperately, I craned my neck in every direction, but saw nobody. Shaking my head, I continued towards the store. Hopefully things would start making sense soon, but until then, Mel and I needed better shoes.

Inside the store I didn't see anyone, and saw no evidence that anyone had slept there or had recently been there. Carefully but quickly, I hurried through the store and grabbed heavy jackets, gloves, and snow boots. Glancing down at my stupid leather leggings, I also made a dash for jeans for both Mel and me. I saw several adorable blouses that were to die for, but resisted taking them. I was only grabbing these things for survival; if the power came back today and everything went back to normal, I didn't want to have to account for stealing tops. As I thought that, I passed several cute long-sleeved shirts. Well, it was awfully cold out there…

I emerged from the store with two bulging duffel bags, feeling confident that we'd definitely make it over to our hotel warmly. Besides, when things went back to normal, we could just bring the items back and explained why I took them.

"Whoa," Mel laughed when she saw me. "You went

shopping? You left me here to go shopping!"

"No way! The way out front seemed clear. There's fresh snow out there and both of us are wearing heels—"

"Stilettos," she corrected.

"Whatever! I got us some snow boots and warm clothes. Let's put them on."

We dumped the contents of both bags onto the floor and sorted through them, dividing up the items among us.

"Nice!" Mel praised as she eyed a scarf. "Good thinking!"

As she draped it around her neck, I swatted it off of her. "That," I explained, "is not for looks. It's for your ankle."

"My ankle?" she scoffed.

"Yes, wrapping it should help it. I think it might heal faster if it's wrapped. It'll help you walk on it too."

"It will?"

"If you believe it will," I said, suppressing a grin.

"Really?" she giggled. "You're something else sometimes."

"I don't know if it'll help you walk, but compressing it does help it heal faster."

"How do you know that?"

Quietly I answered, "My dad taught me."

"Oh," Mel said.

We didn't say anything more as we donned our new clothing. Nick had been right that the building would eventually be cold inside, so we scurried to change clothes, not wanting to be exposed to the cold for long. Gingerly, I wrapped Mel's ankle with the scarf, then slid her snow boot on over it. After we had on the warmer clothes, we packed our old clothes into the duffel bags and put the protection gear back on. As we picked up our guns and slung the bag straps across our chests, I looked at Mel somberly.

"Stay with me as we move. If I get attacked and the way ahead looks clear, make a mad dash for the hotel. Get up to our room and lock the door; don't open it for anything."

"What do you think is out there?" she blurted. "I mean, why all this precaution?"

I stared at her incredulously. "Were you not there last night? Electricity failed. Our power is out, and so are all our batteries. Batteries shouldn't all die like that! Then people freaked. We heard the gunshots and the screaming. When Nick and I went back outside, there were bodies everywhere Mel. There was a weird red glow in the sky and the ground shook several times. All night I slept next to a woman who was dead by morning. Who knows how long I slept next to a corpse? Something freaky is going on. Not to mention, we both saw Nick get attacked. Even if it's just looters out there, I want to be prepared for the worst."

"Yeah, me too," she agreed emphatically, seeming to suddenly realize the direness of the situation. I couldn't blame her for not realizing it sooner; it had only really hit me when I'd seen the bodies in the street.

"Are you ready Mel?" I asked softly.

"Yeah; let's go bestie."

I smiled and hugged her tightly, then we quietly headed towards the front of the store.

"How is your ankle?" I asked as we crept, wanting to know before we got outside.

"It hurts, but I don't want to make you drag me."

"Well I won't leave you behind, either. We'll go at your pace."

We reached the door and each took a deep breath. I poked my head outside, again seeing nobody. I then nodded my head for Mel to follow me, so she stepped through the doorway. When she sighted all the blood on the sidewalk, I heard her gasp.

"Is that Nick's?" she whispered.

"I don't know."

As stealthily as two city dwellers could, we crept down the street towards our hotel. We passed a couple of the holes in the snow where a body had been pulled from, making me further hopeful that someone was working on getting things back to normal. One of them that we passed caught my eye, making me stop abruptly. Mel ran into me, cursing slightly. I knelt down and looked at it, noticing that the smear of blood looked really fresh. If this body had just been hauled off, maybe the person that collected it was still nearby. I glanced around us, but didn't see any other signs of life.

"What is it?" Mel asked.

"I think cleanup has already begun. It looks like someone is taking bodies off the streets."

"Yay!" she proclaimed. "Where is the person?" she asked, also scanning our surroundings.

"I don't know. Let's keep moving for now. We'll figure out what to do once we reach our room."

Together, we continued moving along the street. Our hotel was only a short distance away. I wanted to break into a giddy run and dart through the doors, but I convinced myself that it was probably a bad idea.

As we crossed one of the last intersections before our hotel, Mel gasped.

"What?" I asked, spinning around. I saw her looking down the street to our left, so I followed her gaze.

I inhaled sharply as I saw someone making their way down the street, away from us. I stood frozen as I tried to decide what to do. The person didn't seem to have heard us, and their back was to us. It wasn't too late for us to go on our merry way and pretend we never saw them.

CHAPTER FOUR

"A person!" Mel said excitedly, too loudly for my comfort.

"Shhh!" I hissed, but it was too late.

The person stopped in their tracks, then slowly turned around. They were in the shade of the surrounding buildings, so we couldn't see them very well. I couldn't make out the expression on their face, but it didn't seem to be very pleasant. As we stared, the person snarled at us.

"Mel," I said very quietly. "Move towards the hotel. As quickly as you can."

"What if they can help us?" she protested.

"I don't think they will."

The person started moving towards us, slowly and awkwardly. From the way they were walking, I suspected their leg was broken. I sighed briefly, glad that in a pursuit we could probably outrun them, even with Mel's bad ankle. Still, I wanted her to have a head start.

"Mel, get moving," I urged. "I'll distract them."

As she watched the person, something alarmed her as well. "Yeah, I'll get moving," she agreed. "Be careful. I'll move as fast as I can."

"Thanks," I said, starting to feel my limbs tremble. I had never been in an encounter with another person, and wasn't sure how it would go. I hoped I had what it took to judge when to run and when to fight. What if I hesitated? What if I gave them the benefit of the doubt, then they attacked and shot me with my own gun?

I glanced in Mel's direction, happy to see that her way was still clear. I turned my attention back to the approaching person, but they were gone. I blinked quickly several times, scanning the whole street. The person was definitely gone. Cursing profusely under my breath, I jogged towards my friend.

"What happened?" she asked as we shuffled towards the looming building.

"The person disappeared."

"What?"

"I looked your way, then when I looked back at the person, it was gone."

That seemed to trigger her adrenaline, because suddenly she started moving faster. Together we hurried towards the building. With only a few hundred feet to go, I pondered what we would do when we reached our room. What if someone followed us inside? Obviously we would bar our door, but what if they waited for us in the hall?

My thoughts were interrupted when I suddenly heard a noise behind us. I glanced back, dismayed to see the person following us. Seeing him in the sunlight brought terror to my heart. His leg was definitely broken, and he was slumping after us while snarling. My blood seemed to freeze as I recognized his snarling as being the sound I'd heard the night before. His skin was a dull gray, and his whole body seemed to be bloated. His mouth was covered in blood, and it looked like chunks of flesh covered his face. Fighting the urge to scream my head off and vomit, I grabbed Mel's arm and yanked her along faster.

"We have to move!!!" I thundered.

"Why?" she asked, turning around.

I tried to stop her, but before I could, she screamed bloody murder. Her scream seemed to encourage the thing, for in response it snarled louder and shuffled faster towards us. I pulled us forward rapidly, shrieking as another person walked in front of us.

"Where the hell did she come from?" I yelled, letting go of Mel's arm to raise my gun. With the stock snug against my shoulder, I pointed it at the woman in front of us and squeezed the trigger. My aim was atrocious, but I finally hit the thing and watched it fall to the ground. Releasing the trigger, I swung around to the thing behind us. Hitting him was easier, as he was way too close to us already. As he fell to the ground, I dragged Mel towards the doors of the hotel. Fearfully I glanced back at the woman's body.

"I think that was the woman Nick claimed was dead!" I wheezed in horror as we ran.

Behind us, I swear the two people were still snarling.

Chills soared up my spine as we barged through the front doors of the hotel. I spun around and locked them, hoping nobody else would try to dash in here for safety. I cringed as I imagined someone pounding on the door for help as snarling, blood-smeared people limped towards them.

I should have examined the lobby some, but I didn't. I led us straight to the stairwell and helped Mel start clambering up the stairs. Thankfully, the stairwell had a few windows that let in a small amount of light so we could see. A few flights up, I relaxed a little as my friend begged for a break. Her ankle was really hurting, and we were headed to the twentieth floor.

"If you don't want to me to die of a heart attack before then," she huffed as she tried to catch her breath, "then I need a break!"

I conceded and helped her sit down on the stairs. Uneasily, I paced the landing that we were on.

"What the hell was wrong with those people?" Mel asked, echoing my own thoughts.

"I have no idea," I panted, also out of breath.

"They were scary as shit!"

"Hell yeah they were," I agreed, remembering the man. "Did you see the blood on that guy's face? And the... the bits of flesh around his mouth?"

We both groaned in unison, expressing our disgust.

"Do you think they're connected to whatever happened last night?"

"Probably," I answered. "Unless they're just crack heads," I laughed anxiously. More seriously I added, "But I swear one of them looked just like the woman we saved last night... the one who Nick said was dead."

"Well whatever and whoever they are, I hope they go away soon. That was messed up."

"It sure was." I thought in silence for a moment, then asked, "What if that's what attacked Nick?"

"Then we're probably in some deep shit if even he couldn't fight them off."

"Thanks for the vote of confidence!" I scoffed.

Mel ignored me as she added, "But the guns worked okay on them."

"Yeah," I agreed halfheartedly, remembering how the snarling had continued even after I had shot them.

"Didn't Nick have one when he went out there?" Mel

asked. "Why didn't he shoot his attacker?"

"Dunno," I shrugged.

I kept pondering the woman; having seen the face of someone who I had thought was dead had been scary as hell. "Hey Mel, come to think of it, did you see the woman's body out back of the store?"

"No I don't think so, but I don't remember seeing any tracks in the snow either. That's weird… Do you think Nick actually kicked her out of our group?"

"I have no idea. No matter what the answer is, this is all so messed up."

"Absolutely," she agreed. With a heavy sigh she said, "I'm ready to keep moving whenever you are."

I helped her up and we continued our trek upstairs. A couple breaks and long time later, we made it to our floor. Warily, we emerged from the stairwell and into the hallway. The ends of the halls had windows which also let in a scarce amount of light, like the stairwell. We crept down the hallways, seeing nobody else in them. Along the way, we saw several spots of carpet that were stained with blood. Had people died in here too?

"Maybe they were injured and bled out like the woman we helped," Mel suggested.

"Yeah, but why weren't they in their rooms? If they escaped the panic on the streets and made it up twenty flights of stairs, they could have made it to their room."

The thought nagged at me as we continued, eventually coming to our room without incident. I held my breath as I reached my hand towards the door, hoping to God that it was unlocked. If it wasn't, this was all for naught. Touching the handle, I gripped it and tried turning it. To our thrill, it rotated and the door swung open. Our happiness was short lived though, as we suddenly heard movement inside the room.

"Get back!" I whispered, again raising my gun.

I pushed Mel against the wall behind me, then squatted down and carefully peered around the corner. The curtains were drawn, so the room was pretty dark. I couldn't see anything, but I knew we had heard a sound. Leaning out of the doorway and back against the wall, I pondered what to do. There was no way I was going into that dark room if someone else was in there.

"Hey," I whispered, coming up with an idea as I nudged my friend. "Go back down the hallway a ways and lay flat on the floor. I'm going to try to draw the person out. If it goes bad, you shoot them."

I could tell she didn't like the idea, but she just said, "Okay," and then backtracked down the hall. When I saw that she was lying down with her rifle in the right position, I turned my attention back to the room.

"Who's there?" I called. No answer. "We heard you moving; we know you're in there. Tell us who you are."

Suddenly there was more sound within, and I heard something flying my way. I watched as something flew out of the doorway and past me into the hall, clearly intended to hit me. Squinting in the dim light, I strained to make out the object. Was that... a pillow? Who in their right mind would throw a pillow at an intruder?

"Go away!" a shrill voice squawked.

I grimaced with a smirk as I detected a hint of familiarity in the voice. "Or else what? You'll throw another pillow at me?"

"Don't think I won't!" the voice called, hardly sounding threatening.

I looked behind me and motioned for Mel to come back, then stood. "Calm down lady," I replied.

"Why should I?"

"I'm coming inside."

"Don't you dare!" the voice warned.

"Mom, calm down. It's me."

Suddenly there was a commotion, and my mom dashed out of the room. "Oh darling it's you!" she proclaimed, throwing her arms around my neck. "I was so worried about you!"

"Yes, I can tell," I complained, prying her arms off of me. "Is anyone else with you?" I asked, nodding towards our room.

"Jacques. I don't know what happened to Caleb."

"Are those the guys you were touting around the party?" I sarcastically asked.

In the dim light, I saw my mom frown.

"Anyway," I said, assuming the answer was yes. "Where's Jacques? Why did he let you throw pillows at me rather than doing something himself?"

"He was injured in the commotion. He has been drifting in and out of consciousness since last night."

"Well that's never good," I murmured, walking into the room.

The first thing I did was make my way to the window and throw the curtains open. Bright light flooded the room, bringing with it a tad of warmth. It was hard to tell how much time we had wasted, but the sun was high in the sky, making me estimate that it was around noon. I turned away from the window, seeing that a man was lying in our king-sized bed, bleeding all over it. I tried not to care about the blood; after all, it wasn't our fault and surely the hotel would understand.

I strode to the bed and looked at the man, seeing that his wound seemed to be under his rib on the right side. Tenderly, I lifted up his shirt so that I could see it clearly. As I did so, a horrible stench assailed my nose, making me cough and gag. Jacques moved slightly, seeming to be disturbed. I peered at the bloody wound in horror. Not only did it smell like decay, but it was also a horrible mixture of dismal colors. Blood, flesh and puss seemed to be fighting for dominance within it. I gagged again, then turned to my mom.

"He's not doing well."

"Oh nonsense; he'll be better in no time. He just needs a doctor. They're probably on their way as we speak. I'm surprised they're not here already."

"No," I countered. "There's nobody out there," I said with a gesture to the street below the window. "Well, no one good."

"What do you mean?" she asked with a raised eyebrow. "Are there looters?"

"Worse."

I walked to the bathroom, in search of a first-aid kit.

"What do you mean worse?" my mom asked as she followed me.

"I mean worse. A couple people attacked Mel and me. They... well it was awful, let's just say that."

"How awful?" she dramatically asked.

"Way awful," Mel interjected, hopping towards the sofa

and plopping down on it.

"Did they hurt you?" my mom gasped, finally spotting Mel's hurt ankle.

"Oh, no this is from the earthquake last night. The people didn't hurt us; Addie here popped them both in the face."

My mother spun around, also finally noticing our riot gear and guns. "You shot them?" she exclaimed. "Was that necessary?"

"Uh yeah, it definitely was," I defended.

"Totally was," Mel added. "They were whackos. We think they ate some people."

My mom's jaw dropped as she looked at my friend like she was an alien. "You think they ate people?"

"Yuppers," she replied, not caring about my mom's attitude. "I wouldn't believe it if I hadn't seen it either. They had blood and bits of skin all over their mouths. It was disgusting."

With all the dramatic grace of someone conditioned by showbiz, my mom raised the back of her hand to her forehead as though she may faint.

"If you don't believe us, feel free to go out there," I muttered.

I got a look of daggers from her, but I didn't care. This situation was bad enough without her drama. Finding nothing in the way of first aid, I went back to the bed and looked down at the man. I put my hand on his face, recoiling instantly.

"What is it?" mom gushed, seeing my odd reaction.

"He's burning up!"

"Well, he probably has a fever."

"No, like burning up. The heat hurt my skin."

"I think you're being a little dramatic," my mom replied.

Annoyed by her nerve to say something like that to me, I grabbed her hand and slapped it to his skin. She recoiled too, just like I had.

"You were saying?" I growled.

She said nothing, but I watched her expression turn from disbelief to a mix of fear and sorrow. Sadly, she sat on the bed beside the man.

"I haven't known Jacques that long, but he was a wonderful man," she said quietly.

"I think you meant boy," I quipped, annoyed by her fake sadness.

She furrowed her brows, then looked up at me in anger. "How could you say something like that?"

"Because I can't stand watching you pretend to care about someone. Come on Mel," I huffed, picking up our duffel bags. "Let's leave my mom and her soul mate alone. We'll be in the room next door."

I stomped over to that room, not even taking the time to enter carefully. By the time I realized my mistake, we were already inside. Thankfully, the room was clear. The curtains were wide open, allowing us to see everything well. It looked like the room had once had occupants, but so far they hadn't come back to it. We put our stuff down, then plopped down on the bed.

After lying in the stark silence for a few minutes, Mel turned to me. "So what's next?" she asked.

"I have no clue. I was hoping the power would have come back on by now." Realizing that I hadn't checked my phone in a while, I pulled it out and looked at it. Nothing.

With a sigh, I dropped my head back down on the bed.

"Hey I have an idea," Mel said. "Why don't we go downstairs and check out the lobby? There might be other survivors down there."

"There could also be other crack heads. Not to mention, it's a hella long way down and up those stairs."

"True," she agreed. "What if we just check the rooms on this floor then? There's no way those whackos are wandering around up here. We might find other people though."

"Yeah," I agreed. With a small grin I added, "Now you're having some good ideas."

"Hey!" she chuckled, sitting up. "Thank you for the scarf by the way; it definitely seems to be helping my ankle."

"Awesome," I answered, glad to have helped her.

As we emerged back into the dim hall, I had an idea. "As we search each room, let's prop the door open and make sure the curtains are open. We need some light in this hallway."

"Ohhh, good idea," Mel agreed.

We worked our way down the hall, splitting up. We started at the same end, checking rooms across the hall from each other. We didn't find any people, good or bad. Most of the rooms looked largely untouched. It felt a little pointless, but having all the doors open with light coming in sure brightened up the hall, which was nice. Once we were done, I went room-to-room and peered out each window, hoping to see something insightful. I noticed that the sun had melted the snow, revealing all the bodies that had died the night before. There seemed to be more of them than before, with more blood. I sighed and moved to the next room, saddened by the sight. Ironically, I didn't see anything else until I got back to the room Mel and I had claimed. I gasped when I saw it, then dashed to the doorway, shouting towards the neighboring room.

"Mom, come here!"

A moment later, she appeared in her doorway. Mel had been slumped on the couch, but now perked up as well, wondering what the commotion was for. I pointed to the window, to which they both went.

"What are we doing?" my mom asked.

"Showing you that there are some really weird people out there. Look!" I ordered, pointing down to the street. A handful of people could be seen staggering through it, but without an apparent destination. "Look at the lady by the intersection, on the right."

Our eyes followed my order, spotting the lady I had mentioned. She was stumbling up on a guy who was walking normally. The guy was walking towards her, seemingly asking her for help. As he drew closer, the man suddenly stopped. I recalled the moment Mel and I had realized something was wrong with the person we were facing. The man began backing away, but another snarling person had come up behind him. It grabbed his arms, then suddenly dug its teeth into the man's shoulders.

We shrieked as the man collapsed and blood sprayed from his shoulder. He was screaming, but we couldn't hear it through the sound-proof windows. He violently thrashed and tried to fight off his assailants, but they were completely remorseless. We howled in horror when suddenly one of them thrust their hand into his stomach, ripping it open. I heard Mel retching beside me, and I barely reacted in time to catch my mom fainting. I put her on the bed, gasping for air as well.

With a gulp, I looked back at the scene. I could no longer see the man, as several people were kneeling over him, all feasting on his flesh. I gagged and looked away, darting my eyes elsewhere in the street. Noticing a pattern in the movement, I realized that all the people who been ambling about in the street were now moving towards the scene of the attack. They were probably drawn to the sound. If we hoped to escape from here, we would have to do so really quietly.

I think an hour passed before any of us spoke. My mom lay on the bed in silence, with Mel sitting on the floor under the window. I sat in the window sill with my knees pulled up to my chest. My eyes dully watched the things in the street continue to stumble around aimlessly. Once the group had dissipated from around the man, I could see his dead body. His guts and blood gleamed in the sunlight, sickening me. For a while I stared at him, wondering who he was. Had he just been visiting New York for the holiday? Was he from here? Did he have a family? Was someone waiting for him to come back?

Suddenly feeling sentimental and deeply grateful for the two people I was with, I looked at them. "We have to find Nick!" I professed, standing from the window sill. Both Mel and my mother were startled by my sudden speech. When they realized what I had said, they looked at me like I was crazy.

"Who's Nick?" my mom asked.

"That's a noble idea," Mel said, also standing, "but isn't he dead?"

"Probably. But he might not be. If what attacked him

was one of those… crazy people… then I think his body would still be outside the store. Ripped apart, but still there. And it wasn't, so he must have been able to get away at least for a little bit."

"Then why didn't he come back to us?"

"He probably didn't want to lead his attacker inside." To myself I marveled, "He was still trying to help us, even when he was hurt."

My mom stood from the bed and walked towards us. "Well I like the idea of helping your friend darling, but how are we going to find him? This is a big city with thousands of buildings to hide inside."

"I don't know; maybe we can follow a trail of blood if there is one. Either way, I think we should at least try." I glanced up at the sun, noticing that it had sunk in the sky a ways. "We only have a few hours of light left, at best. Who's coming with me?"

Mel raised her eyebrows, sighing heavily. I glanced at my mom, who wouldn't meet my eyes, but looked horrified.

"You don't have to help; calm down," I grumbled.

"No," she objected breathlessly, pointing past me out the window. "Look at the man! Is he… moving?"

Mel and I spun around, looking down at the dead man who I had been staring at for almost an hour. Sure enough, there seemed to be subtle movements in his limbs. My jaw dropped open as his head turned.

"What… the…" I panted, slamming my palms on the window sill as dizziness took over me.

Slowly, he opened his eyes. We were all the way up on the twentieth floor, but even from that distance I could tell something was very wrong with his eyes. Were they completely filled with blackness? I gawked at the sight, but he blinked and suddenly it was gone. His head had been lying on its side, a result of the muscles relaxing when he had died. Now he turned it straight, and then he sat up. His guts bulged and spilled more when he did so, yanking a shriek from Mel.

"What is happening!" she sobbed, dropping to her knees as her strength left her.

Undeterred by our horror, the man continued moving, eventually getting on his feet. Once standing, it looked like he snarled, then started to shuffle around like the rest of the strange people. We gaped in wide-eyed horror as he just slumped around dully, seeming to have no purpose.

"Oh my God! Oh my God! Oh my God!" my mom bawled, over and over.

As I tried to collect my wits, we suddenly heard a crash in the room beside us. Instantly, we all shut our mouths and held our breath as our eyes darted around at each other.

"Mom," I whispered shakily. "Was Jacques alive or dead when you came in here?"

CHAPTER FIVE

"Mom!" I cried as another crash came from the room next door. "Answer me! Was Jacques alive or dead when you came in here?"

"I'm-I'm not sure…" she stuttered.

I clenched my hands into fists nervously, afraid of what the noise could be. Glancing from Mel's injured ankle to my mom's terror-filled face, I knew I was the one who needed to find out. With a gulp, I walked to where Mel's gun was resting. I wasn't sure how many rounds I had fired from my gun, but I felt safer using hers. Unsure of whether the security guard we lifted it from had used it, I popped out the magazine and checked it. Thirty full rounds. I slid it back into the rifle and jabbed it with the butt of my palm, clicking it into place. As I did so, I could feel the eyes of the other two people in the room darting from me to each other, like I was a barbarian. Yeah, I know how to use a gun, I thought to myself. Did it not already save your life once today? Chill out.

Raising the gun up to my shoulder, I carefully crept towards the door. More sounds came from the room next door, making me wince. Judging from how my mom's friend had looked before, I was guessing he was dead. Or not dead? Undead? Re-alive? Suddenly finding the situation oddly humorous, I chuckled to myself. I'm sure I elicited more weird looks from my two companions, but I didn't care. Continuing to creep towards the door, I picked up on the sound of snarling. Immediately I realized the direness of the situation and blinked determinedly a couple times. If this person wanted to hurt my mom or best friend, there was no way in hell I was going to let him.

Clawing sounds collided with my ears, making me realize that the thing was at the door of the other room. Not wanting it to come into the room where my loved ones were, I jumped into the hallway, instantly backing away from the room. Super thankful that we had opened all the doors to let more light into the hallway, I spotted what had once been Jacques. He stumbled out of his room and into the hallway, snarling like an animal. I cringed as the smell of his wound assailed my nose, seeming to be ten times worse than it had been before.

His snarling grew louder as he stumbled towards me, seeming to be agitated that my flesh wasn't in his mouth. I grimaced with every horrifying movement he made, my mind nearly frozen with fear. He hissed again, lashing his fingers out at me. Straining to get closer to me, he seemed to be infuriated by his own slowness. I was finally able to pull myself from my frozen state and refocus on aiming my gun. With a deep breath, I squeezed the trigger and let the bullets fly. I wasn't a very good shot, but in this close proximity I was able to put several holes through his chest. He snarled loudly in response, then fell to the ground in a heap.

I sighed and strode back to the room to let my mom and Mel know that I was fine. "It's taken care of," I said as I walked into the room.

"Was he...?" my mom dared to ask.

"Yes, he was like the people down there," I replied, nodding to the window.

Mel said nothing, but gulped and furrowed her brows worriedly. "Violetta, how did Jacques get hurt?"

My mom turned to her and shrugged. "I don't know," she answered with a sniffle. "We were in the lounge when the power went out. We lost Caleb initially, but found him in the morning. He... attacked us. It makes sense now, I suppose. I think he may have bitten Jacques. I just don't know!"

"It's okay," Mel soothed, coming over to sit with her on the bed and rub her back comfortingly.

I gazed at them thoughtfully, trying to work out how this all went together. Down in the streets, I could see even more people wandering aimlessly. They all looked changed and rotten. If dead people were coming back to life as these changed things, that was really bad news—there were a lot of dead bodies in the streets. My heart sunk as I realized nobody was out there cleaning up bodies. They were just coming back to life.

"We need to figure out what's going on, and how widespread this is," I proposed as I turned back to my mom and Mel. "Did this just happen here, or is the world normal outside of the city?"

Before they could reply, we heard snarling and saw movement in the doorway. I screeched in terror as I saw the Jacques-thing stumble into the room.

"I shot you!" I bellowed, my mind racing to comprehend what was happening.

I raised the gun and shot him again, right in the head. As blood sprayed all over the wall, the changed Jacques kept coming. I shrieked out orders to my mom and Mel, hardly knowing what I was saying. I think I told them to get in the hallway when they could, as soon I got the thing out of the doorway. I charged him and violently shoved him down to the floor of our room, hoping he wouldn't dig his teeth into me in the meantime. Mom and Mel ran past me, crying out as they darted into the hallway. I jumped off the horrible-smelling thing and dashed for the doorway. As soon as I was out, I grabbed the door handle and yanked the door shut. I heard the thing on the other side snarl and fumble around on the floor. Not wanting to be there if he figured out how to work the door handle, I spun to my companions.

"Ah!" Mel yelled, gripping her ankle. "It wasn't ready for that!"

My mom offered her shoulder to my friend, then darted a worried look my way.

"I'll go get you ice," I said, looking for the sign in the hall that would point us to the ice machine. "Hopefully even though the power is out, the storage bin is still cold enough to have ice inside it."

As I spotted the sign, we heard clawing on the door I had just yanked shut. The sounds were near the handle, telling us that the changed thing had found its way back to its feet and was trying to open the door. I grimaced as it clawed even closer to the handle.

"Mom, help me get her there," I ordered, hurriedly slipping Mel's other arm over my shoulder.

Together, we hobbled down the hallway towards the ice machine. The clawing on the room's door behind us grew louder and more frantic as we went, sending chills soaring down our spines. We moved even faster, finally rounding the last corner. I sighed as I spotted a door, behind which the ice machine sat with the washing machines and vending machines.

"Anyone want to wash your clothes or get a soda?" I joked, slipping Mel's arm off my shoulder.

My mom frowned at me, but I saw Mel crack a smile as she shifted her weight back onto my mom's shoulder.

"Fine, just ice then," I chuckled as I opened the door.

Suddenly a rotting hand shot out at me, making me scream at the top of my lungs. I'm pretty sure I jumped out of my skin, but I know for sure that I jumped backwards several feet. I landed wrong on my foot and fell to the ground, putting my hand out as I did so. Again I landed wrong, this time on my wrist. I shrieked in pain, but there was no time to think about it. A changed thing was coming my way, and so was another… and another. They stumbled out of the dark room, all hissing and snarling at me. One of them didn't seem to have any injuries, but had blood all over its mouth. The other two were covered in blood, probably having been feasted on by the first one. My stomach clenched as I jumped to my feet, trying to overcome the nauseated feeling.

"Mom, get Mel to the stairwell!" I barked.

My mom instantly did as I said, and thank goodness we were right next to another stairway. However, as she moved towards it, the movement caught the attention of the dead things.

"Hey!" I shouted, hitting the wall with my good hand as I tried to draw their attention.

My mom got to the door and pushed herself and Mel through it, then they disappeared. I gulped as the three monsters turned their attention back to me. As my eyes darted to each of them, I realized I no longer had my gun. Not that it stopped them anyway, I thought, remembering Jacques, but at least it slowed them down. I eyed the dark room behind them, almost wanting to dart into it. I could shut the door and hold it shut for as long as possible, hopefully holding it until they got bored and meandered away from it. But something told me that would be a death sentence, and I refrained from doing it.

Suddenly I got an idea. Hoping it would work, I darted down the hall towards the other stairwell. It was on the opposite end of the hallway than the one Mel and Mom had just gone down. Somewhat ironically, the changed things couldn't move as quickly as me, and I had to keep stopping to wait for them. While waiting for them to cover the distance of the hallway, I went back to the room where Jacques was. I may as well test my idea on one of them before trying it on a group of three.

Carefully, I opened the door and then jumped back from it. Out stumbled the thing I had shot earlier, looking and smelling worse than ever. I taunted him to follow me, which he did in a snarling frenzy. His presence seemed to anger the other three; I suppose they were mad that something else might get to eat their dinner.

Eventually getting him to the stairway, I opened the door and held it open as I waited for him to stagger over. He finally did, reaching his hands out in front of himself at me. I flinched as his fingers brushed my jacket, coming way too close to grabbing me. I hopped backwards on the stair landing, letting him follow. Once he was on the landing, I kicked my leg out at him. My foot landed squarely in his chest, making him lose his balance. He fell sideways, to where the downward stairs were. Unable to regain his balance, he toppled over and tumbled down the stairs. I leaned over the railing, peering down the stairs. The sun had lowered in the sky, making light even more scarce in the stairwell. Although I couldn't be certain, I didn't think anything was moving down there. The snarling had stopped too. Well, for a moment it did.

Suddenly the other things were at the door, hissing and clawing their way over to me. I took a deep breath, anxiously wondering if I could take on three of them. I pictured Mel and my mom helplessly making their way down the other stairwell, and instantly I knew I had to come out of this. My mom didn't have a clue how to survive any situation other than a party, and Mel was injured. Glancing up at my foes, I grit my teeth and roared at them.

"Bring it!"

They hissed more at me, and I found myself hissing back at them. They paused for a second in seeming confusion, giving me the opportunity I needed to attack. I shoved one of them into the other two, causing them to all stumble backwards. When the three of them collided, I felt like I was trying to push a wall. Attempting to shove all of them at once may as well have been impossible. Clenching my jaw in determination, I roared as I continued to push. The front one hissed and snarled as I did so, trying to bite my arm. He brought his own arm up, reaching a rotting hand towards my face. I dodged it, but he gripped my arm instead. I shrieked in pain, baffled at how strong he was.

Invigorated by the pain, I hopped backwards and then barreled towards them. My shoulder collided with them brutally, finally giving enough force to shove them backwards. They too toppled over, and then tumbled down the stairs as Jacques had. Not waiting to see the results, I left the stairwell and made my way back down the hall. I stopped at our former room, appalled at how much blood and rotting ooze Jacques had left on the carpet.

I gagged and covered my nose with my shirt as I entered our room, grabbing both our guns and duffel bags. Feeling a moment of nostalgia for the good old times of being nice to my mom when I was a kid, I also went into our first room and looked for any belongings that seemed to be hers. I spotted her purse and grabbed it, also noticing mine and Mel's. Taking all three purses, I shoved them into the duffel bags. Quickly, I also scanned the room for things that might help us survive, and, let's be honest, a few things that wouldn't. There may be dead bodies walking around outside, but a girl's still gotta shave.

Lugging the bags and guns, I made my way to the stairs that Mel and my mom had gone down. When I entered the stairwell, I paused for a moment to see if I could still hear them. Smiling to myself, I heard quite a ruckus down below me. Yup, that was them. I clunked down the stairs in pursuit, hoping nothing was paying attention to all the noise. Once I drew closer, I called out to them.

"Mel, Mom, is that you?"

"Darling?"

"Yeah, it's me. Is Mel okay?"

"I'm fine," I heard her pant.

I sped up my descent, knowing that the panting wasn't good. Although it was a lot of stairs, she sounded very weak. About five flights from the bottom floor, I finally caught up to them. We all smiled and hugged, then took a moment to sit down. By then, the stairwell had gotten pretty dark.

"Where should we stay for the night?" my mom asked, noticing the dwindling light.

"I had wanted to get out of here, but I don't think there's much sunlight left. Even though the sun will be up for another hour or two, it's too low in the sky for the light to make it past all the buildings." I pondered our options for a few minutes, then said, "I'll check out the fifth floor. If it seems okay, we'll stay there for the night. In the morning, though, we have to get the heck out of here."

My mom bobbed her head in agreement, then shocked me by asking, "Would you like me to help you search the floor?"

I smiled warmly at her, touched by the offer. "I would love you to help, but I think someone should stay here with Mel."

"Okay," she agreed with a nod.

Standing up, I grabbed both guns and took the magazines from them. I consolidated all the bullets into one, but even that only filled it halfway. I guess I'd fire only if I had no other options. I pulled the gun into firing position, testing out my sore wrist. Raising the gun made me want to scream, but I might not have a choice. Saving it for emergencies, I lowered the gun and slung it over my shoulder. Nodding to my mom and Mel, I went to the door of the fifth floor and carefully opened it.

First I listened. For many moments I breathed as quietly as I could, listening for any sounds. Next I hit the wall and shouted a couple times. If anything was on this floor, it would respond to the noise. Again hearing nothing for many moments, I finally crept through the door and into the hall. As quietly as possible, I stealthily jogged down the hall, moving from room to room. After opening each room's door, I paused and listened for noises. If I heard none, I moved on. Thankfully, I made it up and down the entire hall without hearing anything. Not wanting to repeat the past, I also crept down to the ice room. Holding my breath, I creaked the door open. Nothing.

Relieved, I went back to retrieve my mom and Mel. Several doors down from the stairwell entrance, we picked a room to stay in. I had tried to say we should get two rooms so we could all sleep on a bed, but both my companions adamantly opposed being separated. We settled on the largest room we could find, which had a king bed as well as a sleeper couch. As they settled in, I went to the kitchenette, thrilled to find a gas stove. When it actually worked and lit a flame, I squealed in delight. I then went to the end table where some fancy candles stood, picked them up, and took them to the stove. After lighting them, I brought them back to the table.

"Now we have light," I said happily.

"Thanks!" Mel exclaimed with a smile.

Seeing her smile reminded me that I had to go check something. I went out to the hall and crept to the ice room, glad to find that it was still devoid of any lurking horrors. Even better, the bin was still ice cold and had chunks of ice inside. I went to the closest room, grabbed their ice bucket, then went back to the machine and filled it up. When I got back to the room, I found a thin kitchen towel to wrap the ice in, then brought it to Mel. Again she smiled and thanked me.

"You are very welcome," I said, grabbing more ice for

my own wrist.

I got another towel and put the ice inside, then plopped down on the couch next to my mom. Mel sat adjacent to us, in a plush recliner. We all sighed and tried to relax as we recalled the horrors of the day.

"What a day," Mel mused.

"Indeed," my mother agreed.

"Hey Vie," Mel said, looking at my mom.

"What?"

"Happy New Year."

I snickered and shook my head as she giggled and my mom chuckled. After letting the ice numb my wrist for quite some time, I stood back up and walked over to the dining table on the other side of the room. I shoved it further across the room, right up against the door. It fit snugly under the door handle, not allowing it to be turned. In addition, I locked the deadbolt on the door.

As I did that, I heard my mom get up and go into the bathroom. I heard a faucet turn, and then water come running out. My mom dashed out of the bathroom, thrill covering her face.

"The water still works!" she proclaimed.

I nodded. "It probably will for a little bit longer. If either of you want to take a shower or… go to the bathroom… now is the time to do it."

They both offered to let the other use the bathroom first, but eventually it was determined that my mom would get the bathroom for an hour, then Mel, then me. In the meantime, I collapsed on the bed and fell asleep. When it was my turn to shower, I groggily shuffled to the bathroom and somehow got into the shower.

As I stood under the steaming water, I marveled at what a mess we were in. None of it seemed real. Here, in the normalcy of a hotel bathroom and hot shower, things seemed okay. It was easy to believe that all of it had been a bad dream, or the result of a bad drink on New Year's Eve that had been spiked with drugs. However, when I stepped out of the bathroom and saw the guns and riot gear on the floor, I knew it hadn't been a bad dream. We were definitely in a weird and awful reality.

When I lay down to sleep that night, I wondered what was next. Mel and my mom seemed to look at me for ideas, and I honestly didn't have any. Where could we go that might be better than a towering hotel? Here we had shelter and, if nobody came back for them, and infinite supply of clothes and toiletries. I rubbed my eyes as I wondered how I was worrying about toiletries when there were walking corpses outside. Because I'm human, that's how, I thought defensively to myself. I felt sleep overtaking me, so I decided I could figure out a plan in the morning.

I awoke to the delicious smell of coffee. I bolted upright, for one second thinking I was back in my home in Texas. When my eyes registered the hotel room, though, I recalled where I was. Wondering how coffee was brewing, I looked at the kitchen. I saw my mother there, standing over the stove. I got up from the couch bed and strode towards her, marveling at her resourcefulness. She had found some coffee on the counter, and had then heated up a pot of water. Once it had gotten hot enough, she had dumped the coffee grounds into the water.

"Want some?" she sang merrily as she produced a mug.

"Uh, sure," I replied.

"You are still a coffee drinker, aren't you?" she smiled, pouring some of the delicious liquid into the mug.

"Well yeah, but... I thought you hated coffee."

"No, I never hated the coffee, just the man who used to make it."

She handed me the mug, which I happily took. Although a bit deterred by her last comment, I chose to ignore it.

"Well thank you," I said awkwardly.

"You're welcome, Adeline."

For the first time in a long time, I smiled at her sincerely. She returned the smile as she pulled me into a warm embrace. I didn't yank myself out of it as I normally would have, but instead chose to enjoy it. I shut my eyes and inhaled deeply, pretending things were as they had once been.

A few moments later, Mel strode into the room, so my mother and I ended the hug. My mom offered Mel some coffee, which she gratefully took as well. As we sipped our warm drink, we all hesitantly made our way to the window. What new horrors did today have in store for us? We looked down at the street, alarmed to see that it was filled with even more walking corpses. I heard Mel groan when she saw the sight, after which she retreated to the armchair.

"What are we going to do?" she asked in despair. "The freaking guns don't even work on them!"

"The guns slow them down, but that can't be our main hope. We have less than fifteen bullets left."

"Great!" she snorted, face-palming herself.

I couldn't help but chuckle at the gesture, but I knew she was serious. I was also wondering how the heck we were going to get out of here. Like I had thought last night, maybe it wouldn't be too bad to stay here for a little while. It was only the three of us, with over twenty floors of hotel rooms to scavenge. My only two concerns were: what happens when the food runs out, and what happens when other people show up? If other hotel stayers came back here, it would lessen the length of our supplies. I frowned as I imagined how frantic people might become if they were afraid they or their families might starve. This city was known for having some of the toughest people around; how might they act if supplies ran low? My mind drifted to the front doors, recalling that I had locked them. Maybe if we barricaded the doors, nobody else could get in… To that thought I shook my head adamantly, refusing to be the one who signed the death sentence for all the people who came here.

"What is it?" my mom asked, seeing me shake my head.

"Nothing," I sighed. "I'm just trying to figure out what to do."

"Talk it out with us," Mel suggested. "It totally helps me when trying to figure out which shoes to buy. Remember last weekend when Saks was having that sale on those adorable booties? I wasn't sure if I should buy them or save the money for textbooks… oh yeah," she said, trailing off at the end as she saw my raised eyebrows. "Sorry, got distracted. Really though, talk it out with us. It helps."

I gave her a small smile and said, "Well thank you for sharing your horrible money-management story with us."

"Hey I didn't say I bought them!" she defended.

"Did you?" I asked, again raising an eyebrow at her.

"Maybe…" she said indignantly, bobbling her head and

putting her nose in the air.

"Well good for you," my mom cheerfully interjected, dismissing my disapproval with a wave of her hand.

"Mom, didn't you have to go to college to get the job you have?" I jeered.

"Yes, but nothing is more important than looking your best."

"Sure…" I replied sarcastically in a low tone. "Except in situations like the one we're in. And everyday life…"

My mom waved her hand trivially at me again, so I decided just to stop arguing with the two fashion lunatics.

"Let's just agree to disagree," I proposed. "Now, regarding real life: I was thinking we have two choices; either leave here or stay here. If we stay, we'll run out of food sooner or later and have to leave anyway. There's also the possibility that other survivors will show up, which will deplete our supplies even faster. There's also the chance that, in this horrible situation, they may not be friendly. On the other hand, if we leave here… well I have no idea how the heck we'll actually accomplish that or where we'll go."

"We could venture out of here and search nearby stores for more supplies," Mel suggested.

"That's a good idea," I agreed.

Mel clicked her tongue and tapped her head with her finger. "I've got all kinds of ideas up here," she winked.

"Wonderful!" I professed with a laugh. "Feel free to start sharing them at any time."

"I just did, and you're welcome."

I snorted with a smile, looking to my mom. "Do you have any ideas?"

"Well, not at this particular moment," she replied, looking embarrassed.

"Mom," I said, leaning forward and putting my hand over hers. "It's okay. I don't know what to do either."

"At least you have some ideas," she answered quietly.

Seeing her embarrassed and vulnerable wasn't something I was used to, and it made me really uncomfortable. I patted her hand, then quickly looked back at Mel.

"So let's talk this out. If we decide to get supplies and bring them back here, we'll have to go out to the streets. We still don't know how to kill those things. We can slow them down, but our method for even doing that is about to be extinguished."

"Extinguished?" Mel teased. "Why do you use such big words? Just talk like a normal person, you dweeb."

I squinted at her playfully, but otherwise ignored her comment. "On the other hand, if we go out there, we might find more weapons."

"But before then," Mel objected, "how are we going to fend them off?"

"Good question; especially since your ankle and my wrist are hurt."

"What happened?" my mom asked.

"I sprained it when one of those things came out of the ice room."

"You should probably ice it and wrap it, like Mel's ankle."

"Yeah, I should," I agreed. "I'll go get some ice."

I stood and went to the door. After removing the barricades, I quietly cracked the door open and listened. Hearing nothing, I slipped from the room and hurried to the ice room. I didn't think anything was in here with us, but haste seemed a good way to err on the side of caution. Once I reached the ice room, I opened the bin. Dismayed, I sighed as I only saw a puddle of water. Yesterday it had contained plenty of ice, but now it was all melted. How had that happened so quickly? The only thing I could think of was that someone else had been opening and closing it, allowing the heat from the outside to flood in and eradicate the cold within. If that was the case, then that meant someone else had been here and they might be staying in the hotel with us.

Rushing back towards the room, I pondered what the heck we should do. Unable to come up with anything, I arrived at the room with a problem but not a solution.

"We need to leave," I urged as I came through the door.

"What? Why?" my mom asked worriedly. "Are there monsters out there?"

"No, but I think someone else has been staying here. If that's the case, we need to leave."

"What if they're nice?" Mel countered.

"That's a possibility, but either way, our supplies will eventually run low. That's when we'll see what they're really like."

"Can't we stay here until then?" my mom pleaded, nervously glancing towards the window. "I really don't want to go out there."

"Neither do I!" Mel gushed, on the verge on whining.

"I don't think we have a choice," I answered as I started to pack my things.

"Addie, think this through," my friend begged. "If we go out there in our condition, we will probably die!"

"I agree with Melanie," my mom added. "We have no

way of defending ourselves, and you two are injured. I think taking our chances with a couple people in a safe place is a much better option."

I paused, looking up at them both. Their faces were both filled with fear, making me realize that maybe I was being hasty. We had cleared the twentieth and fifth floors, so maybe there was nobody here. Maybe the ice had just melted.

"Okay then," I agreed, "But how about this? We make sure our room is guarded at all times. In addition, we check all external doors to the hotel and make sure they're secure so that people can't come inside without us knowing. We barricade all entrances except the front doors. Then we take turns watching them 24/7, with one of us on guard at all times. If another person shows up, we evaluate them and decide if we want to let them in."

My small audience scrunched their brows in confusion.

"When did we become owners of this hotel?" my mom asked.

"That would be the moment we fought our way back here and earned the right to call it ours by making it inside before anyone else," I replied, being shocked by my answer. "I just," I stuttered, feeling like I needed to explain myself, "I just don't want something to happen to either one of you. People rob and kill each other every day in this city under normal circumstances. Now things are bat-shit crazy, and we're expecting them to be nicer than normal? When survival is on the line? No way."

"Okay," they both agreed, somewhat hesitantly.

I nodded in acknowledgment, hoping I was leading us the right way.

"Now let's get down to the lobby and see what we can salvage and use to block the doors."

They agreed, so we all three made our way to the stairs and hobbled down them. Before exiting the lobby stairwell, I opened the door a smidgen and listened. I was about to signal that the coast was clear when crashing sounds met our ears, making us all flinch.

CHAPTER SIX

As my mom, Mel, and I huddled in the stairwell, more crashing noises sounded off in the lobby.

"What is that?" my mom despaired in a whisper.

"I don't know," I answered, closing the door as quietly as I could. When it was shut, I turned to them, continuing to whisper. "I'll check it out, then come back to you. Try to count five minutes in your head. If I'm not back by then, go back up to the fifth floor."

"No—" my mom started to object, but I stopped her.

"If I'm okay, I'll find you up there. If I'm not okay, there's no sense in you also getting hurt."

"But we can help!" Mel argued in a loud whisper.

"Just let me check it out first," I pleaded.

"Why are you the one who has to go first?" she demanded.

"Because your ankle is hurt and I don't think my mom likes these situations."

"Well I don't think you like walking dead people either," my mom defended.

"No I don't," I agreed. "But at least I listened when Dad tried to teach us survival skills," I growled. "All you did was complain about broken nails and dirty shoes. Would you just go back upstairs?"

My mom glared at me in the dim light, then abruptly stood and dragged Mel to her feet. My best friend looked helplessly back at me while my mom muttered to herself and led them up the stairs.

I mouthed, "I'm sorry," to my best friend, then put my hands together in the sign for thank-you.

Sure, I had kind of meant my words, but more than anything I knew they would make my mom mad enough to go back upstairs. With a deep breath, I tried to prepare myself mentally for whatever I was about to experience in the lobby. Once the sound of my mom and Mel had faded in the distance, I cracked the door open again. The crashing had stopped, but that wasn't good. Now I had no idea where the people were.

Carefully, I slipped out of the stairwell and crept along the wall. Thankfully, there was plenty of light, allowing me to see well. On the downside, it also made me highly visible. I tried to stay low and hide behind anything I could, be they armchairs or plants. I made my way from the stairwell, past the elevators, and to the main lobby area. It was a mess, making me remember that I hadn't looked around at all when we had first come inside. There were several blood stains on the floor, but no bodies. I bit my lip nervously as I realized that probably meant that people had died in here. If they had died, they might have come back to life and could still be wandering around in here.

Another crash rang out, making me jerk my glance to my left. I recognized the direction as the club area, so I crouched lower and slunk that way. As I did so, someone hollered at me. Recognizing that they might be in trouble and need help, I sped up. I finally reached the area, carefully peeking around the entrance doors. There was someone behind the bar, who was throwing alcohol bottles at two assailants. I gulped as I suddenly realized that I had left my gun in the hotel room. Cursing under my breath at myself, I looked around for a weapon, spotting an iron fire poker. Why it was this far from the massive fireplace in the lobby was beyond me, but it would be a perfect weapon.

I crept from behind the doors, towards the poker. Unfortunately, the two things saw me. They snarled viciously and stumbled towards me, apparently thinking I would be an easier target than the person behind the bar. Desperately, I grabbed for the weapon and raised it defensively.

"Over here!" the voice called from behind the bar.

I grit my teeth as the things approached me, coming up with a better idea than cowering behind the bar. I backed up as they followed me, backing into the lobby. They followed, emerging from the bar area with me. Once they were at least ten feet from the doors, I lunged at them. I whacked one in the head, making a crack in the skull and spilling blood. I gagged as the dead thing fell to the floor, but I couldn't let my guard down. The other one came at me, so I swung at it with all my strength. The iron bar collided with its head, producing even more of a grotesque result than the first one had. Even though both of their heads were severely damaged, the things still snarled. Fearfully, I darted back to the club. I slammed both doors shut, locking the deadbolt on them and shoving the bar through their two handles.

"It's okay," I called behind me. "They're trapped out there. You can come out from your hiding spot."

Hearing nothing, I warily walked to the bar. Behind it, I found the person who had been yelling. It was a man, and he looked dead. He was still wearing formal party clothes. Although his hair was a little ruffled and eyeliner smudged, I could tell he hadn't been outside. He had probably been at the club when the power went out; maybe he had made his way back to his room during the day, then ended up back down here. I sighed as I knelt down by him, sad that he hadn't made it. On his shoulder there was a huge wound and a lot of blood. The injury looked a lot like Jacques'.

As I eyed the dead man, a wave of sadness suddenly took over me. Unconsciously, I again reached for the necklace hanging around my neck. Tears welled in my eyes, and I found myself saying a hopeless prayer.

"Why in the world is this happening?" I asked, lifting my eyes skyward.

All of the sudden, the sound of splintering wood hit my ears. I jumped up, looking over at the bar's doors. Sure enough, they were breaking under the strain of the things pounding against them. Not for the first time, I marveled in terror at how strong these things were. It was like they died and came back twice as strong as they had been in life. Wondering what in the world to do since I had already attacked them the best I could, my eyes darted around the room. The only other exit was the patio, but going that way meant I would have to go outside where even more of those things were.

As I despaired, I heard a snarl by my feet. I shrieked as I saw the eyeliner guy move. Somehow becoming a world-class athlete, I nimbly leapt over the bar in a split second. As soon as my feet hit the ground, I spun around and saw the man open his eyes for the first time since coming back to life. His eyelids rose, revealing completely black eyes.

I gasped as I recognized seeing the same thing in the man down in the street. This guy blinked once, and then his eyes returned to normal. Well mostly normal; they were glossed over, as one might expect from the undead. Raising my fists defensively, I had no idea how I was going to get out of this. The bar's doors continued to shake and splinter, and now they were starting to fall apart. Pieces of wood flew off the doors, telling me my time was almost up. Gritting my teeth, I glanced around the room again. The thing behind the bar had stood up, but was now trying to figure out how to get over the bar. Thankfully he hadn't made much progress, as he was mostly snarling and reaching his hands my way.

To my left, the doors shook once more, then finally broke open. The two dead things stumbled through, truly looking like something from a horror movie. Both their heads were partially bashed in, causing blood to run down their faces and all over their clothes. Still they came at me, snarling with renewed fury. I cowered backwards, realizing that in front of me the third one had figured out that he could stumble around the bar. They all three came at me, snarling and hissing loudly. My situation seemed hopeless. I wanted to cover my ears and drop to the floor, but that was just a death sentence. There was no way I was going out like that.

Suddenly the head exploded on the thing to the far left of me. A second later, the other one's also did. I gaped at them in shock, barely noticing that a man had come into the room and now aimed his pistol at the third thing. He fired, dropping the last walking corpse. I gaped at that one as well, then finally looked at the man.

"Nick!" I exclaimed, running forward and throwing my arms around him. "We were so worried about you!"

"It's nice to see you too," he replied, returning the embrace.

As I calmed down, I pulled away from the hug, suddenly embarrassed by it. "Thank you for saving me," I sincerely thanked him, nodding to the things. Their hands still twitched, but surely they were no longer a threat without their heads?

"You're welcome," he replied, glancing around. "Where is your friend?"

"Upstairs, with my mom."

"Your mom?"

"Yeah we found her in our hotel room," I answered, looking him over. "Are you okay? What happened after you were attacked? How did you get away?"

"To answer your first question, I am mostly okay. Should we get back to your friend and your mom?" he asked, glancing around. "I promise I'll tell you the whole story."

"Yeah we should get them, but I want to make sure the lobby is clear before I bring them down here."

"It's clear," he assured.

"How did you get inside?"

"A back entrance. Don't worry; I locked it once I was through."

"Oh," I answered. "Well, thank you."

"No problem. I figured you ladies were probably still here, and didn't want to let any of the changed things follow me inside."

"Changed things?" I mused.

"Aye, it's what I decided to call them. What were you calling them?"

"Whatever came to mind at the time of mentioning

them," I chuckled. "Changed things certainly seems suitable."

He agreed and then suggested, "We should get moving. I don't know what you had in mind, but if you wanted to do it today, we shouldn't waste any time."

I nodded in agreement, then headed back to the stairwell. We plodded up the steps to the fifth floor, where I was glad the climb was finally over. Breathing heavily, I led Nick to the room we had been staying in. Before opening the door, I paused and turned to him.

In a whisper so that the occupants wouldn't hear, I advised, "Since you kept referring to her as 'my friend', I'm guessing you forgot her name. It's Mel. She'd kill you if she found out you had forgotten."

"Oh, sorry," he grinned. "Now I recall. I guess I had been so focused on you that I rudely didn't pay as much attention to her as I should have."

I tried to suppress a grin, but failed miserably. He touched my chin gently and gazed at me with his beautiful green eyes. Hadn't his eyes been brown when I had first met him? Feeling like the only person in the world when his eyes were locked with mine, I decided I didn't care what color they were. I felt myself wanting to be closer to him, and almost hoped he would bring his lips to mine. However, he ran a hand over my cheek, then gestured to the door.

"Shall we go in?" he asked with a gentle smile.

"Uh, sure," I answered.

Trying to dismiss my disappointment, I opened the door. Upon seeing us, Mel squealed and yelled a bunch of things about loving us, missing us, wanting to kill us for scaring her, and being happy we were back. My mom stood and graciously introduced herself to Nick, then turned to me for an explanation. When we had all sat down on either the couch, armchair, or window sill, I started talking.

"Mom, this is Nick. We met him in the street at the New Year's Eve countdown. He helped us get to safety the night the lights went out. The next morning, he was attacked and we lost him." I glanced up at where he was sitting at the window. "What happened, Nick?"

"I went outside to see if the streets were clear all the way back to the hotel, since I wanted to make sure you girls got there safely. It looked clear, so I was on my way back. When I was almost at the door to the store, something came up behind me and attacked."

"We saw that happen," Mel gushed. "It was awful!"

"Indeed, it wasn't fun," he agreed. "But I'm glad you listened to me and didn't try to help. That thing was brutal."

"How did you escape?" my mom asked breathlessly.

"When I realized you and Mel," he answered, looking at me, "would have to go out the back door instead, I knew I had to draw that thing away from the front door. There's no way you two would make it across that distance with Mel's ankle being the way it was. So I fought even harder, eventually getting back on my feet and leading it away."

"But there was so much blood outside," I objected. "Was it yours?"

"Some of it, but most of it was the changed thing's. Anyway, after I led it away it took me a while to get back to the hotel. A lot of them seemed to suddenly come out of nowhere."

"It's the dead," Mel offered. "They're coming back to life, creating those—what did you call them—changed things?"

Nick concurred. "It's horrifying."

We all agreed, letting the conversation end there. After a bit, Nick stood up and strode to the window. He put his hands on his hips as he stared down at the stumbling things in the street, seeming to be contemplating something.

"So what was your next plan?" he asked, still staring out the window.

"We were thinking of setting ourselves up on the first floor, keeping the entrances to the lobby guarded at all times."

"Then what?"

"What do you mean?" I asked.

"You can't stay here for long. You'll run out of food eventually, but before then other survivors will come back here and demand to be let in. Not to mention, those things are surprisingly strong. They might be able to break down barricades."

"Well I don't know then," I replied indignantly.

"Hey, take it easy," Nick soothed, coming over and sitting down by me. Putting a calming hand on my knee, he said, "I was just trying to be helpful, uh… you still haven't told me your name. I doubt you want me calling you Deli like Mel suggested."

"Oh just do it," Mel laughed.

"You haven't told this nice young man your name?" my mom dramatically blurted. "That should be a sin!"

"Can you guys butt out?" I asked, putting my hand to my brow in distress.

"Of course," my mom instantly obliged. "Come on Mel; let's work out that ankle in the hall."

"Fine," Mel agreed, letting my mom help her out to the hall. Before closing the door, she glanced back and winked at me.

I bugged my eyes in embarrassment, hoping Nick hadn't seen her.

"They mean well, I'm sure," he chuckled, removing his hand from my knee and standing. He strode back to the window, leaving me uncertain as to what to do.

Nonchalantly, I followed him. We both looked down at the street, at the horrible things out there. A survivor wandered into to view, drawing the attention of the changed things. I inadvertently inhaled, knowing he was probably doomed. Sure enough, when he was focused on the three in front of him, a fourth came up behind him.

I turned away from the sight before the sickening feast started, but I was still jarred. My eyes welled with tears, and they soon began running down my face. Suddenly I felt Nick pull me towards him and wrap his comforting arms around me. It was nice, but I think he was holding me too tightly because the pendant of my necklace was digging into my skin. I pulled away from him, offering a small smile of thanks when I looked into his eyes.

"It'll be okay," he assured, rubbing my arms with his strong hands. "But look at the streets. They're crawling with those things. You have to get your mom and Mel out of here."

"Yeah, I suppose," I agreed, knowing he was right.

"Will you come with me?"

"To where?" I inquired. It sounded like he already had somewhere in mind.

"I need to get to DC."

"As in… Washington, DC?"

"Yes."

I laughed dryly. "And how is that densely populated area any better than this one?"

"I know people there."

"And?" I asked shaking my head objectively. "How do you know they're alive? How are you going to find them?"

"We had a plan. I know where they'll be."

"Assuming they're alive."

"They're alive, trust me. They've always been prepared for something like this."

"Something like this?" I challenged, gesturing to the window.

"Trust me," he insisted again, flashing a charming and reassuring smile at me. He raised his hand to my cheek, gently stroking it. "For some reason, fate happened us to meet two nights ago. I am dying to get to know you. Please don't make me leave you here to fall victim to those things. Come with me. Let me keep you safe." He gazed into my eyes, once again making me feel like the only person in the world. With one arm he pulled me into an embrace, while his other hand stayed gently on my cheek. "Please," he whispered, leaning close to my ear. "Please Deli," he whispered with a smile in his tone.

I chuckled and blushed, baffled at his insistence. "Well, okay," I whispered back, smiling like a fool.

"Thank you," he breathed, pulling me against his chest as he held my head and kissed the top of it.

"There's one condition," I added.

"Anything," he agreed as he held me and softly swayed back and forth.

"Don't call me Deli anymore."

"Well then what shall I call you?" he asked, holding me an arm's length away so that our eyes could meet. "Wait!" he exclaimed with a smile. "I know. I'll call you Eve."

"Eve…? Why?"

"Do you know the Judeo-Christian version of creation?"

"Yeah… In it, Eve is the person who ruined everything."

"Not true," he argued. "And her name wasn't really Eve; that was a poor translation. The Hebrew word is *havah*. It means life. I'm going to call you Eve because you're a survivor. You're going to live, and you're going to help your mom and Mel live. Like Eve, you are a bringer of life."

"Well, okay…" I replied, trying to hide a grin. "How in the world did you know that about her name?"

"What, I can't be an educated man just because of my rugged good looks?" he protested playfully.

I giggled, feeling more drawn to this guy with every passing minute. We locked eyes again, and I felt the moment coming. Our lips were about to meet… or not.

The hotel room door swung open, ending our moment. Embarrassed, I tried to move away, but Nick's strong arms kept me held in an embrace. I looked at him mischievously, but he just winked at me.

"Welcome back Mel and Violetta," he cheered as they came in. He turned me to face them, but kept his arms folded across my chest. "We have some wonderful news for you."

"You're pregnant!" Mel proclaimed. "Oh wait; too soon."

"Shut up!" I snickered, fighting to be free from Nick's grasp. He finally let me go, allowing me to rush Mel and tackle her to the couch.

When she finally quit screaming from my tickle attack, Nick announced his news. "You ladies are all coming to DC with me."

"What's in DC?" they chorused.

"People I know. And shelter. Hopefully some answers."

"Uhhh," Mel said, unsure of what else to say.

"You know, sometimes you can just keep your big mouth shut; you don't have to make noise just to hear yourself," I joked.

"Shush!" she laughed, suddenly swatting me with a throw pillow.

"What about the hotel?" my mom asked worriedly. "Aren't we safe here?"

Nick walked to her, gently placing a hand on her shoulder. Genuinely looking into her eyes, he said, "No love, you are not safe here. I want to get you all out of here to safety."

"Well safety does sound nice," she swooned, sounding like a school girl.

"So when are we leaving?" Mel asked.

Suddenly there was a crash in the street below. We all dashed to the window, but we couldn't see anything from our vantage point. A second later, the ground rumbled and shook.

"Get down!" Nick ordered.

We all dropped to the floor as he shouted at my mom and Mel to get under the dining table. He then grabbed my hand and yanked me to the bed, sliding me under it in front of him. We lay on our stomachs underneath, panting. I kept my eyes on Mel and my mom, trying to reassure them with my expression. It was really hard though, because I kept remembering that the same thing had happened the night the power went out. Then that super-creepy red glow had appeared in the sky, staying there for some time. What in the world was happening?

It seemed like an eternity until the shaking stopped, but in reality I'm pretty sure it was only a minute or two. When it stopped, Nick carefully crawled out from under our shelter, telling the rest of us to stay put. He gingerly walked around the room, checking for fallen objects or broken glass.

"Okay," he called, telling us to come out.

As I slid out from under the bed, he came back into the room and knelt down, offering his hand to help. I smiled appreciatively, taking his offer. We all went back to the living room, where my mom looked exasperated.

"Well what now?" she asked.

"Now we get out of here," Nick answered. "Grab whatever you want to take, but limit it to essentials." Turning to me he said, "There are a lot of stores outside, so you and I will go get any additional required necessities from them while Violetta and Mel wait here."

"We're going… out there? With those things?" I asked with fear tinging my voice. "I mean, I know we have to, but I envisioned it more as running away from here rather than hitting up stores."

"Yes, we will. But first we need to grab a few things. Imagine if one of us gets injured and we have nothing to stop bleeding or stave off infection?"

"Can't we grab that stuff as we need it?"

"No. What if something happens at night? Do you want to try to find a store in the pitch black?"

"No," I conceded. "I just…" I murmured, looking out

the window. "I just *really* don't want to be around those things."

"Nor do I," he agreed. In a quieter voice he added, "But we need to step up for the other half of our party. We seem to be the most capable members, and we need to carry the responsibility that comes with that."

I let his words soak in, knowing they were true. I shook my head in agreement, but was still frightened.

"I'll keep you safe," he assured me with a kiss on top of my head.

A short time later, he and I headed outside. The plan was that Mom and Mel would wait up on the fifth floor while we were out on the run. Once we got back, everyone would spend what was left of daylight sorting and packing our things. Then we'd sleep through the night, heading out at first light.

Nick and I trod down the stairwell, each sporting a set of riot gear. We also both carried a gun, but my rifle still only had fifteen bullets in it. Nick had the pistol he'd shot the things in the bar with; apparently he had found it on a changed police officer, along with several magazines.

"Aim for their heads," he whispered to me. "Without their heads they lose four of their five senses. Without those four, they can't find us."

Sight, sound, smell, and taste. His logic made sense. Whatever revolting force was causing these things to come back to life, there was no arguing that they couldn't get much done without those senses. Not to mention that if we destroyed their head, they'd have no teeth to eat us with. Sure they'd still have their disturbingly strong hands, but we would literally have to run right into them for them to find us.

At bottom of the stairs, Nick paused and turned to me. "Are you okay?"

"Yeah, sure. Why?"

"You were scared earlier."

"I'm still scared. But we have to do this, right?"

"Well, I could make the run by myself."

"Yeah right buddy," I scoffed. "Let's go. Stop coddling me. Aren't you in the military?"

"Yes," he confirmed. "But we take care of our comrades and encourage them when they need it."

"Well consider me encouraged," I insisted, stepping past him to the door. Sure, I was really scared. But having him think I was a frail and helpless woman wasn't going to help anything.

"Hey," he barked in a harsh whisper, slamming his hand on the door so I couldn't open it. Alarmed, I looked up at him. He had a really mad look on his face, and for a moment, I was more afraid of him than the things outside.

"Wh-what?" I asked, cowering away from him.

"This is life or death, Eve."

"I know," I whispered.

"If you're not ready for this, please tell me."

"You were the one forcing me to come out here!" I griped.

"I realize now that it may have been a bad idea. I can handle this on my own if you need to sit this one out."

"I don't."

"Okay," he said, softening his expression. "I can't explain why, but you mean so much to me and I don't want to lose you."

I stared at him in disbelief, wondering if he was telling the truth. I mean let's face it; if he was lying for the typical reason men lie, he'd have a much easier time winning over Mel.

"I appreciate that," I replied, suddenly realizing how close we were to each other. I could feel his body heat radiating towards me. "Should we get moving?" I asked nervously, wondering why I didn't want to kiss him at this moment.

"Sure," he agreed. "Be careful out here, okay? Make sure you stay with me unless I tell you otherwise."

I acknowledged the plan, and we carefully moved to the lobby. As we crept towards the back exit, we heard a low rumbling in the distance. Assuming it was the noises we had been hearing, we kept moving. However, we soon realized that the sound was growing closer. My heart nearly leapt out of my chest as I wondered what it was. Was it an earthquake; a rift in the earth that was coming to swallow us? Or was it… dare I hope it… help? Unable to focus on our mission with the noise growing closer, I darted towards the front of the building.

"Eve!" Nick hissed.

I ignored him, desperately wanting to see what was out there. If it was help, there was no way in hell I was missing it. Seconds later, I got to the front with Nick on my heels.

"You have to be careful!" he whispered harshly. "I told you not to leave me! What if you had run into a bunch of them?"

But I wasn't listening to his lecture, because beyond the windows of the hotel I was watching something incredible. I fell to my knees in disbelief as tears of joy streamed down my face. Upon seeing my reaction, Nick jerked his gaze outside. He cheered and smiled, putting a comforting hand on my shoulder. I put my hand over his, relieved that this nightmare was over.

Outside the windows, five military vehicles had parked. Out of the trucks jumped a dozen soldiers, all of who were wearing jet-black armor from head to toe, complete with gas masks. The soldiers dispersed evenly around the front of the hotel, raising their imposing guns at the approaching dead things as they did so. While they defended the hotel entrance, a single man strode towards the front doors.

"Finally!" Nick cried, dashing towards him.

CHAPTER SEVEN

Although I wondered what Nick had meant by "finally", I leapt up and helped him remove the barricades from the door. I'd love to say that the man on the other side waited patiently for us, but he did no such thing. He tapped his foot in irritation as we scurried to clear the doors. Spewing obscenities at us as we pulled away the last barricade, the man quickly proved to be someone I didn't want anything to do with.

"Maybe we should just leave the doors shut," I whispered jokingly to Nick.

"No way!" he objected. "The major means well, he's just stressed. Look at how many of those things are coming at his men."

I glanced up at the street, noticing that the changed things were coming at the hotel in swarms.

"Oh my gosh!" I despaired. "Even more of a reason to leave the doors blocked!"

"Stop it," he urged to me as the man yanked one of the double doors open.

"How do you know him?" I asked, but there was no time for an answer.

"Into the convoy, both of you!" he barked.

"Why on earth did you bring those ones?" Nick asked, gesturing to the vehicles.

"There were a ton in the metal graveyard. For now, they're all we need."

Nick muttered something quietly that I couldn't make out, to which the man nodded. Then the man looked my way and again ordered me to get in a truck.

"I need to go get my mom and—" I started, turning to dash back to the stairs. Before I could move anywhere, I felt the man's harsh grip on my arm.

"There's no time. Let's go!"

"Without my mom and best friend? No way!" I scoffed, trying to yank my arm free.

"Major Ghost," Nick interjected, "if you let us retrieve them, we'll be quick. You have my word on that."

He eyed Nick somberly, then hollered, "Well then hurry up! Stop standing here wasting time!"

With that, Nick grabbed my hand and yanked me towards the stairwell. We pounded up the stairs in record time. My lungs were working so hard that I wasn't able to talk until we got to the fifth-floor landing.

"How do you know him?" I demanded, wheezing for breath.

"He's part of the group I talked about; the one with a plan. He'll keep us safe," Nick answered as we hurried down the hallway.

"Yeah but he seems like a jerk," I huffed as I followed him.

"Do you want to stay alive?" he asked disbelievingly.

"Sure, but at what cost?"

Suddenly he stopped and spun around to look at me. He gazed at me with his intense eyes, seemingly furious. I eyed him apprehensively, backing away from him slowly.

"What's wrong with you?" I asked, remembering why I hadn't wanted to team up with him in the first place.

At that moment, my mom swung our room's door open.

"There you are!" she called, running towards us. "What's wrong…?"

"Nothing is wrong!" Nick happily promised, turning to her with a charismatic smile. "We were just coming back up here to get you and Mel. Some people have come who can help us. There's no time to explain; we need to get downstairs immediately."

"Really?" my mom asked, looking past him at me.

"Really," I confirmed, not daring to say otherwise in front of Nick.

"Violetta," he said, putting a hand on her shoulder, "you and your daughter need to grab the duffel bags and guns. I'll carry Mel down the stairs. Now please hurry; they won't wait long for us."

She smiled in agreement, dashing back to the room with a squeal. I stepped towards the room, but Nick stopped me.

"I'm sorry for… whatever that was… a moment ago. You know how badly I want to keep you safe, and it pains me that you think I would lead you into a situation that requires a *cost*, as you said. There is no cost for going with old friends. Sure, Major Ghost may not be the nicest guy in the world, but he won't harm you either. Does that make sense, Eve?"

"Yeah, sure. I mean of course it does. Your reaction just kind of… scared me."

"I know; I saw it in your eyes and it nearly killed me. I never want to cause you to look at me like that again. I'll work on it, okay? For now though, will you come with me?"

He nearly pleaded those last words, touching his hand

to my face with the utmost delicacy. I exhaled slowly, wanting to shut my eyes and savor the feeling. Instead though, I nodded and hurried towards the room.

A short time later, we all ran out of the hotel and dove into an armored vehicle. I think it was a Humvee, but honestly, I had no idea. Three men sat in front of us, with a fourth man on a gun. We huddled in the cargo space, hardly able to fit. I looked around, noticing that Nick wasn't with us.

"Where's Nick?" I huffed.

"Here," he assured, getting into one of the backseats. "I had to tell the major that we were about to make a supply run when he arrived. He has agreed to still let us go, and also agreed to let the men in this vehicle guard us."

"Oh," I said, dumbfounded. "Well that was nice of him," I muttered, apprehensively eyeing the weird soldiers and their gas masks. Not being able to see their faces was creepy and a bit unnerving.

"Sure," he chuckled. "Or he didn't want to have to deal with our supply needs. Either way, we need to be quick."

Turning to the soldiers, he thanked them for guarding us. Then he told them the few places he had in mind for us to go. With a jerk, the vehicle was suddenly in motion and moving forward. I marveled at the feeling of being in a moving vehicle, amazed that something I had once taken for granted was now a treat. As we drove, Nick turned to the three of us crammed in the cargo space.

"Eve and Violetta, you'll come with me to grab stuff. Mel, you'll stay with the soldiers."

"Sure," she agreed, "but why do you keep calling Addie by that name?"

"Because you goons wouldn't share her name with me, so I came up with one that I thought suited her."

"So you call her by the name of the woman who is responsible for the downfall of the entire human race?"

"Hey!" I squawked.

"No," Nick defended, shaking his head. "Eve's story is highly misunderstood. Did you know that Adam was standing with her the whole time? When the serpent approached her, when it tempted her, when it gave her the fruit, and when she took the first bite. Adam stood by idly and neither said nor did anything. In no way does Eve shoulder the whole blame. That is a lie that the male-dominated church has spewed for centuries."

"Whoa, calm down," Mel teased. "I didn't know I was asking a religious nut."

"Ha," he chuckled. "I can't say I've ever been called that before. I just happen to know more about the stories in the bible than most people."

Uncomfortable with anything relating to religion, my mom eagerly changed the subject. "What stores are we going to?"

"A sporting-goods, convenience, and grocery store. Major Ghost's base will have a huge stockpile of supplies, but if we bring enough for ourselves to last a good long while, I think he'll welcome the initiative and lack of strain on the camp's supplies."

"How long do you anticipate this situation to last?" my mom breathed.

"I don't know Violetta, but I would like to be prepared for the worst-case scenario. Wouldn't you?"

"Indeed," she quietly agreed, undoubtedly hoping this

horrible reality wouldn't last very long.

Suddenly the driver called out, "We're approaching our first stop. Alpha Team, be ready. Nick, your group has exactly five minutes."

"Which stop is this?" Nick asked.

"The sporting-goods store."

"It's a big place. We'll need at least fifteen minutes."

"No way. We need to conserve ammo and can't spend it all defending this place for that long."

"How about ten minutes?"

"Fine. But that's the max; any faster would be preferred."

"Absolutely." Turning to me and my mom, he said, "Move as fast as you can. We have ten minutes. Both of you need to take one of these," he said, handing us military watches.

As I took mine, I suddenly retrieved my phone from my pocket. Excitedly I checked it, but it was still dead.

"How are these watches working if our phones still aren't?" I asked. "And how are the engines of these vehicles working?"

"Eve, I don't know any more than you do. I'm sure we'll get answers later. Right now, we need to focus."

"Yeah, sure," I halfheartedly agreed. When I had seen the trucks, I had been so elated because I thought this horrible situation was all over. I thought things would be going back to normal. Instead, though, we were digging in deeper. We were desperately grabbing items to keep us alive as long as possible in this weird world, and then we were going to hide at a military camp. It all seemed so bizarre.

Suddenly we jolted to a stop, which told us we had

arrived. Nick instructed my mom and me to set a timer on our watches for five minutes. We did so as the back hatch opened. Before jumping out, we all started our timers. Instantly after that, a frenzy overtook us. We dashed into the store with one soldier, who would take care of any changed things inside. The rest of the soldiers would wait outside and defend us from the things out there.

We all made a beeline for the duffel bags, per Nick's insistence. Each of us grabbed a lot of them, probably about five each. Frantically, we yanked out the filler crap that was inside and threw it to the floor. From there we ran to different sections of the store, making sure we weren't grabbing the same things (another one of Nick's ideas). I pounded up the stairs to the second level with Nick close behind me. He was going for weapons, I was going for meals, and my mom was on the first floor getting clothes and boots. I hurriedly swiped a bunch of MRE's, food bars, and some drinks from the cooler. I filled a bag with food, another with hydrating sports drinks, and a third with water. I lugged them towards the stairs, wondering how in the world I was going to hurry back to the vehicle like this. Looking around me, I found the perfect solution. I grabbed a bunch of the items I had seen, shoving them into a fourth bag. Then I took that bag to the banister and ripped open one of the packages. From inside I pulled rope, then tied it to the banister. I slipped the other end of it through the handles of one of my bags, then pushed the bag over the banister as I held the rope. Slowly, I released more and more of the rope, lowering the bag down. Happy with my pulley system, I hurriedly lowered the next three bags. When I was done, I glanced down at my watch realizing I only had two minutes left.

"Hey!" I called to the soldier downstairs. "Can you drag those back to the truck?"

For a moment he didn't move a muscle or acknowledge that I had even spoken. I scowled at the gas mask, wondering what his expression was underneath it. Again I called down to him, but still he didn't move. I stared at him, thinking he wasn't going to help. But a moment later, to my elation, he strode towards the bags and grabbed them, then dragged them towards the front of the store. Relieved that they were taken care of, I rushed to the hunting section.

Although I was looking for Nick, I also wanted to find a weapon for myself. Sure, he was getting some for all of us, but I wanted to get my own if possible. As I ran by aisles, I glanced down them hoping to see something good. I caught a glimpse of metal down one, so I stopped abruptly and hurried down it. At the end of it, a whole display of machetes stood. I smiled to myself, grabbing a couple and shoving them into the one empty bag I had left.

Off to the left, I heard a noise. I ran that way, eager to find Nick and help him if he needed it. As I did so, I passed the gun counter. The glass on top had been smashed in, presumably when Nick had grabbed us some guns. I kept going, hearing another noise. A couple moments later I reached the aisle where I had heard the noise, but nobody was there. I saw a lantern on the floor and absentmindedly picked it up to return it to the shelf, still used to my old habits. On the shelf where the lantern should have gone, there was a small gun and several boxes of ammo. I glanced around, but didn't see anyone. Why had this been left here? Oddly feeling like I should take it, I grabbed the gun and ammo, shoving it into my bag.

All of the sudden there was a crash on the other side of the aisle. I screamed in shock, dashing around the corner. I saw Nick on the ground, on top of a man.

"Get out!" he roared when he saw me. "Run!"

As I was about to dash away, the man looked up at me. I flinched, expecting him to be snarling and have glossed-over eyes. Instead, I saw fear and terror.

"Nick he's not one of them!" I bellowed, dropping to the man's side.

"What? Yes he is!"

"No, his eyes are fine!"

Nick jumped off the man and spun him towards himself. "You call that fine?" he yelled, turning the man back towards me. Now he was snarling, and his eyes only had a vacant look in them. He hissed and reached his hands at me as I gaped at him.

"But he was fine a second ago!"

"Get back to the group!" Nick ordered.

I complied and stumbled away, eventually regaining my speed. When I got back to the group, I climbed into the vehicle. Our supplies took up a lot of the space, so we were forced to sit with the bags piled on our laps. Moments after getting situated, Nick and the soldier who had helped me came running out and jumped in. We sped away, headed for two more stores. On those stops we filled fewer bags, but the things we needed—like first aid and pills—were smaller than the items we had taken from the first store.

Eventually our time was up, and the driver sped us towards the city exit. When we reached the open expanse of freeway, I was surprised by how empty the roads were. I said this out loud, which made Nick turn and look at me.

"Well, this all started at the exact moment of the year when the least amount of people are driving."

"Yeah, I guess that's true," I agreed.

We drove a long time that night. Thanks to the watch they had given me, I was able to tell that we had been on the road for over three hours. Three hours doesn't seem like much, but when heavy bags are sitting on your lap and you're so cramped that you can't even straighten your legs, a few hours feels like forever. Eventually we reached our destination, and they let us clamber out of the confined space. I desperately asked where I could go to the bathroom, since they hadn't let us stop at all on the way here.

"This way," someone ordered.

I looked up, glad to see a soldier without a gas mask. I hurried after him, barely taking in my surroundings. From what I could tell, we were on a lawn of some sort. Bright lights lit up the area we were in, which seemed to be surrounded by a black iron fence. The person was leading me to a huge old-fashioned house, which looked really familiar. After we had climbed the front stairs and stepped inside, the realization suddenly hit me. I about fell to my knees as my breath felt like it had been knocked out of me.

"Are we… are we where I think we are?"

"Well that depends," the soldier in front of me said. "Do you think we're in hell? Then yes, we're where you think we are."

"No, I meant—"

"I know what you meant; I'm just messing with you. This whole thing's pretty fu—I mean, messed up, huh?"

"Yeah," I agreed, looking around me in awe.

"This place is pretty cool though," he agreed, seeing my

look of wonder. "And the bathrooms are the shit, pardon the pun."

I laughed and looked at him, seeing for the first time that he was pretty young. He couldn't have been older than nineteen.

"What's your name?" he asked.

"I'm uh," I paused, wondering if I should tell him my real name or the name Nick had given me. New world; time for a new identity, right? "I'm Eve," I replied, looking at his uniform. "You're Faulk?"

"All day, every day," he smiled. "Pleasure to meet you madam," he said, shaking my hand.

"You too," I smiled.

"Oh sorry, you were on a mission to empty your bladder. The bathrooms are over there," he said, pointing past us to an ornate door. "I'll wait out here for you."

I thanked him and dashed to the door, finding it to be heavier than I had expected. I marveled when I went inside, awed at how fancy the bathroom was. The floor was marble, the counters were marble; even the stalls were marble! The stall doors were an exquisite dark wood, complemented by a golden doorknob. I entered a stall and emerged a minute later, feeling infinitely better. I strode to the ornate sinks out of habit, forgetting that the world seemed to have ended. However, when I turned the knob, water came rushing out. That's when I realized that the lawn was being lit by electricity... and so was this bathroom!

I ran out to the hall where, true to his word, I found Faulk waiting for me. "You have electricity!" I cried.

"Yeah! Rock on!" he laughed.

"How?" I disputed. "In New York nothing would work,

not even batteries."

"I don't know; I haven't heard anything about New York. Is that where you came from?" he asked with a raised eyebrow.

"Yeah," I replied, barely listening. I glanced to and fro, deciding I had to get back to Mel and Mom. I hurried towards the door, with my escort protesting.

"Hey!" he called as he chased me. "Hey!" he said again, grabbing my arm. "Chill out, okay? You have to be careful around here. You can't just go running around this place. There's security everywhere, and they're trained to shoot sudden movements. You got it?"

"Yeah," I affirmed, realizing my stupidity. "I just wanted to get back to my family. Can we go back out front?"

He took me back to the grand double doors, showing me where Mel and my mom were on the lawn before he went back to his post. I found them sorting the items we had found in the stores, so I helped them out. I made sure that I kept the bag with the machetes and gun I had found close to me. Once everything was sorted, we were told to move inside. I shouldered my bags, then loaded my mom and Mel down with theirs.

Faulk came back over to us and greeted Nick, then led us inside. We rounded a few corners and walked some long hallways, finally coming to a strange door. It opened after Faulk swiped his badge over the glowing blue light to the right of it, revealing a metallic hallway. I walked down it cautiously, feeling claustrophobic.

"What is this place?" I asked, looking at Nick.

"Somewhere you definitely want to be," Faulk answered. "The chompers can't get you down here."

"The chompers?" Mel chuckled.

"Oh yeah," he answered, looking at her with a smile and wink. She giggled and looked away, making me roll my eyes.

We came to a high-tech-looking elevator, into which we all piled. After seeming to have dropped us down a hundred miles, the elevator finally stopped. I glanced at the display pad, which showed that we had stopped on floor "C50". We stepped out and went down a long hallway, in which we passed several doors. When we came to one labeled "C50-F", we stopped. Faulk opened the door for us, revealing a tiny dorm. Inside were crammed two metal bunk beds, a dresser, a desk, and a single chair.

"These are your quarters," he proclaimed.

Mel looked at me like she had never seen something so bizarre, while my mom stared unblinkingly.

"No, there has to have been a mistake," she finally said, turning to Faulk. "Dear, I think there's been a mistake."

"Colonel?" Faulk asked, turning to Nick.

"Colonel!" the three of us exclaimed in unison.

"You didn't tell us you were a colonel!" I balked.

"It didn't come up."

"Well it should have! That's kind of a big deal!" I applauded.

"I don't like talking about myself. Anyway, Violetta, there has been no mistake with your quarters. This is the most room we could spare at the moment, and your gratefulness for it would be much appreciated."

"Oh, well," she replied, slightly embarrassed. "Of course I'm grateful; it's just so... small."

I heard Mel whisper something to Faulk, no doubt

inappropriate, and they both chuckled.

"Faulk," Nick warned.

"Yes sir," he said instantly, stepping away from Mel and standing up straighter.

"Mom, come on," I urged. "Let's just get settled. Nick, or colonel, please tell Major... what was it, Ghost? Please tell Major Ghost thank you for us. And Faulk, nice to meet you."

I gestured to Mel and my mom, so they started picking up their bags and moving them inside. As we did so, I heard Nick dismiss Faulk, who went back to the elevator.

"Hey," Nick said to me, softly, putting his hand on my arm and pulling me into the hallway. He closed the door to the room so that Mel and my mom wouldn't eavesdrop. "Are you okay?"

"Yeah, it has just been a long and strange day."

"It certainly has," he agreed, eyeing me closely. "Is that it though?"

"Mhmm," I nodded, tiredly looking at his eyes.

"Are you sure this doesn't have to do with that guy in the store?"

I grimaced when he mentioned that, frowning. "Maybe a little. I swear that guy was fine. It was like you attacked him for no reason."

"No way! I attacked him because he was changed. Why would I attack an innocent person?"

"So we could get more supplies."

"Eve, listen to me. That is not how I operate; I swear. No sleeping bag or water bottle is worth the life of an innocent person."

"Okay," I conceded, happy to hear his words.

"Do you believe me?" he asked sincerely.

"Yes. Thank you for saying that; it does make me feel better. I guess I had just been seeing things."

"You might have seen what you wanted to see. It has been a strange last few days, and your brain is trying to reconcile all the weirdness."

"Weirdness? Is that the official word for it?" I chuckled.

He chuckled too, softening his gaze. My mind darted to the kiss that seemed to be looming between us. For a split second, I considered grabbing him and getting it over with, but I didn't. If it was supposed to happen, then it would happen when the time was right. Instead, I gazed softly at him too. Our looks seemed to say more than words ever could. Tenderly, his hand found mine, and he laced his fingers with mine. I smiled sweetly at him, amazed that we could create such a beautiful moment in such a harsh setting. A moment later, he brought my hand to his lips, kissing it gently.

"Get some rest," he whispered. "Tomorrow I'll treat you to breakfast and show you around."

"Ohhh," I swooned. "Is that a date, colonel?"

"It definitely is," he smiled, pulling me tightly against him.

We embraced for a long moment, then let go of each other and went our separate ways. I was on cloud nine when I went into the room, and thankfully my mom and Mel had already sunk into the clutches of sleep. I climbed to the top of Mel's bunk, for both my companions had claimed the bottom bed of each bunk. My eyes barely closed as I tried to fall asleep, and my heart raced as I pictured Nick's handsome face. Finally I felt myself drifting out of consciousness, but a huge smile stayed plastered on my face.

CHAPTER EIGHT

Sunlight bathed over me, feeling like a warm and soothing blanket. I drank in the feeling as I sat at a dainty white iron table. Our napkins ruffled in the warm breeze, seeming to come to life in the beautiful weather. My snug fur hat kept my head warm, while my absurdly expensive coat kept my whole body warm. I marveled at the luxurious coat, knowing that its price tag was higher than even my mother's ridiculously expensive taste. I wiggled my fingers in the warm brown gloves that matched my hat, also marveling at how well they fit.

"You like the clothes?"

I looked up with a smile at the handsome, dark-haired man across from me. "I certainly do!" I laughed. "I can't believe where we are, or whose clothes I'm wearing! Why aren't the people here?"

"The First family has been secured elsewhere. They are completely safe at a secret location with all the guards and supplies they'll need for years."

"Amazing," I mused, counting myself incredibly lucky to be at this place.

As I took another bite of our delicious breakfast, someone approached our table.

"Colonel Sir, there's an issue needing your attention."

"Can it wait Faulk?"

"Major Ghost asked me to find you right away."

"Okay, I'll go see him. Eve, I'll be right back. Faulk, will you keep her company?"

"Certainly sir."

Nick walked away, leaving Faulk and me by ourselves. We were on one of the many balconies, but this one was away from everyone else.

"Thank you for staying with me," I said.

"No problem," Faulk answered, peering at Nick's food.

"Do you want some?"

"Oh no, I already had my ration," he said, putting his palm up in protest.

"Ration? You're on rations?"

"This whole place is. How else are we going to survive?"

I looked down at my plate. "Is this a ration?"

"It's about five of them. The good stuff too."

"Then why am I eating it?" I asked, jumping from my seat. "I don't want Major Ghost yelling at me!"

"Major Ghost?" Faulk laughed. "You don't have to worry about him if Colonel Kadav gave it to you."

"Whoa whoa whoa!" I protested. "Two things! First, did you just say Nick's last name is cadaver?"

"No, but close. Just drop the r sound. Kadav."

"That's creepy…" I muttered. Faulk just shrugged, so I asked my next question. "Is Nick a higher rank than Ghost?"

"Oh yeah, he outranks him twice. Colonel is two ranks above major."

I pondered his words, shocked again by Nick's background. "Is Nick in charge here?"

"Yup; sure is."

I felt a small smile creep over my mouth, which I tried to hide, especially when I saw Nick coming back. He dismissed Faulk, then retook his seat.

"Everything okay?" I asked.

"Aye, there was just a slight miscommunication."

I tried to keep eating, but I didn't do very well at acting normal.

"Is everything okay with you?" Nick asked, eyeing me with suspicion.

"Oh absolutely," I beamed. "In fact, a little birdy just told me that you are the highest-ranking person here!"

He laughed in amusement, revealing his pearly teeth. "Yes, that would be true."

"Why didn't you tell me?" I grinned, slapping his arm playfully. "Do I have to call you sir now?"

"Only if you want to," he winked, electrifying me with his allure. Suddenly I felt breathless. I barely heard him when he asked if I wanted to take a walk, and am afraid I agreed a little too enthusiastically.

We stood from our meal and went down to the lawn, then walked leisurely in the garden. The walk was good for me; it was a good distraction from Nick's charm. We strolled among the bright flowers and towering trees, loving the sights. Here and there a bird sang, making me feel relaxed. I sighed happily, glad for the peace of this place. At an iron bench, we took a seat and leaned back with ease. Nick put his arm around me, so I snuggled warmly against him. Whatever secrets he had, I found myself not caring. Sure, he had some oddities about his character, but don't we all?

Seeming to read my mind, he said, "I'm glad you're here with me."

"Me too," I agreed, wrapping my arms around him and

snuggling closer. We sat in silence for a few moments, but then I had another question. "So how does a colonel end up bartending at a New Year's Eve party?"

He chuckled and said, "I knew the owner of the place. I used to bartend a while back, so thought it might be a fun time to pick it back up for the night."

"I take it the owner didn't... survive the night?"

"He actually flew to Italy for the week, so I don't know. He might still be alive."

"Speaking of which," I said, sitting up and looking him in the eye, "how is there electricity here? How do the vehicles work?"

"We aren't certain, but we think a lot of cities were unaffected by what happened. New York and DC were hit hard, but we think other places weren't hit as bad. It seems like there were a few scattered blasts of some sort that knocked out most of the electrical devices in the areas they affected. For example, DC was hit hard, but Major Ghost came from a small town that was barely hit. All the vehicles and electricity there continued to work, so he packed up his guys from his base and headed this way, per our emergency plan. When they got to DC, they realized this house was the only place in the city that was still operational."

"If their town wasn't affected, how did they know anything happened?"

"They still experienced an earthquake. And all of the major New Year's celebrations were being broadcasted on TV and radio, so when those went out they knew something was up. He tried calling a lot of us, me included, but couldn't reach anyone. The base even tried to connect to bases all over the country of every branch, but could only reach a handful of them."

"Which ones?"

"Uh, one in Oregon I think. A few in the Midwest. One in Texas."

"Texas? Which one?" I huffed.

He looked at me strangely, but still answered my question. "Lackland. It's an air—"

"Air Force base, I know that. Can we go down there? Or can I call there? Please!"

"Eve, honey, calm down. Do you know someone there?"

"Sort of; my dad lives nearby in San Antonio." I gasped as guilt flooded me for not even having thought to call him. "Oh please let me borrow a phone!"

Nick pulled a cell phone from his pocket, handing it to me. I frantically jumped up and dialed my dad's number, praying as I paced that he would pick up. The phone rang and rang, but nobody answered. When it beeped, I left a frantic message. "Dad, it's me! Please, please, please call me back at this number. I love you Dad!"

Having heard his voice in the voicemail prompt, I suddenly felt weak. Nick caught me as I stumbled back to the bench, catching me halfway in his lap.

"Hey," he said soothingly, running a gentle hand down my face, "at least the phone rang, right? If it was off or fried, it would have gone straight to voicemail."

"Yeah," I agreed, slumping against him and draping my arms around him. "I hope he's okay."

"How about this," Nick proposed. "You give me his address and I'll ask someone at Lackland to go check it out."

"Really?" I squealed, instantly feeling better. "Oh thank you!" I gushed, hugging him tightly.

"You're welcome, Eve."

I wrote down the address for him, but he insisted I go inside with him to give the order. Happily, I bounded alongside him with my fingers interlocked with his. We reached the inside of the house, where we came up on several guards. Like everyone else, they wore all black rather than normal military uniforms. Glancing at Nick, I realized that he was wearing the same thing as them.

"What branch are you guys?" I asked, glancing around at more of them.

"What?" he asked as we came to a door.

I didn't get to ask my question again though, for the door swung open, revealing a room full of important-looking people. My eyes bugged as they stared at us, but Nick kept his hand clasped over mine as we walked to the front of the room. When we got there, he greeted the person who had been speaking, who happened to be Major Ghost. I did a double take at the major, realizing that he was much younger than I had thought he was. When I had first seen him yesterday, I'd guessed his age to be in the mid-fifties, if not older. Now he looked like he was the same age as me and Nick, in the mid-twenties.

"Major Ghost, I would like to apologize for interrupting, but this is an emergency." Nick turned to the people sitting around the long table and asked, "Who is in charge of communications with other bases?"

"I am sir," a young man replied. "Second Lieutenant Rodriguez."

I blinked in disbelief as I realized he was as young as Faulk. Scanning the entire room, I realized everyone was extremely young. How had they come to these ranks so soon in their lives?

"Second Lieutenant Rodriguez, please take this address and make contact with Lackland." The young man hurried to the front of the room where Nick stood and took the note. "Ask them if they have any people available to go to this house and secure the man within. His name is..." he paused, looking at me.

"Bruce; Bruce Homes," I gushed.

"His name is Bruce Homes," he continued, "and he is very important to us. If they could do this, it would be an enormous favor to me."

"Roger sir," Rodriguez assured as he took the note.

"As you were Major Ghost," Nick said, patting the man's back.

He nodded, then continued speaking to the room as we exited. I expected us to go back to the garden, but Nick paused in the hallway.

"Want to see the presidential room?"

"Uhm, am I allowed to?" I laughed nervously.

"They're long gone; I don't see why not. Come on, it'll be fun," he grinned, taking my hand.

Together we ran across the front room, then down a luxurious hallway. At the base of a grand staircase, several guards made us briefly stop. Since Nick was in charge though, they easily let us pass moments later. We giggled as we skipped down the hallways, feeling like two teenagers ditching school. Nick led us to a closed door, pausing dramatically in front of it.

"May I present to you, madam, one of the most exquisite bedrooms in the entire world!" he said, bowing low dramatically.

I laughed out loud and clapped my hands together. "Bravo monsieur! I am ready!"

He took my hand again, then opened the door with his free hand. I inhaled sharply as he led me inside, oohing and aahing all the while.

"Quite something, isn't it?"

"Oh yeah," I agreed. "But it's kind of…"

"Old?"

"Yeah!" I laughed. "I thought they would have modernized it a little more. Don't get me wrong—it's incredible—but it looks like it's stuck in the wrong century."

"Well, once you get settled in, you'll see the modern improvements."

"Once I get settled in?"

"Oh! Come look at the balcony!"

He trotted across the room with me in tow, opening a French door to reveal a majestic balcony.

"Wow," I said in awe, "the view up here is amazing!" As I said that, my eyes scanned across the lawn to the fence, where a crowd of changed things stood snarling and swaying. "Ehh, kind of."

"Oops, that sure ruins the fun," Nick laughed, ushering me back inside. He shut the doors as I continued to marvel at the room within. "Check out the bathroom," he said, walking past me to another heavy door. He swung it open, revealing one of the nicest bathrooms I'd ever seen.

"Wow," I chuckled. "Now I see the modern stuff," I said, pointing to the TV over the bathtub and LED panel in the shower. I ran my fingers over the edge of the tub, still in awe of where I was.

"Would you like to use it?" Nick asked.

"Me? Oh no, thank you though."

"Why not?"

"Are you kidding me? It wouldn't feel right!"

"My dear," he smiled, placing reassuring hands on my arms, "they aren't coming back here for a while, even if this whole thing resolves itself tonight. Come on; it'll be the best bath of your life!"

I grinned and looked down at the tub, still hesitant. "What about my mom and Mel?"

"You can bring them up here and take turns. The other two can just lounge in the bedroom and watch TV in the meantime."

"Really?" I beamed.

"Really," he smiled in return. "I'll call someone to go get them."

A long time later, I emerged from the steamed-up bathroom in an impossibly plush robe and soft slippers. I dreamily waddled to the bed, where my mom and Mel were lazily watching a movie. I plopped down onto the bed, letting out a long and relaxing sigh.

"My turn!!!" Mel squealed, jumping up with enough force to fly to the moon. "I mean uh, Vie, do you want to go next?"

"No," my mom laughed, graciously pawing her hand at my friend. "Go ahead sweetheart."

Mel excitedly dashed to the bathroom, slamming the door shut behind her. We heard the surround sound system kick on, and music started blaring. Mel bellowed her heart out, and sure did her darndest not to be outdone by the speakers. My mom and I laughed happily as I settled more comfortably onto the bed.

"I can't believe this place," my mom commented.

"Me neither. I can't believe we're here."

She looked at me seriously, putting her hand over mine. "And I'm glad it's *we*, not one or the other."

I studied her face for a moment, trying to decide if she was being fake or not. I squashed my lips together, deciding she had no reason to be disingenuous here, in front of only me. "I'm glad too," I finally said, daring to inch closer and snuggle with her.

That made her smile like I hadn't seen her do in a long time. Quite content, we turned our attention back to the movie and watched it with happy hearts. A while later, Mel emerged from the bathroom, looking as relaxed as I had after my bath. My mom excitedly got up and took her turn in the bath. Mel and I popped in a new movie, not seeing my mom again until about halfway through it. We all snuggled on the bed, cozy as ever. Towards the end of the movie, there was a knock on the door. Mel called the person inside, and a moment later Nick walked in.

"Well look at you ladies," he smiled. "I'm glad you enjoyed the bath."

"Oh did we!" my mom expressed.

"Thank you!" Mel professed, jumping up and bounding over to him. She grabbed him and pulled him into an embrace, planting a kiss on his cheek in the meantime.

He laughed a little uncomfortably, saying, "You're very welcome. I'm happy to have made your night." He then looked at me and asked, "Can I talk you for a minute?"

"Absolutely," I agreed, getting up and going out into the hall with him. "What's up?" I asked when he had shut the door. He started walking slowly down the hall, so I followed.

"I have news on your dad."

"And…?" I asked breathlessly.

Nick turned to me, pulling his lips tight against his teeth. "They found him."

"Is he okay?"

"Indeed."

I let out a huge sigh, slapping Nick on the shoulder. "Why did you do that to me?" I laughed, so relieved to hear that my dad was alive.

"I'm sorry," he grinned. "I suppose I have a flair for the dramatic. Anyway, they found him. The problem is, he doesn't want to come here."

"Why not?" I asked in alarm.

"I don't know. In the morning I'll take you downstairs and have you call him again."

"Can't I call him now?"

"No, sorry. The guys I've been communicating with over in Texas are off duty right now."

"But I have his number."

"I think the guys have his phone right now. They wanted to charge it up, and make sure he got some sleep."

I scrunched my brows in confusion. "Are you saying what I think you are? Is my dad a prisoner?"

"No! They detained him for the night, just in case he tried running. Eve, it's for your benefit. Don't you want to see him? That won't happen if he tries to run off and gets killed in the night."

"Why would he run off? What aren't you telling me?"

Nick sighed. "I didn't want to upset you. When they made contact with him, he flipped out. He started swearing and shooting at them."

I suddenly laughed, despite myself. Nick looked at me like I was crazy, so I explained, "Yeah, I guess that sounds like my dad."

"Does he hate the military or something?"

"No, not exactly. He used to be in it, as a matter of fact."

"Oh. Well my hat's off to him. What changed?"

"Something happened a while ago, when I was younger. He suddenly became paranoid and wouldn't let my mom or me go anywhere without him. He was obsessed with making the house safe, and making sure we were prepared for what he called the end of the world."

"Is that so?" Nick asked with a raised eyebrow.

I didn't notice, since I was lost in memories. "Yup. It drove my mom crazy. That's what caused their divorce. I stayed with my dad. Some of what he said made sense. He taught me a lot of useful survival skills, and seemed to genuinely think there was something out there. He cared about my safety."

"How'd you end up in New York?"

"Oh, it was always a dream of mine to be there on New Year's Eve. My mom pulled some strings and got us a free room at that amazing hotel, and well, you know the rest." My face fell a little as I thought of my dad, hoping he was okay.

"Hey," Nick whispered, stopping our stroll in the hall and turning to me. "He'll be fine. You'll talk to him in the morning, I promise."

"Thank you," I sighed, looking up at his eyes.

"In the meantime, I want you to get some rest."

"Yeah, I'll gather up my party and go back to our room."

"Or," he smiled, turning and opening the door we stood by. He walked into it and flipped on the light, revealing another majestic, slightly smaller room than the presidential one. "This is the secondary master bedroom. Your mom and Mel can stay in it tonight."

"Wow! Thank you! Wait; Mom and Mel…?"

"Yes. You can stay in the other one."

"I don't want to stay in there by myself!" I laughed in protest.

"You won't be alone," he said sweetly, taking my hands in his.

"Oh. Uh…" I gulped, darting my eyes around the floor.

"Not like that," he said softly, taking my face into his hand and tilting my chin up towards him. "I'll just be there beside you; that's all. I don't like you down in that bunker, so far from me. You, your mom, and Mel deserve to be up here."

"Why?" I challenged him, starting to feel like he was trying to flatter me.

"Why?" he laughed. "Because you're survivors! You have survived this so far; why shouldn't you deserve the best rewards for it?"

"Isn't life reward enough?"

"It's a reward, but why not take more when it's just sitting here, waiting to be used by someone as beautiful as you." He suddenly pulled me close, tightly against him. "Please Eve, allow me this honor."

A few minutes later, I was trying to explain to my mom and Mel the plan. Their reactions were both along the same lines, although I'm not sure why that surprised me.

"Hell yeah lady!" Mel cheered, giving me a high five and

then slapping my backside.

I rolled my eyes at her as my mom swooned, "Oh darling, you've made quite the catch!"

"Would you both stop," I begged, giggling as Mel made absurd faces at me. "I'm serious; nothing is going to happen."

"I've heard that before," Mel smirked. "From myself. Doesn't happen."

"Well I'm not you," I countered, raising my eyebrows at her and turning on the sass.

"Whoa, excuse me!" she said, putting her hands up in defense. "I'll just grab my clothes and head to my own room. Come on Vie!"

They both continued making ridiculous comments at me, making me wonder if at some point their personalities had been switched out with men's. A few minutes after they left, Nick came into the room.

"Hey," he smiled.

"Hey," I replied, trying to play it cool.

"I brought these for you," he said, holding up a stack of clothes. "It's sleeping attire that we found. I think it's all, uh, appropriate."

"Thanks," I said, grabbing it and dashing to the bathroom. To my relief, he had been right when he said it was appropriate. I happily put on long flannel pants and a long-sleeved flannel shirt, then went back out to the room. As I got into bed next to the person I hardly knew, I suddenly felt like an idiot. What if he forced himself on me? He didn't hide the fact that he liked me; maybe he didn't care what I wanted. And who would do anything about it if he did? He was the highest-ranking person here, whom everyone seemed to respect.

"Uh, I'm actually going to sleep with my mom and Mel," I said, quickly getting out of the bed and making my way to the door.

Nick jumped up and beat me to it, standing in front of it so I couldn't leave.

"Eve," he pleaded. "Don't do this. I know what you're thinking. I don't want to hurt you honey. Haven't I helped you and saved your life? Why would I do that just to hurt you?"

"I don't know, but I do know that we're nearly strangers."

"Fine. Please stay in this room. I'll go sleep elsewhere."

"Don't be absurd," I opposed, but he cut me off.

"I'm serious Eve. I want you to trust me. I'll go sleep downstairs. See you in the morning," he said, kissing the top of my head.

With that, he left the room. I stood in the dark silence for a moment, trying to decide what to do. I really didn't want to sleep alone, but I also didn't want to go get Mel or Mom and make one of them sleep alone. Sighing, I went back to the comfy bed. Cracking a small smile, I leisurely stretched out across it, sprawling my limbs to every corner.

I didn't even realize I'd fallen asleep when I opened my eyes to sunlight. I rolled to my right, feeling something beside me. I screamed as I flung my eyes open, seeing Mel lying there staring at me.

"What is wrong with you?" I groaned, clapping my hand to my forehead.

"Lots of things," she laughed. "I see you ran off your lover already."

"Ugh, don't say that it word, it's so gross. And you don't know if I ran him off; what if he's just in the bathroom?"

"Mmm nice try, but he's the one who woke us up."

"What did you do to him?" my mom inquired, making me realize that she was sitting on my left side.

"Jeeze you two," I laughed, sitting up. "It just didn't feel right sleeping next to a stranger."

To that, I saw them exchange strange looks. "Sure, whatever," Mel murmured. "You hungry? They made us breakfast."

I dressed in record time, happy to have a set of new clothes from our supply grab yesterday. Once dressed, I hurried downstairs, eager to find Nick before I ate anything. Finding him in a room with several others, I waved to him from the doorway. He gave me the signal for one minute, so I eagerly paced the hall until he came out. Knowing what I wanted, he led me to the communications room.

Along the way, he asked, "How did you sleep?"

"Excellently, thank you for asking. How about you?"

"Decently. I'm glad you slept well Eve," he said sincerely.

We reached the room, where there were two people working. One of them was repeatedly making SOS calls to other bases, while the other seemed to be waiting for us. He dialed Nick's people at the base where my dad was, then handed the phone to Nick and excused himself. Someone picked up on the other end of Nick's phone, making my heart skip a beat. He spoke to them for a minute, then was put on hold.

"They're going to get him," he explained to me.

I smiled at him happily, anxious to talk to my dad. However, a moment later someone came back on the phone. Whatever they said made Nick frown, which made me worry.

"What is it?" I whispered.

"I see," Nick said into the phone, signaling for me to wait. "Okay, I'll call you back as soon as we decide. Thank you."

He hung up, then turned to me with his brows furrowed. "They said he wouldn't come to the phone; that he said there was no way his daughter was really calling for him. He said it was a 'trick of the enemy' and demanded that they release him."

"No," I moaned, trying not to cry. Had he finally gone mad?

"They asked if we wanted to come get him."

I snapped my gaze from the floor to Nick's eyes. "Can we do that? Is that really a possibility?" I asked excitedly.

"Maybe," he said with a long sigh. "Although we don't have many people here as it is, and I don't want to spend more on a side mission."

Always one for paying attention to the smallest of details, I raised my eyebrows. "Side mission? Then what's the main mission?"

"Classified," he answered with an apologetic expression.

"What about the people who picked us up? Can you spare them?"

"No, they're one of my best teams. Major Ghost and his men only risked themselves because I was out there."

"You said it might be possible to get my dad though," I pleaded, gripping his arm with both of my hands. "What makes it possible? What can I do? I'll do anything!"

I saw something flicker in his eyes, but it was gone in an

instant and he didn't say anything about it. He clenched his jaw, then looked at me somberly. "There is one thing, but it's dangerous."

"What? Anything?"

"Maybe if you could find more survivors and we trained them, I could spare the bodies to go get your dad."

"Sure!" I agreed instantly, not letting myself think about the fact that I'd have to go out there with the changed things. "Where do I start? Should I go now?"

"No way," he chuckled. "You need training first. A lot of training."

"Training? I don't have time for that!"

"You have nothing but time, Eve. Your dad isn't going anywhere. Lackland will keep him there if I ask them to."

I scrunched my face up, picturing him held there for weeks. "That might be the end of him," I whispered. Looking back at Nick, I asked, "Will you call them again? Ask them to bring the phone to him. He needs to hear my voice. Please?"

Nick nodded. "I need to call them back anyway. I'll ask them to do that."

I anxiously waited as he called them and asked them to do what I had requested. After a few moments, Nick handed me the phone. Gingerly, I took it and placed it against my ear.

"Hello?" I softly called. Hearing nothing, I again said it.

"Who's this?" a panicked voice asked.

"Dad!" I whimpered, sinking helplessly into the chair beside me. "Dad it's you!"

"Is this the thing they got to impersonate my kid?" he growled. "How dare you!"

"No! Dad it's me! I promise!"

"Of course it would say that. I suppose you have normal eyes, too."

I gulped and frowned in confusion, trying to figure out what he meant. Suddenly I remembered the changed things' eyes, and how they were black when the things first changed. Somehow I knew that's what he was referring to. "Yeah, my eyes are normal Dad. They're not black. How about yours?"

"Mine?" he asked, sounding surprised. "Mine are... mine are fine."

"So are mine."

"Oh my gosh," he muttered in realization. "Is it really you?"

"Yes Dad," I eagerly assured. "I swear it." He didn't say anything, but I heard labored breathing and a few sniffles. "How are they treating you in there?"

"Well enough I suppose," he answered, trying to sound strong.

"They found you because I asked them to Dad. Do you mind staying there until I get there?"

"You're coming here?" he gasped. "No darling, don't!"

"Dad it's okay; I'm coming with friends."

"You can't trust them!" he insisted. "Anyone who survived this isn't right!"

"You and I survived though," I argued.

"Yeah, but they were prepared, weren't they? The people you're with have gear and strength, don't they?"

I didn't say anything, but wondered how he knew that. Sure it was obvious that they were military and could communicate with the base, but did that automatically mean they had been prepared?

"They got us and they'll get you too!"

"Us? Who's us? Please calm down," I begged. "You're wrong about them being dangerous; the man I'm with has already saved my life several times."

"Even worse! Has it happened in a strange situation each time? Have you seen things you can't explain?"

"Uh yeah; the dead rising and eating the living!" I countered.

"They're heading it! I told you they'd come one day; don't trust them!"

"Dad—"

Suddenly the phone dropped and I heard a commotion. My dad yelled something out, and I could tell the soldiers were trying to restrain him. I broke into tears, barely able to hand the phone back to Nick. He said a few more words to his people, then hung up. I miserably made my way back upstairs with his help, finding Mel and Mom in their room. Nick dropped me off with them, then let us have our privacy.

"What happened?" Mel asked venomously, looking towards the door where Nick had been. "Did he do something to you? I don't care how hot he is; if he did I'll kill him!"

"No," I groaned. "Not him." I brought my eyes up to my mom's. "Mom, I talked to Dad."

"Your dad?" she exclaimed. "How on earth did that happen?"

"Nick has been in contact with the base by where Dad lives. I asked him to go to the house…"

"Oh darling, you had to know he wouldn't react well to

that."

"I know; but I had to find out if he was alive! It turns out that he is, but they had to lock him up to make him stay. He thinks they're behind all this. He got all crazy and they had to restrain him…"

I started crying again, so my mom got a pillow and had me lay my head in her lap on the comfy bed. Mel sat beside us, watching my mom tenderly stroke my head.

My mom looked at Mel and asked, "Do you know about her father?"

"No, she doesn't talk about him much."

"He used to be an incredible man; loving, handsome, and so very noble. He was even a highly respected military man, having the rank of major general. Major General Homes." She smiled fondly, remembering the good times. Then her face fell as other memories surfaced. "But then, something happened about fifteen years ago that made him lose everything."

"What was it?" Mel asked.

"I'm not sure; he never told us. All I know are scattered details. He was supposed to have been on a deployment somewhere in Africa, but while he was gone he sent me a postcard from Nordkapp. It's a tiny little town in Norway, at almost the northernmost part of the country. The post-card didn't make any sense. Not only was he supposed to be in an entirely different part of the world, what he wrote was completely unlike him."

"What did it say?"

"Nothing he'd normally say. He was always a loving and valiant man, usually writing in a serious tone. But this note was absurdly cheerful and bright. I thought he was crazy.

When he finally got home, he told me the postcard had been some sort of code. He started ranting and raving about a conspiracy. He started watching us like hawks, not letting me or Adeline out of his sight. He'd watch for cars following us and people outside our house. I never got a straight answer out of him about what he was doing in Norway."

"Wow, that's straight out of a movie," Mel breathed.

"Unfortunately. But life doesn't play out like the movies. He ended up getting dishonorably discharged from the military. I couldn't take his erratic behavior anymore and took a trip to New York."

"And never came back," I said angrily, sitting up from her lap.

"I tried taking you!" she countered. "He wouldn't let me!"

"Thank goodness. You just left us Mom. Who does that?"

"I had to get away from him!"

"You just left us!" I reiterated. We stared at each other in silence until I decided to finish telling my story. "Nick said we can go get him if we train and recruit more guards."

"Pardon me?" my mom scoffed.

"Recruit guards? I like the sound of that," Mel said playfully.

"This is serious Mel," I said, looking earnestly at her. "He wants us to train a bit before going back out there though."

"How long is a bit?"

"I don't know. We didn't get into details. What do you guys think?"

"I think I'm not risking my life to bring a lunatic here,"

my mom said coldly.

I curled my lip angrily at her, resisting the urge to unleash a string of verbal lashings on her. "He was your husband!" I thundered.

"Was."

I flinched and curled my lip again, getting up and leaving the room. Mel chased after me, not letting me shake her.

"Hey, I know your mom made you mad, but don't push me away." She grabbed my arm as I reached the door to the room I had slept in. "So," she inquired, "how do we do this? What's first?"

I allowed myself a small grin, looking her in the eyes. "I don't know. Let's ask Nick."

Ask Nick we did, who was happy to start us in training. First he had Mel work on physical therapy for her injured ankle while I practiced my marksmanship. When we started I was concerned about wasting ammo, but he said not to worry since they made all their ammo on-site. Where they were getting the supplies to do so I had no idea, but he didn't seem worried about it so I wasn't either. I practiced on a rifle and handgun in several different stances: standing, kneeling, and lying down. Nick also had me practice hand-to-hand combat with a rather large knife, insisting that I needed to know it. This was my favorite, although I wasn't sure why. Something about the blade and being in such close proximity to your enemy was so primal and thrilling.

Mel's ankle healed nicely, which allowed us to start running together. Nick had us do a ton of physical training, and sure as hell didn't go easy on us. Several times he had the instructors run us to the point of vomiting. After heaving our guts up, he made us rehydrate and then keep running. We also lifted weights and tried to do things like push-ups and pull-ups. At first it was more of a joke than anything. Sure, both Mel and I were thin, but that didn't mean we had the strength to do these things. As time passed though, we eventually did develop said strength.

I saw Mel go through a staggering change, too. She became tough as nails. Never had I seen her apply herself so wholly to something other than drinking and flirting. I marveled at her changes, hoping I was as tough as her.

My mom watched us, from a distance at first. She didn't want anything to do with the training initially, but slowly we started to win her over. Never one for wanting to be left out, she eventually started doing training with us. I was awed by her devotion, too. Watching her train made me admire her for the fighter spirit she apparently had. Sometimes I would chuckle to myself, amazed that both my parents were so resilient. I was ever grateful that they had passed that gene on to me.

Together, the three of us grew stronger. We even moved back down to our tiny room so that the frills of luxury wouldn't distract us from how bad things were outside. Enviously, the three of us would watch as soldiers would get called out beyond the gates. Every time we would ask Nick if we could go, but each time he would say that we weren't ready.

I got to talk to my dad a few times a week, thankfully. I had hoped that maybe the world would right itself before we got to him, but it didn't look like that was going to happen. As days and then weeks passed by, I started to lose hope that the world was going to go back to normal anytime soon. Every week, Nick's people lost touch of another base. Rather than returning to normal, it felt like the world was getting worse.

At least the people I cared about were getting stronger—even my dad. The soldiers wouldn't release him from their custody, saying he was a danger to society, but they allowed him freedom on base. He kept up his own marksmanship and physical strength, sounding as though he was training as hard as we were.

One night, we finally got the chance to prove ourselves. I was woken by the ground shaking, which I was used to happening pretty often. This time though, our hall alarm started sounding. Hurriedly, I threw my uniform on and shouted at mom and Mel. They were already on it though. Mere moments later, we grabbed our gear and dashed to the elevator. I prayed it would work as I pushed the button, relieved to see it light up. It shot us to the ground floor, where we ran out to see the house in panic. We thundered up the stairs towards Nick's room, but met him hurrying down.

"What's happening?" I yelled over the commotion.

"We aren't sure," he said quickly.

We followed him to the command room, surprised that they let us in.

"Major Ghost," Nick said immediately upon entering.

"Colonel Kadav," he barked. "We're concerned that our perimeter has been breached. We saw a horde stumbling this way last night, but didn't think—"

Whatever the rest of his sentence was, I didn't care. I slipped from the room, causing Mel and my mom to follow. They shuffled after me in their combat boots with their rifles ready.

"Where are we going?" Mel shouted.

"To see what's going on!"

"Shouldn't we wait for orders?" my mom objected.

"No," I said determinedly. "They need help outside. We'll find whoever's in charge out there."

We hurried towards the front door, but suddenly there was an explosion. The entire front of the building exploded into a million pieces, the shockwave of which hammered us to the ground. Debris rained down around us, making us cover our heads protectively. I darted my eyes to the front of the building, raising my gun as I did so.

"Stay alert!" I shouted to my two comrades.

Smoke and debris filled the air of the gaping hole in the building, but the huge lights out front lit it up quite well. Within the smoke, something huge was moving. I grunted as I rolled over and squirmed on the ground, trying to steady myself and my gun atop the rocky debris. Holding my breath, I kept my eyes on the smoke as the massive shape drew closer. My heart pounded as the thing came to the edge of the haze, revealing itself. My jaw dropped in terror, and all my strength momentarily left me.

"What the shit!" Mel whispered shakily.

I gaped and shook my head slowly, wondering what in the world to do. Before us stood a ten-foot-tall rotting chomper that was growling and dragging two dead soldiers in each of its mammoth hands. It looked around the room, spotting us. Suddenly it snarled and stepped our way, roaring mightily.

CHAPTER NINE

Making the mistake of knee-jerk reacting and not thinking, we all unloaded a magazine at the thing. It had no effect other than making it even angrier. It bellowed out another roar, swinging the dead bodies that it held and then throwing them at us. We dodged them and ran for the stairs, but one hit Mel, making her plummet to the ground. My mom and I stopped instantly, turning around to grab her.

"Go!" she hollered. "I'll figure it out!"

"No way!" I bellowed, rolling the body off of her as my mom pulled her to her feet.

The thing barreled towards us, reaching us just as we got her free. It reached a grotesque hand at us, swiping me off the ground. I screamed as I dangled from its hand, yanking out my knife. With all my might I jabbed it into the thing's flesh, making it growl and drop me. I fell a couple feet to the floor, landing with a thump.

Forcing myself to dismiss the pain, I scrambled back to the stairs and suddenly heard a hollow thunk just above my head. I looked up, relived to see Nick standing there with a grenade launcher. I spun around just as the grenade exploded on the beast, somehow setting it ablaze. The thing screeched and ran back outside, tumbling to the ground a minute later. I dashed out there, amazed to see it engulfed in flames. As it burned, it didn't snarl or move.

"Fire!" I roared, turning to the personnel around me.

"These things can be killed with fire!"

"Chompers!" Faulk suddenly called from beside me, pointing at the massive hole in the fence that the behemoth had made.

I yanked a grenade from my belt, sending it flying towards the group. A few seconds later it exploded, also mysteriously lighting them on fire and stopping their movement. I laughed and threw another grenade. "Take this you bastards!"

It took some time, but we were able to completely halt their advance on us and barricade our fence. As the fires dwindled, I noticed that the bodies burned down completely, leaving nothing but ash. I pointed it out to Nick, but he didn't find it odd.

"Human bones don't burn down entirely from a normal fire," I stated.

"Agreed, but they also don't usually come back from the dead."

"True," I agreed with a dry smile. "But normal grenades also don't light flesh on fire."

"Sure they do."

"Only in Hollywood. Shouldn't you know that?"

"Of course; I'm just joking with you. We specially make our grenades."

"You make your own grenades? Why?"

"In case we ever needed to burn things, I suppose. Good thing too, because they sure came to our aid tonight. You did a brilliant job discovering that the fire harms the changed things."

"Thanks," I grinned.

"Can you help us get this place cleaned up? We'll need

all the help we can get," he said, looking around before pulling me into an embrace, "and nice work tonight."

I smiled and he released me, then made his way back to the house. As I turned to the giant thing that was still burning, I noticed that it was finally almost done burning down. I decided to stay and watch it, since I'd probably clean it up right afterward.

Just as the fire burned up the last bit of the body, I could swear a dark shape rose from it, then darted off into the night. I blinked several times, looking at the smoldering pile of ash. It was dark outside and impossible to say if I had really seen anything, so I didn't tell anyone about it. If I ever saw it again, then maybe I'd bring it up.

After an exhausting night of cleaning up and re-securing the fence, my mom and Mel exhaustedly went to bed. I didn't join them though; instead I offered to take the first night watch so that someone else could sleep. That someone else happened to be Faulk, who thanked me profusely. Of course, he refused to go inside and instead slept on the ground next to his post, where I kept watch. The next few hours were pretty dull, and I found myself fighting to stay awake. I tried pacing, tossing a rock between my hands, and counting the stars.

Eventually I landed on getting out my awesome night-vision binoculars and scanning the grounds. I spotted a group of changed things about a block from our fence, heading our way. I was about to tell someone when I saw a small group of soldiers hurrying that way. There were about five of them, all wearing full gear and gas masks. I frowned when I saw them; I hated those gas-mask guys. They were so creepy. Not all of the soldiers here wore them, like Faulk, but a good number of them did. Once I had asked Nick about it, but he wouldn't answer. I guess it was part of their classified mission or something.

As I watched the men, I was expecting them to throw a grenade towards the group of changed things. However, I was shocked to see them continue to get closer to the things. As they drew even closer I watched in horror, afraid that the soldiers didn't even know how close they were to the things. To my great shock, they jogged right up to the things. I cringed in horror, waiting for them to get ripped apart.

But they didn't. The changed things continued to meander around as if they didn't even see the soldiers. At first I was really confused, but then I realized what had happened. Nick's people had found a way to blend in with them! I kept watching them, but soon the soldiers went around a corner and disappeared from my sight. I anxiously waited for my watch to be over. As soon as it was, I woke Faulk and dashed off to find Nick. He had just awoken and taken a shower, but called for me to enter his room after I knocked.

"You did it!" I congratulated as I paced the room.

He came out of the bathroom in a plush robe, running a towel through his wet hair. "Did what?" he asked.

"Don't pretend you don't know!" I laughed, skipping over to him and looking into his eyes. "You found a way to blend in with them!"

"With who?"

I blinked confusedly. "The changed things."

"I did?" he asked skeptically. "Then this is news to me."

"But I saw them!" I insisted.

"Saw who?"

"Your people. Last night they were right by the changed things and the things didn't attack them."

Slowly, he lowered his arm. "Where did you see this?"

"Beyond our walls."

"What were you doing out there?"

"I wasn't. I was watching them with my binoculars."

"Which direction?"

"North."

"Thank you for bringing this to my attention. I'll ask Major Ghost about it and who the men were."

I nodded, hesitating to mention my next concern.

"What is it?" he asked, striding over to me. "Don't you want to get some rest?"

"Yeah, I do. I'm so tired… but I wanted to ask you something."

"Ask away," he smiled, taking me into his arms.

"I'm filthy," I objected, looking down at my dirt and ember encrusted uniform that was dangerously close to his glistening white robe.

"Like I care," he chuckled. "Want to shower and sleep up here today?"

"No," I answered firmly. "I want to keep focus. Speaking of which…"

He cracked a smile, knowing what I was going to say. "Yes, I agree."

"You do?" I breathed.

"Of course. You did well last night. I think you've got this down. Violetta and Mel have morphed into capable soldiers as well. You have my permission to make a run today."

"Oh thank you!" I cried, jumping up and down like a foolish school girl.

"Now will you allow yourself to sleep up here?" he quipped.

"Sure, if it'll make you happy!"

"Of course it would. I love seeing you comfortable. I'll get a bath filling for you while I get dressed."

I smiled and he disappeared back into the bathroom. I heard water come on behind the closed door, so I started removing my gear. I put most of it on top of the bedside table, which I also leaned my gun against. I then carefully removed the rest of my gear, and finally my boots. Happily, I curled my toes up and squashed them into the soft carpet, sighing in relaxation. A moment later, Nick came out of the bathroom in his own uniform. I lazily walked that way to say bye to him.

"Take a nice bath and get some sleep," he urged, pulling me against him again. "I'll send a message to your comrades," he grinned. "When all of you are ready, head out on your mission. I don't want you going too late in the day, so you won't get to sleep that long. Unless of course, you'd like to go tomorrow."

"No way," I replied. "I've waited long enough."

"Just be careful," he said, taking my chin into his hand. He looked longingly into my eyes, then brought his mouth to mine. I hungrily kissed him back, surprised by how much I wanted him. I think I was in the process of nearly eating his face off when he pulled away with a huge smile. "Wow," he exhaled.

"Yeah," I agreed breathlessly.

"You're so beautiful," he whispered, stroking my face

with the back of this hand. "Unfortunately I have to get to work. Come find me when you wake up."

"Absolutely," I said dreamily.

I watched him go sadly, but plunged into my steaming bath with a renewed zest for life. I scrubbed myself clean with a bounty of suds, then leapt out to dry off and dress in record time. I tried to lie down and sleep, but it was impossible. Not feeling like my heartbeat would slow down to below 140 beats a minute anytime soon, I put my filthy uniform and gear back on, then dashed down to get Mom and Mel. They could tell I was walking in the clouds, and swooned with a bunch of guesses as to what had happened.

Fed up with their absurd guesses, I finally blurted, "We finally kissed!"

We all squealed and jumped around, remembering a minute later that we were supposed to be soldiers. Grinning like crazy, we calmed down and went to find Nick.

"Colonel Kadav," my mom said when we found him. He turned around to find three women grinning at him like lunatics.

He looked around in playful fear, asking, "Uh, yes?"

"We're ready for our mission," I said.

"I'll bet you are," Mel teased from the side of her mouth.

"Shhh!" I hissed, elbowing her.

Nick chuckled with raised eyebrows, looking at me and shaking his head. A few minutes later, he produced a map that had red lines and arrows drawn on it.

"The red marks on this map," he explained as we looked at it, "are the roads you should take. The X marks are places we expect you to find survivors."

We all asked a few questions, including how many changed things he expected us to run into.

"It's hard to say," he answered grimly. "Mel and Violetta, we've added a grenade launcher to your rifles. They're single shot only, so beware of that. Eve, we're giving you a stand-alone launcher. You've got six shots before needing to reload that one. Hopefully you won't need more than that. If you do, you're each going to take a bandolier with extra grenades. Use them wisely and sparingly because we don't have that many. Of course, you'll all be sent out with a melee weapon as well."

"What about the cloaking technique your men used last night?" I asked.

Nick looked around uneasily, lowering his voice. "I think you were mistaken, Eve. We didn't have any patrols up in that area last night."

"But I saw them."

"You must have seen something else, or maybe you were looking a different way than you thought you were."

"No, I'm sure I saw them. They were the gas mask—"

"Eve honey, let's talk about this when you get back," he said firmly, placing a hand on my shoulder.

My blood seemed to suddenly run cold in my veins. I knew what I had seen, and it had definitely been the creepy gas-mask soldiers from our camp. They had walked amongst the dead like they weren't even there. My mom and Mel didn't catch the significance of Nick's words, so they kept talking as I stood there speechless.

"Do you expect us to run into one of those giant things like the one that attacked last night?" Mel asked.

"We haven't seen any on patrols, but hell, we didn't even

see that one coming."

Finding my voice again, I assured them, "We'll be ready for whatever we encounter."

"Your truck is number four. You'll have a driver and gunner."

"That doesn't leave us much room," I said.

"Would you rather not have either of those men?"

"No, I'm just wondering how we're going to get a bunch of people back here."

"We piled in when we were brought here," Mel noted.

I looked around incredulously. "We're only hoping to find three people? Are you crazy?"

"What number were you expecting?" Nick asked.

"More than that! How are three people going to help?"

"For now, we only need as many people as we'll be losing when we go get your father. A handful of people will work."

"Okay," I agreed, hoping it was true. "Let's go. We're burning daylight."

We left the room and walked outside to where our guns were. We got some frighteningly brief training on the grenade launchers, received our bandoliers, then were sent on our way. We walked to where the vehicles were parked, feeling a bit fearful about our mission. Regardless, none of us were going to say so or back down from going. At the row of trucks, we found number four, greeted our driver, then realized our gunner was missing.

"Where the hell is he?" the driver growled.

"Here sir!" Faulk panted as he ran up. "Here I am."

"Get in," the man barked.

Faulk looked at us and raised his eyebrows, then jumped

in the truck and got on the gun. We looked among ourselves, happy that someone else we knew was coming with us. I slid into the front passenger seat, then narrowly passed the driver our map over all the gear between us. He studied and memorized it, then threw it on the dash.

I looked back at my mom and Mel as we started rolling, being both eager for our little group to prove itself and afraid of death. Sure we had been through some training, but not that much... And no amount of training could prepare someone for the real thing, could it?

As we neared a group of changed things, I nervously looked up at Faulk. He seemed to enjoy his spot though, for he launched obscenities and rude names at them as he fired away on the gun. I cracked a small smile to myself, glad for his enthusiasm.

We soon arrived at the first spot, which was an abandoned warehouse building. The driver and Faulk stayed at the truck to defend it and be ready when we came back. I jumped out of the vehicle with my companions, shocked at how shaky my legs were. Taking a deep breath, I told myself to focus. The three of us came together, stealthily creeping towards the building. So far, there didn't seem to be changed things or survivors here. We made our way inside, carefully sticking to our training on how to clear buildings. Although I appeared okay, my palms were sweating like crazy, filling my gloves with sweat.

When we made it through the small front-office rooms and emerged into the large cavern of the main warehouse, we were awed by what we saw. In the middle of the floor was a huge crevice that spanned the entire warehouse. We guardedly crept towards it, hearing a strange noise coming from inside.

Suddenly the ground shook, and then a red light started emanating from the crevice.

"What could be down there?" Mel whispered.

I gulped as we crept closer, terrified at what we might see. A dark feeling was coming from it, seeming to pull me closer. I inched forward, swearing that I heard it call my name. My real name; not the nickname I told everyone. Sounds reached my ears; sounds of crawling and groaning. I braced myself for what I might see, peering over the edge.

A scream erupted from my throat, and I scurried backwards as fast as I could go. In the pit were faces; hundreds of dead faces clambering towards the surface. I shrieked as I envisioned the horrible things crawling from the chasm, seeing their rotting hands reach up to the surface.

My mom and Mel dashed to my side, checking me for a wound. My mom tried to calm me as Mel went back to the chasm, which made me even more frantic. I wildly ran towards her, grabbing her hand and yanking her away from the pit. Seconds later, Faulk and the driver came running inside.

"What is it?" the driver demanded.

"In the pit!" I despaired. "Hundreds of them in the pit!" I panted.

He and Faulk hurried to the edge, looking down. I watched in agony, but was confused when they shook their heads and turned towards us.

"There's nothing down there," Faulk said.

"What?" I wheezed, rapidly crawling over to the edge. When I looked down there, all I saw was darkness. "They were there!" I reiterated to everyone, looking frantically from face to face. All I saw was doubt. "What happened to the red glow?" I muttered.

"What red glow?" my mom asked.

"Didn't you guys see it?" I anxiously asked. "It was right after the ground shook."

Mel's eyebrows twitched, then she sighed sadly. "Addie, the ground didn't shake and there was no red glow."

My eyes darted around the floor in sudden realization. I stomped back to the truck in embarrassment, not saying a word. I guess the rest of them decided the mission was over, so we headed back to our camp. My mom and Mel tried talking to me, but I made it clear that I wanted to be left alone. I went to our tiny room and plopped down on a bottom bunk. I tried not to let them, but I felt hot tears forming in my eyes. Rage filled me as I recalled this happening countless times in my teen years. It was always the same outcome; nobody else saw the weird things either. Just the weird girl with the weird name.

I scoffed as I thought of my name. *Yirah*. As if the name weren't weird enough, it was supposedly Hebrew for the awe and fear of God. Who names their kid that? A while ago, someone suggested that my visions were related to my name. Sure, who wouldn't fear a god that was making them see visions and feel like an outcast and psycho? So I had ditched the name and ignored my visions. Eventually they went away and I found normalcy. Now they were back, just in time to make the end of the world even worse. I recalled what Nick had said about me being mistaken about seeing his soldiers walking with the chompers last night. I guess I was seeing things then, too.

There was a knock on the door, to which I yelled, "Go

away."

But my plea went ignored, and the door opened. Expecting my mom or Mel, I was surprised to see Nick walk in. I rolled over to face the wall instantly, not wanting him to see my puffy eyes.

"Hey," he said gently, sitting down on the bed beside me. I stayed facing the wall. "Want to tell me what happened out there?"

"No."

"Eve, honey, come on."

"Don't call me that," I commanded, not wanting to be called anything relating to the cause of my craziness.

"Should I call you Addie?" he asked, lying down beside me. He tickled his fingers down my arm, which felt so nice and soothing. "Or..." he pondered, "What about Deli? You like that one don't you?"

"I told you not to call me that," I answered, trying to hide the smile in my voice.

"Well you're not leaving me many options," he argued, pretending to be distressed.

"Sorry," I replied dryly.

"How about something else?" he grinned, kissing my arm. "Sugar? Sweetheart?" He pulled the hair back from my face, allowing him to see my eyes. "Come on love, talk to me."

"Don't call me love," I ordered.

"Honey? Babe?" he asked, kissing the side of my face. He pulled me into his arms, and I guess I let him. It was nice how much effort he was putting into cheering me up.

"Mm mm," I shook my head. "Not babe either. I hate that one."

"I can think of a few more, but you aren't ready for them," he grinned, biting his lip.

I tried not to smile, but ended up laughing. "Shut up," I said, pulling away from him and standing up.

"Want to get some air?" he asked. "You've been down here a while."

A few minutes later, we were sitting on the edge of the balcony of the presidential suite. We had our legs through the railing, letting them dangle freely in the cold air. I stared up at the stars idly, trying not to think about anything. Nick patiently sat beside me, hoping I would talk to him, but also seemed to be content that I was no longer crying. Eventually I looked over at him, shocked to see that he was staring at me.

"I haven't seen you move out of the corner of my eye in a while. Have you been looking at me all this time?"

"Absolutely."

"Why?" I laughed nervously.

"Because your beauty is divine."

"It's not divine," I laughed. "Careful what gods you may offend."

"Oh, I think God would take it as a compliment of his fine handiwork."

"You believe in God?" I grunted.

"Of course. Don't you?"

"Yeah, I suppose. Sometimes. But if he's real, why does he let crap like this happen? Why has he let so many people die? Why all the terror and suffering?"

"Some people would argue that it's because we wanted it."

"Who wants to suffer?" I objected.

"Quite a number of people," he said with a playful grin and wink.

"I'm serious," I laughed. "Stop being a pervert."

He laughed too, then said, "I am serious though. God made humans to be his companions, right? He had absolutely everything; heaven, a whole slew of beautiful angels at his beck and call, and the entire universe. But still he had to create humans. He had a relationship with them like he hadn't had with anything before, especially not his other created beings who loved him. But what did people do with that? They threw it away. They wanted to be mightier than him, so they forsake him. That's why there's suffering; people chose it. They chose to be separated from God, which is the very essence of suffering."

I looked at Nick skeptically, trying to decide if he was serious. When I saw a strange gleam in his eye, I knew he was. "Whoa," I laughed. "I didn't mean to strike a nerve. Did you go to seminary school or something?"

"Something like that," he smiled apologetically. "Sorry. I get so impassioned when people ask questions like that because the answer has been right in front of them for centuries, yet still they ask as if they don't have a clue."

"Well sorry I'm clueless."

"No, it's not you. It's the whole culture of this world. I don't blame you," he assured, smiling warmly at me. A moment later, he asked, "It's cold out here; want to head inside?"

"Sure." As we stood to go inside, I chuckled and asked, "So are you going to start a church for us all?"

He laughed out loud and said, "I'm not so sure that's a good idea."

We went inside and shut the doors. I sighed as I realized I needed to face my mom and Mel, but still didn't have the heart to. My mom was used to these episodes; maybe she filled Mel in for me.

"Hey," Nick said, looking earnestly at me. "Now this is just an idea, don't get upset. I won't be offended if you say no. But I would really like it if you would consider staying up here with me tonight. That way you don't have to explain anything to anyone. Just rest here tonight and face it in the morning. If you want, I'll even go sleep elsewhere."

My pulse quickened as I considered his offer. Not seeing anyone else tonight sounded so good... and he had offered to sleep in another room. "That sounds wonderful," I answered, stepping closely to him. "And it would be even better if you stayed here with me."

To that he smiled from ear to ear, pulling me close.

"But—" I started to say, but he cut me off.

"Nothing will happen. I just want you here with me," he breathed.

After a long embrace, he went to one of the dressers in the room, producing more nightclothes for me. I gratefully accepted them, changed in the bathroom, then crawled into the warm bed with him. I snuggled next to him, happy to have his strong arms around me. With my ear against his chest, I fell asleep listening to the pounding of his glorious heart.

CHAPTER TEN

During that first night that I slept next to Nick, I had the most bizarre dreams. They reminded me of the vision I had seen earlier that day; horrible dead faces groaning and wailing in misery within a pit. I tossed and turned like crazy, but Nick remained at my side. When we finally woke for the day, we were both haggard from a fitful night of sleep. To my amazement, Nick wasn't irritated with me at all.

"Every time you turned restlessly, thrashed your arms, or whimpered in despair, I tried to pull you closer," he assured.

I gazed into his eyes, awed by his true concern. Who else would have tolerated that all night?

"Not me," Mel replied when I told her about it.

We were in truck four, again trying to look for survivors. My mom was with us, as was our driver and Faulk.

"No funny business today," the driver had said gruffly when he saw me. I had nodded quickly in embarrassment, also hoping for nothing odd to happen.

So there we were; cruising down the road back to the place we had gone yesterday. We figured that maybe my screaming had scared off any survivors, so we wanted to do a more thorough check today to make sure none were in the warehouse. It was nice to be with Mel and Mom again, since I had avoided them all night. Thankfully, they both seemed to understand why I had been distant. My mom had seen me like this before, and once she had explained it to Mel, they both sympathized with me. Sympathy or not though, they both begged me never to ditch them like that again.

"I don't care what weird things you see or do," Mel said, "you can count on me, and especially Vie, to be there for you. Okay?"

"Okay," I had smiled.

"I like Nick and all, but how dare you turn to him instead of us!" she added, sniffling crossly.

"I'm sorry Mel," I apologized. "You too Mom; I really am sorry. I just feel like such a lunatic when those hallucinations happen."

"It's all right," my mom replied sweetly. "Just promise to not shut us out next time, okay?"

"Of course," I confirmed with a smile.

Soon we arrived at the warehouse, where Faulk offered to come in with us. We assured him we'd be fine on our own; besides, it was more important for him to guard our escape vehicle, should the need for it arise. Carefully, as we'd done yesterday, we crept through the front offices towards the main warehouse. Since I had gone a little crazy yesterday, I let Mel and my mom take the lead while I covered their backs. We opened the last office door that led to the warehouse hesitantly, hopeful to find survivors. Stealthily, we crept forward. This time, I wasn't the one who freaked out first.

"Fall back! Fall back!" Mel suddenly whispered over and over until we were all hiding behind a stack of pallets. "Shit!" she cursed.

"What?" my mom and I demanded.

"The whole damn warehouse is filled with changed things."

My mom gasped, and I immediately peered around the corner of the pallets. Sure enough, covering the whole warehouse floor were those rotting creatures, all facing our direction. They were just standing there swaying, sending a multitude of chills down my spine. My jaw suddenly dropped in horror as I realized some of them looked familiar. I had seen them before, in my supposed hallucination.

"What the hell!" I shouted in a whisper, leaning back from around the pallet.

"What?" Mel hissed.

"I saw those things yesterday! In the chasm. They were crawling out of it!" I received skeptical looks from both people, but I didn't care. "Those damn things weren't here yesterday. Now when we come back today, the ones I saw in a vision are here? You don't find that weird?"

"I find that freakishly weird," Mel frantically replied. "Let's get the hell out of here!"

Everyone agreed, so we carefully and quickly made our way back outside.

"We have to get out of here!" I thundered as we neared the truck. "Let's go!"

"What happened?" Faulk asked.

"The whole warehouse is filled with chompers," Mel answered.

"Whoa!" he exclaimed. "Since we were here yesterday? That was fast!"

"Wait," I called, pausing. "Should we destroy them?"

"They're not harming anyone just standing there," Mel said.

"Yeah but what happens when they leave?" my mom countered. "That was an awful lot of them, and right now, we have the jump on them."

I looked to Faulk and the driver, whose name tape I finally glanced at. "Smith," I said as I looked at him, "and Faulk. What do you think? You two have way more experience than the three of us."

Smith glanced at the warehouse, then all around us at the roads. "I think we should leave them."

"Are you shi—er, kidding me?" Faulk protested, trying to reform his language for the fairer sex that stood around him. "A whole warehouse of them? Do you realize how much damage they can do once they get out of there? Why the hell would we just leave them?"

"Because," Smith said gruffly, "right now, there are only a few of those things in the roads coming towards us. If we blow up a whole damn warehouse, they will come out of the woodworks towards the explosion. Since our camp is less than half a mile from here, I'd say that's the worst idea of the year."

"That's not bad, considering we're only a few days into the year," Faulk quipped. Upon Smith's scowl, he lessened his humor and grew more serious. "Like you said though; our camp isn't far from here. What happens when those things wander out of the warehouse and head our way?"

"Who says they're going to move? And if we blow them up, we'll draw the attention of everything in this area. Then we'll have a lot more of them to deal with. Now we're leaving; let's go."

Hesitantly, the rest of us followed his lead. We sped towards the next destination on our map in silence. I think each of us was simultaneously worrying about all those changed things that we had just left behind, while also hoping that we'd find survivors at our next stop.

Ironically, the next stop was a sporting-goods store. I guess Nick thought that survivors would gravitate to somewhere like that to gather supplies. I could see the logic in that; now that we were actually going on missions, there were a few more things I wanted to grab. Since we had found many changed things inside the last place we went, Faulk insisted on coming inside with us. We didn't want to leave Smith alone outside, but he grumpily shooed us away. We demanded that he come in with us, but still he resisted. Finally, Faulk told us to give up and just get inside.

We snuck into the store, carefully checking the entire bottom floor as thoroughly as possible. When we were sure it was clear, we headed upstairs. Hearing hissing as we neared the top of the stairs, we all prepared for the worst. Coming onto the landing, we recoiled as we saw about fifteen people stumbling around snarling. Blood ran down all their clothes, and a horrible stench filled the air.

As Mel and my mom were about to fire their guns, I urged, "Aim for their heads."

In this close proximity, my grenade launcher was totally useless, so I had to just stand there and watch as my three comrades fired away. Thankfully Faulk was with us, because I think he hit most of them. Mom and Mel tried their best, but they just weren't very good yet.

"We only had a few weeks of training, okay?" Mel said defensively.

"Hey, it's fine," Faulk replied. "I'm just happy I came in with you ladies."

"We're not ladies," my mom said dramatically as she reloaded her gun. "We're females."

"Well excuse me," Faulk chuckled. Leaning close to Mel, I barely heard him whisper, "I'm glad you're all right."

I grinned to myself as Mel scrunched up her face in confusion. "Let's keep moving," I suggested. "Although, we just announced our presence quite spectacularly…"

We pressed onward, carefully checking every aisle for more offenders. Some of the ones we had shot still twitched on the floor, but with their heads out of commission, we were pretty sure they were harmless. Eventually we came to the manager's office, which we found locked.

"There's either a survivor back there, or…" Faulk stated.

"Or a chomper," Mel said, completing his sentence with the word he had coined. He looked at her with an impressed expression, to which she winked.

"Can we focus?" I quipped.

They both nodded quickly, seeming to be embarrassed. We all got ready, then Faulk kicked in the door. He led the way inside, and we started our search of the room. Since it was pretty small, the search was brief. We swept our flashlights back and forth systematically, skeptical when the light beam landed on flesh. To our joy, the flesh was the face of a living person, who looked relatively healthy.

"Don't hurt me!" he begged, jabbing a knife out in front of him.

"We're not here to hurt you," I assured him. "Are there more of you here? Survivors?"

"Who are you?" he asked, eyeing me and the others apprehensively. "Are you here to… to save me?"

"Yes, we are!" Mel answered.

"Why is the power still out?" he asked with a raised eyebrow.

"Uh, what?"

"If you're here to help, why is the power still out?"

"It's back on in other places," my mom offered.

"You're dead, aren't you!" he murmured, jumping up from where he sat on the floor.

At that moment, we all felt fear, but I felt something else. Outside, down in the street… it felt like there was an approaching darkness out there. I shook my head. This wasn't the time for hallucinations.

"Sir, we are not dead, I promise," Faulk said. "We can take you somewhere safe if you want."

"Nowhere is safe!" he proclaimed. "Especially not with her!" he bellowed, pointing a finger at me.

I looked around in confusion, realizing he was pointing my way. Then, before any of us could react, he raised his knife and stabbed himself in the throat. Three of us screamed in horror as the man fell to the floor. Faulk dropped to his knees and felt the man's pulse.

"It's weak; we might be able to save him if we hurry back right away."

My mom and Mel agreed, so they rushed to help Faulk pick the man up. I stared in a daze, struck by the man's chilling words. Why was nowhere safe with me? I tried to forget it as I hurried to help my group, but his words and accusing look stayed with me.

As we made our way to the stairs, we suddenly heard a low noise.

"What is that?" Mel whispered.

We glanced around, seeing no other changed things. Then I realized. I looked down at the man, who was opening his eyes. They were covered completely in black, like the others I had seen. Shrieking, I released my hold on him. Everyone else had the same realization at about the same time, also dropping him. The man blinked and snarled, reaching a dead hand out for any of us. Faulk pulled out his pistol, making the rest of us cringe and look away. We heard a couple deafening shots, then silence.

With our ears ringing, we made our way back to the front of the store. We walked out the doors, not seeing the truck where it had been when we had gone inside. Glancing around for a moment, we spotted it parked a little ways away. Figuring Smith had needed to circle the building for security reasons, we jogged that direction.

As we got closer, I saw Smith standing with his back to us, leaning against the truck and smoking a cigarette. From out of nowhere, a changed thing suddenly came around the corner of the truck. The thing was only inches from Smith, and I didn't have a rifle. Even shouting to him wouldn't help in time. I watched helplessly as the thing approached him, seemingly in slow motion. But then, the thing walked past Smith as if it hadn't even seen him. Instead the thing snarled and ambled our way.

"Look out!" I roared to my group.

Snarling reached our ears from our left as well, making us spin that direction. There were a bunch of them stumbling through the street towards us. I looked back to the direction of the truck and Smith, now seeing more of them in the road than just the one. I unconsciously whimpered in fear, horrified by the sight.

"Blast the bastards!" Faulk yelled at me, pointing to the ones on our left.

I complied and raised my grenade launcher, hoping to

make my first shot count. I held my breath and fired, thankfully landing an explosion in the middle of the group. I spun back towards our truck, dismayed to see even more of the things shuffling towards us. To my horror, I saw Smith walking away from us casually, right in the midst of them. He was heading towards... the warehouse... which was also the direction the changed things were coming from. My mind spun as I tried to comprehend what the hell was happening. Had our driver led us into an ambush?

"Addie!" Mel wheezed as she struggled to reload her single-shot grenade launcher. Apparently she and my mom had had to fire a couple off while I was in la-la land.

Cursing at myself, I came back to the present situation and fired off a couple more shots. I tried to keep the shots as far from the truck as possible while still being effective on the chompers, since we needed the truck to get back to camp. When we had thinned the group closest to us somewhat, Faulk commanded us to get in the vehicle. We had to fight our way there with our knives, having to stab and slice several rotting people. After a couple of them, I suddenly heaved, barfing up everything in my stomach. It spewed all over the changed thing in front of me, seeming to confuse it. I shoved it down and dashed away, not having the heart to stab another one.

When we got to the truck, I was afraid Smith had somehow sabotaged it. To my surprise, Faulk jumped in and was able to speed away almost instantly. As soon as we were moving, Mel released a whole slew of obscenities that made even Faulk grimace.

"What happened?!" she bellowed, pounding her hand on the seat beside her.

"Did any of you see Smith?" I asked cautiously, wondering if it had been a vision or if I had really seen him.

"I thought I did, but I guess it wasn't him," my mom answered.

"Same here," Faulk seconded.

I sighed heavily. "No, it was him." I explained to them what I had seen, making Faulk slam on the brakes.

"Are you saying that son of a… witch… ambushed us?"

"It sure looks that way!" I fumed. "He did nothing while we were being attacked! And he walked among them like… like…"

"Like he had found a way to blend in with them," Mel said, finishing my sentence. "You mentioned that to Nick the other morning. You said you saw the same thing the other night."

"Yeah; I did."

"Where? When?" Faulk asked.

"The night I was keeping watch for you while you slept. I saw some soldiers beyond our northern perimeter. They snuck past the changed things without a problem."

"Maybe the chompers can't see in the dark."

"Maybe," my mom interjected, "but it was broad daylight just now when Smith walked away from us."

"How much you want to bet that warehouse is empty now?" I scowled. "He was the one who didn't want us to destroy them!" I slammed my fist down on the dash and groaned in anger, unable to express myself in any other way.

Faulk nervously checked our mirrors, then kept driving so that we wouldn't get swarmed. As we sped away, I also looked in my rearview mirror. Several fires from our grenades still burned, destroying the rotten flesh of our attackers. Just as several bodies crumbled into pure ash, dark shapes rose from them. I gaped in the mirror, squinting in disbelief. The dark things swarmed over the ash piles for a second, then lurched towards our truck. Hurriedly, I rolled my window down and stuck my head out. The things weren't in my imagination; there was no mistaking the dark shapes.

"What are you doing?" Faulk demanded, desperately looking in the rearview mirror.

"Addie!" Mel cried. "What is it?"

"Do you see those?" I hollered, ducking back into the vehicle.

"What?" they echoed, since they couldn't see in the mirror or see out the back of the truck.

Before I could answer, our vehicle suddenly rocked to the side, as if we had run something huge over with only the left tires.

"What the…?" Faulk muttered, casting a confused glance at me. "I didn't see anything in the road."

I looked in the mirror, but no longer saw the dark shapes. Again I stuck my head out the window, spotting them. They no longer pursued us, but hung back in the road, hovering in the air. I trembled at the change, wondering why I preferred them chasing us. Now it seemed like they were… waiting for something. I jerked my face back into the truck, then turned to my group.

"When the bodies finish burning, dark shapes come out of them."

"Dark shapes?" Faulk scoffed. "Like squares and triangles?"

"No," I hissed. "Dark shapes like clouds or something. A

few just came out of the burning bodies and started follow-ing us. I think they're what hit the truck."

Nobody said anything, but instead glanced around at each other skeptically.

"I'm sorry," I said irately, "but dead people are coming back to life, and you find what I just said hard to believe?"

"Uh yeah," Mel concurred. "That's super weird."

"So are walking bodies!" I gushed, wanting to pull my hair out. Was I going mad?

"It's super weird," Faulk agreed, "which is why we don't want to believe it. It scares us."

"Yeah," I murmured, slouching into my seat. "They also have black eyes when they first change."

"They what?" my mom asked.

"They have black eyes. The whole eye is completely cov-ered in black when they change."

Suddenly, Faulk slammed on the brakes, sending me flying towards the dashboard. I threw out my hands and screeched in pain, but knew I wasn't injured beyond a massive bruise on my hands. After checking them for cuts, I glanced up to try to see why Faulk had stopped so suddenly.

"Oh," I grunted. "That's why."

In front of us in the road stood dozens upon dozens of changed things. They weren't snarling at us, they were just standing there swaying with their heads tilted down, but eyes cast up at us. And guess what? All their eyes were completely black. I gulped at the sight, knowing this was hardly the time to say anything remotely close to I-told-you-so. Unable to resist, I glanced over at Mel. She solemn-ly shook her head, so I didn't say it.

Faulk glanced in our mirrors, trying to see if we could

take another route. "Shit!" he cursed, slamming his hands down on the steering wheel.

I glanced in the mirror, seeing that a huge group was now behind us in the road too.

"Where did they come from?" my mom blurted. "The roads behind us were clear a second ago!"

"This is so weird," Mel said quietly, trying to mask her fear.

"What can we do?" I asked, looking to Faulk.

Panic ran across his face as he realized that in this group, he had seniority. He needed to be the leader.

"Hey," I said reassuringly. "You've got this Faulk. We all respect you. Tell us what to do and we'll do it."

He nodded and swallowed nervously, then took a deep breath. "Okay," he said in a strong voice.

I smiled to myself, knowing that his moment of doubt in himself had passed. I marveled as I watched him make a plan, always impressed by how men were capable of stepping up when they had to.

"Here's the plan," he said. "These things can't move very quickly. They're not even moving towards us right now, so we'll use that to our advantage. We're all going to exit the truck on the driver's side. Vie, you use Mel's door. Eve, you climb into the back seat and also go out Mel's door since there's no way you'll get over the gear that's up front. Once we're out of the truck, we're going to head down the alley on our left. We'll move quickly and carefully. Call them out as you spot them so we're all aware. Obviously, use your grenade launchers carefully in the alley. We're going to head west to get home. If we get separated, God forbid, keep heading that way. Do not come back for anyone."

"But—" we instantly objected, but he put his hand up.

"No time for objections," he said quickly. "Now let's go."

Mel opened her door and jumped out, with my mom following behind her. Faulk popped his door open as he signaled at me, so I tried to scramble to the backseat. I almost got over it, but my gear got stuck on something. I yanked at my side, but it was caught on something. Cursing profusely, I backtracked and just jumped out my own door.

Instantly I was blindsided by something and fell to the ground. I heard screaming; I think it was my mom and Mel. I struggled to open my eyes, desperate to figure out which direction was up or down. There was a deafening sound piercing the air, making all my senses run haywire. Groggily, I tried to move, but I also couldn't feel my limbs. I groaned weakly, hoping I wasn't dead. I didn't want to become one of those things.

Barely, I could feel myself being dragged along the ground. With all my effort, I tried to open my eyes. Finally they opened, and as my vision came back to me, I wish it hadn't. I was being dragged through the mass of changed things, all of which were staring at me with their horrific black eyes. Weakly, I rolled my head to the side, trying to catch a glimpse of what was dragging me. It was dark and very tall, but that's all I could see.

After a while the movement finally ceased, and I felt my feet get released. I whimpered weakly and shut my eyes, unable to do anything else. There was a strange feeling in the air, like the one I'd had when we'd been in the sports store… just before the first group had attacked us. Slowly I made the connection, realizing that I could feel these things when they were nearby. I already knew that I was in the midst of them, but there was something more than that. The strange feeling was all around, but strongest was right in front of me.

My heart pounded as I wondered what the thing was. I fearfully pictured it being another one of the giant monsters that had attacked our base, wondering how in the world I might hope to escape from this. I lay still for a bit, not wanting the thing to know that I was awake. Before moving, I wanted to come up with some sort of plan.

Ever so slightly, I opened my eyes again. I was hoping that the thing had moved to where I could see it, and wasn't disappointed. It now stood in my line of sight with its back to me. I trembled in shock when I saw it, for it wasn't one of the changed things. The foe was a tall person, clothed in all black. It was standing at some sort of industrial table, seeming to be making something. Were we… inside the warehouse? I clenched my jaw as I thought of Smith's betrayal, wondering how in the world he had gotten others to help him.

I slammed my eyes shut again as the person turned towards me. It walked to where I lay, then started fumbling with me. I prayed it wouldn't do anything horrific, realizing a few moments later that it was removing all my gear. My weapons and protective gear were ripped off of me, leaving on only my clothes and boots. Shortly afterward, I heard voices approaching. They were muffled, but as they came closer I was able to pick up a few words.

"Good work, Smith."

"We weren't able to get them all."

"That's all right; this one will do." Bitterly he added, "She's the special one, after all."

Footsteps came my way, and I felt someone kick my foot. Everything in me wanted to fight back, but I made myself keep pretending to be unconscious.

"She's still out, huh?" the voice asked, coming closer to my face. I imagined the onlooker bending down and peering at me. "Well," he smirked, "let's see if we can't fix that."

CHAPTER ELEVEN

My captors cackled all around me, making me feel like I was either in a tacky TV drama or a real-life horrible situation. I decided on the latter as I felt someone grab my foot again.

"Yes sir," replied an impossibly deep voice. I think it was the person that had dragged me inside. "I'll make her wake up."

They cackled again, giving me a sinking feeling in my stomach.

"As much as I'd love to stay and watch," said the voice belonging to the person who had kicked my foot and called me special, "I have matters to discuss with Smith. I'd advise you not to make too much of a mess, but it would be a lie. Make all the mess you desire. I want him to mourn her," he paused dramatically, then seethed, "I want him to know that he failed."

"Of course," the person by me responded, again dragging me by my foot.

I cracked my eyes open a tiny bit, seeing Smith standing a short ways from me. Beside him was the other man. It took everything in me not to shriek when I saw his face, for at first I thought it was Nick's. Then I realized it wasn't, but it very closely resembled his. That man had to be related to him. As I was dragged away, I saw the man and Smith walk out of the room.

Carefully, I turned my attention to the person dragging

me. I peered at him and beyond, noticing that he was taking me through the doorway of a rather small and dark room. I couldn't see much in the dim light, but it looked like there was nothing inside the room, save for a few chains dangling from the ceiling. And a drain. There was a drain in the middle of the floor. I swallowed fearfully and glanced around, trying to figure out how I was going to get out of here. The person let go of my ankle and reached for one of the chains, making me realize that my window of opportunity was about to close.

As soon as his full attention was on the horrible metal things, I violently kicked both of my feet towards him. He staggered forward, caught off guard by my sudden move. As he spun around to face me, I jammed one of my boots towards the back of his knees. My plan worked, causing his legs to buckle. When he fell to his knees, I leapt off the ground and seized the chains. I viciously hooked them around his throat as I stood behind him, crossing them over one another at the back of his neck. His arms thrashed wildly, but I held on with all my might, hoping he would pass out soon. Still he thrashed and weaker my arms grew. He was a mammoth of a person; excessively muscular and terrifyingly tall. My arms shook and burned, but I refused to let go.

I suddenly wasn't given a choice as one of his fierce hands grabbed my left leg and yanked me sideways. I fell to the ground, screaming in pain. I think he had just broken my leg. He growled in anger as he rose to his feet, letting me see just how alarmingly tall he was. His face towered above me, shrouded in shadows. All I could see was the white of his eyes and glistening white teeth. Sharp teeth, I might add.

"Bad idea," his deep voice rumbled, sounding like the ethereal voice that movies like to use for dragons and demons. "We know who you are, Yirah," he seethed, shocking me with the use of my real name.

He knelt down on my right side, leaning in closely to me. In the dim light of the room I still couldn't see his face clearly.

"How," I breathed, still reeling from the pain in my leg. "How do you know my name?"

"Ha!" he laughed, cupping my face with his left hand and reaching his right hand across to my left hip. I cringed, feeling as though I were held in an odd embrace by him. "We know much about you," he said quietly, sliding his hand down my leg. I jerked away, but it was useless. His hand ran down my leg, stopping where the break in the bone was. "We know your name," he whispered still cupping my face. "We know who you are. We know who you care about. We know what causes you pain." With that, he suddenly gripped my leg as tightly as he could.

I screamed with all my might, feeling the wear in my throat immediately. He released his hold, then did it again, this time with a cruel laugh. I screamed and screamed, but he wouldn't stop. My body pumped adrenaline through my veins, giving me the energy to keep screaming and feel the pain. I cursed and bawled, but the pain just kept coming. Finally, after who knows how long, the adrenaline wore off. I wearily sobbed and whimpered, having no energy left for anything else. The man seemed to finally be satisfied and let go of my leg.

"There you are," he chuckled, stroking my sweaty face.

"In your rightful state: broken and miserable."

"Please stop," I croaked, for once bringing my eyes to his. In them, I saw only hate and malice. Not an ounce of compassion.

"There will be no stopping," he promised. "Only more pain," he seethed, bringing his face even closer to mine. "I'll bet that pathetic heart of yours is pounding and working its hardest to keep you alive," he laughed, trickling a hand to over my heart. "I'd love to hear it," he breathed, licking his lips nauseatingly.

I cringed as he brought his ear to my chest, resting it against my shirt. Suddenly, he screeched in pain and leapt away from me, snarling viciously. "Get her out of here!" he bellowed before turning into a cloud of black smoke. I blinked in disbelief, suddenly finding myself back in the street by the truck.

Confusedly, I looked all around me and realized that I was sitting on the ground outside the truck, as if I had just fallen out of it.

"Addie!" Mel shrieked. "Come on!"

Someone rounded the corner and came running at me. My mom lifted me up, apparently possessing that superhuman strength they say pours into mothers when their kids are in trouble. I can definitely confirm that's true, because she scooped me up from the ground and dashed down the alley like I was just a doll that weighed half a pound.

"I can run myself!" I professed, insisting that she let me down.

When we were a ways from the horde of changed things, she complied and let me down. I instantly shrieked in pain, collapsing to the ground.

"Arhhh!!!" I bellowed, hitting the ground with my fist.

"What's wrong?" everyone chorused.

"My leg is broken."

"How did you break your leg getting out of the truck?" Mel asked, looking at me with a raised eyebrow. "Clumsy much?"

"It wasn't the truck. I think I... went somewhere."

"Like where?" Faulk asked.

"As soon as I got out of the truck, I was knocked out and dragged to the warehouse. Smith and two other men were there. One of them started torturing me. He broke my leg."

"Uh yeah, I think you just fell and got knocked out," Mel said.

"No!" I roared, suddenly passionate about what I was saying. "This was real!"

"Adeline," my mom said softly, "That's impossible. Only seconds passed between when you jumped out of the truck and when I picked you up. There's no way you were taken somewhere, tortured, and brought back that quickly."

I glowered at her, knowing she was making sense, yet I hated her for it. "I did not break my leg jumping out of the truck," I hissed.

Ignoring all of them, I hobbled down the alley towards our base. Thankfully we didn't encounter many more of the changed things and made it back relatively quickly. When Nick saw us, he unleashed several obscenities and rushed over.

"What happened?" he inquired.

"We were am—"

"Nothing," I said quickly, cutting off Faulk. "We just

came across more of them than we could handle." Everyone looked at me oddly, wondering why I was lying.

"Where's Smith?" Nick asked hesitantly.

"He didn't make it, unfortunately."

Nick cursed again, rubbing his brow worriedly. "Are you all right though? All of you?"

"My leg is broken."

"Well let's get you examined by the medic."

"Yeah," I agreed, hobbling towards the house. I glanced back at my group fiercely and shook my head, warning them not to say anything to Nick about what really happened. That man had looked too much like Nick to be a coincidence. I wasn't so sure we could trust him.

I made my way to the medic, finding that I was his only patient so far that day. I changed into one of those annoying paper gowns, then carefully got onto the exam table. He came in and introduced himself as Mortimer, which made me chuckled.

"Mortimer the doctor?" I asked. "Sounds like you're in the wrong field. Mortimer the mortician sounds better."

"Indeed," he smiled oddly. "But alas, here I am. I trust you are ready for your exam?"

"Uh, sure," I answered, making a strange face to myself at the way he talked.

"Let me see here," he muttered, wheeling over to me in his stool. He looked closely at my leg, poked and prodded the area, then sighed and looked up at me. "It's certainly broken, of that there can be no dispute."

"Don't you want to take an x-ray?" I asked.

"A what? Oh, yes, yes. No, an x-ray isn't necessary, I assure you. I know bones like you wouldn't believe. And this one is definitely broken."

"Okay," I sighed. "So what do I do?"

"Stay off of it for many weeks."

"Uh, no can do," I countered. "That'll be a death sentence in this world."

"I'm sure Colonel Kadav will ensure that you're kept safe," he said, offering a peculiar smile.

"Kadav," I mused, suddenly realizing how many strange names there were around here.

"Pardon?"

"Oh, I was just repeating Nick's last name. Kadav. Sounds pretty close to cadaver, don't you think?"

"Hmm, now that's an interesting observation," he said in a high-pitched voice.

"And yours," I mused. "Like Mortimer the mortician."

"Ah ha ha!" he laughed, a little too loudly.

"And then there's Major Ghost," I said, looking at him intensely. "Isn't that strange?"

"A coincidence, I'm sure," he insisted, fidgeting under my stare.

I felt something welling up inside me; I think the word for it was rage. I felt rage welling up inside me, for it seemed like everyone was making me feel like a lunatic.

"You know something," I whispered, leaning towards him.

"Uh, what?" he scoffed, backing away from me.

I hopped down off the table on one leg, lunging towards him. Gripping both of his shoulders with my hands, I shoved him against the counter, hissing as I leaned into his face.

"What the hell is going on here?" I demanded. "Tell me.

Tell me!"

He cowered in fear, making me even angrier. I bared my teeth at him, suddenly wanting to hit him.

"Eve?" a voice called, startling me out of my anger.

I let go of Mortimer and spun around, seeing Nick standing in the doorway.

"Hey," he called, putting out his hand as he walked towards me. "Are you okay?"

"I'm fine," I spat, looking down at Mortimer.

"Okay," Nick said skeptically, looking at me with a critical eye. "Come upstairs with me," he insisted, and I knew I didn't have a choice.

He draped a robe over me, then helped me get up the stairs. We came to the master bedroom, where he helped me get into the bathroom. I carefully changed into night clothes, then emerged from the bathroom and Nick helped me hobble to the bed.

"Why don't you get some rest?" he said, helping me get into it.

I slid under the warm blankets, grateful for their softness. I gulped as I stared out the glass of the balcony doors, remembering the pain I had felt earlier.

"Do you want to talk?" Nick asked, placing a hand on mine.

I jerked it away instinctively, not even meaning to. Almost feeling sorry for doing so, I heard him sigh slightly. When I glanced at his face though, all remorse disappeared. He looked too much like my captor.

"Who are you?" I suddenly asked.

He flinched in surprise, then looked at me inquisitively. "What in the world would make you ask that?"

"Answer the question."

He gazed at me for a moment, then asked, "Is this perhaps prompted by your vision during your run?"

I glowered at him unbelievingly, aghast that my mom and Mel had betrayed me. So they had told him what had happened.

"Eve, people deal with betrayal in different ways. What Smith did to you guys is unforgivable. What you thought you saw may have been your way of coping with it."

"I know what I saw," I growled, leaning towards his face. "None of you have a clue! Except you," I glowered. "I think *you* have a clue, *Colonel Kadav*," I added, my words dripping with accusation.

"And what do I have a clue about?" he asked wearily.

"I don't know, but my captor looked a lot like you."

"Eve!" he cried sadly, taking my face into his hands. "My dear," he breathed, suddenly looking as though he was about to cry. "It was just like a dream; dreams capture and exploit our fears! I think you trust me and look to me for safety, so your worst fear is that I will abandon you. I shall not though, my dear! I swear I will never leave you."

I recoiled at his words, truly surprised by them. What he said seemed to make sense; visions and dreams seem to capture one's worst fears and make them feel like a vivid, horrible reality. It certainly seemed likely that in this strange new world, I was very afraid of losing Nick. Never before, even in the normal world, had I met someone like him. Yet, just before this awful new world, I had found him. He was like a godsend; an angel in disguise. Of course I was afraid of losing him, or worse, him leaving me.

My eyes fluttered shut in embarrassment as I touched

the back of my hand to my forehead. "Forgive me Nick," I whispered, feeling like a fool. Of course it had been a vision. Nobody knew my real name besides my mom, so how would captors know it? They didn't break my leg either; I obviously broke it jumping out of the truck, at the same time I knocked myself out. Strange things happen when the mind is under stress, so when I was unconscious I had bizarre dreams.

"Of course I forgive you," he answered, kissing my forehead.

"You'll…" I murmured, afraid to ask.

"What is it?"

"You'll… you'll really never leave me?"

"I will never leave you," he confirmed. "I know we only met a short time ago, but the moment I laid eyes on you, I knew I would never let you out of my life."

I laughed out loud, amazed by his words. "There is no way you're real," I breathed, pulling him close.

"I assure you that I am," he smiled.

Gazing at his perfect face, I pulled him close for a kiss. Our mouths collided in passionate unity again, filling me with burning desire. I greedily pulled him closer to me, paying the price a second later when soaring pain shot through my leg.

"Are you okay?" he gushed, instantly placing his hands on my hips.

"Yeah," I winced, trying not to pay attention to the fact that the person in my vision had touched me the same way.

"I should let you rest," he said with a smile.

"No," I groaned, trying to pull him back to me. "Don't go."

"I'll be back soon to check on you, I promise."

He kissed me lightly once more, letting me savor the delicious taste of his lips. Then he tucked me in and left the room. I happily slipped into sleep, having quite different dreams than the ones I'd had earlier. This time, I dreamt of delectable and sultry days spent with Nick.

When I finally woke up next, I could see through the windows that it was dark outside. On the nightstand across the bed from me, a lamp was on. I looked around for Nick, but didn't see him anywhere. As I pondered getting up, he entered the room.

"You're awake," he said happily when he saw me looking around. He sat down on the bed beside me, letting me hug his waist tightly. "I came in to check on you several times, but you didn't wake up at all."

"I was having the loveliest of dreams," I breathed.

"About what?"

"You."

"Oh," he grinned. "Anything good?"

"Absolutely," I answered, returning the grin.

"I'm glad to see you're feeling better," he said, running delicate hands through my hair. "I have to admit that I was a little worried about you."

"Yeah I was pretty freaked out earlier, there's no denying that."

"Oh I almost forgot," he said, pulling away from my embrace to get something out of his pocket. "Doctor Mortimer asked me to give this to you."

"Mortimer," I groaned. "I need to apologize to him."

"Don't worry about it," Nick assured me. "He's used to seeing people under duress. Talk to him when you can, but don't worry about it right now. If he hated you, would he be sending you medicine?"

"If you made him," I chuckled.

"Well I didn't," he replied, setting a little bottle of something on my nightstand.

He then stood up, so I asked, "Are you coming to bed now?"

"Yup. My watch is over." He walked over to his side of the bed and started removing his gear, carefully placing it in an orderly fashion on the bench nearby. I dreamily watched him pull his jacket off, then his boots... then he stood up and walked towards the bathroom. "I'm going to shower," he said, stopping by me and kissing my shoulder.

I said okay and watched him go into the bathroom and shut the door. I gingerly rolled over with a sigh, careful not to agitate my broken leg, then fell back asleep. Sometime later, I felt Nick crawl into bed beside me. He gently snuggled up against my back and wrapped his muscular arms around me. We fell asleep breathing at the same tempo, sending me into a blissful night's sleep.

Yells and screams reached my ears, making me think I was having another nightmare. As I woke, though, I realized it was real life. I nudged Nick, trying to wake him up.

"Nick, wake up; something is going on."

He jerked awake, finally hearing my words and the screams. He dressed hurriedly, gave me a quick kiss, then dashed downstairs. I sat up in bed worriedly, looking at the balcony doors. It was light out, so I knew morning had come. I got out of bed and dressed in my crusty clothes from yesterday, then carefully hopped over to the balcony.

Peering out the curtains, I hoped to be able to determine if it was safe out there. Tanks were parked on the lawn, making me cock my head in curiosity.

I opened the doors and went onto the balcony, realizing the screams had stopped. I think they had just been cries of alarm from our soldiers as they tried to figure out who the people in the tanks were. It looked like the tanks had plowed through the iron fence, demolishing that element of security.

Off in the distance I also saw smoke on the horizon. Since it was so far away I wasn't sure if the two events were related, but I didn't like either of them.

I fearfully turned back to the room and wondered where my mom and Mel were, wishing I had a phone to call them on. I hoped they were all right. Briefly I considered going down to their dorm, but with all the commotion going on and my broken leg, I didn't want to end up in the way. Maybe I could just go outside the room and look down at the first floor from the banister? I went to the door and opened it, shocked to find two guards standing there.

"Get back inside!" they barked.

Frowning, I shut the door and stood there. Why wasn't I allowed to leave? Since when were there guards outside the room? Well, Nick slept in here so maybe he had asked for the room to be guarded at all time. He was the highest-ranking person here, after all. And maybe he had told the guards to make sure I didn't leave the room for my own safety.

With a sigh, I shuffled back to the bed, recalling the medicine Mortimer had sent to me. I sat down on the bed, swiping up the little bottle from the nightstand. It was a strange vial; definitely not one I had ever seen a prescription in. For some reason it reminded me of ancient healers, like those of the supposed pagan world.

The bottle was made of clear glass, shaped like a weird figure. It was a beautiful piece of art, but seemed strange choice for storing something that was supposed to be beneficial. The shape was… a goat's head? A ram's head? Unable to figure it out, I looked past it at what was inside. It was a white, nearly grey, liquid that made me think of liquid bones. I supposed I had been around all this strangeness for far too long. Why was everything reminding me of weird things? I shrugged to myself and popped the lid off the bottle, wondering how much I was supposed to take. There were no instructions, so I figured I should drink all of it. But first, I sniffed it. I had learned long ago to always sniff medicine before taking it, that way you know what you're in for. Some medicine was worse than alcohol! To my delight, this stuff smelled wonderful. It had an aroma like vanilla, mixed with sugar. I happily swigged it back, almost disappointed that it was gone so quickly.

With that drank, I wondered what to do next. Delicately, I lifted up my leg to the bed, straightening it out before me. I looked at the horrible swelling that was halfway down my shin, encompassing my leg all around the broken bones. Stupidly I poked at it, grimacing as I felt something squish. The liquid below the skin pushed away under my finger's pressure, but when I pulled my finger away it instantly filled the indent. There was lots of discoloration in the area; all the lovely hues of bruises were present. As I eyed the dark spots, I started noticing a pattern. Was it a pattern, or just anomalies? Anomalies? Since when did I think of words like that?

I shook my head, realizing that it was swimming. I lazily glanced down at the empty glass bottle, wondering if whatever I'd drank was making me feel weird. Looking back at my leg, I recalled where I had left off in my ponderings: anomalies. I giggled at the word as I peered closer. Yes, there were definitely strange marks in all the bruising. Looking closer, I realized they were little ovals. Blinking quickly as I stared at it, I recalled the supposed dream I'd had. In it, my leg had broken because that person had yanked me sideways.

Suspiciously, I lifted my hand and put it towards my bruises. I recoiled as my fingers covered them. There were five little ovals that were bigger than my tiny fingerprints, but they were definitely in the pattern that fingers would be.

Peering closer, I noticed a few more patterns of five marks; probably formed by all the times the man had grabbed my broken leg to make me scream. I wheezed as my head swam, trying to make sense of all this. If there were fingerprints on my leg, that meant I had really been in the warehouse. It hadn't been a dream. The person torturing me had been real, and so had the other man's resemblance to Nick. Did that mean Nick's insistence that it had been a dream was spurred on by a sinister motivation? My thoughts felt foggy again, so I leaned over and lay down on the bed. My leg was tingling like crazy. Maybe if I just lay here for a bit, my mind would clear…

I jerked awake to the sound of my door bursting open. With a start, I sat up and blinked as I tried to look at the intruders.

"Mom!" I huffed. "Mel!" They both ran towards me,

donned in full gear and each carrying a gun. "What's going on?"

"Smith," Mel spat. "He's here! He's the one who broke through the fence with those tanks."

My jaw dropped open. "And Nick arrested him or something, right?"

"No!" my mom snorted. "They're talking. That's why we came to get you. We expressed our dislike for the situation, but Nick wouldn't listen to us. Maybe he'll listen to you."

I nodded emphatically, but gestured to my leg. "I would love to, but you'll have to help me down. Check out all the bruising. Oh, I need to tell you two something!"

"Hey!" Mel mused. "Your leg looks great!"

All eyes darted to my leg, which looked completely normal. There was no bruising or swelling whatsoever.

"What the...?" I breathed, feeling it with my hand. Everything felt fine and there was no pain.

"Maybe you didn't really break it?" my mom asked. "Maybe it was just a sprained ankle."

To that, I glowered at her. She and Mel both fidgeted, knowing that I had definitely broken my leg.

"The doctor!" I exclaimed. "He gave me some weird drink in a strange bottle..." I looked around for the container. "Ah! See!" I proclaimed, holding up the bottle. "I drank that and then passed out. It made my thoughts really fuzzy and my leg tingle. I just woke up when you came in here."

"That's some awesome medicine!" Mel cheered. "Can you walk on your leg?"

"I hope so! Help me up."

They helped me like I asked, propping me into a standing position. Ever so lightly, I put some weight on the leg. It felt fine. I put a little more weight, then a little more, until I was standing on it completely. With a huge smile, I took a step. Once I had walked around the whole room, I jumped for joy.

"It's better!" I celebrated.

My mom and Mel cheered with me, really glad that I wasn't going to be bed-ridden for months.

"Awesome!" Mel laughed. "Now let's get down there and deal with that traitor."

"Whoa whoa whoa!" I yelled, dashing in front of them before they could get to the door. "Wait, I need to tell you something."

"What is it?" my mom asked.

Knowing there were soldiers on the other side of the door, I walked my two visitors across the room to the sitting chairs by the balcony.

In a whisper I said, "It wasn't a dream. I was really in that warehouse."

"Addie—" Mel objected, but I cut her off.

"I know we've already been over this. Nick talked to me and had me totally convinced that I just bonked my head and had a whacko dream while I was unconscious. But," I said earnestly, leaning towards them both, "there was bruising on my leg consistent with fingerprints. Several of them. In my supposed dream, my torturer first broke my leg by grabbing it, then kept hurting me by strongly gripping the broken spot. I saw the bruises! But now my leg is healed and I have no proof." I saw skepticism in their eyes, which was like a dagger in my heart. "Please," I pleaded, "just consider it. The man in charge of both Smith and the man who broke my leg looked a lot like Nick. I think they're related." Both of them opened their mouths to protest, so I emphasized, "That would explain why he's talking to Smith, even after the bastard betrayed four of his own people!"

Mom and Mel thought about what I said, turning their eyes from me, then each other, then the floor, then back to me.

"You don't have to believe me," I said, trying to hide the hurt in my tone, "just think about it before you decide."

I got up from where we were sitting and walked to my side of the bed. Looking around on the floor for a minute, I tried to remember where I left my gear. With a sigh, I turned around. "Do either of you happen to know where I left my gear?"

Mel shook her head, and my mom frowned. "Actually, I don't think you wore it back yesterday."

I gasped and bugged my eyes, then dashed back over to both of them. "Mom, was I wearing it when you carried me away from the truck yesterday?"

She scrunched her brows together, trying to remember. "Uhm, I'm not sure, but I doubt it. I probably wouldn't have been able to carry all that weight."

"That's it!" I squawked, smacking my palm to my forehead. "Before they tortured me, they ripped off all my gear. That's your proof! I know I wore it because it got caught on something when I was trying to get to the back of the truck. That's the whole reason I went out my own door."

Mel looked like she wanted to object, but couldn't think of anything to say.

"Maybe you just slipped it off when you were getting out of the truck," my mom weakly offered, knowing that was absurd.

"Mom, you are the one who said hardly a few seconds passed between when I tried getting out Faulk's side of the truck and when you came to get me. How the heck would I have taken off all that gear in that short of a time?"

"I don't know, but it seems a lot more likely than you being dragged off to that horrible warehouse to be tortured!" she thundered, suddenly trying to hold back tears.

I recoiled slightly, all of the sudden realizing why she and Mel were so upset with what I was saying. "Mom! Mel!" I exclaimed, rushing to them and putting a hand on each of their shoulders. "Do you think you're guilty in this? You are not to blame in the slightest!"

"Like hell we aren't!" my mom sobbed, all her tears bursting forth. "You tell me you were dragged off and hurt, and I wasn't able to help? I couldn't do a single damn thing to protect you!"

"Mom," I breathed, hugging her tightly as she sobbed. "I'm a grown up now; your job is done."

"A mother's job is never done Adeline. I wasn't there for part of your childhood, and now as an adult I can't even take care of you. I'm just one massive failure as a parent."

"No mom," I said sincerely, stroking her hair and looking into her eyes. "Please don't feel that way."

Suddenly there was a rumble outside, making us all remember what was going on.

My mom flicked her hand at me, nodding her head a couple times as she did so. "I'm fine," she sniffled, hurriedly drying her tears. "Let's go. I'm okay, I promise."

"Okay," I said. "Mom, know that I love you."

Warmth appeared in her eyes and a sweet smile covered

her mouth. "I love you too darling."

We locked hands for a second, then all three of us looked at one another.

"Now let's go find out why that bastard is back at our camp," I growled, leading my pack of wolves towards the doors.

CHAPTER TWELVE

Determinedly, my mom, Mel, and I stormed across the presidential suite. At the magnificent double doors, we paused to nod to each other. I then threw the doors open, startling the two guards on the other side.

"You ladies aren't permitted to leave," one started to say, but Mel and my mom raised their guns.

"You were saying?" my mom hissed with a vicious expression.

I grinned to myself, wondering when she had become such a badass. The men put their hands up in surrender, so I grabbed both of their guns. I slung one over my shoulder and raised the other one defensively.

"Inside!" I barked.

The men complied and entered the room. Quickly, I grabbed some plastic ties that I saw hanging from their belt. I reached up and grabbed the hands of one guard, quickly zipping a tie around each hand and linking them together. My mom followed my lead and worked on restraining the other man. We led them to the bed, sitting them on the floor at the foot of it. We made them sit back to back, locking their hands together with another tie. Not wanting them to have any chance of coming after us, I also tied one of the guy's feet together then tied that to the bed post. Again, my mom followed my lead and did the same to the other guard.

Without a word to their protests, we hopped up and

dashed from the room. Once we got out to the hallway, we heard a lot of chaos. Matching the speed of the other soldiers, we hurried down the hall and made our way downstairs. I figured Nick would be in the meeting room where I had seen him a couple times with Major Ghost, so I led us that way. Sure enough, we burst through the doors to find him in a private discussion with Smith.

"Eve!" he greeted when we came in, not getting up from his seat.

I nervously curled my lip, wondering why he was so calm. If he had assigned guards to our room and didn't want us getting out of there, shouldn't he be worried that we escaped?

"You shouldn't be down here," he said coolly. "It's dangerous right now."

"Yeah I noticed!" I snorted, striding over to Smith. I don't know who I thought I was, but for some reason I was acting like I had as much authority as Nick. I planted my feet widely as I stood in front of the betrayer, indicating that I wasn't going anywhere any time soon. "Thanks to him."

"Eve, I've been talking to him. I think there was a misunderstanding."

"A misunderstanding?" I scoffed. "He betrayed us! He left us when waves of changed things were coming at us! He released them from the warehouse!"

Smith looked at me tranquilly, not saying a word. I think I saw a hint of a smirk on his face.

"That's not what happened," Nick countered. "Smith was waiting for you outside when he saw some of those things approaching. He actually ran away to try to lead them away from you guys. Unfortunately he wasn't able to distract them all. He did run back towards the warehouse, but he had gotten disoriented. Luckily for us too, because he found more of our group out there and was able to bring them and all their gear back to us. The man's a hero."

I snarled at Nick's words without meaning to. But the yelling that came next? That was all intentional.

"A HERO?" I thundered, turning my full fury towards Nick. "You weren't there Nick! You didn't see what we did! Smith betrayed us and left us to die!!!"

"No, he didn't," Nick replied as he shook his head.

"Were you there?" I growled, trembling with rage.

Suddenly the door opened and a soldier dashed in, stopping instantly when he saw us. "Oh, uh Colonel Kadav, they need you out there. Sorry to interrupt."

"That's okay; we were about done. Smith, you'll accompany me. Eve, please get Vie and Mel somewhere safe."

With that he stood up and walked towards the door. Smith also stood, but I gripped his arm.

"If you think for a second," I quietly warned so that Nick couldn't hear, "that you're going to get away with this, you're dead wrong."

He smirked and leaned close to my face, whispering, "What are you going to do about it, *Eve?*" Then he jerked his arm from my grasp and left the room.

Never in my life had I been so furious. I bellowed in utter fury, slamming my hands down on the table over and over. I ranted and raved to my mom and Mel about how Smith was going to pay, unable to calm my rage. Venomous words and pure hatred flew from my mouth, as did spit and slobber. My audience nodded in agreement, because even if they were on the fence about my weird warehouse experience, they sure as hell knew Smith had betrayed us; of that there was no doubt.

Finally, when I had calmed down slightly and was once again thinking straight, I wearily sank into one of the plush leather chairs. "What are we going to do?" I weakly asked, having worn myself out with my tirade.

"Calm down, for one thing. Sheesh," Mel answered.

I laughed and shook my head at her in embarrassment. "I'm sorry. I felt so helpless. Nick holds all the power here and he's totally siding with the man who tried to kill us."

"Maybe Smith is jelly," she shrugged.

"Jelly?" my mom asked.

"Yeah; jealous. Maybe he's jealous of Addie, since she's close to Nick. Maybe he's jelly of how much all three of us get to do since we're in with Nick. So he tried to get us killed, and now he's totally discrediting our version of the story."

"Yes, maybe," my mom agreed. "That's certainly a possibility."

"He has turned Nick against us," I said sadly.

"Nick isn't against us," Mel countered. "He's just not against our enemy. The non-enemy of our enemy is our... friend?"

"That's not how it works," I laughed, shaking my head at her.

"Hey!" my mom exclaimed, clapping her hands together. "We should go find Faulk. Maybe Nick will listen if Faulk tells the same story."

"Yeah!" Mel agreed.

"You just want to see him!" I jabbed.

"Well duh," she grinned.

To that we all laughed and strode to the door. "Stay alert," I cautioned, since we had no idea what was going on outside. If Smith had brought back more of Nick's supposed men, they were probably all on Smith's side. Nick didn't even realize that he was inviting a potential revolt into his own camp.

We exited the room and made our way through the main areas of the house, finding a lot of men hurrying to and fro. Although we saw a lot of familiar faces, we also saw a lot of new ones. They kind of glared at us, probably wondering what the odd group of women was doing. That's okay; we just stared back. I will admit that I felt a little out of place since all I had on was clothing when all people around me had on full gear.

"Maybe Faulk has some spare gear I can borrow," I murmured to Mel.

She agreed as we came to the back doors of the house. They were thrown wide open, allowing us to have a clear view of the back lawn. It looked pretty hectic. There were several new tanks parked on it, along with half a dozen more trucks. Men sporting gas-masks dotted the perimeter, causing a knot to form in my stomach. Those men were so uncanny. Why did only some guards wear masks and not others? And come to think of it, the masked men never seemed to do much. I had pretty much only ever seen them standing still or walking slowly between their posts. They moved weird too; almost like they didn't know how to work their bodies. They were so flipping creepy.

Past them, we could see that the iron fence had been mowed down. I frowned at the sight, wondering how Nick was okay with that. The huge thing that had attacked a while back had blasted down the front fence, and now these idiots had plowed through the back fence. I scowled at the mistake Nick was making. How could he not see that Smith and his goons weren't friends?

"Hey there!" someone called as they ran over to us. We looked their way, happy to see that it was Faulk.

"Hey yourself," Mel swooned, batting her eyes and running her fingers through her hair.

Faulk grinned bashfully, darting his eyes to the ground.

"Hey Faulk," I said as normally as possible, hoping to make him comfortable again. "What's going on out here?"

"What isn't going on is a better question. These whack-os drove right through our fence, then demanded to speak to the person in charge. Guess who their leader is?"

"Smith," we all growled.

"Whoa!" he defended, backing up a step from us. "I guess you already knew. He and Nick are on good terms."

"Yeah," I seethed. "Nick called him a hero; said he tried leading the changed things away from us."

"Load of horse shit; excuse me ladies," Faulk fumed.

"Don't apologize to us," my mom agreed. "It's exactly that. Nick is making a mistake by welcoming them."

"So what's the plan?" I asked, nodding to where I saw our people bringing out blankets. "Are these guys going to camp on our lawn or what?"

"Yup; that's the plan."

I shook my head in anger, determined to speak with Nick again. "I'm going to find Nick," I said lowly. "But first, Faulk, do you know where I can get some spare armor?"

"There are a few spares down in storage. Take the ele-

vator to level E60; the whole floor is storage," he said, and
then I thought I saw him wink.

Unsure of what the heck that meant, I just ignored it
and said, "Awesome, thanks. Mom and Mel, are you okay?"

"I'll take care of them," Faulk promised.

I thanked him and then dashed towards the house, uneasily glancing all around myself. I tried to chill out a little
with how I was constantly ready to fire my gun if necessary,
but it was hard. Even if these people meant well towards
Nick, I was one of the very few females around. Being
around a group of tough men that outnumbered me a-hun-
dred-to-one was a little worrisome. I hurried to the elevator,
allowing myself a sigh of relief when I reached it. I punched
the button for E60, then felt myself plummet downwards.
A dizzying time later, I arrived at my floor. Cautiously I
stepped out of the elevator, unsure of what to expect.

At first the room was entirely dark. Once I started
moving, the light sensors ignited and lit up the part of the
room that I was in. I marveled at the size of it; even though
most of it was still dark, I could tell that it was a massive
warehouse. It had to be at least 20,000 square feet. I blinked
and looked around, wondering where in the world armor
might be. I could see that everything in here was in tidy
containers, stored in rows upon rows of racks. However, a
few feet from the elevator, a lone table stood with a single
box on it. I walked towards the table, realizing it was probably for sorting purposes. If someone grabbed a container,
they could bring it here to sort through the contents.

I cautiously walked towards the table, flinching when
another light came on above me, activated by my movement. Once I reached the table, I noticed that the storage

container on top of it was open. Cautiously, I peered over the top to see inside. With an unexpected frown, I lowered my gun and reach both hands towards the box. Pulling out file folders, I scrunched my brows.

"Files?" I asked myself, looking at them.

Each folder was labeled with a name. I flipped through them, learning that each one was a profile of a specific person. Inside the folder there was a picture of the person, their name, medical history, professional history, education, and pretty much anything you could want to know about someone. As I looked through them, I noticed most of them were stamped with either a big red X or the word Acquired.

Suddenly I thought I heard a noise. I glanced up with a start, but didn't see anything in the darkness. I went back to looking through the folders, realizing moments later what I had seen. Gasping, I looked up again. About halfway through the giant warehouse on my right, a light had come on. That meant something was moving. Suddenly something caught my eye on the other side. I jerked my head to the left, seeing another light coming on even closer to me. The sound of snarling hit my ears, making me cringe. I swallowed fearfully and looked down at the folders, seeing more lights coming on out of the corner of my eyes. Apparently there were snarling things down here, and they were on the move.

I flipped through the folders again, feeling like they were significant somehow. I didn't want to just leave them. Faulk had sent me down here for armor, but there was no way I'd find armor in this huge warehouse. Had he wanted me to find these files? After all, he had winked at me. All of the sudden I stopped flipping, alarmed by the name I saw.

Major General Bruce Homes.

"Dad?" I gasped, yanking the folder open. The inside wasn't stamped with anything.

Snarling reached my ears again, this time only a few feet from me. I shoved the folder into the back of my pants, not knowing where else to put it. I raised my gun and unloaded a clip at the things coming at me. My aim was getting better, but I still wasted a lot of ammo. As I fired, I skipped backwards towards the elevator. I hammered a few of the changed things, which were ironically all wearing guard gear. Of course I wanted it, but hopefully I'd find a better option upstairs. Just as my first magazine ran out, the elevator opened for me. I jumped inside and pounded the ground level button, panting as I watched the doors close and cut off my view of the things.

"Whew!" I huffed, trying to catch my breath. As I did, I untucked my shirt and tried to re-tuck it over the folder. With all the strangeness that was going on, I didn't want anyone to know that I had found it.

The elevator slowed and stopped, alarming me at first. Then I realized the next level up was lit up on the keypad. The doors opened, letting a hulking man get on board. I acknowledged him, to which he replied with a grunt. As I worked on discreetly finishing tucking the shirt, I looked up at the man. He had his back to me, but somehow he looked familiar. His height was astounding, almost like… no, it couldn't be. I gulped and kept staring at him, seeing something weird on his neck. Was that what I thought it was?

As though he could read my thoughts, the man calmly reached out and hit the emergency stop button. We jerked to a stop, making me sway and fling my arms out to steady myself.

"Whoa, careful there," the man said, having turned around to face me and catch my arms.

He held my arms firmly, helping me steady myself. I would have thought it was nice of him if he didn't have massive bruising around his throat. Bruising from where I had tried choking him with chains.

"I see you looking at my throat," he seethed. "That's right love; we have some unfinished business."

"No," I whimpered without meaning to.

"Oh yes," he grinned, slowly reaching his hand toward me and slipping the guns off my shoulder, tossing them to the other side of the elevator. "Your leg seems to be better. Can I fix that for you, dear?"

"No!" I screamed, trying to wrench myself away from him. He was infinitely stronger than me though; I may as well have been a child's doll in his grasp.

Panting through gritted teeth, I looked up into his hateful face. It was covered in ill intent, making my insides knot up. There was no reasoning with this man. He didn't want anything except the pleasure of harming me. I wheezed for air, feeling like I was on the verge of a panic attack. I begged myself to calm down; panic sure as hell wouldn't get me out of the situation. Well maybe... maybe if I passed out, there wouldn't be any enjoyment in it for him. I shook my head to dismiss the idea. If I did that, there was also the chance that I would never wake up. I desperately scanned his face for any ounce of compassion.

Sympathy I didn't find, but I thought I saw something interesting. Burned into his skin... was that the shape of my cross necklace? Suddenly I remembered how our last encounter had ended: he had put his face to my chest, then he had started screaming. Had my necklace been the cause?

"Hey just out of curiosity," I jeered, not seeing the harm in antagonizing him since he was going to torture me anyway, "do you not like crosses?"

He recoiled from the question and growled. "Shut your mouth."

"I couldn't help but notice there seems to be one burned on your face. That wouldn't be from my necklace, would it?"

"I said shut your mouth," he seethed, leaning his hulking frame down towards me.

I cowered back and complied, letting my self-preserving sense of fear wash over me. Maybe I should shut my mouth. Maybe I should just let him do whatever he wanted and not fight back. If I did that, perhaps he would let me live. I didn't want to die like this; alone with a killer in an elevator. It seemed like a ridiculously sad way to go out.

Suddenly the man gripped my face with one of his massive hands, slamming me back against the wall of the elevator. The handrail jabbed into my back, making me scream. His lips curled back into a sickening smile, and in that moment I knew without a shred of doubt that he was going to kill me. I shrieked and violently thrashed to get free, but his grip was too strong. I launched kicks at him, somehow managing to land a satisfying blow to his groin. He recoiled and backed up, dropping me as he did so. I scrambled towards the keypad to get the elevator moving again, reaching a desperate hand out to the button. Just as I felt it brush my fingertip, the man grabbed me and threw me to the floor.

The air was knocked from my lungs, leaving me to lie

there helplessly. The man's face loomed over mine, viciously growling at me. In this moment, possibly one of my last, I suddenly felt the urge to pray. It was overwhelming and seemed to hit me like a train. I heard a voice telling me to call out to God; a voice so powerful it seemed to be on a loudspeaker. I blinked and looked around, wondering what I had just heard. I didn't pray though, and felt foolish for even having the urge.

Suddenly the elevator doors flung open, shocking both me and the man. Had I actually pushed the button and gotten us to the next floor? Someone stepped inside and savagely yanked the man out. A barrage of curses followed, allowing me to recognize the voice. Nick. I exhaled in relief, so glad that he had been there in time. Weakly, I stood up and peered out of the elevator. Nick was screaming at the man so profusely that I couldn't even understand what he was saying. Then he grabbed the man's collar and yanked him down the hall.

I stood on trembling legs and followed, wondering where Nick was taking him. He dragged the huge man along, making me marvel at the fact that the man wasn't even fighting back. The colonel led him outside, barking an order to someone that he passed. As he stopped in the middle of the front lawn, a soldier came darting up to him with a megaphone.

"Everyone, come to the front lawn!" he yelled into it.

Slowly, everyone around the camp made their way to the front as Nick shoved the man down to his knees. I didn't go out there, but watched from the front doors of the house. When the majority of our camp was present, he continued to yell into the megaphone. His voice carried across both lawns, and even miraculously into the house.

"This man was caught attacking one of our female soldiers. Bullshit like this is sickening and absolutely will not be tolerated! Is that clear?" Murmurs echoed through the crowd, making Nick even angrier. "I said is that clear?" he bellowed.

I recoiled from his fury, frightened by the level of it. Apparently the soldiers had the same feeling, because a unified and loud, "Yes sir!" shouted from the crowd of them.

"In case it isn't," he growled, "I want to make sure it's crystal clear." He suddenly raised his pistol and put it to the man's head, then pulled the trigger.

I yelped and covered my mouth grievously as the man's brain splattered into the air, and his body slumped over. Wanting to be as far from that situation as possible, I turned and ran up the stairs to the bedroom. Thankfully, the guards must have escaped because there was no sign of them anywhere. I threw myself down on the bed and wept, having no idea why. That man was awful; he would have killed me if he hadn't been stopped. Nick had saved me just in time. But had he needed to execute the man in front of everyone like that? It seemed unnecessarily cruel and barbaric.

After getting out most of my tears, I finally picked up my wet face from the pillow and wearily rolled over onto my back. As I did so, I felt a crunch. I weakly reached underneath my back, pulling the file out of my clothes. Wiping my eyes on my shirt so that I could see, I opened the folder and looked through it. Why in the world had it been in that storage bin? Had it been there before, or had Nick's group brought it here?

I heard footsteps in the hall, so I hurriedly shoved the folder into the drawer of the nightstand beside me. A moment later, Nick walked into the room.

"Oh Eve," he breathed, striding towards me. "Honey look at you."

I wiped my eyes again. "I'm okay," I insisted.

"No sweetheart, you're not," he countered softly, pulling me close to him. I noticed that he was only wearing an undershirt. He probably had to take off his uniform jacket because that man's brain matter was on it.

"Why did you do that?" I moaned, unable to stop myself.

Bafflement covered his face. "That man attacked you!" he roared. "That's why!"

"But did you have to just… execute him like that?"

"Eve, an example needed to be made of him. Do you want every man to treat you like that? Because I sure as hell don't. Baby, I did it for your safety. And your mother's. And Mel's. I did it for all three of you." He tenderly stroked my hair and gazed at me, hoping his words were having an effect.

"Okay," I consented. "I suppose I see what you're saying. Thank you, I guess."

"Trust me Eve, it was the best option. Would you really be happy knowing that guy was around here?"

"No, but you could have kicked him out of the camp."

"To certain death by the changed things? I think what I did was much kinder. At least he had a quick end and wasn't eaten alive by rotting humans."

"True."

"All things considered, are you okay?"

"Yeah, I guess so. I have a ton of questions about today. Especially about Smith and why the hell you trust him."

"Who said I do?"

"Uh, that's exactly what you said," I barked, annoyed to see him grinning.

"Honey," he soothed, taking my hands into his. "I only said that for him. The man rolled into our camp with tanks and soldiers. To refuse him would have meant certain death for us. I'm telling him what he wants to hear."

I gawked, staring at him in disbelief. "Seriously?"

"Yes, seriously. You think I would ever take his word over yours? No way."

I rolled my eyes and laughed, falling back in joy. "Oh my goodness you have no idea how freaking relieved I am to hear you say that!" I exclaimed, punching my arms towards the ceiling.

Nick laughed merrily, laying down beside me and propping himself up on his elbow. "I'm glad. I'm sorry I had to make you think I was against you. And I'm so very, very sorry that I wasn't there for you sooner today. That man in the elevator," he fumed, suddenly sounding furious, "that worthless human being! I can't believe I almost wasn't there for you in time. I'm so sorry baby."

"It's okay," I beamed, reaching a hand up to his face. "You saved me in time."

His eyes were glossed over with tears, but he smiled in response to my words.

"How'd you know where I was?" I asked.

"I was looking for you and Faulk told me you'd gone down to your old room. When I saw that the elevator's emergency stop had been pressed, I knew something was wrong. My guys tapped into the audio feed and heard your screams… it was awful!"

I thought back to the horrible event from earlier, recalling the words that the guy and I had exchanged. "Did you hear anything else?" I asked softly.

"No, why?"

"Just curious," I lied. "I thought maybe you picked up something that would indicate why he did that to me."

"Some men are just lunatics. I'm so happy that you're okay Eve."

"Me too," I smiled.

He gazed down and stroked my hair, then leaned in for a kiss. We'd barely kissed like twice since we'd met, so his gesture was absolutely delicious. I hungrily kissed him, yanking him as close as possible. He climbed on top of me, making me nearly die of happiness. I clawed at his shirt, ripping it off of him. He kissed me harder, never missing a beat as he pulled my shirt off. Then someone knocked on the door.

I groaned in annoyance, making him smile. After a moment, he cleared his throat and asked who was there. Someone claimed that they needed him, so he told them he'd be there soon.

"But I need you," I said glumly as he pulled his shirt back on.

"I'll be back soon," he promised, kissing my shoulder.

"Okay," I murmured, hardly able to protest to anything when he was being so sweet.

He put his boots back on, gave me a quick kiss, then left the room. I sighed and put my shirt back on, feeling silly sitting there shirtless by myself. I looked around the room, wondering what to do until he came back. It was nowhere near as fun as what I'd just been doing, but I figured I should go check on my mom and Mel. I left the room, again surprised to find two guards outside the doors. Thankfully, they let me leave this time. They were even helpful.

As I left, one of them said, "If you're looking for your companions, they're in the room down the hall."

I raised an eyebrow, thanked the man, then went to the room they had stayed in when we first got here.

"There you are!" my mom exulted when she answered my knock. "We were so worried about you! We tried to get to you but the guards outside your room said you wanted to rest."

"When Nick shot that guy on the lawn and said there was an attack on a woman, we knew it had to have been you!" Mel cried, rushing to the door and hugging me. "Are you all right?"

"Yeah, sort of." I came into the room and shut the door. "You guys, it was that guy from the warehouse. The one who broke my leg."

They both looked at me with raised eyebrows, unsure of what to say.

"I might be able to prove it," I gushed. "Nick said they had audio of the elevator of when he attacked me. Maybe they recorded it. When he first confronted me, he said we had unfinished business. If that's on the recording, it'll prove what I'm saying."

"Whoa…" Mel mused. "Creepy!"

"Yeah," my mom agreed. "But even without that, we believe you. You know that, right?"

"I'm not sure," I replied. "I thought you were skeptical."

"Well yeah, what you're saying doesn't make much sense," Mel sang. "But we don't think you're crazy, and we agree that the story of you simply knocking yourself out doesn't make much more sense."

"Oh, but there is good news!" I proclaimed, suddenly remembering. "Nick doesn't believe Smith. He just needs him to think he does so that he doesn't attack us. Don't say anything!"

"Awesome!" Mel laughed. "Because the way he acted earlier was not cool."

"Not at all," my mom agreed.

There was a light knock on the door, which Mel answered.

"Hey," Nick said. "Have you seen a gorgeous woman with red hair?"

I giggled and stepped forward, making him smile.

"My lady," he smiled, offering me his hand.

Mel squealed and ushered me forward, making me laugh. I took his hand and bid Mel and Mom goodnight, then went with him back to our room. Once we got there, he dimmed the lights.

"Mood lighting?" I whispered hesitantly.

"Sort of," he smiled. "After this long day, though, I think we could both use a relaxing, hot bath. What do you say?"

"Uh, maybe…"

He blinked seriously, then said, "Eve, there's no pressure from me. I just thought it was what you wanted."

"It is," I said uncertainly. "I mean, I think it is…."

"We can wait darling," he said, holding me at arm's length and smiling warmly.

"No," I objected, pulling him back towards me. "I want this."

"Are you sure? I don't want you to feel pressured at all."

"I know. But I would love nothing more than to have, what did you call it, "a hot, relaxing bath," with you."

He chuckled and kissed me passionately, then swooped me into his arms. "All right then!" he proclaimed, carrying me to the bathroom. I giggled and laughed merrily, then kissed him all the way there.

CHAPTER THIRTEEN

Morning greeted me with a lovely kiss, delivered from the lips of what I thought was an angel. I smiled as I emerged from my slumber, wrapping my arms around Nick.

"Good morning beautiful," he breathed.

"Good morning," I giggled as he pulled me close.

"How'd you sleep?"

"Sleep!" I laughed. "I barely recall sleeping."

He chuckled and sultrily put his lips to my neck. "Is that so? What do you remember?"

"Many amazing things," I murmured, fluttering my eyes shut as I felt his lips move across my skin.

He kissed me softly several times, then leaned back to look at me. "You're such a beautiful woman Eve; I daresay the most beautiful creature on this earth."

"Awww!!!" I gushed, feeling so wonderfully lovely. "You really think so?"

"Of course," he smiled.

"Well," I chuckled, "I guess that's easy to do now that the earth is filled with rotting corpses."

"Oh love!" he exclaimed, slapping his palm to his forehead. "Way to ruin my compliment!"

"I'm sorry," I giggled. "I promise not to do it again."

"You better not," he said dangerously, raising an eyebrow at me.

"Oooh Colonel Kadav, are you going to punish me if I do?"

He looked as though he had a delightful response to my dare, but before he could answer there was a knock on the door.

"Always," I sighed. "You are one very important person."

"And you are the most important person," he proclaimed, pulling me close for a kiss. "Get yourself ready for the day; I have another mission to send you on."

"Okay," I beamed, ready to face any challenges that the day might throw at me. Well, I thought I was ready. Little did I know what the day had in store for me.

I dressed quickly, then headed downstairs. Unsurprisingly, I found two guards outside my room. I scowled as I walked past them, not liking the way they looked at me.

"What are you looking at?" one growled.

"Nothing," I muttered.

"That's right. Be on your way before your boyfriend accuses me of attacking you."

I recoiled from his words, shocked by what they implied. With a frown, I walked towards Mel and Mom's room. Were there two guards outside their room too? Yup, there sure were. When I got to the door, the guards stopped me from entering.

"The women already left," one of them said gruffly.

"Where did they go?"

"Downstairs."

"Well can I go inside anyway?"

"No."

I dipped my brows into a V, wondering why they wouldn't let me in. Should I keep insisting? "Why not? I left something in there yesterday and need to get it."

"Tell us what it is and we'll retrieve it for you."

"What is the big deal?" I scoffed, trying to push past them and get inside. They were way bigger and stronger than me, so that didn't happen.

"I am advising you to stop," the other one said to me. "Be on your way."

I scowled at them and puffed up my chest, wondering what their deal was. Angrily, I marched down the hall to the stairs and began my search for Nick. I found him by the front doors.

"Seriously!" I griped, walking towards him with quite a bit of annoyance.

"What?" he asked, perplexed.

"First the two guards outside our room had quite an attitude with me, implying that I lied about that guy attacking me. I didn't even say a word about it! You found me being attacked by him!"

"I know, I'm sorry Eve," he soothed, putting a hand on my shoulder. "A lot of the men are upset about what I did. If they take it out on you, be sure to let me know and I'll make them regret it."

"Well, okay," I muttered. "But secondly, the two guards outside my mom and Mel's room wouldn't let me go inside."

"That's simply because they're both down here already," he said with a nod towards the back lawn. "They're practicing their hand-to-hand fighting."

"Well why wouldn't the guards let me into the room? Are they hiding something?"

"Not that I know of," he chuckled, putting his arm around me and walking towards the back of the house. "They're probably just taking their security duty seriously."

"I guess that makes sense," I conceded. "After all, you did put the fear of God in everyone when you executed that guy."

"*The fear of God,*" he chuckled. "That's one way to say it." For some reason, his tone made the hairs on the back of my neck stand on end.

We walked to the back of the house, where Nick pointed to the right. "Your friends are over there. But, you'll need to replace your gear, which is that way." He pointed to the left, where I saw a truck with its back hatch open. A man stood by it, handing out supplies to men as needed. "Now if you'll excuse me, you stunning creature, I have to get back to work."

"Okay," I exhaled dreamily just before he kissed me goodbye. I turned and watched him walk away, grinning to myself at the sight. Once he turned a corner and was out of my view, I made my way out to the lawn. I went to the truck where the man was standing.

"Hi there," I greeted.

"What do you need?"

"I uh, Colonel Kadav, sent me over to get gear and a gun."

"Sure." The man turned around and barked something, making me realize there was someone in the back of the truck sorting for items as they were requested. I waited patiently, realizing a moment later that the man in the truck looked familiar. It was dark in there, making me squint in order to see him better.

"Faulk?" I called. "Hey, how are you?"

"Don't talk to him," the man ordered, making me give him a questioning look.

I looked back at Faulk, who discreetly acknowledged me with a small nod. What was wrong with his face? Was that… a black eye?

"What—" I started, but the man cut me off by jamming my new gear into my hands.

"Here you are. Next!"

I scowled at him and glanced behind me, surprised to see that a line had formed. Oddly, everyone in line wore a gas mask. I shuddered at the sight of so many of them being near me. With a sigh and resolution to find out what had happened to Faulk, I strode away and donned my gear. With all of it on, I slung my rifle over my shoulder and made my way to Mom and Mel.

"There you are!" Mel squealed when she saw me. She bound my way, throwing her arms around me. "You dirty girl," she chided with a wink.

"Hey!" I cried, looking around anxiously. "Shush!"

"So it finally happened, huh? Tell me everything!"

"Oh don't do that," my mom opposed as she reached us.

"How the heck do you two know what… what may or may not have happened last night?"

"Well for one, those guards at your door wouldn't let us in for the world last night!" Mel said indignantly.

"I don't think that was the reason, although if they knew about it—gross!"

"And for two," Mel continued, "I can see it in your eyes and the ridiculous smile plastered on your face."

To that I couldn't help but laugh and giggle, making my mom and Mel squeal a lot and demand tasteful details.

"How was it?" Mel demanded. "I bet it was uh-may-zing!" she sang. "Was he all bossy and man-in-charge like?"

"Stop!" I laughed, playfully pushing her away. "Don't we have an assignment today? We should go find out what it is."

Mel made some horribly embarrassing comment, making me flush red as I laughed and practically ran away from her. We went back inside, learning that Major Ghost had our orders. Apparently we were making another run today to look for survivors. I sighed as he told us. Yes, I wanted to find more to replace us so we could go get my dad, but it was starting to feel hopeless.

"Wait!" I protested, accidentally interrupting him. He scowled deeply at me, eliciting an apology from me before I then asked my question. "With the men Smith brought here now, can't the three of us get permission to leave?"

"No."

"Why not?"

"You just can't."

"Why?" I asked, stepping towards him.

"I've given you the answer. I don't have to give you the why. You have your orders... what's your last name, Homes? You have your orders Homes. I suggest you carry them out."

"Orders?" I growled. "I'm not a soldier, and I don't have to listen to you."

Anger raced through his eyes, and I swear for a second they flashed black. I blinked in terror, unable to confirm what I thought I had seen.

"You're absolutely right," he said calmly. "You're not a soldier. You're not helpful. You know what you are? A leech. You consume resources, yet you do nothing for this camp."

"What do you do?" I argued. "You're always here, in this comfortable house."

"I do more than you could imagine," he hissed and leaned towards me. "Now I suggest you either carry out your orders or remove yourself from this camp."

"That's not your call," I sneered.

With that, I spun around and left the room with Mel and my mom following behind me. We didn't go very far though, because I didn't have a plan. We stopped in the hall as I wondered what to do.

"What was that about?" my mom asked.

"It feels like they're keeping something from us," I said quietly. "Everything here seems so weird. Mel, have you seen Faulk this morning?"

"No, why?"

"He's like, in trouble or something. They have him hidden in the back of that supply truck and I think he has a black eye."

She raised her eyebrows in concern, quickly looking towards the truck. "Well let's find out why," she said angrily, starting to walk that way.

"No!" I objected, darting in front of her. "They don't want us to know it's him or talk to him. We'll have to catch him later or distract the guy at the back of the truck."

A few minutes later, I walked back over to the truck. Oddly enough, the entire long line of gas-mask guys was gone.

"What do you want now?" the guy demanded.

"I was just wondering if you could help me and my mom adjust our armor."

"I don't babysit," he said incredulously, shaking his head at me.

"Just a moment of your time darling," my mom

swooned, coming out of nowhere. She turned on the charm and smiled at him sweetly, looking as helpless as possible.

"Well, okay, but make it quick."

I tried to hide a grin. Never underestimate a man's desire to feel useful for a damsel in distress. Carefully, I glanced at the side of the truck where Mel was sneaking up to one of the doors. As gently as possible she opened one and leaned inside. Hopefully she could get Faulk's attention and ask him some questions. A few moments later, I saw her walking away. I excused myself from the rude man and my mom's nauseating flirting and went over to where Mel was.

"What did he say?" I asked in a whisper.

"He wants to talk to you at midnight. He said it had to be you." She frowned, trying to hide the hurt in her voice.

"Me? Why?"

"I don't know," she spat, suddenly mad. "Why don't you ask him tonight on your little midnight date!"

"Mel!"

"Leave me alone," she said, swatting her arm at the hand I had reached towards her.

She walked away from me angrily, making me clench my fists. Why had Faulk only wanted to talk to me? I glanced over at my mom, seeing her still talking with the man at the truck. With her occupied and my best friend mad at me, I wondered what to do. Suddenly I recalled the file upstairs in the room. With a purpose, I strode back into the house and up the stairs.

At the doors of my room, two new guards gave me looks as dirty as the other guards had. I ignored them and went inside, loudly locking the doors after doing so. Then I went to the nightstand and pulled the drawer open, gasping. The file was gone. I yanked open the other drawers, finding nothing. Madly, I dashed to all the other cabinets and dressers in the room. Nothing. I ripped open the dresser and closet, and even dashed to the bathroom and searched through all the counter drawers. I dropped to the floor and looked under the bed, then under the mattress. The file was gone.

Who would have taken it? I scowled with realization. Those damn guards! I bet they came in here and searched the room every time we left for the day. Fine, if they wanted to take it I would just go get it back. Sure, there had been changed things down in that room, but I was ready to take my chances. Any amount of danger was worth finding out what was in that folder.

Fuming with anger, I unlocked the doors and stormed from the room. I thundered down the stairs to the elevator, punching the button for E60 as soon as I could. I tried to ignore the memories of what had happened in the elevator, but it was pretty hard to dismiss the memory of almost being murdered. By the time I got to the level I wanted, I was shaking pretty badly. Determined not to let that affect me, I stepped from the elevator as soon as the doors opened. The lights came on above me, then lit the way as I walked forward.

I gasped when the light above the table illuminated. The table wasn't there anymore, and neither was the box. I strode past the spot to the nearest row of racks, which towered above me to the tall ceiling. The lights came on as I walked, again making me gasp. The racks were completely empty.

"No, no no no!" I muttered, running down the aisle to make more lights come on. Sure enough, all the racks were empty.

I ran down several more, hoping to find at least one with content left on it. No such luck. All the racks were empty. I stopped running as I accepted the fact that this whole massive room was probably empty. I panted and keeled over, leaning my hands on my thighs. As I tried to catch my breath, I wondered who in the world had done this. How had they cleared out 20,000 square feet of storage so quickly? This place had been jam packed with containers when I had been in here the other day! Where were all the bins that used to be in here? Had they moved everything because I had discovered it?

With a gasp, I realized that this was probably related to how Faulk was being treated. I thought back to how Nick had said he found me; Faulk had told him I'd gone down to my old room. Not this floor. Faulk had tried to cover for me, and now he was being punished for it. If that was the case, then something big was going on here.

Suddenly I heard movement behind me. I cursed, realizing that I had been lost in thought and hadn't been paying attention to my surroundings at all. Before I could even spin around, a grip strong as iron clenched onto my shoulder. I howled as the thing snarled and dug its fingers into my skin.

"Ahhh!!!" I bellowed as searing pain shot through my shoulder.

I fought to spin around, seeing a snarling changed thing. Its impossibly strong fingers pierced my skin, making blood spurt in four little streams. I screamed again, yanking my knife from my belt. I violently swung it at the thing's arm, slicing it off of the body. Instantly I ran away, with the hand still implanted in my shoulder. I clenched my jaw and groaned in agony as I ran, wondering if I should yank the thing out of my shoulder or leave it. It hurt like hell, but wouldn't taking it out make me bleed even more? With one glance down at the hand, I decided to yank it out. It was covered in grime, crusted blood, and some black goo. That shit wasn't staying in me for a second longer.

When I had started running, I had made the mistake of not making an educated choice of which way to go. As I slowed, I saw that my mistake had put me deeper in the room, rather than closer to the elevator. I growled in anger to myself, annoyed with my own stupidity. Hadn't Nick trained us to stay level-headed in even the worst of situations? Apparently I had failed hard. I tried to steady my breath and dismiss my angry thoughts. Being mad at myself and doubting my decision-making skills wasn't going to help anything.

I looked at the ceiling, hoping that the lights that were on would show me which way to go. It didn't look like that plan was going to work though, because most of the lights were on. I gulped, wondering if they had been activated by me running, or if this place was crawling with changed things. Of course the person who had removed all the storage bins hadn't killed the things. I mean why would they; that would have just made things too easy on me.

A wave of fatigue washed over me, making me remember my wound. I looked down at it, gulping when I saw how much blood I was losing. I opened one of the pouches on my vest, elated to see what I was hoping for. Pulling out the packaging, I ripped it open with my teeth and pulled out the gauze inside. I brought it to my shoulder, cringing in pain as I did so. As my hand pressed down on the four holes, I grimaced and grit my teeth. The sound of snarling interrupted me, making me whirl around. Sure enough, three horrible things were shuffling towards me. They were at the far end of this aisle, with me on the other end.

Finally feeling like the situation was in my favor, I reached into another pocket on my vest. I yanked the pin out of the thing, then sent it flying down the aisle. I dropped to the ground in the fetal position, covering my head and facing my back to the explosion. Sure, my back made a pretty big target, but it and my chest were the only places where I had armor covering me. A second later there was a bang, then two unconscious grunts left my mouth as I felt two shrapnel impacts with my back. The sprinkler system instantly activated, sending torrents of water down on me. Cautiously, I peered at the scene behind me. Chunks of flesh and blood littered the floor, as well as surrounding racks. I grimaced from the carnage, horrified that seconds ago the gore had been three people. Granted, they more resembled flesh-eating monsters than humans, but they had once been people.

I jumped up and started jogging again, this time heading the right direction. Lights lit up with me as I ran through the spacious room, thankfully illuminating potential foes before I reached them. I dodged a couple groups of them, hoping I'd get to the elevator long before they caught up to me. Others were too close to dodge, forcing me to yank out my knife and sever their head from their spine. It sickened me each time, and getting to the elevator couldn't have come soon enough.

When I got to the elevator, I pounded on the button. Expecting it to open immediately, I picked up my foot and ran right into the door. I recoiled slightly, almost laughing at my stupidity. Now wasn't the time for humor though. The doors still weren't opening. I spun around and looked behind me, seeing a horde of changed things stumbling towards me. All the ones I had dodged, left behind, or just pissed off were coming for me. I trembled and jammed on the elevator button over and over, desperately hoping it was on its way.

In the meantime, I pulled out two more grenades and lobbed them towards the group. I hit the floor again, cringing as two booms went off. Snarls and sickening sounds of wet matter splatting to the ground echoed through the air, making me glance at the group. It was much smaller now, but looked even more like a horror show. Some of the things only had parts of them blown off, so they were still coming at me. A mass of things with broken limbs and slopping black blood slowly moved my way.

Unexpectedly, I felt sick and retched. I heaved and heaved until nothing came up, but still I couldn't stop. Every glance up at the moving mass made me feel like I was in hell. Hell... Suddenly I had the urge to pray, like I'd had when the man attacked me. This time I didn't hesitate, but said a prayer. What's the worst that would happen; I'd feel foolish? I said a quick prayer that was completely awful. It had been a long time since I last prayed, and I had forgotten what to say.

However, as soon as I said amen, the elevator doors went ding and opened. A sigh of exultation escaped my lungs, and I leapt into the elevator. I pounded on the ground floor button and watched as the doors closed and shut out the things. Just as they were almost out of my sight, I swear I saw a white light flood the room, knocking all the changed things to the ground. I stared at the now-closed doors in disbelief. Surely I had just been seeing things. I had lost quite a lot of blood, after all.

As soon as the metal doors opened at my floor, I stumbled towards the doctor's room. Several soldiers saw me and raised their guns. I was hobbling like a changed thing and was covered in blood, so I guess I couldn't blame them.

"No," I weakly grunted, raising a hand out in front of me in defense.

One of the soldiers realized who I was and lowered his gun, shouting at the others to help me. They all rushed forward and picked me up, quickly carrying me to the doctor. I heard some shouting as my eyes drooped shut; I think the men were telling me to stay awake. I struggled to keep my eyes open and watch the ceiling pass by as the men carried me, but it was hopeless. Sleep seemed so much sweeter…
I hadn't realized I'd passed out until I jerked awake. It felt like eons had passed, but when I opened my eyes I still saw the ceiling passing by. Someone was slapping my face, probably to wake me.

"I'm awake," I mumbled, knowing that they hadn't heard me. I had barely heard myself.

They must have seen my eyes open though, because they stopped trying to wake me up. Moments later, I saw the frame of a doorway pass by. I felt myself being put on top of a table. My head lolled to the side as they set me down; I was too weak to stop it. Now I could see that I was back in the doctor's room. The men were leaving as someone in a white coat was walking up to me. I couldn't see their face, but I could read the name tape: Mortimer. I sighed in relief. He had fixed my broken leg in one day, so I knew he'd have me patched up in no time.

Unfortunately I was wrong about that. After Mortimer's initial exam of my shoulder, I heard him sigh heavily. He called someone on a phone or radio, then my droopy eyes barely saw him make some notes at his desk. I tried to call out to him and ask if he could at least stop the bleeding, but I was too weak. Sometime later, somebody else came into the room. Mortimer and the man came to my side, and I was elated to see that it was Nick.

Weakly, I tried to take his hand in mine, but I could barely move. He and Mortimer peered at me and exchanged words, but my head was too foggy to understand what they were saying. Nick looked rather grim. He said something solemnly to Mortimer, gripped his shoulder, then left the room. I groaned, but it was too faint for anyone to hear. The doctor came back to my side with a needle, also looking rather sad. He looked down at the needle hesitantly, seeming to not want to use it.

Although I couldn't hear him, I saw him mouth the words, "Forgive me."

I tried to thrash and squirm away from him, but I just didn't have the strength. I watched in horror as he raised his hand, and then shoved the needle into my arm. Seconds later, I felt myself weakening even more. With the liquid drained, Mortimer dropped the empty needle. It clanged to the floor as he turned and walked to the door. He flicked the lights off, then stepped from the room and shut the door. I heard the bolt of the lock slide into the door frame and then footsteps echo away from the room.

Panic washed over me as I glanced around in the pitch black. I tried to remain calm, but so many strange things had just happened. Had Nick ordered Mortimer to kill me? Had I been drugged and then left in this room to die? I growled at the thought—well tried to growl, but I was too weak to make a sound. My fighter spirit raged inside of me, but it was hardly effective against my weakened body. Everything in me wanted to get up from the table, but my body wouldn't comply. Over and over again I tried to move my limbs, only able to wiggle my fingers or change my facial expression. Still I grit my teeth and kept trying.

As I struggled, sweat broke out over my whole body and a dull ache formed in my head. At first I thought it was from how hard I was struggling, but then I recalled the liquid Mortimer had shot into my veins. With that thought, I fought even harder to move. Although it still felt pretty much useless, I think I was making a little bit of progress. My fingers were moving more, and I could groan now. Sweat continued to form on me, soon feeling like it was pouring out of every pore. I started gasping for air, even though I wasn't actually moving. My veins burned, seeming to carry a fire throughout my blood. Soon the dull ache in my head had turned into a full-blown migraine. I winced from the pain of it, feeling the pulsing pain every time I tried to move. Still I continued to sweat, drenching the table I was on. Hotter and hotter I grew as the pain in my head grew even worse.

I don't know how long passed by as waves of pain and heat washed over me. I think it was hours, but it felt like eternity. Eventually I gave up trying to move because it hurt my head so much. I just kind of surrendered to my fate and lay back on the table. Enduring the pain passively didn't make it any less painful, but it also didn't add to it like struggling did. As the horrible agony increased over the hours, I grew more and more weak. Once again, I felt myself drifting out of consciousness, hopefully for the final time. I had already passed out twice, but jerked back awake both times. This time I hoped it would be different. I hoped it would be the end.

As I exhaled for possibly the last time, I heard a snarl. In my weakened state, I almost didn't care. Maybe there was a changed thing in here with me. Maybe it would eat me and end my misery. Then I realized where it had come from. Me. I had snarled.

CHAPTER FOURTEEN

Alarm suddenly seized me, making me flinch. The snarl had come from me! Were they trying to make me one of those things? Whatever Mortimer had given me was to turn me into a chomper!

Everything in me fought to move, and to my immense surprise, I actually succeeded. It was slow, but I was able to sit up. I groaned heavily from my massive headache, raising a hand to rub my head. A second later I frantically brought my hand back to where I could see it. All of the veins in my hand were showing through my skin and they were black. They weren't the normal dark blueish color of veins; they were black. As I watched them, though, they faded back to their normal color. Then the next surprise hit me. I could see in the dark just fine. I inhaled deeply and darted my eyes around the room, seeing everything as vividly as if the lights had been on. I trembled fearfully, hoping that this didn't mean I was already one of those disgusting creatures. With a chuckle, I asked myself if I suddenly had an all-consuming desire to eat human flesh. *Nope.*

"I guess I'm safe for now," I muttered to myself somewhat dryly.

Carefully, I put one of my feet on the floor, then the other. I tested out the strength of my legs cautiously, gripping the side of the table as I stood on them fully for the first time. To my surprise, I wasn't weak at all. In fact, the more I moved around, the greater I felt. My headache melted away and my limbs felt strong. The only ailment I had was thirst; I was insanely thirsty. I staggered towards the sink, not caring that the water was probably dirty. As I made my way across the room, I realized that all my gear had been removed. All I had on was a paper-thin gown, like the one they had put me in when I had broken my leg.

At the sink, I turned on the water. I cupped my hands under the ice-cold liquid, which felt like heaven on my burning skin. I dropped my hands and instead put my whole head under the water. The shock of the cold hit me like a train, jolting me even further awake. I let the cold water pour down over my head and face, then turned my head to drink some of it. After gulping down quite a bit, I stood up and put my hands under the water, cooling them off.

As I did so, I thought of how nice a freezing-cold shower would feel. With that idea, my thoughts drifted to my room... and Nick. I knew Mortimer had drugged me, but had Nick told him to? I doubt it; I mean Nick wouldn't do that to me, would he? I remembered last night and the sacred time we had shared. After such a personal experience together, he wouldn't leave me for dead—or worse—would he?

I recalled all of the beautiful things he had said to me since we had met, including that he would never leave me. No, there was no way this was what Nick had ordered Mortimer to do. Nick was on my side, but I wasn't sure who else was. Maybe all of the men of the camp, including the doctor, just wanted me dead.

With that conclusion drawn, I knew I had to get to Nick. I couldn't just go find him, could I? If the other soldiers saw me, they might detain me on sight. I looked around the room for a phone or radio, but didn't find one. As I started to wonder what in the world to do, I saw a clock sitting on the counter. It was a digital one with big red letters, so there was no mistaking what it said. 23:49. My jaw dropped in surprise; I had no idea it was so late in the day! The hell I had suffered through when I couldn't move had felt like it lasted forever, but I hadn't realized that it had actually spanned across the whole day. I recalled that Faulk had wanted to meet at midnight. I was pretty sure I could trust him and that meeting with him would be a good idea. With only about ten minutes to go, I needed to hurry up and get out to the yard.

Carefully, I unlocked the deadbolt of the door and slipped it open. I breathed as quietly as I could, listening for footsteps. I heard one man pacing the halls to my left and another man to the right. Their patrols were staggered well, so that when one was at the far end of his route, the other was near me. No problem, I thought to myself, hoping I was right.

I quietly pulled my head back inside the room and shut the door. I then looked around the room for what I needed. Upon finding it, I cracked the door back open and studied the men. As soon as the one on the right started to walk away, I crept down the hall towards the one on the left. Sneaking up behind him, I jumped up and covered his mouth with the towel I had covered in chloroform. I threw my other arm around his chest and dragged him back towards the room. Although he was tall and muscular, and thus heavy, I was somehow able to move him without a problem. He thrashed and kicked at first, but after a few seconds he passed out. I waited for a few moments, then pulled the cloth away from his mouth.

Dashing back to the door, I quickly locked it. Hopefully the other guard knew this door had been locked before and wouldn't try to bang it down looking for his other patrol-man. I hurried back to my unconscious guard, yanking off his gear. Every time he started to move a little, I put the cloth back over his mouth for a few seconds. Once all his gear was off, I grabbed his handcuffs and pulled his hands behind his back. I slid the cuffs closed over them, making sure they were snug against the smallest part of his wrists. Then I took off his socks, tying one around his mouth as a gag and the other around his eyes as a blindfold.

"Sorry man," I whispered. "Hopefully your feet don't smell too bad!"

I quickly put on the gear I had taken from him, un-surprised to find that it was way too big for me. Hopefully it was better than nothing and wouldn't get in the way. I pulled on his boots, laughing at how big they were com-pared to my tiny foot. I usually wore a women's size 6, and this guy's boots were a men's size 11. Still, hopefully they were better than nothing. Once I had on all of the gear, I picked up his gun and slung it over my shoulder. I checked his vest pockets, happy to find at least a couple grenades.

Ready to go meet Faulk, I reopened the door and checked outside. The other guard wasn't nearby, so I slipped from the room and hurried to the back of the house. Hard-ly any guards were inside, so I easily escaped out the back door. Out on the lawn, there were a few guards by the fence, but they were all watching outside the perimeter. Although none of them were looking for perpetrators inside the fence, I still stuck to the shadows and carefully made my way to where I had last seen Faulk.

When I got to the truck, I didn't have to wait at all. Someone whispered my name, calling me over to the shadows closer to the fence. I crept over there, spotting Faulk in the darkness. He motioned for me to follow him, so I did. We snuck over to another truck, where he quietly opened the back hatch and told me to get in. After me, he climbed in and slowly closed the door.

"It's easier to talk in here," he whispered once the latch of the door had clicked. "We should still whisper, but we're a lot less likely to be heard in here."

"What the hell is going on?" I blurted in a whisper. "Who did this to you?" I asked, putting a gentle hand to his face.

He looked at me strangely. "Did what?" he stammered.

"The shiner you have!"

"You can see that in this light?"

"Uh, kind of; it's a long story that probably goes together with your story."

"Okay…" he mused.

"Well?" I asked expectantly. "What's going on?"

"A while ago, when we first came here, I discovered that giant storage room that I directed you to."

"E60?"

"That's the one," he affirmed. "I saw some pretty weird stuff in there. I had no idea who to tell or talk to about it. Then when I saw how well you, Mel, and Vie had trained, I knew it would be one of you who I could trust with it."

"Why me? Why not Mel? She was pretty hurt that you only wanted to talk to me."

He sighed. "I like Mel, a lot. But I just had this feeling

that you were the one I needed to tell. You seem pretty smart and capable. I have no doubt that Mel is smart, but you seem to possess more of a survival instinct than she does. I didn't want her to get hurt."

"Just me," I laughed bitterly.

"No, not at all!" he countered, but I stopped him.

"It's okay Faulk, I was only kidding. So they did this to you because you told me about that room?"

"I think so."

"And who are they...?" I asked, afraid to hear the answer.

"Major Ghost did the actual discipline, but I'm sure Colonel Kadav put him up to it."

"Why would you think that?"

"Because," he said quietly, "I know things, Eve."

"What... kind of things?" I asked slowly.

"Too much to tell you now. But I wanted to let you know that this place isn't what it seems."

"Ha! That I believe. I spent all of today turning into a changed thing."

"What?" he asked confusedly. "What in the world does that mean?"

"This morning I went down to E60 again. It was completely empty." I heard Faulk let out a string of curses, but I continued. "There were changed things down there. One of them snuck up on me."

"Did it bite you?"

"No, but it put its fingers through my shoulder."

"Aw Eve, I'm so sorry!"

"That was nothing compared to later. I barely escaped the room from them and was taken to Mortimer."

"Curse that man," Faulk whispered.

"Yeah, I wish I had known that. Anyway, I had so much blood loss that I could barely move. At one point Nick came in and conferred with the doctor. Next thing I know, Mortimer says "forgive me," and jabs me with a needle. Then he leaves the room and locks me inside in the dark. The rest of the day I spent in agonizing, excruciating pain. I think I was about to die when I heard myself snarl."

"Snarl?"

"Yeah. Like one of them. I think he gave me a shot of something to change into one of them. My skin has been burning all day. The first person I saw change into one of those things had hot skin just before he turned."

"Why would they do that?" he murmured to himself.

"I don't know," I sighed, but he didn't seem to be listening to me.

"They knew it wouldn't work on you…"

"What?" I asked sharply, suddenly alarmed. "What did you just say?"

"Me? Oh, nothing."

"Faulk," I growled. "You just said they knew it wouldn't work on me! You mean this was planned?"

"Eve, please calm d—"

"No way!" I yelled, backing away from him. "What the hell is the matter with you people?" I frantically turned and looked for the latch to the door. I had to get away from this psycho!

"Eve!" he growled in a whisper, throwing his arms around me from behind and yanking me backwards.

We both toppled backwards and fell to the floor of the truck on our backs, with me on top of him. I tried to scream, but he covered my mouth with his hand.

"Eve!" he whispered harshly. "Please listen to me! Don't run from me; I am your only friend right now. I can help you!"

"Mrmbrml!" I grumbled through his hand.

"Shh!" he hissed. "Seriously, please quiet down! If you want your mom and Mel to get out of this alive, you need to listen to me!"

At the mention of my loved ones, I calmed down to consider his words. A moment later, I grunted. Ever so slightly he removed his hand, gauging how likely I was to try to run again.

"Okay," I whispered angrily as I sat up and moved away from him. "I'm listening. Speak."

"Like I said, I know things. I will gladly share them with you when we're safe. But we're not safe here. You guys need to leave."

"What about Nick?" I asked sadly. "Is he my enemy too?"

Faulk didn't answer my question, but just stared at me for a minute. "We can get out of here if we plan it right. We'll just need to work together."

I thought about what would happen if we left. We'd lose the security of this place, plus we'd have living enemies. Then I remembered Lackland.

"What about my dad?" I croaked. "I found a file with his name on it in that storage room. I took it to my room and now it's missing."

Faulk let out several curses, gripping his forehead in the meantime. "That's why they went on the offensive with you. Look, I can get him out of their clutches, but I can't bring him here."

"Will you help me go find him?"

"Eve, Texas is a long way from here. We aren't going to have many supplies to begin with and should use them to survive, not go on a manhunt."

"Then stay out of my way; I don't need your help." I turned back towards the door, but he stopped me.

"Yes, you do need my help."

"Faulk, I think you need *my* help." He grimaced at the words, looking shocked. "You could have disappeared a while ago if you didn't like this place, but for some reason you wanted to meet with me and offer your help to me. Maybe you don't believe you can survive on your own. Maybe you just want to hook up with my best friend. Maybe you want to escape with all three of us and then murder us. Or maybe, just maybe, there's a bigger reason—and I'm inclined to go with this theory: you're afraid of these people. I think you've wanted to leave for a while but weren't sure how, and now you see a way out with me and my group. Am I right?"

"Uh," he stammered.

"I think I'm right. You said I have a knack for survival, and you were right, because I also have a knack for seeing through bull crap and reading between the lines. So I'm reading between your lines Faulk. I want to be on your side and I believe you're on our side. I want to help you. But for me to agree to help you, you have to agree to help me. Help me find my dad and I'll help you get out of here."

Faulk eyed me for a while without blinking. Then finally he blinked and smiled. "Well I'll be damned Eve. You are certainly the right person to team up with. I'll help you find your dad."

I sighed with a small smile and a gulp. "Okay then. What's next?"

"We need to talk to Mel and Vie, but you can't let anyone see you. If they locked you in that room, they've got a death wish for you."

"But what about Nick? I don't think he's against me."

"Eve, I don't know if that's true or not, but I'm pretty sure you can't trust him."

"Can I at least… check?"

"No because if he is what I think he is, he'll take you out as soon as he knows you're onto him."

"And what do you think he is?"

"This isn't the time or place for that conversation. We need to talk to Mel and Vie."

"Now?"

"Hell yeah. Do you want to be here in the morning when they find out you escaped that room? The whole place will be on a manhunt for you."

"Okay," I concurred. "How do we get into their room then? There are guards outside their door."

"There's a balcony outside their room. We'll sneak in that way."

I nodded, and Faulk edged past me to open the door. I inhaled deeply as he crept by, for he was so close that I could see the pulse on his neck. My thoughts went to Nick and the delicious night we had spent together. I felt a knot in my stomach at the thought of him betraying me. I hardly ever believed men's lies, and had done so well my whole life at not giving myself to liars. Although I'd had my suspicions of him, I had allowed myself to think he was special. Most of the time he had seemed so genuine and caring… I really,

really hoped that Faulk was wrong about him.

We stealthily left the truck and worked together to move across the lawn. Since everyone was still watching the perimeter and not the lawn, it was a relatively easy task. As we rounded one of the corners of the house, I realized we were by the presidential room's balcony. A light was on inside, making me want to see what Nick was doing. I relayed this to Faulk, but he shook his head.

"Come on," I whispered from our vantage point. We were by the fence, hiding behind crates of supplies. "I can easily climb up the wall and get on the balcony to look inside."

"No," Faulk objected. "What happens if he comes outside?"

"He won't," I said. "I just want to see what he's doing."

Despite Faulk's protests, I made my way over to the wall and climbed up to the balcony. He ended up helping me do so, and once I was up there I pulled him up with me. Together, we peered into the room. To our horror, we saw that Nick wasn't alone. In the room with him was Mel, and they were kissing. A hiss left my mouth, and I started to raise my gun before I even realized what I was doing. Faulk yanked me away from the window, and ordered me to climb back down the wall. I complied until we were both hiding in the shadows under the balcony, then I spewed curses at them both, wondering who I hated more.

"Eve!" Faulk cautioned. "I know you're hurting, but you need to calm down. I'm not happy about this either."

"Did you give yourself to Mel last night?" I fumed. "Did you trust her and surrender to her and share something sacred not one night ago?"

"Eve, I'm really, really sorry for what we just saw, but if we sit here swearing and letting emotion blind us, we're going to get killed."

"Yeah whatever," I murmured.

"You still want to save your mom, right?"

"Yeah," I sighed.

"Then we need to move."

I grunted, so he looked me sternly in the eyes and put a hand on my shoulder. I sighed and decided to change my attitude. "I'm ready," I promised. "I won't get you killed."

"Now that's what I like to hear!" he laughed.

I chuckled and made my way across the lawn with him. As he moved ahead, I carefully checked behind us. Soon we reached the next balcony, which thankfully wasn't guarded. We climbed up the wall as we had on the other one, happy to see that the light was also on. I told Faulk to hang back while I peered in, just in case my mom was changing or something. He agreed and I looked inside, happy to see that she was just sitting in bed reading. I turned around and signaled to Faulk, then turned back to the balcony door. Lightly, I tapped on it.

At first my mom didn't hear it. I tried to keep the tapping light enough so that the guards outside the door wouldn't hear, but so that she would. I tapped on the door again, making her look up. I saw alarm in her eyes, but I had to knock again. This time she put her book down and looked at the bedroom door. I tapped again more urgent-ly, praying she wouldn't go get the guards. Thankfully, she cautiously got up and crept towards the balcony. As she drew closer, I tapped on the glass again. When she got to it and pulled the curtain back, I waved anxiously. Right away she opened the door. She was about to say something, so I immediately covered her mouth.

"Stay quiet!" I whispered. "Can we come in?"

She agreed quickly, so Faulk and I crept inside. Faulk then led us to the spacious bathroom, where we all filed inside and shut the door.

"Talk in a whisper," Faulk said quietly.

"What is the meaning of this?" my mom asked.

"Vie, I want to get you and your daughter out of here."

"Out of where?"

"This base."

"Why?"

"The people are dangerous."

She looked him up and down, noticing his black eye for the first time. "Did they do that to you?" she breathlessly asked.

"Yes, they did."

"Why?"

"Because I tried to tell Eve the truth."

"Don't call me Eve," I demanded. "Call me Adeline."

"How about, well, never mind…" Faulk said.

I agreed, assuming he had wanted to call me Addie but stopped because that's what Mel called me.

"Where are we going to go?" my mom questioned.

"Texas," I answered.

"Texas?" she scoffed.

"Yes. To get Dad."

"Oh darling," she sighed, putting an arm on me. "He always warned us of this day, didn't he?"

"Yeah and we called him crazy," I lamented.

"How are we going to get him? Isn't he being held by

people who know Nick?"

"I'm going to send a message supposedly from Nick ordering his release," Faulk answered. "Then Adeline will call his cell and tell him to lie low."

"Well what about Mel? Have you talked to her?"

"No," Faulk and I chorused together.

"Do you know where she is?" I asked her.

"No, she was upset all day. I think Nick noticed because he came by earlier and said he knew how to cheer her up."

Both Faulk and I rolled our eyes and cursed, drawing a bizarre look from my mom.

"Yeah he had the perfect freaking way," I grumbled.

"Mel is with Nick in his room," Faulk angrily stated.

"Oh my!" my mom blurted.

"Yeah neither of us are too happy about it, so it's best that we don't talk about it."

"Oh sweetheart I'm so sorry," my mom gushed. "I know how much you cared about him, especially after…"

"Mom," I insisted, "please stop. I can't deal with this right now."

"Okay," she conceded. "So what's the plan? Are you just going to leave her here?"

"Well we need to get out of here as soon as possible, and she's with Nick right now."

"Is Nick one of the… bad people?" she asked skeptically, gesturing at Faulk's black eye.

"He's the leader," Faulk replied gravely.

I gasped and darted a look of daggers at him. He had pretended not to know that a few minutes ago when I had asked if Nick was on my side. I guess he hadn't wanted to tell me, but once we saw Nick kissing Mel, there was no point in not telling me.

"Oh heavens," my mom despaired. "Well we can't just leave Mel here!"

"I'm pretty sure she's upset with both Faulk and me for a misunderstanding. I don't know if she'll come with us, especially if Nick has filled her head with lies. Like he did mine."

"She's your best friend Adeline; you at least have to try!"

"I know!" I agreed. "But if we ask her and she says no, our cover is blown."

"Is the situation really that dire?"

"Mom," I gulped, stepping towards her and looking at her intensely. "They tried to kill me."

"They what?" she squawked in shock.

"So yes, the situation is that dire."

"Oh my goodness!"

"Stay calm, please," I asked. "I'm alive, right? We just need to get out of here ASAP."

"Yes, yes," she agreed, nodding as she took in what I had just said.

"Vie, maybe you can help us save Mel."

"How?"

"Adeline and I can go down to the truck and get some gear together. We'll work on clearing an escape route out of here. In the meantime, you can go to Nick's room and tell Mel you want to hang out and go for a walk. You can lead her to where we are, and then we'll all go from there."

"When she sees us I doubt she'll come with," I sighed. "Nick's lies are intoxicating and convincing."

"Then we force her," Faulk said.

My mom and I both glared at him, but I knew that

might be the only way. "Yeah," I agreed. "Faulk, are you supposed to be locked up or anything?"

"No, I can move around freely."

"There's some chloroform in the doctor's office that you might want to grab. Hurry though; the guard I locked in there has probably woken up by now… Oh crap!"

"We have less time than I thought," he said suddenly. "If that guard tells anyone that you escaped, this place is going to go in full lockdown mode."

"Not good!" I exclaimed. "What can we do?"

"Can we break into Nick's room and grab Mel?" my mom asked.

Faulk and I looked at her like she was crazy.

"Break into Nick's room?" Faulk asked in disbelief. "You have no idea how powerful that man is."

"Well how are we going to do this then?" my mom demanded.

We all frantically racked our brains, hearing only our pounding hearts in the silence. I wholeheartedly agreed with my mom that I couldn't just leave Mel here. However, she was pissed at me and Faulk, as we were at her. Even with that in mind though, it wasn't right to just leave her here to possibly be killed. I found myself praying again; this time for real and not just in passing. I was still unsure of what to say, but I dared to ask God what he thought we should do. My heart knew the answer. Even if it risked my life, it was wrong to just leave my best friend here.

With my mind made up, I whispered to Mom and Faulk. "We need to try to get her."

They looked at me blankly, both of them unsure of whether or not to object. Miraculously, we were interrupted by the sound of the bedroom door opening and shutting.

"Hey, I'm back," Mel's voice called.

All of us took a deep breath.

"Tell her you need to talk to her where the guards won't hear," Faulk urged. "And tell her she needs to see something. Then lead her in here. Warn her to be quiet, no matter what she sees in here."

"Okay," my mom agreed, nodding quickly.

She left the bathroom and shut the door behind her. I nervously swallowed as I heard her and Mel's voices go back and forth, growing progressively quieter. It sounded like Mel had agreed to coming in here, because footsteps soon headed our way. Making sure that Faulk and I didn't look at all like we were romantically interested in one another, we prepared for Mel to see us. The door swung open, and in she stepped. Her appearance was absolutely haggard; her eyes were red and puffy and she looked miserable. When she saw us, she looked incredibly shocked.

"Addie!" she squealed to my surprise, dashing towards me with open arms. She wrapped me in a tight embrace, which I happily returned. "Nick said you were dead!" Well I guess that explained her appearance.

"Oh god," Faulk groaned, gulping and starting to pace. "That confirms it."

Mel looked at him questioningly, so I gripped her face and directed her gaze back at me. "Mel, we have to leave here."

"Why?"

"Because I'm pretty certain it was Nick who ordered to have me killed."

"Don't be absurd!" she laughed. "He just saved your life

the other day."

"It doesn't matter. I found something I wasn't supposed to, and I don't think he liked it."

"What did you find?"

"A whole floor of storage deep below us. I found files in there... one of them had my dad's name on it. I took the file and it disappeared from my room. After that is when Nick told the doctor to give me the injection that almost killed me."

"B-b-but he said you went past the perimeter on your own and got attacked; that they did everything they could to save you," she stammered in horror.

"Did he tell you that before or after he kissed you?" I asked quietly.

She recoiled and backed away from me. "You know?"

"Yeah. We saw." I gestured towards Faulk.

She looked over at him, then cast her eyes at the floor. "I'm so sorry," she said with tears in her eyes. "I was so confused. I thought Faulk liked you, then I thought you were dead..."

"It's okay," I croaked, knowing she had been a victim of his lies just like I had been. "We can talk about all this later. Right now we need to get out of here."

"Yeah, okay," she agreed. "How do we do that?"

The three of us turned to Faulk for that answer. "Right," he said, then began to outline his plan.

A short time later, we all four snuck out the balcony doors. Even though Mel and my mom weren't wanted like I was, we didn't think the guards would let them go outside this late at night. The three of us women would sneak down to the supply crates and take as much food, fuel, and ammo we could manage. Then we would bring everything back to the two trucks Faulk had designated for us to take. One of the vehicles was the truck the men were handing out gear from, so it had all the extra gear we would need on the road, as well as some boots that would actually fit my feet.

While we did that, Faulk would sneak into the doctor's room and get as many medical supplies as he could as well as knock the guard out again. Then he'd go to the communication room and send a missive to Lackland ordering the release of my dad. On his way to our trucks, he would throw a grenade at the front lawn. That distraction would cause most of the guards to direct their attention there, allowing us to escape out the back way relatively easily.

As the three of us crept towards our destination, I peered up at Nick's room. The light was now off, which was a good thing for us. We had soon made it to the supply crates as planned, without incident. I marveled at the lack of internal security around this place. Although it was bad for them, it was definitely good for us. We found bags to put everything in, then loaded them full of supplies. Carefully, we lugged them back to the trucks and slipped them inside. We had decided that since we were taking two vehicles, Faulk would drive one with Mel as his passenger, and I would drive the other with my mom. Before leaving the room we had briefly discussed which way we'd be going, but it made me nervous to be doing this at night. I hoped everything would go to plan and we wouldn't end up shot to death by the people we had once trusted or eaten by changed things.

The three of us crouched down in between the two trucks, eagerly waiting for Faulk to return to us. We sighed from time to time, wondering why it was taking him so long. Hopefully he hadn't been caught. As I was about to stand up and go look for him, a tremendous boom shook the ground. My mom, Mel and I glanced to one another quickly. It was time.

CHAPTER FIFTEEN

Moments later, Faulk came running through the shadows towards us. We all clambered into our designated vehicles, trembling with anxiety. Faulk jumped in his as well, but didn't start it. I nervously stared him down through the window, trying my best to follow his lead. I knew he was waiting until all the guards ran to the front of the house, but waiting felt so counter intuitive. Finally, a few moments later, he started his truck. I hurriedly started mine as well. We backed up one by one, then floored the gas and sped towards the hole in the back fence. I don't know how many people noticed, but not enough for them to do anything about it. In all the confusion, they probably thought we were a response team.

We sped down the road away from the camp, making me feel a surge of thrill. Although I was scared, I looked over at my mom with a stupid smile on my face.

"This is fun, huh?" I laughed.

"Uh sure," she answered, sounding thoroughly terrified.

"Don't worry Mom," I assured. "I'll keep you safe."

"I know darling; I know."

We cruised along the road behind Faulk. It felt like we were going way too fast, yet not fast enough at the same time. I didn't want to be caught by Nick's men, but I also didn't want to crash. I wanted to radio Faulk and ask him to slow down, but he had specifically told me not to use the radios. Not wanting to be the cause of them finding us, I readily complied. I followed behind him for the better part of an hour. Our truck's compass told us we were heading west and just slightly south.

Finally, Faulk turned off the highway and headed south. Soon we came to a neighborhood, where he sped down the streets with a purpose. I cringed as we plowed over changed things, wondering how many we were attracting to us as we drove. He made several left and right turns, seeming to know where he was going. Eventually we came to a sprawling gated estate. He and Mel jumped out of their vehicle a moment later. He dashed to the gate as she jumped into the driver's side of the truck. Faulk messed with the lock on the gate, popping it open moments later. Then he yanked the gate open and hollered something at Mel. A second later, their truck drove forward through the gate. He then waved me on, so I also drove through.

In the mirror, I saw him slide the gate shut quickly. Then he ran back to the truck and hopped into the passenger's seat. Their truck sped up the driveway towards a massive garage, which I realized a minute later was actually a small hangar. Again he jumped out of the truck and ran to the human-sized door at the side of the building. He picked that lock as well, then disappeared inside. A moment later, the main hangar door began to open. As soon as it was high enough, Mel sped her truck inside and parked. I pulled in as well, parking beside her. As we exited the vehicles, Faulk shut the massive door. With the trucks off, we turned on our flashlights for light. Once the hangar door was secured shut, Faulk jogged over to us.

"How did you know about this place?" I asked.

"I used to know the people who lived here," he answered as he started leading us towards it.

"Do Nick's men know about it?"

"No."

"You swear?"

He abruptly stopped walking and turned to me. "I told you the truth about Nick. I just risked my own life to break you out of that place. Why would I do that if I wanted to lead you into a trap?"

"I don't know," I grumbled indignantly. "It seemed like a reasonable question though. I have no idea who to trust now."

"Well you can trust me, I promise," he assured, putting a hand on my shoulder. Looking back towards the house he said, "We should get inside. I doubt the owners were here when everything happened, so I don't expect us to find any changed things inside."

"What about all the ones we just led here?" my mom asked.

"The fence should hold them," he replied uncertainly. "We're not staying here for a while; just long enough to get some sleep. All of us had a rough day; especially Adeline."

Everyone looked at me, making me cringe. "I'm fine," I assured, but none of them bought it.

"We want to hear exactly what happened to you," Mel said, walking to me and draping her arm around my shoulder.

"No you don't," I said with a dry laugh.

"Yes we do," Faulk agreed. "You told me some of it, but I want to know more."

"You have your own bit of information to share," I mentioned.

"And I'll tell it to you, as promised."

"Good," I nodded. "Shall we head inside?"

"Yes!" my mom eagerly agreed. "That truck was so uncomfortable."

"I hate to break it to you," I said, "but we have a lot longer drive ahead of us in a few hours."

She groaned, making us all chuckle. We grabbed what provisions we would need for the night, then headed towards the house. Faulk made us all turn our flashlights off, so I insisted on leading the way since I could see best in the dark. I didn't tell any of them that, but I didn't stop insisting so they agreed to let me lead. We crept towards the house, noticing that quite a few changed things were gathered at the gate. As we entered the house, I glanced back at them worriedly. I hoped they wouldn't break through the gate during the night.

Once inside the house, we determined it was clear with relative ease. The house was huge—more than 8,000 square feet—but we had eventually searched the entire thing. When that was done, we all sighed in relief. The power didn't work here, so none of us were able to shower or turn any lights on, but that was a good thing. Faulk didn't want us to turn any lights on anyway; if Nick's men were looking for us in this neighborhood, lights would be a dead giveaway. We had secluded ourselves well behind a gated house and had hidden the vehicles in the hangar, but turning lights on would negate those efforts. I voiced my opinion that the changed things gathered at the gate would give us away, which he agreed to surprisingly quickly.

"I'll go take care of those," he said, standing from the place where we were all sitting.

"Whoa, what?" both Mel and I objected.

"You can't go out there alone," my mom added.

"Not to mention that if you blow those ones up, more will just flock to the area."

"I'm not going to blow them up," he replied. "I'm going to chuck a few grenades a few blocks from here to attract them, then sneak back over here."

"I don't know if that's a good idea either," I said. "What if Nick's men are on the road? They'll see the explosions and know we're nearby."

"Is that a risk you want to take? Or would you rather have those things both announcing our presence to his men while also trying to break in all night?"

I sighed and cocked my head, unhappy with both options.

"What about flashbangs?" I asked. "The noise would attract them."

"No, they let light off also."

"I say we just do that," Mel said. "It's a quick flash of light that would draw them away. Even if Nick's men noticed it, it would be too short for them to be sure they saw something. They wouldn't even see it long enough to know where it came from."

"They're highly trained men," Faulk countered. "But like you said, if they just saw it out of the corner of their eye, they might not be sure if they even saw something. If they try to check it out, there won't be any damage to tell them where it actually went off. Good thinking. I'll release one or two of those."

"I'll go with you," Mel said as she stood up.

"No; you're not coming with me."

"Listen buddy," she countered, "you took us out of that base and told us that we're in danger. Now we're on the road with you. We need to help each other survive, so don't coddle us. What happens if you get taken out? Do you want us all to just roll over and give up if that happens?"

"Heck no."

"Then give us the credit we deserve, as well as the training. If you can help us get better by watching the way you handle missions, please do so."

He stared at her for a moment, then grinned. "Well all right," he agreed. "You can come with me."

"Yes!" she squealed, grabbing her gear to put it back on.

"You guys be careful," I commanded. "You better make it back safely."

They assured me they would, then grabbed their guns and headed out. My mom and I anxiously waited for the better part of an hour before they returned. I don't know why, but I had been expecting them to come back tired and somber. However, they burst into the house laughing and joking.

"Well I see you two are having fun," I commented somewhat jealously. "Did you draw the things away?"

"Yeah, mission accomplished," Faulk answered.

I saw Mel look at me sadly, clearly wanting to say something. "We should all get to sleep," I said before she could say anything.

"I agree," Faulk said. "I'll take first watch."

I offered to take the next one, but nobody would let me help. They all insisted I needed a whole night's sleep and that they'd take care of keeping watch.

Unable to win that argument, I at least proposed that

we figure out sleeping situations. We all picked beds in the spacious rooms. My mom and I shared a king bed in one of the master suites, while Mel and Faulk took the suite beside ours. Climbing into that bed had never felt so relaxing. My heavy eyes couldn't wait to be shut, and my weary body couldn't wait to rest. Even though countless worries plagued my mind, I was exhausted. As soon as my head rested on that pillow, I was out.

I woke up the next morning to the sound of talking. Groggily, I opened my eyes and saw scarce sunlight streaming through the windows. I looked around, seeing that I was alone in the room. I crawled out of bed and put on a super fluffy robe, then strode over to the next room. In there, I found my companions sitting on the couch of the suite talking.

"You're awake," my mom smiled. "Come in, come in. We were waiting for you."

I made my way over to them and sat down on the love-seat next to my mom. At the table, I saw four steaming cups of coffee and some food.

"How'd you make that?" I asked. "I thought there was no power here."

"I made a small fire in the backyard," Faulk replied. "Small enough so there's no way it could be seen from the road. The smoke dispersed in the air before it rose high enough to be seen from there."

"Nice," I replied, picking up a piece of toast and taking a sip of the coffee that was on the table in front of me. Nobody said anything, making me feel like I had interrupted something. "I can leave if that'll make you all more comfortable," I offered.

"Oh cut it out," Mel replied.

"Were you all gossiping about me?"

"No," my mom answered.

"It wasn't gossip," Faulk said.

"Oh yeah? What was it?"

"Faulk asked me what happened between me and Nick," Mel replied.

"Awesome," I said bitterly, suddenly not wanting to be in the room anymore.

"Addie, I'm so sorry—"

"I really don't want to have this conversation here," I said in a shaking voice.

It both surprised and embarrassed me, so I got up and quickly went back to the other room. I slammed myself face-first on the bed, trying to stifle my tears. Mel followed me into the room, sitting down on the bed beside me.

"Addie," she whispered, delicately stroking my head. She gingerly played with my hair, running her fingers soothingly through it. "I'm so sorry Addie."

"Yeah, I know," I groaned.

"He told me you were gone… he said you betrayed us all and just left. He claimed he tried to get you back but that you got killed in the process."

"Then what happened?" I growled. I didn't want to know, but I also needed to know.

"Then he kissed me. I admit I kissed him back. I felt so confused and alone. First I thought I lost the guy I liked, then I lost my best friend. Nick was right there to comfort me."

"Then what?"

"Then we talked. That's all."

"That's all?"

"That's all Addie, I swear. We didn't do anything more."

"What a scumbag," I vented. "He's such a bastard."

"Yeah he is," she agreed. "I'm so sorry for what he did to you."

"Did Faulk tell you anything?"

"No, nothing."

"Then you don't even know the whole story. Let's go back in the other room so I can tell you and my mom at the same time. Then Faulk can tell us everything he knows."

She agreed as I sat up, then leaned over to give me a hug. We embraced tightly, as only the best of friends can. Afterward, we got up and strode to the neighboring room. Once we were seated, I took a deep breath and began the tale of what happened to me the day before. I told them every excruciating detail, making them grimace and cringe more than several times. My mom nearly wept when she heard what I had gone through, but I adamantly tried to convince her that it wasn't her fault. Eventually she seemed to believe that, but her eyes remained cloudy at the thought of my misery.

When I was done, I looked up at them all. "And here we are," I concluded.

"Wow," Mel mused. "That's awful. Truly awful. But at least you have a new super power! Who doesn't want to be able to see in the dark; am I right?"

I chuckled at her crazy perspective, ever grateful for the odd way she saw things. "Yeah, sure," I shrugged with a smile.

"Why in the world did they have a folder with Bruce's name on it?" my mom wondered.

"Good question," I agreed. "And that's where Faulk's story will come in useful."

All eyes darted to him. He inhaled deeply, then leaned forward. "In due time I will tell you everything. For now, I am only going to tell you part of it."

"Oh come on," I argued. "You said you would tell us everything!"

"By the time we reach your father, I promise to have told you everything. Believe me; you are going to need to hear this in small pieces. I can explain every single weird thing that has happened. I can tell you that you're not crazy Adeline. You need to know that every strange thing you picked up on was significant. Just because others may not have noticed doesn't mean that it didn't happen."

I leaned forward in the same manner he had, in response to his enthralling words. "You gotta give me something now," I demanded.

"Of course," he said with a gulp. "The first thing I can tell you is that Nick didn't just happen upon you. He knew you'd be at that New Year's Eve party and purposefully ran into you."

I huffed out a quick sigh, pressing my hands together and putting them to my mouth thoughtfully. "That's why I didn't notice him when I first got to the bar. He wasn't there yet. And that's how he found us out on the street; he followed us." Faulk nodded. "But why? Does it have to do with my dad?"

"Yes."

"How?" my mom asked.

"It is a long story, and not one I will tell you now. Let's just say it has to do with what he saw all those years back."

My mom inhaled sharply. "Was Nick with him on that mission? The one where he was supposed to be in Africa but was actually in Sweden or something?"

"Norway. And yes, Nick was there."

"So Nick knows my dad? He was in the military with him?"

"Yes and no. They did not serve together; Nick was in a different military."

"Which one?"

"I can't answer that yet. But it's the same one that I'm from."

"It's some weird military, isn't it?" Mel asked. "That's why your uniforms are so strange?"

"Yes," Faulk confirmed. "Adeline, several times I heard you ask what branch Nick was in. He conveniently didn't answer you each time, because he's not from the American military."

"Why can't you tell us which one? It's not like knowing that he was in the Norwegian army is going to hurt the world any more than it's already hurting."

"It wasn't the Norwegian army," he assured. "I promise I'll tell you soon. Like I said, I need to ease you into this."

I clenched my jaw, fighting the urge to scream at him and demand that he tell me everything right this minute. Forcing myself to stay calm and believe that it would all make sense soon, I sighed and said, "Okay, fine. So Nick knows my dad from some mysterious event in Norway; the event that coincidentally drove my dad crazy. Years later, Nick finds me at a New Year's Eve party just before the end of the world happens. My dad always warned us about the world ending... did Nick somehow... no, there's no way that's possible."

Faulk looked at us solemnly. "What you're thinking is absolutely possible. And it's the truth."

"What's the truth?" my mom whispered.

"Nick knew," I murmured. "Nick knew the world was about to end."

Again Faulk confirmed my suspicions, drawing a gasp from my mom and Mel.

"And I take it he didn't find Addie out of the goodness of his heart?" Mel questioned.

"No, not at all."

"Was I a bargaining chip to use against my dad, since he knew something about all this?"

"In a manner of speaking, yes."

"Good grief!" I snorted, getting up from my seat and pacing the room. "If that's true, then why did he go through the trouble of saving Mel and protecting my mom?"

"Probably so he could earn your trust and keep you with him willingly for as long as possible."

"Ugh," I groaned, remembering the moment when we had slipped into the bathtub together. I cringed at the memory, wishing I hadn't been so foolish.

"Don't beat yourself up too badly," Faulk urged. "Nick has deceived and persuaded people his entire life. It's what he does. He has honed the skill unbelievably well over the cen-, uh, decades."

"What?" my mom interrupted.

"What?" Faulk echoed.

"You were going to say something else. You weren't going to say decades. Were you going to say… centuries?"

"What? No way!" he laughed.

"Yes you were!" she insisted, leaning forward and clasping her hands over his. "Please, tell me!"

"Mom, why are you so adamant?" I asked.

"Because of something your father said. One of the things he carried on about the most, actually."

"Which was…?"

"That they found something, someone, rather, when they were in Norway. He said that the being was hundreds of years old. Faulk was about to say that Nick has spent centuries honing his skills."

We all looked expectantly at Faulk. He gulped, then said, "I wanted to break this to you slowly."

"You mean to tell me that Nick is hundreds of years old?" I scoffed. "How is that possible?"

"I cannot tell you everything today; you wouldn't believe me. But yes, he is much, much older than he looks."

"How the hell did he know about the blackout ahead of time?" I demanded, having a sinking feeling that his true age and foreknowledge were related in the worst way.

"I'll tell you when I tell you how he's so old," Faulk replied, confirming my fears.

"Fine," I agreed. "But I gather this means he's way more dangerous than a normal person?"

"Way more," Faulk affirmed. "Thankfully for you though, you're with me."

"What does that mean?"

"It means I have been in Nick's company for quite some time and know many of his moves and ways of thinking."

"Faulk," Mel said quietly. "Are you as old as he is?"

He stared at her unblinkingly. "Yes."

We all gasped, completely surprised by his answer. Suddenly we all feared him and grew nervous in his presence. I think he knew this, because he excused himself and then left the room. When he was gone, we all anxiously looked around at each other.

"What in the world is going on?" my mom sighed, sinking back onto the couch.

Mel glanced from spot to spot on the floor, trying to accept what Faulk had just said. "How in the world can what he's saying be true? It isn't possible!"

"Why would he lie?" I asked.

"Maybe he's just crazy!" she professed. "Maybe he lost his mind when all of this happened!"

"I don't think so," I said, shaking my head. "Everything else makes sense."

"Everything else is just what you wanted to hear," Mel argued.

"What do you mean?"

"It means he could have made up a nice convincing story so that you'd believe him."

"Convincing? So he decided to throw in that little bit about him and Nick being hundreds of years old?"

"Well if he's crazy, he's not all that smart."

"Mel, I don't think he's crazy."

"Nor do I," my mom said, taking us both by surprise.

"Vie, you believe him?"

"I might. I can't deny that his details about Norway coincide with what Bruce said happened."

"He only said a couple things! He could have read those things in the weird file Addie found."

"Yeah, maybe," I agreed.

"What do you propose then?" my mom asked Mel.

"That we ditch him?"

"I don't know!" she cried confusedly. "If he's crazy, I don't think it's exactly healthy to stay with him."

"Well if he's not crazy, I don't think it's exactly healthy to *not* stay with him. He has a lot of military experience, as well as knowledge on Nick that may help us escape and avoid him."

"Information that might all be horse crap."

"Might be, but I don't think it is," my mom said. "I think we should continue trusting him."

I agreed and looked at Mel, who still seemed skeptical. "Don't you want to trust him?" I asked.

"Well yeah; I really like him. But he's claiming he's hundreds of years old Addie. You don't find that a little unbelievable?"

"I find it incredibly absurd. But I also find corpses rising from the dead to eat us absurd. I find the things I've seen and experienced the last couple months completely absurd. But that doesn't make them any less real. We can't watch—with our very own eyes—dead people walk around, yet refuse to believe that a human can be hundreds of years old. If this grisly nightmare that we're living is real, then a really old person can be real."

"Yeah, I guess so," she hesitantly agreed.

With that decided, I left the room to go find Faulk. We needed to get out of this place and back on the road as soon as possible. I wandered the enormous house looking for him, finally realizing that he was probably out back. I went out to the luxuriously landscaped yard, indeed finding him there. He was sitting on a low stone bench by the fire pit.

"Hey there," I said, sitting down by him.

"Do you all think I'm lying?" he asked.

"No. The jury was out for a little bit, but we all decided you're a good egg."

He laughed out loud and looked at me with a smile. "Why do I have a feeling that you voted in favor of not crazy?"

"Because I did. So did my mom."

"So Mel thought I was a loony person?"

"She doesn't believe in much, Faulk. Just what she sees in front of her."

"Gotchya. I don't know if we're going to work out then."

"That doesn't seem like a good attitude."

"There's way more that I need to tell you ladies, and if she found that little bit hard to believe, then she's going to absolutely flip about the rest of it."

"Well you never know," I offered, but felt like he was right.

"If only she were as open minded to things as you," he said, gazing softly at me.

"Stop," I said instantly, standing up and backing away from him. "Don't you dare look at me like that."

"I'm sorry," he said sincerely. "I didn't even realize I was doing it. It's the darkness in me."

"Darkness?" I sneered.

"Yeah," he said. "I mean it Adeline; I'm sorry. I didn't mean to do that. It won't happen again."

"It better not. Don't turn out to be a scumbag like Nick."

"No; I promise I'm trying not to."

I didn't say anything, but eyed him keenly for a moment.

"Oh," he said. "I almost forgot. I was able to find a working phone in the house." He took a cell phone out of his pocket and handed it to me. "We couldn't bring one from camp because they're all traceable, but this one is good. Call your dad."

I excitedly took the phone from him, pounding my dad's number into the keypad. The phone rang several times on the other end, making my stomach knot up with anxiety. Finally there was an answer.

"Hello?"

"Dad!"

"Adeline?"

"Yeah it's me, Dad. How are you?"

"I'm all right."

"Did they let you go home?"

"Yeah; they just released me a little bit ago."

"That's good. Now I need you to listen to me very carefully. Get your things together and get out of there."

"What? Why?"

"The people I was with turned out to be really bad. I escaped them, but I'm pretty sure they're going to come after you."

"Oh my gosh!" he gushed. "Addie are you okay?"

"Yeah Dad I'm fine, but I'm really worried about you. Please get out of there."

"Of course I will. How can I find you?"

"Remember the camp you used to take me to when I was little? Can you make it there?"

"Yeah; I think so. If that's not possible, meet me at our church, okay?"

"That sounds good. I love you Dad."

"I love you too darling."

"Get moving Dad, please. You can lay low for a day or two; we won't be there before then."

"Who's we?"

"Me and a couple friends, and Mom."

"Your mom is with you?" he breathed.

"Yeah."

There was silence for a few moments, then sniffling. Was he crying?

"Hey Dad, are you there?"

"Yeah, I'm here," he answered quietly.

"Get out of there; I'll see you soon. I'm going to keep this phone on me, but it'll be off most the time to save battery. I'll check the messages every eight hours."

"Good idea; I'll do the same."

"Okay. I love you Dad; I'll see you soon."

"I love you darling; see you soon."

I hung up with him, fighting back the urge to cry. Then Faulk and I walked back inside, finding my mom and Mel already dressed and ready to go. I rushed into the bedroom and quickly changed, then scooped up my things and met everyone in the hangar. We left the house just as the sun was rising above the distant mountains. Although it was still pretty dark out, we didn't turn our headlights on so that we wouldn't attract unnecessary attention. Our plan didn't go so well though, because as we were leaving the neighborhood two black SUVs pulled out in front of us.

With the two SUVs blocking our path, my heart skipped a beat. Were we trapped?

"Don't you dare stop!" Faulk squawked over the radio.

"Roger that, over!" I exclaimed in reply.

Faulk barreled his truck into the back of the SUV on the left, and mine followed right after. That vehicle seemed to be pretty damaged, but the other one peeled out and followed behind us. Although our trucks were armored and powerful, I think the SUV had more speed to it. I floored my truck, but still our pursuers kept up with us. They didn't ram us or anything, probably knowing that doing so would be useless.

"What are they doing?"

"Probably staying with us until we run out of gas," my mom said fearfully.

"That's a dumb idea," I said with a frown.

The back driver's side window of the SUV started to roll down, revealing a soldier within. He raised a massive gun to his shoulder, making Faulk shout something over the radio.

"RPG! Evade!"

I bellowed out an incoherent reply, slamming on my brakes as the man fired. Thankfully we skidded to a stop just in time, and the grenade missed and flew by us harmlessly.

"Mom! Gun!" I yelled.

She jumped up and went to the gun spot, taking aim at the SUV. Our truck had a mean gun on it, as well as a grenade launcher. She fired a couple at our enemies, making a solid hit with one of them. The grenade exploded, blasting the SUV open. I tried not to think about the horror the people inside were experiencing.

"Nice shot Vie!" Mel's voice said over the radio.

"Thanks!" I shouted into it for her.

"Back to radio silence now," Faulk ordered. "But let that be a lesson to whoever is listening. You can't stop us!"

CHAPTER SIXTEEN

We soared down the road as fast as we could, hoping to get as far away from the area before Nick sent out reinforcements. I nervously checked my mirror every few seconds, afraid that I'd see a black SUV or another truck in pursuit. My mom noticed and tried to calm me, although I could tell she was jittery as well.

"If they do catch us, we'll put up one hell of a fight," she assured, putting her hand on mine.

I smiled in reply, so glad to have my normal mom back. Whatever she had become in New York wasn't her, and I was glad that the effects of high society were leaving her character.

A few minutes later, Faulk and Mel's truck began to slow. I wanted to get on the radio and ask what was wrong, but resisted the urge. Whatever it was, I'd either find out for myself or Faulk would tell me. We came up on a freeway exit, which Faulk took. He drove down the ramp, took the first right, then pulled into a shopping center. I unconsciously held my breath as we drove, wondering how many changed things would be here and why Faulk was taking the risk of coming in here. We traveled down the main road of the center, which eventually faded away and turned into a golf course. Faulk ramped his truck up onto the sidewalk, then shamelessly plowed onto the golf course. As we went, I realized that the course backed up against a river. The truck in front of me sped across the course, towards one of the furthest holes. Finally Faulk pulled to a stop, right next to the river.

We all got out of our trucks somewhat confusedly, including Mel. I figured Faulk had told her why we were here, but it didn't look like it. Faulk strode towards the edge of the course, stopping right where the water lapped against the structure. I nervously glanced behind us, seeing only a couple changed things straggling around the course. However, the clubhouse had probably been hosting a party when the blackout had happened, which meant there were probably a ton in that building. Thankfully, Faulk had driven to the spot on the course that was furthest from it. The things had probably still seen us though and were shambling towards us; we just couldn't see them yet. With a gulp, I turned towards Faulk.

"Why are we here?" I demanded, gagging as I realized that the river stank horribly. "Hundreds of changed things are probably coming towards us right now, as well as Nick's men. We don't have time for golf or scenic routes."

I had kind of hoped he'd chuckle or smile, but he did neither. He looked solemnly at the river, seeming to be in another place in his mind. I glanced at Mom and Mel, who both had concerned looks on their face. I nervously bit my lip, wondering what we should do.

"I know our time is limited," Faulk finally said, still staring at the river. "We needed to stop here though. All of you, come to the edge with me and look at the water."

I skeptically glanced at the other two people, wondering if this was a trick. What if Faulk was on Nick's side and was going to push us into the river or something?

"You can trust me," he said, sensing our hesitation. "I'm

helping you. I want to help you. But to tell you everything, you need to see a few things first."

I locked eyes with Mel, who shrugged and nodded. I gave her a small smile, then hooked my arm with my mom's. We all stepped closer to the river as Faulk instructed.

"Now look at the water. You smell that awful stench?"

"Uh yeah, it's kinda hard not to," Mel gagged. "My eyes are watering."

"It's the smell of death," he replied. I glanced over at him, seeing a tinge of regret in his face.

"Death?" my mom asked. "Like dead fishes and other things that were in it? Are they affected by all of this too?"

"No, it's not just the smell of dead fish. Their stench certainly adds to it, but it's mainly human."

Before I could stop myself, I heaved and suddenly barfed into the river. Something about his words had brought the most revolting images into my head. I pictured masses of dead bodies floating in the river; rotting and bloated. Grey skin decayed and fell apart, slipping off of bodies and flowing down the river on its own.

My mom knelt down beside where I trembled on the ground, still heaving. I tried to stop; throwing up in front of people was pretty embarrassing. I felt my mom's hand on my back, rubbing it soothingly.

"What are you saying?" Mel asked. "They dump bodies into the river?"

"No. I'm saying that the cause of all of this started in rivers."

"What?" we all three echoed.

"There were many sacrifices made by a powerful being—"

"Being?" I panted. "What does that mean?"

"I'll explain in a minute. This being sacrificed animals with tainted blood, then gave them to the rivers to pollute the water supply. He did this in several places, making sure to spread the infection across the land. Source water is heavily filtered and cleaned, but he planned for that. He made sure the contamination could slip through a percentage of the time, and it did. Several thousand people got infected with it. Sure enough, they died one by one. The deaths were excruciating and painful. Many of the people who caught it were nobodies, missed by no one. So once they died, we stole their body and took it to our secure facility. Sure, it would have been easier just to kidnap people and inject them with the taint, but he thought it would be more amusing to watch them catch it of their own free will. Watch them drink from the river of their own choice, never realizing what poison they were ingesting."

Faulk paused in his tale, glancing up at all of us. We all looked quite horrified, I'm sure. He must have been expecting this, because he had no reaction when he saw our faces. When he saw that we were all still listening, he kept talking.

"Once Christmas rolled around, the last of them had died and gone through the change. He decided New Year's Eve would be the perfect time to release them on the world."

"Who is he?" I asked fearfully, climbing to my feet.

"The one we work for; the one Nick reports to."

"What was in this tainted blood?" my mom asked. "A virus?"

"No. It was a different sort of infection. It was a special blend of blood from various predators, such as wolves, bears, lions, and jackals. That blend was fused with the last ingredient."

"Which was…?"

"Our blood."

"Our blood?" I scoffed. "How would our own blood make us die and come back to life?"

"Not your blood; our blood. The blood of my kind. The blood of me, Smith, Nick, Ghost, Mortimer, and all the others from that camp. Including the man who tortured you."

My brows furrowed and twitched as we all backed away from Faulk. "And what the hell are you?" I whispered.

"It will be hard for you to believe," he cautioned.

"Tell us!" Mel hissed.

His gaze quickly turned to her, causing sorrow to show in his eyes. "I'm sorry Mel," he confessed. "I truly am. But I got you away from there because I want to help you. I don't believe in their cause anymore."

Mel's face was covered in fear, and her eyes were brimming with tears. "Just tell us what you are," she begged.

Faulk gulped, then opened his mouth to speak. Suddenly though, he jerked his head towards the road, back in the direction of the camp. "They're coming!" he exclaimed. "I can't go with you; they can track me."

"What?" I cried.

"That's why we're parting ways here. You guys need to leave! Take both trucks and all the supplies."

"What about you?" Mel objected as tears streamed down her face. "You can't stay out here with nothing."

We all glanced up the golf course, seeing that dozens of changed things were ambling towards us. My eyes widened in fear as I suddenly realized we needed to get moving.

"We need to leave now!" I yelled, turning back to Faulk. "Are you really not coming with us?"

"It will endanger you if I do. They can track me no matter where I go. I only stayed with you last night because I jammed the device they use to track me, but I knew they'd probably fix it by today. You need to get in the trucks and leave me. Don't worry about being tracked in those; I completely disabled the GPS in them. Once you're away from me, you'll be safe."

"Can't we disable the chip or whatever they're using to track you?" Mel quickly asked, grabbing his arms and looking at his wrist.

"No, I'm sorry Mel," he answered gently. "It's not a device. It's in my blood."

The mention of his blood made me remember that his story wasn't over.

"What are you?" I urgently asked as I inched backwards towards the truck. We could see Nick's vehicles on the freeway now. Our time was quickly running out.

He looked sincerely into Mel's eyes, then nudged her towards the trucks. My mom took hold of her and pulled her along, but all eyes were on Faulk. He looked down at the ground, then back up at us. My jaw dropped open and I nearly fell over. His eyes were completely black.

"I am one of the fallen," he said in an impossibly deep voice, much like the one of the man who had tortured me. "I am powerful and dangerous, like Nick and all of his men. Except, they are thoroughly evil. They will stop at nothing to see this world burn, and all of those within it. Get to your father, Yirah."

I gasped, as did my mom. "How do you know my name?" I wheezed.

"Hold to the meaning of it, and you will get through this. Now leave me and go find your dad; he can help stop all of this. That is why they had the folder on him. You need to get to him before they do."

I could only stand there panting as I absorbed his words. He was walking towards me now; those evil black eyes of his were on mine. I screamed and backed away, but he caught me. His strong fingers gripped around my arm, and he looked into my eyes. Suddenly his human eyes showed again, and he looked relieved.

"Go!" he roared. "My true nature is trying to take over. They can see everything that I can when my eyes are black."

I frantically complied and spun around, making sure my mom had gotten into her vehicle. When I saw that she had, I yanked open the door to mine.

"Yirah," Faulk panted, dropping to the ground for some reason. He looked weak.

"Yeah?"

"Nick's real name is Necromarthe. Remember that."

With that he clutched his side in pain and thundered at us to leave. I gaped, wanting to help him, but he had adamantly told us several times to flee. I jumped into my truck, glancing over at the other one. My mom was in the driver's seat, and had managed to get a very sad Mel into the passenger's seat. I signaled to her and we took off. We plowed through the changed things that were on the golf course, splattering blood and guts all over our trucks. I cringed with every hit, but knew that I couldn't slow down. I glanced back in the mirror, seeing the things surround Faulk. To my surprise, they didn't attack him. They surrounded him, but that's it. Like they had done with Smith, they just meandered around him without any interest.

Once we got out to the street, we sped to the overpass and hid under it. A minute later, several trucks got off the freeway and sped towards the golf course. Once they were out of sight, we floored our trucks and got back on the freeway, heading west. Although I felt better about leaving Faulk since the chompers hadn't attacked him, I was afraid of what Nick, or Necromarthe, rather, would do to him when he found him.

We sped down the highway as fast as we could, but the damn trucks topped out at like 67 miles per hour. I desperately hoped that Nick's men wouldn't come after us, or we'd be dead. Up ahead, to the north of the freeway, I could see a sprawling forest. Part of me considered exiting the wide open road and trying to hide in there. Would our pursuers expect that? Would they find us? I anxiously glanced in the rearview mirror again, still seeing nothing. Whatever they were doing to Faulk must be truly awful, because if they had gotten on the road right away they would have caught us by now. When they were done punishing him and decided to chase us again, we'd be sitting ducks. Well, speeding ducks, but slow ducks that would be overrun by faster ducks.

Deciding we had a better chance hiding in the forest for a bit, I steered my truck over to the exit. Mom followed me, undoubtedly wondering what I was doing. We drove a couple miles before coming to the entrance of the forest, where an abandoned guard booth stood in the middle of the road.

I carefully drove around the extended arm, making a wide arc around it and going up onto the sidewalk. I hoped that if the barrier arm remained down and undamaged, then this place would continue to look abandoned and our pursuers wouldn't suspect that we were in here.

We followed the road for a bit, which led deeper into the forest. After a while it began to get a little rough, then the asphalt started looking poorly maintained. I slowed down, figuring dirt was coming. Sure enough, the road soon turned to dirt. Right away I veered off of it into the forest, not wanting to stir up any dust. If they saw that in the air, it would be a dead giveaway to our location. We carefully crept through the trees, trying to avoid treacherous cliffs and sinkholes. For hours we went, and all the while I was tracking the location of the sun. Getting lost in the forest wouldn't help me save my dad any more than getting caught by bad people would.

Eventually we came to a stop. Right away we grabbed leaves, dirt, and wood and did what we could to hide the trucks. I looked at the ground grimly, hoping these guys wouldn't find our original trail. They could probably track like pros. After doing what we could to disguise the trucks, we all quietly climbed into one of them. I wouldn't say we were exactly eager to talk, but we needed to go over some things.

"So…" I started somewhat awkwardly. Mom and Mel had been in their truck for hours, and I wasn't sure how much Mel had talked about her sadness for losing Faulk.

"I'm okay," she said with a weak smile, having that famous best-friend telepathy.

"Are you sure?" I asked, taking her hand in mine.

"Yeah. I talked with Vie a lot; I feel better. I mean I didn't even know him that well."

She shrugged like she didn't care, but I knew better. She had met a lot of losers over the years, but she had seemed to really like Faulk. He had really seemed to like her, too. He had helped us escape and it had looked like they could've had a chance to be together. But then... then we found out all that weirdness.

"I can't believe all this," my mom said dramatically with a wave of her hand.

I chuckled despite myself. Although her character had infinitely improved over the last couple months, she still had her little showman moments.

"Which part?" I gawked. "The part where Faulk told us that Nick helped start all this, or the part where his eyes went black and told us that he was one of them?"

"And what does that even mean?" Mel gushed. "One of them. One of them what?"

"He said a *fallen one*," my mom quickly replied.

"Yeah," I agreed anxiously. "What did that mean?"

"And how," my mom breathed, "did he know your name?"

"I didn't even know that was your name!" Mel blurted. "What was it?"

"Yirah," I answered. Faulk had also said something else about my name; what had it been...?

"So whatever those fallen ones are, they started all this," my mom stated.

"And there are tons of them," Mel added.

"How do you know that?"

"Faulk said thousands of people were affected and that

his group monitored each one of them. He said they were nobodies, so it sounds like maybe they were homeless. You can't track homeless people with surveillance of their phones and computers because they don't have them."

"So to track thousands of homeless people, you actually have to physically have an eye on them, which means they could possibly have thousands of people on their team."

"I don't think the word is possibly. I think it's *probably*, or even *definitely*."

"This group is no joke," I whispered fearfully.

"And somehow Bruce knows about them, or what their plan was...?" my mom mused.

"Yeah he definitely said your dad was in the know," Mel echoed.

"We have to get to him," I said determinedly. "He might know how to reverse all this."

"Ugh," Mel groaned. "Is there any reversing this? Is there ever going back to normal after seeing what we've seen?"

"I don't know," I shrugged. "But I know it's what Faulk wanted us to do. He wanted us to beat these people."

"Fallen ones," my mom corrected with her index finger in the air.

I chuckled and leaned into her shoulder. As silence flooded the truck, I saw Mel's face fall. I could tell she was thinking about Faulk.

"Hey Addie," she whispered, looking up at me with glistening eyes. "What did he say to you when we were about to leave? I saw him call you back."

I took a deep breath and let it out slowly. "He told me that the others could see everything he saw when his eyes were covered in black." Both my mom and Mel gasped.

"So they know what he told you about Bruce," my mom said, leaning away so that I sat up. "They know exactly where we're going."

"They probably knew before," I sighed. "Nick knew I wanted to get to Dad."

"Is that all he told you?" Mel asked.

"Yeah. Oh wait, no. He also told me that Nick's real name is Necromarthe."

Mel frowned and raised an eyebrow. "That name gives me the chills."

"Same here. I have no idea why; I've never heard of it. Have you Mom?"

"No, I can't say I have."

"We can ask your dad when we get to him," Mel suggested.

"Definitely," I confirmed. "It was certainly important. Faulk told me to make sure I remembered it."

"I can't believe it," Mel whispered. "I can't believe they were all in on this. Why the heck did they take us in?" She looked up at us with anger in her eyes. "Was it just to... to toy with us? Have some women around for when they got bored?"

"Perhaps it was to use us as leverage," my mom said.

"What?" I asked.

"If they were after Bruce and realized that we both knew him, maybe they kept us to use against him if necessary."

"Yeah, probably," I agreed sadly. My mind flashed to memories of the night I had slept with Nick, striking a deep pain in my heart. Fighting the urge to burst into tears,

I looked back up at everyone. Eager to distract my mind from that subject, I brought up another one. "I uh, didn't have a plan when I drove us into this forest. I figured hiding in here might give us a better chance than staying on that wide open highway with us being in slower vehicles than them."

"That's okay," my mom smiled warmly as she patted my hand. She must have known that I'd been thinking about Nick and was trying to cheer me up. "You don't always have to be the leader. Mel and I know how to make plans too."

I smiled in appreciation. "Thanks Mom."

With that, we set about making a plan. Thankfully we had some low-tech items in the truck, such as an old-school paper map and magnetic compass. I remembered which exit we had taken and that we'd entered the forest from the east, which help us roughly estimate where we were.

"It looks like we can escape out the northwestern side of the forest," Mel said as she peered at the map. "The 259 freeway will take us southeast, joining back to the I-81. And that will take us… pretty much the whole way to San Antonio."

"That's probably our best option," my mom said. "If we go straight back the way we came, there's a good chance they'll be monitoring the roads."

"What do you think Addie?"

"I think it sounds like a plan. Want to wait until night-time? It'll give us the cover of darkness. We have night vision to help us navigate in the trucks."

"So do they."

"Yeah but it still seems like a better idea than just going out there in broad daylight or using headlights at night-time."

"But then we'll lose the entire day," my mom countered. "They could be on their way to your dad right now."

"Well hopefully the place we chose to meet up at will be a good hiding spot. I told him to meet us at the campground we used to go to."

My mom smiled warmly, fondly recalling precious memories. "That's a good place," she said quietly to herself.

Suddenly I remembered that I still had the cell phone Faulk had given me. "Hey, I can try calling him; duh!"

I eagerly pulled out the phone and pushed the power button. Nothing happened. I pushed it again and again, but still it didn't come on. I stared at it sadly as worry washed over me, hoping Dad would stay hidden and not give up on the fact that we were coming for him.

"The phone won't work?" my mom asked.

"No," I sighed. I wrinkled my brow as I stared at it, remembering Faulk's words when he'd given it to me. "He said we couldn't take a phone from camp since the soldiers could track the GPS. He said he had found this one."

"In the house we stayed at?" Mel asked.

"Yeah, but nothing in that house worked," I countered. "None of the power worked, just like the rest of the places we've been. In fact," I realized, looking up in realization, "the only things that have worked have been things that Nick's men possessed."

"Do you think they know how to fix them?"

"Something like that," I said. "How else do we explain that only the things they have work, while nothing else does?"

"They knew this was going to happen. Maybe they protected all their electronics from whatever knocked out all of ours," Mel proposed.

"Yeah that would explain a lot, but not where this phone came from. It worked fine when Faulk gave it to me. Now it won't turn on. There's no way the battery is dead because it has been off, not using any power."

"Are you thinking the phone only worked around Faulk?" my mom asked with a raised eyebrow.

"Maybe. I mean, he did have some other pretty strange features. He claimed to be centuries old and could turn his eyes completely black. Doesn't seem too far-fetched to think he had influence over electronics."

"Good grief," Mel groaned. "This reality just gets stranger every hour."

"That it does," I agreed.

"What about you though?" Mel asked. "If you almost became a changed thing, are you still changing? Are you going to turn into one of them?"

"I have no idea," I replied grimly. "When I told Faulk about it, he said something weird like they knew that it wouldn't work on me. I think the taint ran its course on me and already had all the effects that it's going to have."

"Like your super cool night vision?" she asked, raising her eyebrows at me.

"Yeah, like that," I chuckled.

"Do you feel different otherwise? Do you have any spidey senses or green skin?"

I laughed and rolled my eyes. "Not that I know of."

"What about more serious things," my mom asked hesitantly. "Have you had any urges to…"

"Eat people?" I finished her sentence. "No; thankfully."

"Have you had a fever?"

"I did while I was on that table for hours of agony, but not since then. If it comes back, I'll be sure to let you know."

"Yeah if you're going to eat our faces off, we'd like a warning," Mel chided.

I laughed and hooked my arm around her neck, pulling her down playfully. Soon we got out of the trucks and walked around a little, happy to stretch our legs out. Although we would have all liked to relax and waste the day away, I figured it could be better used. We had a good supply of water, but it wouldn't last forever. Since we were in a forest, we knew there were streams nearby. Hopefully we could get drinking water from them. We spread out carefully, each searching for a stream. I made sure each of us had a compass and knew exactly how to get back to the trucks. There was no use looking for water if the cost was losing one of us.

The forest was a beautiful place, and I loved meandering through it. The trees and lush ground was a wonder to me, since I had grown up in a mostly barren area in Texas. I trudged along, soon realizing that I could hear water gurgling. Eagerly I went towards it, elated to see a bubbling stream in front of me. I smiled as I knelt down and brought my canteen to it. For the most part, flowing water was pretty safe to drink. Although, Faulk had just told us the taint had been spread through the rivers. Which rivers? Was any water safe to drink? Seeing no other option for quenching our thirst, I decided to get the water. We would just boil and filter it really well.

As I filled my canteen, I suddenly felt a crushing presence all around me. I panted and fell forward, throwing my hands out in front of me to stop myself from falling in the water. Frantically I regained my balance and glanced skyward, wondering what in the world was causing that feeling. I couldn't see anything, but suddenly the sound of whooshing air reached my ears. I spun around and looked behind me, gasping at what I saw. Nick.

CHAPTER SEVENTEEN

I gasped as I stood from the stream, gawking at the sight in front of me. Nick stood before me, standing with his feet planted wide apart. He looked powerful and mighty, making me gulp in fear. I had always found him attractive, but right now it seemed to be amplified tenfold. His hair looked darker, his eyes more glorious, his smile more enthralling, and his muscles more powerful. I stared in awe, wondering what was happening. Was this a vision?

"Eve, my dear!" he said kindly, not moving. "I was so worried about you! What a relief it is to have found you."

"Is it?" I hissed, finding it hard to resist his words.

"Of course it is. Come to me, darling."

"No," I said shaking my head. "Get away from me!"

"I can't do that Eve."

"Why don't you call me by my real name?" I snarled. "You do know it, after all."

He grinned slyly, making his perfect face look even more alluring. I blinked fiercely, feeling as though I was under a spell.

"Come over here," he insisted. "Let me wrap you in my arms, love."

"No," I muttered, realizing that I really wanted to walk over to him. Like really wanted to.

"That's it," he smiled. I looked down, realizing that I was walking towards him. "Surrender to me Eve; let me take you into my arms and keep you safe."

"Safe!" I barked, finding the will to stop walking towards him. "Safe from whom? You are the enemy!"

"Oh no," he chuckled. "I'm afraid you're mistaken my dear." He extended his hand towards me.

I looked at it longingly, greatly desiring the safety of his touch. When my hand was in his, I always felt so protected. Surely that was still the case.

"There we are," he cooed as I continued my approach to him. "Let me hold you sweetheart. I miss you being in my arms."

"Do you really?" I breathed. "Because I've missed you too Nick."

"You disappeared; I've been looking for you all this time. You just left me after our precious night together."

"I didn't leave you," I whimpered.

"You did, and it really hurt me."

"But I didn't," I defended. "You locked me in a room."

I finally reached him and wrapped my hungry arms around him. He swept his strong arms around me, pulling me tightly against him. I rested my head against his chest and fluttered my eyes shut, recalling all the glorious moments of our night together.

"I did no such thing," he assured. "You lost a lot of blood when those things attacked you. I had Mortimer nurse you back to health. When I went to check on you, you were gone."

"No," I muttered, realizing my memories of it all were getting hazy. "I don't think that's what happened."

"It is," he said, stroking my hair with one hand. The other firmly held my waist.

"I don't think so," I mused, scrunching my brows. I

struggled to remember the events as my head swam.

"I promise you, it is," he assured. "You were kidnapped by a crazy man. Now help me find Mel and Vie," he said smoothly. "They want to go back to the house. Help me get you all back to safety. It isn't safe in this forest."

"Kidnapped?" I asked.

"Yes, by Faulk."

Faulk. An image came to my mind; the last one I had of him. He was collapsed on the golf course with chompers surrounding him. What was he doing on a golf course…? Some of his last words came swirling into my thoughts. He had said them right after I asked how he knew my real name. "Hold to the meaning of it, and you will get through this."

I took one of my arms from around Nick and tried to lean back to grip my little cross pendant, but he held me too closely against him. That's when I realized he was holding my waist too tightly. It wasn't in an adoring manner, it was possessive. My pulse quickened as it struck me that I had just literally walked into the arms of the enemy. I desperately said a silent prayer, awed when a moment later my head cleared. All my thoughts became clear again, and I recalled exactly what had happened. At the same time, Nick flinched. Just as his grip on me weakened, I wrenched myself away from him.

"You!" I thundered as I backed away from him. "You were behind all of this!"

He didn't say anything, but glared at me as he contemplated his next move.

"Get away from me!" I repeated from earlier.

"I can't do that Eve."

"That's not my name."

"Oh I'm sorry; *Yirah*," he said condescendingly. "Do you even know what it means?"

"Of course I do."

"Then you know that it's bullshit! Why would you want to be called that?"

I gulped and tried to recall what Faulk had told me about Nick's name. Not much except that I should remember it.

"How about your real name, Nick?"

"Ha!" he said dryly as he rolled his eyes. "You'll never learn my real name."

"Oh really?" I growled, stomping towards him.

"Really," he said with all the smugness in the world. "Now come back with me," he ordered, gripping my arm. He ran a finger down my face as he whispered, "I'm going to make you regret ever leaving me. I'll take you back to our room and open your eyes to all the horrors of this world." His hand continued down my face, then throat... "I'll teach you never to defy me again."

I bared my teeth at him and shouted, "Get away from me, *Necromarthe!*"

Instantly he recoiled and leapt backwards. He snarled viciously at me, then suddenly disappeared into a poof of black smoke. I yelped and fell to the ground, panting as relief washed over me. I clenched my eyes shut, trying not to imagine all of the horrible things he would have done to me if he'd gotten me back to camp. Why using his real name had had such an effect on him, I had no idea, but I sure was glad for it. Taking a deep breath, I tried to calm my trembling limbs and pull myself together. I had to get my mom and Mel out of here.

A short time later, I had found them and gotten them into the trucks. We were tearing through the forest, heading towards our planned escape route. It was still day light, but Nick had found me easily enough. There was no way we were going to sit here for the rest of the day. Even though I had somehow gotten rid of Nick, his people were probably pouring into the forest through the entrance we had taken earlier. Since they knew we were headed for Texas, we hoped they might not expect us to head north out of the forest.

We charged through the trees, trying to both hurry past them while not hitting any of them. Some parts of the forest were dense with them, so a couple times we were forced to stop and back up, then find another way around. Eventually though, we emerged from the sea of green and found ourselves in open air.

I stopped my truck and my mom stopped hers right behind mine. Quickly, I jumped out of the truck and dashed to the back. Mom and Mel did the same, grabbing the gas can I handed them. As we filled up the tanks, Mel looked at me inquisitively. I had barely told either of them anything, other than the fact that I had seen Nick. She watched my shaking hands try to fill the truck's tank, which I was doing a pretty bad job at. When my hand slipped and spilled gas everywhere for the second time, she walked over to me and took the can from me. She took over filling it as she looked up at me.

"Are you okay?" she asked.

"Yeah."

"I don't think you should be driving. I'll drive for you."

"I don't want you to leave my mom alone."

"I'll be fine," my mom pitched in.

"Vie is fine. Let me drive for you."

A few minutes later, we were speeding along the 259. Mel was at the wheel of my truck, with my mom following behind us. I slouched in the passenger's seat, trying to calm my erratic emotions.

"You want to talk?" Mel asked from somewhere on the other side of all the gear that was between us.

"Yeah I'm fine."

"You just said yeah but that you're fine. You're not making sense, which means you're not fine."

"Letting someone into your heart is always a mistake. Always."

"Not always."

"Oh that is such crap. They either lie, cheat, or do both. They're all pieces of crap. Every single one."

"That's not true," she disagreed.

"Even Faulk," I griped. "Even if he meant well for you, he turned out to be some weird thing that helped bring about the end of the world. Tell me that's not wrong."

"It is wrong. But not every person is bad."

I didn't say anything, indicating my disagreement with that statement.

"Am I bad?"

"No," I said instantly. I leaned around the gear and looked her in the eye. "I love you Mel. You know that. Men are just... unbelievable!"

Suddenly I was in tears and couldn't stop them. I sobbed and sobbed, much to my embarrassment. I knew Mel understood, but it was the only sound in the car. There was no radio or music, or anyone else talking. It was just me sobbing like a big baby. And what was I sobbing about? A man who lied to me to get me in bed. It was the oldest story in the book and here I was crying about it.

I guess I said sorry for crying, because I heard Mel telling me it was okay and to shut up with the apologies. She said she'd been through this more times than she wanted to admit, and that she completely understood what I was going through.

"Oh but it's so much worse this time," I panted as I tried to catch my breath. "When he found me in the forest, he made it clear that he wanted a night with me again… but just for the chance to make me miserable!" I cried out in a sob, shaking profusely. "He took something precious that I had given him and totally turned it around. The pain of knowing that is so unbearable!"

"Oh Addie," Mel comforted, reaching her hand over to mine.

I felt our speed decrease, instantly making me look over at her. "Don't stop this truck."

"We need to share this with your mom."

"And we will, but not now. We need to get away from the psychos that are chasing us."

"Are you sure?"

"Absolutely. I'll be fine. There'll be time for talking later. Before that though, we need to survive."

I convinced her that I'd be okay until we could stop safely. Once she was solely focused on the road again, I managed to stop crying. Tears still streamed down my face as the ache in my chest lessened. I was determined not to let Nick, or Necromarthe, hurt me too deeply. What he had done was nearly unforgivable, but I was going to do my best not to let it destroy me.

We drove for several hours before we finally took a break. Quickly we filled up our gas tanks, realizing that we had used nearly the whole supply of gas that we'd stolen from Nick's camp. We tried not to think about what would happen when we ran out as we emptied our bladders and then jumped back on the road.

As we drove, I stared out the windows at our surroundings. Like there had been for the past few months, heavy smoke hung on the horizon. Here and there cars and trucks dotted the roads. They had obviously been stopped dead in their tracks, for none of them were pulled over; they were just stopped in the middle of the road. Some of their doors were opened, and most of them looked empty. I wasn't sure if they had gotten out while they were still alive, or had been dragged out.

The cities that we passed all looked relatively the same: desolate, except for the changed things that wandered the streets. I felt pity as I watched some of them bumble around aimlessly, wondering if they were conscious of what was happening. Were they really dead, or was there still a person in there? Could we save them? Although we had gone on several missions for Nick, I was grateful that until now we hadn't really had to be around them. I was glad that at least for a time, Nick had kept us safe.

"Hey you two," Mel squawked over the radio.

We had decided that if we changed frequency and used them rarely, it was probably okay to use them. I wasn't sure how far of a range they had, but if Nick's people were still pursuing us, they probably would have overtaken us by now. I didn't want to call us safe prematurely, but after my encounter with him, I was wondering if they were even still bothering to chase us. I still wasn't exactly sure how I'd gotten rid of him.

"Yeah?" I answered, looking over at my mom who was driving our truck. She and Mel had switched vehicles a couple hours ago.

"There's a small town coming up. Want to stop in it to look for supplies?"

"Don't we have everything we need?" I asked, glancing back at our stockpile.

"Uh, hello, we're running short on gummy bears."

"Gummy bears huh?"

"Yup. And Skittles. I'm pretty sure it would be a crime to run out of those."

I smiled and looked at my mom. "What do you think?"

"I think Skittles sound wonderful right about now," she sang.

I squished my lips together and considered stopping. It didn't seem like a good idea, but I also had to admit that the sweet taste of candy sounded really good right now. I sure could use some sugar.

"Okay, but we have to be fast," I answered into the radio.

"Yay!" Mel squealed. "I see a gas station right off the freeway. We'll be in and out."

"Park in the back."

We pulled off the highway and drove up to the gas station. After parking in the back, we jumped out of the trucks. Mel and my mom had grabbed their guns, but I just grabbed a machete. My grenade launcher wouldn't be much good inside a store, and regular bullets didn't stop them. I thought about telling them it was pointless to bring the guns, but I didn't. Even though I knew the rifles were pretty much useless against chompers, it was still comforting to see them being carried.

Before rounding the corner to the front of the store, I paused and whispered, "In and out!"

My mom and Mel agreed, then we all carefully hurried towards the doors. They were automatic sliding glass doors, which were frozen shut. I pressed a palm to each of them and pushed them apart, grunting as the heavy doors begrudgingly slid open. As soon as they did, the snarls reached our ears. If these doors had shut when the power went out at the stroke of midnight, then I figured there weren't many changed things in here. Thankfully I was right; we only found two of them wandering around the store.

I charged the first one, whacking my machete towards it like a bat. Apparently my aim was horrible, because the blade struck the thing in the shoulder. I tried pulling it back, but it was stuck in the rotting flesh and bone. I grimaced as I pulled on the handle, putting a foot on the thing's torso. Bodily fluids squelched under my boot, making a horrid sound. With all my might, I yanked backwards, finally prying my blade out of the thing. I gagged when I saw the blade; a nasty dark sludge covered it. Blood and guts seemed to have merged together, creating a gruesome type of glue.

There wasn't time to gawk though, because the thing came at me, snarling angrily. I swung my blade again, this time hitting its neck and separating the head from the body. I cringed and closed my eyes as they both fell to the ground. Even though the thing had been trying to eat me, it was still hard to do that to something that resembled a person.

Glancing over at my mom, I saw that she had disposed of her foe easier than I had. I sniffled indignantly to myself, embarrassed by my mistake of hitting the thing in the shoulder. Shaking off the feeling, I hurried up and down the measly aisles of the store. Mel and my mom did the same. It was quickly cleared of all candy, which Mel shoved into her backpack. My mom went towards the back of the store to check out the beverage section. Although the power had been off for a couple months, some of the drinks would still be good warm. Mel called to me as I jumped behind the clerk's counter to see if there was anything useful back there.

"Catch!" she laughed, tossing me a bag of candy.

I snagged it from the air, ripped it open, and poured the Skittles into my mouth. "Mmm," I mumbled as I squatted down behind the counter. There was a shelf back here that had some personal items on it.

"Anything back there?" Mel asked, peering over the counter at me.

"Mehmahbeh," I said through the candy.

"Talk like a normal person," she chided.

I scarfed down the sugary goodness then said, "Yeah, a knife and a gun. Looks like whoever was here left in a hurry. Who would leave a gun?"

Mel shrugged, so I picked up the items and dropped them in her backpack. In the next moment, we heard the sound that I'll never forget. My mom suddenly shrieked.

Adrenaline filled my limbs, and in a split second I jumped over the counter and flew towards the drink section.

"Mom!" I wheezed.

We reached her in seconds. I gaped in horror when we rounded the corner; a chomper had grabbed her from the other side of the drinks, in the refrigerated area. It had yanked her halfway inside and was rabidly feasting on her arm. I dashed towards her as she screamed her lungs out and thrashed to get away. I yanked out my machete and jabbed it into the thing's head as many times as I could. Still it kept tearing off her flesh with its grotesque teeth. I roared and stabbed with all my might, but the thing just looked up at me and kept ripping and devouring. With a savage growl, I got up and ran around to the back of the store. In seconds I was behind the thing, and viciously sliced its head off. By then, Mom had stopped screaming.

As fast as I could, I ran back around to where she lay on the floor. Mel had pulled her out of the doorway of the refrigerated area, and now sat with her cradled in her lap.

"Mom," I whimpered when I saw her. She wasn't moving.

I dropped to the ground and leaned towards her, but Mel shook her head. My lips and jaw trembled as I reached a hand towards her. My eyes burned with tears; I couldn't see anything. But I felt her. I put my hand on her neck and felt nothing. Nothing except coldness starting to spread through her body. A shudder coursed through me, and in the next second I was wailing.

"No!!!" I bellowed, slamming my fist onto the ground. "Why?" I spat towards the sky. "Do you enjoy watching us suffer? You are such a cruel god!"

At those words, I instantly felt regret for saying them. But I was furious just the same. Faulk had told me to remember the meaning of my name. The awe of God. Yeah, it's real easy to be in awe of a harsh being who just watches us suffer and die. He probably wasn't even real. If he was, then he definitely wasn't the god I thought I believed in. Angrily, I ripped the necklace from my neck. The tiny little cross clinked to the floor, ending up in a pile of blood. How appropriate. My faith and mom died on the same day.

Oddly, though, I recalled Nick's words the night we'd talked about God on the balcony. He said that maybe God let us suffer because we chose to be distant from him. We had rejected God first, not the other way around. When had I rejected him though? I was a good person. I was nice to people. I helped old ladies carry groceries and I returned stolen wallets.

Even as I thought that though, I felt my heart expose the truth. Acting decently towards fellow human beings didn't mean you hadn't rejected God. There were plenty of nurturing, giving, and kind people who didn't believe in God. Choosing to avoid church, which I did, and ignoring his laws were acts of rejection. How many times had I called a law of his old fashioned and acted against it, even though I knew I was wrong? How many times had I used logic to justify doing something I knew would break his heart? And deep down, I knew that every single thing he told us not to do was for our own good.

I groaned as I sadly looked down at my mom. Whatever the reason for her death, I knew I shouldn't blame God. I had every right to be furious at the changed thing that had killed her, but blaming God was just childish. Gingerly, I reached over and picked up my necklace. What was more; Faulk had known my name and its meaning. Somehow all of this was connected to that.

"Addie," Mel said softly, placing a hand on my arm. "We can't stay here. You know what happens."

"I can't let her go through that," I sniffled. "The serum Mortimer gave me made me suffer through the changes of becoming one of them. I know the pain and agony that comes before the change. It has probably already started," I sobbed, picking up my machete. With a gulp, I glanced over at Mel. Her eyes were red and puffy as well. She looked very concerned.

"Can you really... do that?" she asked in disbelief.

"I have to," I said quietly. "I refuse to let her change into one of those things."

We didn't have long to ponder it though, because a second later, a sound came from my mom.

Warily, I looked down at her. Her chest was rising and falling again, and a slight snarl was coming from her lungs. Again my lips started to tremble, and I broke down into tears. I blinked and wiped them away, knowing I needed to be strong right now. With a gulp, I forced myself to grip my machete. As I brought it towards her, she opened her eyes. They were glossed over, but they weren't black. Her face turned my way, and her hands slowly raised towards me. I let out a loud sob as the hands that had once reached for me so lovingly—that had carried and protected me when I had come into this world—now reached towards me to rip off my flesh.

I couldn't do it. I dropped my machete and wept, not flinching as her hands came closer. Mel yelled something, and then was suddenly behind me dragging me backwards. I would have let Mom claw her dull fingers through my skin. I would have let her sink her teeth into my muscles and rip them off my bone. How the hell was I supposed to cut the head off of the person who had brought me to life?

Suddenly there was noise outside. I glanced towards the door, not really caring what was out there. What, death? Bring it on. I changed my mind a second later when I saw the look on Mel's face. Outside, a group of changed things had come to the doors. I guess we hadn't noticed them in all the commotion with my mom. There was a ton of them, and I knew Mel was scared. No not scared; terrified. I looked down at my snarling monster of a mom, deciding that even though I couldn't save her, I should still try to save my best friend. And get to my dad. He still loved Mom, and I didn't think he should have to lose both of us in the same day.

With a gulp, I wiped my tears away again. I put a gentle hand on my mom's forehead.

"I'm so sorry," I whispered, then ripped my machete across her neck. I let out an involuntary cry, then used every ounce of energy I had to keep from falling apart again.

Looking away from the heart-wrenching sight, I grabbed Mel's arm and pulled her to her feet. She followed me as I dashed to the back of the store, hoping there was a way out. Thankfully there was, and it was clear of those things. I rejoiced at my idea to park around the back as we hopped into the trucks. I didn't want us both to be in a separate vehicle, but it seemed like having two military trucks was a really good idea.

We sped away and back towards the freeway like there

was no tomorrow. Well, there was no tomorrow for one of us. I grimaced as I imagined the moments when those things would break through the doors and spill into the store. Since my mom had been one of them for a short time, I hoped they would leave her alone.

I drove for as long as I could, but a few hours later I couldn't take it anymore. We had crossed into Tennessee when my mom was still with us, so I think by now we were around Nashville. As the sun started to disappear behind the horizon, I exited the freeway and headed towards some neighborhoods. I went to an area that looked secluded; hopefully there would be less changed things there. Along the way, we came across a number of them in the road. I hit every single one that I could, feeling a sick gratification as the truck collided with their rotting bodies.

A couple curved roads and turns later, I realized we were definitely in Nashville. Huge houses dotted spacious properties on either side of the road. I drove around a little more, having a feeling that there was an even nicer gated area nearby. Sure enough, we soon came to a wall and gate. It was still shut, so I hoped that meant that it was relatively untouched. I jumped out of my truck and glanced around carefully, then dashed to the gate. It was heavy. Thankfully, Mel also rushed to it and helped me pull it open. We quickly pulled our trucks through, then shut the gate. If Nick was following us, I wanted to make it look like we hadn't been this way.

We slowly rolled through the neighborhood as we tried to determine which house would be the best pick for us to stay at. Did rich people typically have house parties for New Year's, or did they go somewhere? As we moved slowly through the neighborhood, I grit my teeth as I saw bodies on the ground. They weren't normal people; they were definitely changed things. Someone had killed them.

"Mel," I whispered over the radio. "Maybe we should leave."

I think she saw the things too, because she didn't answer right away. But when she did, she tried to sound like it didn't matter. "Why? Someone did the hard work for us! Now we just get to pick which mansion we want to be ours."

"What if it's more of Nick's men?"

"What if it's not? Wouldn't it be awesome to find some other survivors?"

"Yeah, actually it would be."

"Oooh!" she squawked suddenly. "Look at that one."

I glanced to my left and right, seeing a spectacular mansion on my left. It was made of grey brick, stood three stories high, and had quite a grand entrance. A long driveway, or small road, rather, led up to the house, where it met with a circular drive. Lush greenery stood in the middle of the circle, as well as all around the house. From the circular driveway, a cobblestone path led up to a grand brick stairway, surrounded by white railing that resembled Greek pillars. Up on the third floor of the structure were three distinct balconies dotted equally across the front of the house. It looked like a beautiful castle.

"Oh yeah," I agreed.

Suddenly feeling oddly giddy, we both floored our trucks and raced each other up the long driveway. We laughed as the side of our trucks bumped into each other, feeling like we were playing bumper cars. At the circular driveway, Mel kept her pedal to the metal and peeled out as she did donuts. I laughed and parked haphazardly on the lawn, running over shrubs and pretty flowers. As I got out of the truck, I was going to joke with my mom that I knew she wanted the bedroom on the third floor with the middle balcony. Then I remembered that she wasn't there with us.

Sadness washed over me as I walked towards the front of the house. Mel got out of her truck and skipped towards me, but slowed when she saw my face. Soothingly, she draped an arm around me. I leaned my head onto her shoulder, thankful for her friendship.

"Give me a minute," I asked as we ascended the stairs and came to the front door. "I can't clear a house like this."

"Yeah," she concurred. "Take all the time you need."

But that wasn't an option, for suddenly we heard a crash inside the house. Grief was shoved to the back of my mind as we both raised our guns. Mel looked at me and I nodded, so she swung the door open. Stealthily we crept inside. Unfortunately for Mel, it was pretty dark in the house. Thanks to Mortimer's failed attempt at turning me into a changed thing, I could see just fine in the dark. I took the lead as we went room to room and cleared them. With most of the first floor cleared, we heard another crash above us. With caution, we made our way to the stairs and went up them to the second floor. Snarling reached our ears, filling me with dread. I tried not to remember my mom making that same sound.

When we heard a scream, we instantly picked up our pace. If there was a person in here, we weren't going to let them get eaten by these things. It was a little brighter up here, so Mel could see more easily than on the first floor.

She charged forward with me as we approached the room where the sounds were coming from. I dropped my rifle and slung it back over my shoulder, wondering why I'd even had it raised in the first place. It would take a bunch of bullets directly to the head to stop these things. As I pulled out my machete, I motioned for Mel to do the same. She copied me as we came to an open doorway, where another scream reached our ears.

We peered around the corner, horrified to see like ten changed things in the room. They were surrounding a barricade of some sort, which I was guessing the person was behind. I think the person saw us, because they suddenly started making a lot of noise and banging on the barricade. They were distracting the chompers so that they wouldn't see us and we'd get the drop on them. I chuckled in amusement despite myself. A smart survivor? This was awesome.

I swung my machete around in practice, then darted towards the things. In an amazingly cool move that quite surprised me, I swung it perfectly and was able to lop off three heads in the single swing. Needless to say, that caught the attention of the rest of them pretty quickly. Mel was right there with me though, and we easily took down a couple more. Now that the person wasn't horribly outnumbered and pinned down, they jumped up and helped us take the rest of the things out. Soon enough, ten rotting bodies filled the floor.

As I panted and marveled at our improved survival skills, my attention instantly went to the newcomer. I hoped he or she meant us well. Just in case, I raised my machete as the person walked towards us.

CHAPTER EIGHTEEN

The survivor walked towards us as I glanced at Mel and held my machete defensively. I hoped they meant us well, but you could never be too careful.

"Thank you for your help," the person said, extending a hand towards me. It was a man, and he was gorgeous... almost like Nick. Did only the beautiful survive the apocalypse?

"Uh you're welcome," I grunted, not trusting him. His staggering looks reminded me too much of Nick and his people. Was he one of them?

"Who are you?" Mel asked, as if reading my thoughts.

"My name is Mikael."

"Kale?" Mel frowned. "Nasty."

The man laughed, sending a melodic sound throughout the air. It made me feel safe, and seemed so very familiar. I wanted to curl up and listen to it all day.

"No, not kale. Think of it like the name Mckayla, but without the 'a' on the end."

"And you're a dude, right?"

"Mel!" I exclaimed. "You can't just ask people that!" I turned to the stranger, "I'm so sorry, she has no filter."

"That's all right," he laughed. "Yes, I am a male."

"So what were you doing here?" Mel asked.

"I likely had the same goal as you; trying to seek shelter. Unfortunately I discovered a greater number of those things within these walls than I expected."

Mel glanced over at me and raised an eyebrow. I forced myself not to laugh; I knew she was mocking the formal way he was talking.

"Well good sir," she mused, "do we thouest have your permission to take shelter within thine walls for the night?"

He looked solemnly at her for a moment, then grinned. "Of course you may. And there is no need to mock my way of speaking. Although, now that I am outside my normal surroundings, I suppose my speech could use an update."

"She didn't mean any harm," I offered, but he put his hand up.

"You saved my life; you don't have to apologize for her words."

"Well I'll apologize then," Mel said. "I didn't mean any harm."

"I know," he smiled.

I knew that she was swooning at his charming smile, so I yanked her from the room and down to the trucks.

"We need to leave," I urged. "He's weird. And last time I had a weird feeling about a guy, he turned out to be a super-old person that wanted to kill me."

"Yeah he's weird," Mel agreed. "But he seems cool... and this house is so nice."

"We need to go Mel," I said resolutely.

She sighed but conceded, so we started getting into the trucks. At that moment Mikael walked up.

"You're not leaving are you?" he asked.

"We uh..." I stammered.

"Please stay," he asked. "You know this house is safe; you already cleared it and know there is no danger within."

"Do we?" I quipped before I could stop myself.

"Yes, you do," he said sincerely.

Suddenly all my fear and distrust melted away. Something in his eyes seemed so calming and safe. I grit my jaw as I pondered staying, but it seemed Mel had experienced the same feeling. She looked at me expectantly, then proclaimed that we would be staying. I agreed numbly, unsure of whether or not it was a smart idea. Regardless of my hesitation, Mel and Mikael began unloading our things from the vehicles.

A few moments later, I shook my head and participated in the unloading. Then I suggested that we park our trucks around the back so that if anyone saw the house, they wouldn't immediately know we were there.

After that was done, Mel had a good idea to barricade the front door. Once we were inside we moved a bunch of furniture in front of it. As we worked on that, we saw Mikael coming down the stairs with a few of the bodies of the changed things. He dragged them to the back door and out to the backyard. By the time we had secured the front door, he had made several trips up and down.

I trudged up the stairs to help him, but was surprised to find the room already clear of all the bodies. Mikael came in behind me, panting slightly.

"I wanted to help," I said, turning to him.

"That's all right," he panted. "It's done."

"Well… thank you for taking them out of the house."

"No problem. I didn't want that foul presence in here with us overnight."

Chills soared down my spine as he said that. They were the good kind though; the kind you feel when you know without a doubt that you're with someone of like mind.

Without meaning to, I found myself walking towards him.

"I'm Yirah," I said, nearly gasping from my own words. I hadn't introduced myself with that name for over fifteen years.

"Nice to meet you Yirah," he said with a smile.

I wanted to shake his hand, but refrained since he had just been dragging chompers around. He saw me glance at his hands, then let out a slight laugh.

"I wrapped my hands in plastic bags from the kitchen before I touched them," he assured. "And it's definitely time for a change of clothes."

He pulled off the outer shirt he had on, revealing a sleeveless undershirt. "I'm going to change," he said, then turned and walked towards the door of the room. As he went, I saw something on his skin. It was on both shoulders, and I soon realized it was a tattoo. I could only see the backs of his shoulders, but it was apparent that the tattoo was a pretty big one that covered a large part of his back. I felt drawn to it, and again found myself walking forward.

To my shock, he turned around and smiled warmly at me. "Wait, Yirah," he whispered.

I stood there stunned as he kept walking and soon disappeared from my sight into one of the bedrooms. Musing to myself, I went downstairs and found Mel snoozing on a couch. She looked exhausted. Although I really wanted to talk with her, I decided to let her stay there. With a sigh, I figured I should boil us some water. I went to the back patio in search of somewhere to make a fire.

Sure enough, the mansion was complete with a huge covered patio that was adorned with couches, fire pits, grills, and a brick oven. I went back inside and dug through my backpack, happy when I found matches. Then I went back outside and lit a fire in the brick oven. Since it was wholly covered except for the door, it was a safe bet that nobody would see the light. Once it was lit, I went inside and grabbed a pot from the kitchen. As I was about to go to the toilet for some water, I laughed. There on my left was a bottled-water dispenser, and the bottle was full of water. I went outside and extinguished the fire, then went back to the kitchen.

Happily, I filled three cups with water and put them on a tray. I grabbed some candy and beef jerky from my backpack as well. As I was rummaging through kitchen drawers, I found a plethora of candles. I lit a couple and put them on the tray, then walked to where Mel was sleeping. I put a cup of water, some candy, and a single candle on the coffee table by her. Since she couldn't see in the dark very well, a candle would be a nice treat for her.

Next I made my way upstairs and to the room where Mikael had gone. Gingerly, I knocked on the door.

"Yeah?" he called. He sounded as though he'd been asleep.

"Sorry for waking you," I called. "I don't know how long it has been since you've had water, but I wanted to bring you some."

"Oh, thank you. That's very nice of you," he replied.

"Can I come in?"

"Yes, certainly."

I opened the door and entered the elaborate room. Sure enough, the man was in bed and tucked under the sheets.

"I'll just put it on your nightstand," I said quickly, feeling like I was intruding.

"Don't worry about it," he said, sitting up. The sheet fell from his torso, revealing ridiculously sculpted muscles. I quickly looked away and focused on what I was doing. I didn't want to be interested in him.

As soon as I set the food and drink down, he hungrily reached for it.

"Thank you for the food," he huffed as he ripped open the package and downed it in one bite. "I'm starving."

"Oh, well I have more," I said, gesturing behind me. "I can go get some of it."

"Thank you!" he professed as he looked at me eagerly.

I left the room with a small smile on my face, wondering how long it had been since he'd eaten. I went to my pack and removed a few more snacks, but then had a thought. I strode to the kitchen and opened the pantry, finding it completely stocked. I grabbed a few things from it for Mikael, then made my way back upstairs. I guess he had probably been pinned by the changed things as soon as he had gotten in the house, so he hadn't had time to raid the pantry.

When I got back to the room, I was disappointed to find him asleep. He breathed shallowly and quickly, telling me just how exhausted he was. I put the snacks down on the nightstand, then looked once more at him before I left. He was facing away from me, but his whole back was exposed. I could see the tattoo. Inching closer to him, I peered closely at it. It seemed to be a pair of wings, covering his entire back as I had suspected. It was a beautiful tattoo; the artist had truly created a masterpiece. Although it was dark, the ink added to the majesty of the wings. It looked opalescent, like a pearl.

Suddenly I didn't want to leave his side ever again. A wave of comfort and safety washed over me, imploring me to stay next to him for the night even if I had to sleep on the floor. I shook my head at myself, knowing that was a stupid idea. First of all, I couldn't leave Mel downstairs. Second, how much of a creeper would I be to sleep on the floor in his room?

I sighed and left, heading downstairs. Before I settled in for the night, I made sure all the doors were secure and that all the shutters were closed. If there was anything out there, I didn't want them being able to either get or see inside of the house. With that done, I tiredly sunk into a sofa across from Mel and fell asleep.

Irony is a funny thing. When I awoke in the morning, I saw Mikael's face hovering over me. As I woke up more, I groggily looked around and saw that he was sitting on the coffee table staring at me. Now who was the creeper? I widened my eyes a couple times and sat up, trying not to look as gross as I felt. Who wants to be stared at first thing in the morning?

"Good morning," he greeted with a smile. He smelled wonderful.

"Morning," I mumbled, hoping he wasn't close enough to smell my morning breath.

"I found a stream nearby and hauled some water back here. I plugged up a couple bathtubs and sinks and poured the water in, so you're free to bathe and brush your teeth."

"No way!" I cheered.

"Absolutely. Mel is in one of the second-floor bathrooms. I filled up the third-floor tub as well; the one in the middle bedroom."

I looked at him in awe, wondering if he somehow knew that my mom would have loved that room. Of course there was no way he could know; that was a silly thought. All the same, I was awed by his kindness.

"Thank you so much!" I cried, leaping up and throwing my arms around him. Feeling the warmth of his body underneath mine gave me the most unexpected sensation. Again I felt an overwhelming sense of safety, as well as love. Pure love and strength was emanating from this guy. I pulled away from the hug in tears, baffled by my bizarre and sudden feelings. What was stranger, though, was the way he responded. He put one of his hands over mine, then brushed the tears off my cheek.

"It's okay," he assured with a smile as if he had expected my reaction. "You should get upstairs to your bath though, Mel will soon be done with hers."

I nodded and stumbled up the stairs, wondering what in the world was going on. Nick had made me feel crazy things, but nothing like that. I had never broken into tears just by hugging him.

When I reached the exquisite third-floor bedroom, I was awed by its grandeur. All the rooms were nice, but this must have been the master. It was huge and ornate, with elegant furniture and décor. I walked around the room for a minute, examining its luxuries. Stopping at the closet, I threw open the door. My jaw dropped as I went inside, marveling at all the fine attire and enormous closet. Eagerly, I sorted through some of the clothes and found some that I thought would both fit me and be practical.

I threw them onto the bed, then strode to the marble bathroom and walked through its double-door entryway. I ran my hand over the expensive counters, laughing at the fact that I had never been anywhere as nice in my normal life as I had been in the couple months since the world had ended.

I dug through the bathroom cabinets, happy when I found what I was looking for. I ripped open the packaging, pulling a fresh toothbrush from it. Then I found a new tube of toothpaste and happily set about scrubbing my pearly whites. I leisurely strode around the room as I did so, even walking out to the balcony. From way up here I could see for miles. I eyed our immediate surroundings, glad to see that only a couple changed things were meandering in the streets. A couple minutes later, I strode back to the bathroom and rinsed out my toothpaste. With a fresh mouth, I shed my clothes and sunk into the chilly bath.

Although it took a couple moments to adjust to the coldness, I soon relaxed and enjoyed the luxury. When we'd been with Nick, we were almost able to live in ignorance of what was going on in the world. We had electricity, plenty of food, and most of the amenities we were used to in our normal lives. But now, being out on the road and in the thick of things, I realized what the new reality was. Our world had changed. Even if all of this ended tomorrow, would we go back to our normal lives? Would we be expected just to go back to school and work like this had never happened? What about all the losses? I sighed sadly as I thought of my mom. I really missed her. It had only been one night, but it felt like I hadn't seen her in years.

I soon found myself sobbing like a child. I cried and cried, also wailing and calling out her name. Such pain coursed through my heart that it felt like it was going to explode. The things that had happened seemed too horrific to be real, but they had been. If they hadn't been, she'd still be with us. I cursed Nick and his men for bringing this plague to humanity and ripping families apart like this. What did they hope to achieve from all of it?

There was a knock on my door, making me calm down. With several sniffles, I stood from my bath and threw on a thick robe. I went over to the door, cracking it open.

"Hi," Mikael said gently. "Are you okay?"

"I'm fine," I muttered.

"Do you want to talk?"

I glared at him for a moment, trying to decide if he was serious. Most men didn't genuinely offer to talk. "Only if you really mean that. If it's an empty gesture, forget it."

"Of course I mean it."

I sighed and opened the door, letting him in. I then walked to the balcony, slumping down onto an armchair that sat on it. As I stared at the ground, I saw something between the two chairs. I picked it up, seeing that it was a bottle of whiskey. As I raised it to my lips, Mikael came over and took it from my hands.

"Excuse me?" I growled.

"You don't need that."

"I don't need someone telling me what to do, that's for sure."

"Do you really want to be drunk right now?" he asked, gesturing to the ground below us. I knew he was reminding me that anything could happen and we could find ourselves in a dangerous situation at any moment.

"No I suppose not," I muttered.

"Did you lose someone?" he asked softly.

"Yeah."

"Who?"

"My mom."

"I'm so sorry to hear that," he breathed, and I sensed that his entire heart was in that statement. I looked up, surprised to see as much pain his eyes as there was in mine.

"Why do you care so much?" I asked reproachfully.

"I uh, I'm sorry," he said, darting his eyes away from mine. "I have an uncanny ability to relate with people; to feel their pain as my own. It freaks them out many times and sometimes makes them skeptical and untrusting of me. That hurts though, because I just want to help."

"You have helped," I offered, wanting to make him feel better. "Thank you for the water, it was wonderful to take a bath again."

"How long has it been since your last one?" he chuckled. "You didn't look that crusty."

I laughed out loud at his word choice. "Crusty, huh? Yeah it hasn't been that long; only a couple days actually."

"Wow, you're lucky," he remarked. "How did you accomplish that?"

Something in his tone sounded faked. I looked at him as I jumped up in alarm. "Why do I get the feeling you already know the answer to that question?" I demanded.

Shockingly, he didn't deny it. Instead, he stood as well and looked sincerely at me. "I am on your side, Yirah."

"Yeah, how do I know that?"

"Let's go downstairs and include Mel in this conversation so I don't have to re-explain everything."

"No!" I barked. "You're not going anywhere near her until you explain this to me!"

"Please reconsider that," he urged.

I dipped my eyebrows at him, scowling. Had I been wrong in calling him a friend, too? Suddenly the sound of a motor came to my ears and my gaze darted to the road. I sharply inhaled as I saw five trucks exiting the freeway. All my fury and fear channeled towards Mikael.

"Did you lead them here?" I thundered, wishing I had my weapons on me.

"Absolutely not!" he replied. "Go get dressed; we need to leave as soon as possible. I'll tell Mel to pack up."

I bared my teeth at him, but then rushed into the room. He darted downstairs as I rapidly pulled on the clean clothes I had found. I grabbed the rest of the clothes, then ran down to the first floor. There I found Mikael and Mel making an escape plan.

"He's not coming with us!" I hollered as I ran to my pack and shoved the clothes into it.

"What?" Mel scoffed.

"He knows where we came from."

Mel recoiled and backed away from him, the pain of betrayal in her eyes. "Is that true?"

"Yes, but it's not in the way that you think."

"Yeah, how's that?" I growled, grabbing my machete and marching towards him.

"I'm on your side!" he roared, suddenly reminding me that he was way stronger than me.

"Maybe he's like Faulk," Mel breathed. I could tell she really wanted to trust him.

"I am *nothing* like Faulk," he growled, much to our surprise.

"Faulk helped us escape from Nick," she objected.

"Did he?" the man mused. "Well that's interesting. And Nick, huh? That's what he calls himself?"

"We know his real name," I growled.

He raised an eyebrow. "Do you know how to wield a true name?"

"Uh… no, but I'll find out your true name too if you're one of them."

"I am not one of them, I assure you."

"Then what are you?"

"We don't have time to stand here and argue," he protested.

"Addie, maybe you should let him come with us."

"So he can lead Nick to us again? No way!"

"I didn't lead him to you!" he thundered, making us both shudder yet also feel inexplicably safe. I gaped at him, baffled by the power he seemed to possess. "Now get to the truck, both of you!"

"T-truck?" I stammered, picking up my bags and doing as he said. "Singular?"

"You two are taking one and I will take the other to lead them away."

"Will we see you again?" Mel inquired, seeming to be afraid of the answer.

"Yes, you certainly will," he assured, and I heard her sigh in relief.

We all dashed towards the front door, but before we could get to it, it opened. In filed a dozen men wearing all black, with guns raised to their shoulders. Gas masks covered all of their faces, making me cringe.

Upon seeing them, Mikael protectively shoved me and Mel behind him. I trembled and glanced at my friend, seeing the same fear in her eyes as was probably in my own. Without a word, we both reached a hand towards each other and locked them together. Moments later, Major Ghost strode through the doorway. His face was covered in a smug expression, and he didn't even look up at us as he patted one of his men on the back. When he did look up though, his arrogance disappeared instantly.

"Y-you!" he stammered at Mikael as he cowered back in fear. "How did you get here?"

"I warned all of you as to what would happen if you tried this," he replied, sounding awesomely powerful. His strong voice seemed to reverberate off all the walls and echo through our bones.

Major Ghost snarled and snapped his fingers, causing all his men to raise their guns. Mel and I whimpered, but our protector didn't even flinch.

"You don't want to do that," he cautioned.

"Why not?" Ghost taunted, sounding quite evil. I can't say I've ever used that word to describe somebody, but in that moment, I felt pure evil radiating off of him. Suddenly I realized what he was. What all of the men surrounding us were.

"Oh my gosh," I panted, collapsing to my knees.

Ghost's men thought I was retaliating, and suddenly they fired on us. Bullets flew at us from every which direction, making me and Mel shriek in fear. Suddenly there was a massive pressure in the air, then silence. Seconds later, a deafening explosion blasted all around us. We covered our heads and kept screaming, having no clue what was happening or if we would live. Moments later, all the commotion was over.

Cautiously, we raised our heads and looked around. The whole room was blackened and smoldering, as if a great fire had ripped through it. All the men were dead; their bodies burnt to a crisp. Ghost was dead too; I could see his smoking body on the ground. Where we stood was completely untouched. All three of us were fine.

"What the hell was that!" Mel screamed, her voice raw with emotion. It wavered as she yelled, telling us all how terrified she was.

"We need to leave," Mikael urged, starting to walk towards the door.

"What was—" Mel sobbed, stumbling forward.

I put her arm around my neck and helped her out the door. "It's okay Mel; we're okay. We're safe now."

"Aw; too bad that isn't true."

I gasped and looked up, horrified to see Nick standing in front of us. He was leisurely leaning against the hood of our truck.

"That was quite a show," he chuckled, nodding towards the house.

"Do you not even care that your own men are dead?" I hissed.

"Oh they'll be back," he said with a wave of his hand.

I gulped, remembering what I had realized just before the explosion. His 'men' would be back, because they weren't men. They were beings, like Faulk had said. Evil beings that could inhabit bodies and turn eyes black. Evil beings that could turn into beautiful human forms. They were demons.

Fearfully, I turned my gaze to the man who had protected us. "Mikael?" I whispered. Was he one too?

"Mikael?" Nick mocked with a laugh. "You changed

your name just slightly? We still know it's you, Michael. What are you doing on this plane? Did you get demoted?"

I wheezed, looking Mikael up and down. Michael was his real name? Like... the archangel Michael?

"I have not been demoted, I assure you," he thundered, once again sending his powerful voice out from his body like a force field. "I am here to protect those whom you hunt. If you know who I am, then you also know that you are no match for me."

I grinned despite myself, taking pleasure in seeing Nick belittled.

"We'll see about that," he snorted.

"Be gone Necromarthe," Mikael ordered.

"About that... I would be, but your buddy upstairs made a deal."

"What?" the archangel glowered. "Explain yourself."

"While you were down here blowing things up, my leader and yours made a deal. I get Yirah. You can keep the friend."

"You speak lies, deceiver!"

"If that were the case, I would've had to leave when you told me to, wouldn't I?"

I saw Mikael's powerful jaw clench. Fear wrapped its sickening tendrils around me. In watching his expression, I knew Nick spoke the truth.

"No," I whimpered, clinging to Mikael. "Don't let him take me!"

"His words are true; I have been told such just now."

"Why?" I moaned, breaking into tears. "Why is he letting this happen?"

"Necromarthe, take your human."

As Nick strode towards us, Mikael looked sincerely into my eyes. "Be strong Yirah. This deal would not have been made if it wasn't to your benefit."

"How is this to my benefit?" I screamed as I felt Nick's hands on me. I shrieked and violently fought him with all my might. I heard Mel screaming too, but Mikael held tightly to her. "No!" I despaired, wrenching myself free. I ran, but Nick caught me almost instantly. "NO!!!" I roared over and over.

Nick dragged me to the truck, then slammed me into the side of it. My face smashed against the metal as tears streamed down my face. With one hand, Nick pinned both of my hands. With the other, he pulled something from his vest. A second later, I felt a needle sink into my neck.

As my world went black, I felt myself collapse into the arms of a demon.

.

CHAPTER NINETEEN

My life was a failure.

I had failed to protect Mel. I had failed to save my mom. I had failed to get to my dad. I had failed to evade my sick captor. Everything I had set out to do had failed. And now, I was going to pay the price of my failure. Endless torture and misery were undoubtedly in my immediate future, and I knew that any cries to God were going to go unheard. He had brokered this deal, after all. I had been wrong to not blame him for my mom's death. He probably made that happen too, just like my capture.

As I emerged from the drugged state that Nick—no, Necromarthe—had put me into, I started to regain my bearings. I could feel movement below me; we must be in a vehicle. I moved slightly, sensing that my hands were tied behind me. Groggily, I opened my eyes. I was in the cargo space of one of the trucks. With great effort, I turned my head towards the front of the vehicle. There was only one other person in it with me, and he was in the driver's seat. Necromarthe.

With a growl, I worked my hands down around my feet, bringing them in front of me. Then I rolled onto my stomach to clamber to my knees. To my immense surprise, I saw my cross necklace dangling from my neck. That made me furious. How had it gotten back on me? Although I had grabbed it out of the pool of my mom's blood, I hadn't put it back on. Necromarthe must have found it in my pocket and put it on to taunt me. It wouldn't work though; his cruelty just fueled my rage. Once I was on my knees, I carefully moved into a kneeling position. When I felt like I was steady and strong enough, I suddenly lunged towards the man driving.

With a roar, I threw my bound hands around his neck. I yanked backwards with all my might, hoping to choke him. My mind flashed back to when I had tried this before with the guy who had tortured me, but I was determined for it to work this time. Seconds later, I realized it didn't matter if I choked him or not, because he was so distracted by my attack that he lost control of the truck. In his thrashing, his knee hit the steering wheel and jerked us sideways. The truck spun sideways, then flipped over. I screamed as I hit the ceiling, then fell back to the seat, then back to the ceiling. We rolled over and over, off the freeway and down to the ground below. I think we had been on an overpass.

We landed with a tremendous crash, which bent the metal of the truck around me. Somewhere in my body there was a horrendous pain; something sharp had stabbed through me. I wearily glanced down, seeing a huge piece of metal jutting out of my stomach. I whimpered weakly, then lay my head back down. The truck was crushed around me and I was impaled.

Seconds later, a trickling sound reached my ears. At first I thought it was gas leaking, then I realized it was my own blood dripping out of my body and onto the surface below. I groaned in agony, too weak to scream or care. My death was here; there was no way I could survive this. Surprisingly, I sighed happily. I might be at death's door, but at least I was free from the clutches of a demon. Gingerly, I closed my eyes and said a prayer. I asked God to forgive me for being mad at him. I asked him to protect Mel, and to defeat the evil that was on the earth. Then I blacked out.

Sometime later, I opened my eyes. I expected to see the pearly gates, but instead I was still in the truck. I was still in the back, tied up. Attacking Nick had just been a drug-induced dream. I groaned to myself, wishing it had actually happened. I'd rather be dead than with this monster.

Like the dream, I pulled my hands down around my feet and to the front of me. The demon must have heard me moving, because he looked back and smiled.

"Morning sunshine."

"Shut up," I mumbled, rubbing my aching head.

"You can sit up front with me if you want," he invited.

"I'd rather die."

"Oh sweet thing, there's a time for that, but it's not yet."

I grimaced at his words, appalled by his cruelty. I guess I shouldn't be surprised, I mean, he was literally from the depths of hell. Still, it was hard to accept that someone could be so blatant about their foul intentions for you.

"I'm sorry I drugged you," he called, sounding sincere. "I knew there was no other way I'd get you in here though."

"Uh huh," I agreed, crawling towards the back of the truck. I gripped the release latch to open it, but it didn't do anything. With a grunt, I moved towards the passenger doors for the backseats. They wouldn't open either.

"Those aren't going to open," Necromarthe stated cheerfully. "They're locked from the outside. Welded shut, actually. The only door that will open is mine." He looked back and winked at me. "If you want out, you better crawl into my lap."

I threw a string of curse words at him, which made me cringe. I didn't want to sink to his level and needed to control my anger. Becoming as hateful and foul as him would just bring him more satisfaction.

He laughed in reply to what I said, sounding thrilled by it. With a gulp, I decided to take a different approach. Stay calm, play nice, and go along with whatever he said until I saw a chance to escape. That was a good plan, right?

With a deep breath first, I made my way to the front of the truck and climbed into the front passenger's seat. The gear in the center console had been ripped out, so I could see Necromarthe as easily as if we had been in a normal car. He glanced over at me with a warm smile.

"It was nice of you to join me," he beamed. "Buckle up; I wouldn't want you getting hurt if we crashed." He stared at me knowingly, making me squint at him. Did he know about my dream?

Forcing myself to adhere to my plan, I weakly reached for the seatbelt and buckled it. "There," I said gravely.

"Thank you," he swooned, reaching over and putting his hand on mine.

I flinched, but made myself put my hand back underneath his. I saw him grin out of the corner of his mouth.

"You know you're special to me, right?" he asked, looking at me again.

"Oh yeah? Why's that?"

"Because you are, Eve."

"Please stop calling me that."

"I suppose I can. I lied to you about why I came up with that name for you anyway."

"Big surprise," I seethed.

"Want to know what it really means?"

"No."

"Okay, I'll tell you." He gripped my hand tighter. "I told you it was because Eve means life, and that you were a survivor. You kept life with your mom and Mel." He laughed cruelly. "That was wrong anyway; I see you got your mom killed."

"No I didn't," I objected angrily, yanking my hand away from his.

"Anyway, you're not a life bringer. The reason I called you that is the reason you first said when I told you the name. Do you remember what it was?" When I didn't answer, he said, "Because Eve was responsible for the downfall of humanity. She was created as the pinnacle of creation; the most beautiful and wonderful thing God created. And then she let everyone down—her creator, her husband, and the entire human race. She is the reason humanity crumbled, and so will you be."

"What?" I scoffed, looking at him with disgust. "How can I possibly be the downfall of humanity? You and your demented kind started all this."

"And you, Yirah, could have stopped all this. If your faith had been stronger to begin with, you could have risen above all this and brought mankind back from it."

I looked at him in disbelief, my jaw hanging open.

"You were chosen long before you were born to be the savior in this apocalypse, so to speak. You noticed weird things happening from the very beginning of this. Hell, you saw weird things your whole life. Instead of accepting and studying them, you brushed them aside and believed the lies. I'll admit we hit you pretty hard with doubtful thoughts, but if you had prayed even just a little more every day, or gone to church and been in the presence of God more often, you would have believed. You would have been ready when we launched our attack."

His tone changed, and I could see his chest rising and falling more now. He was getting mad. "But, like all you pathetic humans, you were a fool and rejected God. You rejected the being who created and loved you greatly for no damn reason. He created us first, and we were wholly loyal to him. But that wasn't enough, was it? He had to create you pieces of shit and love you more. We were completely devoted to him while your kind scorns him every single day! You think you're so wise and all-knowing, yet in your arrogance you repeatedly reject the being who loves you most and only wants good things for you." He growled and looked at me hatefully, baring his teeth as he thundered, "You are all such fools! Every single one of you deserves the misery that you bring upon yourself!"

I cowered back from him, pressing myself against the door. After those words, he didn't say anything more. He fumed to himself as he drove, gripping the steering wheel with white knuckles. I turned towards the window and shrunk down in my seat, hoping not to attract any further attention from him.

As I watched towns and fields pass by the window, I thought about what he had said. I felt a sense of... shame? Embarrassment? Deep in my heart, I knew he was speaking the truth. We had been given everything by our creator, and yet most of us chose daily to throw it away.

Unconsciously, my left hand went up to my necklace. As I gripped it, I was grateful for its presence. It was only an item; it didn't have spiritual powers, but its presence around my neck made me feel better. So many times the only sense we could detect God with was our feelings, and oftentimes even that failed us. Having something I could touch to remind me of his existence was nice. I smiled to myself, glad for however it had ended up back around my neck.

After quite a while in silence, Nick pulled off the freeway. He stopped in front of a restaurant, then got out of the truck. He offered a hand to me, which I gingerly took to help me climb out his door. As I stepped onto the ground, I glanced around wearily. Chompers were all around us. They started to stagger our way, but Nick just grabbed my arm and yanked me towards the front door of the restaurant. He marched through the group of things, astounding me with their reactions. When he got close to any of them, they recoiled and backed away. I gulped as we made our way into the building, wondering how I should feel about it. He could keep me safe from changed things, but he fully intended to kill me himself.

As we went, I suddenly recalled back when this had all happened. That day when we were in the toy store... had he not been attacked by a chomper? With a scowl, I realized it had probably been a fake attack. It had probably been orchestrated for Mel and me, to ensure that we had no idea who he really was. I glowered at him, hating him even more.

We reached the inside of the building, causing the electricity to suddenly flicker on.

"If you need to use the restroom, go now," he ordered as he strode towards the kitchen.

Hesitantly I walked to the bathroom, still baffled by

the fact that Nick's presence could turn electricity back on. As I turned the corner to the hallway, I was suddenly face-to-face with a changed thing. I screamed and lunged backwards, but it had already grabbed onto me. I stumbled and fell to the floor with the thing falling on top of me. I shrieked as it viciously chomped its jaw at me, eager to rip my face off.

All of the sudden its head exploded. I cried in disgust as blood and brain flew all over my face. Frantically I shoved the body off of me and clambered away from it. A strong pair of hands lifted me from the floor and carried me towards the bathroom. Nick sat me on the counter and holstered his gun, then wet some paper towels as I sat there shaking. Tenderly, he brought them to my face and wiped the blood off of it. He added a tad of soap and scrubbed some more, making me feel like I was truly rid of that thing's filth. A few minutes later, he told me to use the restroom, then left the room.

I did as he said, then went to the sink to wash my hands. To my surprise, he came in carrying clean clothes. As he left the room again, I yanked off my bloody clothes and put on the clean ones. I hated the outfit though; it was the black uniform of Nick's men. As I turned to leave, I caught a glance of myself in the mirror. The person staring back at me didn't look very familiar. I guess I hadn't used the mirror much when we were staying in DC, because I looked way different than when all this had started. I was never super girly, but now I looked tough and… determined?

The line between my lips had usually been curled up in a smile, but now it was arced downward. My eyes looked hardened; not as compassionate as they had once been. I looked like a soldier. What kind of soldier, I still wasn't sure, but I knew conflict was in my future. If what the demon had said was true, then I was destined to do something big in this bizarre new world.

I chuckled to myself, wondering if my enemy knew that he had inspired me. He shouldn't have spewed all that information at me; it had just made me stronger. How had he said it… if my faith had been stronger, I would have been ready for this? Then I would work on my faith; every second of every day I would strengthen it. I would look for lessons in every situation and try to obtain wisdom from every awful thing that happened.

That started right now, with this situation. Mikael, or Michael, had said this deal had been made for my benefit. My spirits dared to soar as I realized what that benefit was. Dare I think it…? Was it to make me aware of my purpose and strengthen me for the coming war? A gentle tug on my heart seemed to answered yes, making me suddenly brim with tears. A sense of purpose unlike anything I'd ever felt surged through me. Suddenly I knew what I was put on this earth to do. I felt like I could fly. I knew I wasn't invincible, but I sure would start acting like it. If I was here for a divine purpose, planted in the midst of an evil war, then I would fight with all my might. Evil may have started all of this, but I would make sure that good ended it.

I marched to the door and yanked it open, shocked to see Necromarthe standing there. He looked surprised by the look on my face, and for a second, fearful. However, he looked me up and down once, then gripped my arm and dragged me back to the truck. I climbed back into it, ignoring the fact that he was staring at my backside. Nothing he could do would deter me, and no harm he inflicted on my body would diminish my spirit.

We sped out of the parking lot and back to the road. Interestingly, we didn't go back to the highway. He directed us towards the city, where we drove to a towering building. He dragged me inside the skyscraper, which hummed to life as soon as we entered. We marched towards the elevators, then entered them. I looked over at him, wondering what he was up to.

"Where are we going?" I asked.

He didn't say anything. His demeanor had dramatically changed at the same time mine had, so I figured he knew I'd had a revelation.

"Whatever sourpuss," I laughed, thinking of all the popular memes of a crabby cat.

The elevator dinged and opened, revealing that we were on the roof. As we exited the elevator, I heard the sound of a helicopter. I gawked as it came our way, then landed on the helipad in front of us. Necromarthe dragged me towards it. Moments later we reached it and I was shoved inside, belted in, and then handcuffed to my seat. I glowered at the pilot and co-pilot, wondering if they were demons too. How come I couldn't sense it? I used to be able to feel evil around me.

Necromarthe got in and sat beside me, belting himself in. He gave the pilot a thumbs up, so we took off. As we flew, I gasped at the sights below. Many cities and small towns that we passed over looked annihilated, like someone had bombed the crap out of them. My mind recollected how often the ground had shaken since all of this started, and finally it made sense. The rumbling hadn't been an earthquake or any work of nature, it had been bombs. That also explained all the smoke I had seen off in the distance. I eyed Nick, wondering if it was his group that had been dropping them. Killing off the monsters they had created didn't seem very productive to their sick cause. If it hadn't been them though, did that mean there was somebody else out there fighting back? Excitement at the possibility danced in my chest, and I felt even more hopeful about winning this war.

The man to my left saw me look his way, and I guess he thought it was a good opportunity to start talking to me. He leaned his evil body against mine, making me shudder in the worst way possible. We had headsets on to drown out the deafening sound of the helicopter, but he slipped mine off. Leaning closely to my ear, he whispered chilling words to me.

"Where are we going, you asked? We are going to get your father, of course. You didn't really think I'd forgotten about him, did you?"

"No!" I gushed, looking pleadingly at him. "You have me! Isn't that enough?"

"No way," he smiled, running a finger down my face. "We need him. Don't worry; no harm will come to him unless he refuses to cooperate."

"He'll never help you," I spat.

"Oh I think he will, especially if you beg him to."

"Why in the world would I do that?"

"Because if you don't, I'll torture you."

"I still won't help you."

"That's what they all say before the pain starts."

My lip trembled and I looked away. A moment later, I

turned back to him. "What in the world do you need his help with anyway?"

"Rebuilding."

"I thought you wanted to destroy us."

"No, just those of you who love our God. See, we made a wager with him that in the face of catastrophe, his precious little sheep would turn from him faster than the blink of an eye. And they pretty much have. Before starting this, we recruited some of the smartest minds from around the world to help us rebuild. Engineers, scientists, doctors, scholars, politicians, teachers, and so on.

"What do they have in common? At one point in their lives they all used to believe in God, and now they don't. After the trials and hardships they've faced in life, they've abandoned all belief in a loving father-like god. Who can blame them? That's what most of you pathetic creatures do when things get hard. Blame God for it, then ditch your belief in him.

"Anyway, these wonderful non-believers are going to lead the new world. The rest of the survivors will turn from God as well; they have already started to. The only catch is *you*. I have a feeling that tearing down your faith will be more of a challenge. To win the wager, we have to turn every heart against him. So you see, that's why you must suffer like no other."

I shuddered from his words and stared out the helicopter. Fear wrapped around my being, but I fought not to let him see it. I was determined to stay strong and find a way out of this. However, I was a bit dismayed to hear that they had made a wager with God. Really? Were we just little playthings to him that he could make bets on? I recalled the story of Job with a sinking feeling in my gut. Yup, he sure would make bets on us and let us suffer unbelievably just for fun. Maybe I was on my own and just needed to look out for myself.

Not soon enough, the helicopter landed. Rather than the skyscraper we had taken off from, we touched down in what looked like a farm field. To my left was a barn and small house, and to my right was a forest.

A forest. If I could make it there, maybe I could lose these things. I looked away from it as someone came to unlock my handcuffs. I groaned as I stepped from the helicopter; my whole body was stiff and my back ached. I hobbled towards the house, per the man's lead. Inside, I was taken to a quaint bedroom. They shut the door behind me and then locked it. I sighed and sat down on the bed, rubbing my wrists that had been freed from their handcuffs.

In the silence of the room, I carefully listened to the chatter that was going on outside in the hall. I heard a couple men talking; one of them said we were only a few miles from San Antonio. I gasped, suddenly more determined than ever to escape. Stealthily, I walked to the window and pulled back the curtain. My room faced the forest. It was a good half mile away, but there was no way I wasn't going to at least try to make a run for it when the time was right. Gingerly, I tried to open the window, baffled when it actually opened. I guess the guys—demons, rather—had just stopped here along the way. For some reason I had been thinking it was a safe house or something.

With that in mind, I went back to the bed to sit down and think. I hadn't seen anyone else around when we got here, and if this was just a stop along the way, then there were probably just the three men from the helicopter in the house with me. That meant that if I figured out where they all were, I could determine if it was safe to escape. I turned my attention back to the conversation outside my room, knowing that two of the men were nearby. But where was Necromarthe? He had gone into the house first, and I hadn't heard him since.

My question was soon answered when my door opened and he walked in. I gulped as he strode towards me, hoping he didn't have anything too horrible planned for me yet. When I eyed his face, I was surprised by the lack of malice. He offered me his hand, which I almost took. Instead though, I just stared at him.

"Would you like dinner?" he asked.

"Sure," I replied apathetically.

"You have to convince me."

I scowled and looked up at him, shocked to see him smiling charmingly. "What are you smiling about?"

"Just remembering all the nice evenings we had together."

"Yeah, which were all a lie."

"That's not true love," he breathed, kneeling down in front of me. He took my hands in his as he gazed up at me. "You are such a beautiful and smart woman. You are a prime example of what makes us angels jealous of humans."

"Fallen angels," I corrected. "Demons."

He ignored my words and carried on. "We watch as human men defile you women and take your beauty for granted, both exploiting it and selfishly devouring it."

"Yeah men suck," I agreed. "Especially the evil kind," I growled, trying to yank my hands away from his.

He held them tightly though, not letting them free. His eyes gazed into mine, seeming to pierce my soul. I looked away uncomfortably. He leaned forward, making me cringe. I felt his lips brush my cheek, planting a kiss on it. Then he leaned back and stood, pulling me with him.

"I know you're hungry; let us dine together."

I went with him to the dining room, where platters of food sat. I looked at them in confusion, wondering where they had come from.

"Sit," Necromarthe instructed, standing behind a chair that he gestured to.

Hesitantly, I sat down and then he pushed the chair in. He went to his own chair, then started scooping out food.

"Where did this come from?" I asked.

"It is courtesy of the owners of this house."

I frowned and looked around, noticing blood on the tablecloth. I groaned as I understood what he meant. The people who lived here had just sat down for dinner when we arrived. Necromarthe had barged inside and killed them.

"I can't eat this," I gagged, standing from my chair and dashing into the kitchen.

I wish I hadn't. I screeched as I rounded the corner, seeing three bodies on the floor. They were practically shredded; there was blood and flesh everywhere. My hand shot to my mouth, and suddenly I turned to the sink, heaving up whatever was in my stomach. As I did so, I felt his hands clasp my shoulders. I wanted to scream at him, but I couldn't stop throwing up.

"Shhh," he soothed, patting my head and making my whole body reel.

Finally I stopped barfing, but I was so weakened by it

that my shaking legs gave out and I slid toward the floor. I groaned miserably as the puddles of blood and chunks of flesh came back into my sight. Necromarthe knelt down beside me, gently pulling my hair out of my face.

"Shhh," he soothed again. "Don't worry darling, they were dead almost instantly."

"Did you…" I wheezed, unable to complete my sentence.

"Of course. That was me, in my true form. Darling," he said, tilting my jaw towards me so I'd look into his eyes. "I need you to know what I can do. If you cross me or try to escape, I won't hesitate in doing that to your dad."

My jaw trembled, and I found myself weeping at the thought. The disgusting being in front of me picked me up and carried me back to my room, gently setting me on the bed. He pulled the covers back and tucked me in, then kissed my sweaty forehead.

"Goodnight my angel," he whispered, then left the room.

I hate to admit it, but I broke down in tears yet again. I wept and wailed like I had when my mom died. Reality was too much to bear. I was in the clutches of a sadistic monster, and if I tried defying him he would slaughter the one parent I had left. I knew I should be praying, but I couldn't bring myself to do it. What was the point? He was the one who had struck the deal to let me go with Necromarthe, so what was the point of crying out to him?

Much later, I wore myself out and exhaustedly sunk into a deep sleep. I would have predicted nightmares in my future, but instead I had the most marvelous dream. I was atop a beautiful mountain at sunset. I was the only human up there, and had the majesty of the place completely to myself. Beautiful scenery stretched as far as the eye could see, and glorious hues of red, purple, and orange were strewn across the sky. In front of me, a breathtaking sunset sat as the provider of all the glorious lights.

Down the mountain on my right was a shore of the ocean. Splendid waves crashed against the beach and seagulls cawed in the air. Wildlife dotted the fields down in front of me; I could see an adorable family of deer bounding across the land. I smiled happily, gazing at all the beauty. Nothing tangible happened, but I suddenly felt an overwhelming sense of peace. I soaked in the serenity and harmony around me, feeling incredibly blessed to witness it. I lay down and stared up into the colorful sky, hoping this would last forever.

But at that moment, I woke up. I woke up from the most wonderful dream I'd ever had and was dropped back into reality. I groaned as I rolled onto my side, not wanting to face my life. My mom was dead. Mel and I had the great fortune to happen upon an angel—an archangel, no less— and then I got ripped away from them. Now the demented, evil angels were on their way to my dad to con him into helping them shut God out of the world. They were going to use me to get his help, and then kill me… and I was just lying there, like an idiot.

I bolted upright with sudden realization. I was being weak. Hadn't I told myself in that restaurant bathroom that I was going to be strong and build my faith? Yet, when the very first test came my way, I failed miserably. No, I shook my head, that's not who I wanted to be. Eagerly, I said a prayer asking for forgiveness for having been so stupid and for pushing him away, yet again. When was I going to learn not to blame him? I also asked for the courage and strength to do what needed to be done.

After saying amen, I quietly stood from the bed. I crept over to the window as my pulse raced. Fear coursed through me, but I pushed it deep down inside. Carefully I pulled back the curtain, seeing nothing outside the window. The moon was nearly full, illuminating the fields beyond the house. My eyes scanned them all the way to the forest. There were a few changed things ambling about, but nothing I couldn't handle.

Ever so carefully, I backed away from the window and poked around the room. I was looking for a weapon of any sort. Something told me to look in the bottom drawer of the dresser, underneath all the clothes. There, I found a machete exactly like the one I had been using before Necromarthe had taken me. A grin covered my mouth from ear to ear as I looked skyward.

"Thank you," I whispered with all my heart.

I quietly went back to the window. My heart thudded in my chest as I carefully slid it open, desperately hoping it wouldn't make an awful screech like many windows did. To my delight, it slid open without a problem.

A sudden noise in the hall nearly stopped my heart. I glanced towards my door, trying to decide if I should pretend to be asleep or jump out the window. Deciding on the first choice, I flung the curtains closed and leapt into bed, sliding the machete underneath it.

My door creaked open. I inhaled fearfully as someone walked inside; I think it was one of the other demons. The door shut behind him, making me gulp again. What was he going to do? He arrogantly strode towards me, sitting on the edge of my bed. I tried to pretend I was asleep, but it was really hard with him so close.

"So you're the human Necromarthe is all worked up about," he mused, leaning over me.

I was lying on my back, so he planted a hand on the bed on either side of me. I felt my throat constricting, making it hard to breathe. He leaned closer to me, allowing me to smell his scent. To my surprise, it smelled wonderful. Alluring, even. Of course it does, a voice in my head told me. That's how evil gets a foothold in your life; it disguises itself as everything you've ever wanted.

Slowly, as if I was just waking up, I opened my eyes. The perfect man's face hovering over me smiled.

"I'm glad you woke up," he grinned. "It wouldn't have been as fun if you were asleep."

He winked at me, then brought his mouth towards mine. At the last second, I jerked myself sideways, reaching for the machete under the bed. Before he could even protest, I gripped his hair and sliced the blade through his neck.

I tried with everything in me not to cry out or make a sound as I wormed my way out from under his corpse. Hurriedly I went back to the window, then slipped out it. With a deep breath, I started my mad dash for the forest. I ran with all my might, not bothering to pace myself. The sooner I could get away from that house, the better.

Suddenly I saw that there were way more changed things in the field than I had thought. They seemed to be rising from the ground. I groaned as I ran, realizing that this was Necromarthe's insurance policy against me fleeing.

He had littered the field with changed things, hoping they would deter me. No way. I flew past them, only beheading the ones that I couldn't slip by.

Halfway to the forest, I heard shouts behind me at the farmhouse. A car engine roared to life, and lights flooded the field. I pressed myself to run harder, crying out determinedly. Any chomper that crossed my path was cut down immediately, preceded by a vicious roar from me.

As the car sped my way, I reached the forest. I wildly dashed through the trees, trying to head for ones that were too close together for a vehicle to fit through. Once again grateful for my peculiar night vision, I darted through the trees even without the light of the moon. Ahead of me I could see a dense area of trees, combined with shrubbery. It wasn't a good place to hide, but maybe I could lose them in there.

I didn't dare glance behind me as I ran; the sounds were enough to tell me that I better not let them catch me. Necromarthe and the other demon were in furious pursuit, yelling curses and threats at me. I no longer heard the car, so it seemed like I had succeeded in forcing them to abandon their vehicles. I dared to hope that they couldn't see me, and that I was getting away.

Suddenly I felt myself falling. I tumbled and rolled down a steep hill, flailing my limbs in every which direction and hitting my head countless times. It felt like I fell forever. Finally, I came to a stop. I was dizzy beyond belief, and every part of me hurt. Hesitantly I sat up, afraid that I'd have several broken bones. To my surprise, everything felt intact. I sighed with relief, also thankful that I hadn't impaled myself on my machete. I looked around for it, but

I'd probably never find that thing. Shouts reached my ears, but they were in the distance. I scrambled from where I was on the ground and kept running, trying to fight off the dizziness.

In the darkness, I saw a log that seemed like a good hiding spot. I sunk to the ground and crawled under it, panting in the silence. My heart and lungs worked in overtime as I tried to catch my breath. Moments later, I held my breath as I listened for sounds. I heard shouts, but they were even further away now.

I waited there for a long time. It ended up being the entire night. Eventually I had fallen asleep, waking up when the first rays of dawn crept through the trees. With many grunts and groans, I crawled out from under the log. I had no idea where I was or what direction was north or south.

With a sigh, I stepped towards a tree and started climbing it. Painful limbs eventually carried me to the top, where I scanned the area around me. My eyes surveyed the surrounding area. To my right was the dreadful house where Necromarthe had kept me. The helicopter was still there. With a gulp, I kept looking around. When I looked to my left, I exhaled with joy. There was San Antonio, only a couple miles away.

Quickly, I scampered down the tree and jumped to the ground. I felt a pain in my ankle as I did so, but I didn't care. With renewed determination, I bolted towards the direction of the city. If those monsters thought they were going to find my dad before I did, they were dead wrong. They weren't going to use him for their demented rebuilding of the world, and they sure as hell weren't going to use me. Before I knew it, I reached the highway. I hurried down it, eager to meet my dad at the campground we'd decided to meet at.

When I got there, there was no sign of him. I frantically looked all around for any clues that he might have left, but there were none. I wanted to sink to the ground and despair, but I made myself carry on. I trudged closer to town, towards our secondary meeting spot. Our church was on the outskirts of the city, but I still worried about my lack of weapon. Surely I would run into too many changed things to make it there in one piece?

Miraculously, I was wrong. I brushed past a handful of chompers, but nothing I couldn't dodge. With the church in sight, I ran forward. My heart pounded as I approached it, desperately hoping he was in there. I thundered up the front steps and yanked the doors open. My eyes took a moment to adjust to the lighting. I squinted as I stepped into the building, trying to figure out what I was seeing. It looked like the pews were filled. Did our whole town survive the catastrophe?

I stumbled to the front of the church, where someone was standing. My dad! I ran towards him and threw my arms around him, but instantly recoiled. As I pulled away, Necromarthe's face came into view. I was hugging him, not my dad. With a cry, I wrenched myself away from him. That's when I realized the whole church was snarling.

I slowly turned around, aghast to see that everyone in the pews was a chomper. I fell to my knees in hopelessness. There was no way I was getting out of here without Necromarthe's say so.

He knelt down and put an arm around me, gesturing to the crowd with his other hand.

"Aren't they lovely?"

The doors suddenly burst open, and in two demons came, dragging a man with them. My dad.

"Dad!" I bellowed, jumping to my feet.

He tried to cry out as well, but his mouth was gagged. He fought and grunted, but his captors were strong. As they passed the pews, the chompers hungrily sniffed at him. Slowly, they started to stand. My heart nearly leapt from my chest as they shuffled from the pews and down the aisle, following the sweet scent of a living being.

As the men brought my dad to a stop in from of Necromarthe and me, the chompers gathered around them. They snarled violently, obviously ravenous for fresh flesh. Every time they tried to reach out to him, they recoiled from the presence of the demons. The evil beings were keeping him safe, for now.

Necromarthe turned to me with a sadistic smile. "Now, sweetheart," he cooed, walking around behind me and leaning his face over my shoulder. "I believe you were about to tell your dad why he wants to help us?"

I stared at the chompers in horror, darting my eyes from them to my dad. I had no idea what to do.

CHAPTER TWENTY

I had to save my dad at any cost.

Right?

Currently, that cost seemed to be convincing him to join evil beings in their quest to end the world. No big deal.

"Dad, these men need your help," I panted. My eyes darted worriedly to the chompers standing behind the evil soldiers. Only they stood between my dad and a horrific death.

"My help?" he asked knowingly, nodding slightly to me. I had told him days ago that I was running from people, and surely he had figured out these were the ones of which I had spoken.

"Yes," I replied, confirming both his spoken and unspoken question.

Nick—Necromarthe, rather—impatiently shifted his painful grip on me. I heard the faintest of growls rumbling in the depths of his throat, intended for my ears only. I knew he was warning me not to try anything. Of course I wouldn't; I wasn't that stupid. I'd wait until a better time.

"So how about it?" he asked my dad, not waiting for me to speak again.

My dad's eyes met his for the first time. Suddenly I saw my father start to tremble, which triggered a deep sadness within me. Fear lit up his eyes as he tried to back away from the monster. Unfortunately, all that was behind him were more demons and the savage undead.

"Dad, stop!" I called, but he wouldn't listen. Still he backpedaled, pushing himself past the demons and right into the hungry hands of the changed things. "Dad!" I shrieked, just as their skin met his.

Somehow I fought my way free of Necromarthe and grabbed my dad. At the same time, the evil people around us shoved the chompers back. They stumbled briefly, recovered, and then came at my dad again. This time though, they suddenly stopped. I glanced over my shoulder, seeing Necromarthe step towards the commotion.

"Enough," he said quietly, barely above a whisper. All the changed things froze in place, cowering and shifting their gazes to the ground.

Chills broke out all over my body.

Necromarthe looked up at my dad, who still trembled. "Bruce," he hissed like a serpent. "Your darling daughter has beseeched you for help. Surely you cannot deny her?"

With those words he grabbed my waist, pulling me closely to him. I grit my jaw, but kept my eyes on my dad.

"Please," I mouthed. "Come with me."

He stared at Necromarthe with all the hatred he possessed, occasionally darting his eyes to me, then the henchmen, then chompers, then back to the instigator of it all.

"Looks to me like I don't have much of a choice," he finally said.

"*Au contraire* my dear man," Necromarthe replied. "You can choose not to come with us, but it will be the end of your life. And your daughter's." He paused to dramatically kiss the top of my head. I recoiled and fought him, doing it more for my nerves than expecting him to stop.

He let out a disgusting chuckle that enraged me further,

but I ceased my struggle nonetheless.

"Anyway," he chuckled again, "Bruce, you are a smart man. You are also a very valuable man. Choosing to let yourself and your only offspring get torn about by the former living is a foolish thing to do."

My dad looked at me once more, to which I nodded. He looked back at Necromarthe and said simply, "Okay."

I felt hands grip my arm, and saw that the same was being done to Dad. The sidekicks were guiding us through the changed things, leading us out of the church. When we got to the street, they led us towards the forest. We all walked in silence for a while, eventually emerging into a field. I groaned when I saw our destination; that dreadful farm house.

Without meaning to, I turned to Necromarthe to complain.

"Save your words," he ordered coldly, showing none of the fake affection towards me that he had demonstrated in the church.

He marched on ahead of us, leading the way to the building. Once we arrived and were inside, they took my dad and me down the hallway. They shoved me towards the room I had formerly stayed in, and my dad towards another.

"No!" I yelled. "Let us stay in the same room!"

I fought them viciously, not wanting to be alone in that room again.

"Stop!" Necromarthe thundered, suddenly there with us. "Do you really expect us to put you together after you already escaped from here once?"

I saw my dad glance at me, pride twinkling in his eyes.

"I won't flee again," I panted, breathing heavily from my

struggles with his men.

"Damn right you won't," he hissed. "If you try—or I even think you tried—I will make you *pay*." He spat the last word at me, thoroughly removing any doubt from my mind that he would do just that.

"Okay," I nodded furiously. "I swear to it Necro—uh, Nick. We won't try to break free. We just want to be together."

He inhaled deeply, held it for a moment, then slowly exhaled. Turning to look at his men, he jerked his head towards my dad and the room he was next to. I was shoved that way, and next thing I knew, we were both inside. The door slammed shut, then several locks clicked into place.

My dad and I both cried out in a weary release of emotions. We threw our arms around one another, then fell to our knees. We sat on the floor, where I cried and he gently wrapped an arm around me. I apologized a hundred times for getting him into this mess, to all of which he insisted it wasn't my fault.

Eventually I stopped my tears and was able to wipe my eyes dry. As I emerged from my pity party, I glanced around the room. It was pretty dark; only two lightbulbs on each end of the room provided all the light. The window was boarded up, obviously to prevent escape. There was a simple nightstand with a basin atop, and a bed like the other room.

I looked at my dad, who also looked like he'd been crying although I hadn't heard it. I snuggled my head into the nook of his shoulder, taking comfort in being next to him.

"I'm so glad I found you," I breathed.

"As am I," he replied softly. "I was worried about you."

"No reason to be; you raised me to be as tough as you."

He laughed lightly, although it didn't sound as merry as it normally did.

"I love you Addie."

"I love you too Dad."

We sat there in silence, but several times I could tell he wanted to say something.

"What is it?" I asked, sitting up and leaning away so I could see his face.

"It's just… are you… are you the only one who made it?"

Pain struck my heart. I suddenly realized I'd have to tell him the horrible news. As my face wrinkled up in pain, he knew what the answer was.

"Oh Addie," he breathed, pulling me back into a hug. This time, the embrace was more for his comfort than mine. I felt a sob rock his body, then a strangled wail came out of his mouth.

"I'm not the only one," I groaned, "but Mom…" I couldn't finish the sentence.

For the second time within the hour, we both fell apart and let our sorrow run rampant. We sobbed together, our hearts breaking for the woman we had loved. It didn't matter to my dad that she had left him; that they hadn't worked out; that she wanted nothing to do with him. He still loved her. To me, her absence had never been more obvious than right then, sitting with my dad.

I grieved as though I had just learned of her death, like my dad. When it had actually happened, I hadn't had the time to mourn properly. Since then I'd had to constantly move on to the next survival situation. Now, in the relative safety of our location and the comfort of being together, I could give in to the sadness. I could recall the good times with her, the bad, of how she had shown up in my hotel at the start of this all, how she had been obnoxious at first but then developed into an incredible comrade. How we had grown closer after being distant for so many years. Then... then how she died. I groaned, sobbing harder.

Somehow I managed to blurt out how it had happened. My dad hadn't asked, but I figured he had to be wondering. I spared him having to inquire. He didn't say anything, but held me tighter. I knew he was trying to tell me it wasn't my fault, but I wasn't sure if I believed that.

Finally, after hours, we had cried ourselves dry and exhausted our ability to feel sadness. Numbness was setting in, allowing us to focus on the world around us once again. Sometime during our cry-fest, someone had apparently come in and brought us food. Although neither of us felt hungry, we knew we should eat. Dad grabbed the tray that had two plates and water bottles, then brought them to me on the floor. Neither of us wanted to sit on the bed, like the simple pleasure of being more comfortable was blasphemy during grieving.

We ate in silence, chewing the food we couldn't taste and drinking the water that we knew should have been refreshing. When we were done, my dad collected the plates, put them back on the tray, and put them by the door. As if they'd been waiting for that, someone walked in and then collected them. Then another person came in and pronounced that it was shower time. My dad volunteered to go first, to make sure it was what we thought and not a horrible trick. I lay on the hard floor and waited for him to come back.

When he returned looking clean and a tad refreshed, I

perked up a little. He nodded with a small smile, so I followed Necromarthe's man to the bathroom. It was tiny and quaint, but the shower was stocked with all kinds of delicious shampoos and soaps, and the water pressure was great. After scrubbing off grime, I stepped out of the shower and dried off, spotting fresh clothes on the counter.

I, too, came back to our room a little happier than when I'd left. There was more water waiting for me, which I eagerly drank. My dad was pacing the room, eyeing every inch of the ceiling, walls, and floor.

"We can't," I croaked. After reliving the pain of losing my mom, I didn't want to do anything that would risk losing him.

"And we won't," he assured me. "Just a habit to know what my options are."

I nodded, and we decided to try to get some sleep. It was probably only midday by now, but since we had no idea when they'd move us, getting some sleep seemed like a good idea. Dad made me take the bed, and he lay on the floor beside it on top of a spare blanket. For a while we lay in silence, thousands of thoughts coursing through our minds.

"I'm glad we're together Dad," I said, unable to fall asleep without expressing it.

"So am I Addie. So am I." I felt his hand on the side of the bed, so I rolled over and put mine in his.

"Dad… what do you know about him?"

I didn't need to use his name; my dad knew exactly who I was talking about.

He let out a long breath. "Whew Addie, that is a loaded question. The answer ruined my life. Made me lose your mom…"

"I know," I strained, barely able to hold back the tears. "You were right though. Everything you saw and tried telling us was true. I'm so sorry for what you went through."

"It's ok kid," he said, patting my hand. I could hear the pain in his voice.

"What did you see in Nordkapp?"

He snorted bitterly; not to me but to the memory.

"Strange and horrible things."

"Was he there?"

"Oh yes. Like he is now, he pretended he was an officer in some army. I suppose he is, just not the kind we all expected."

"How did you know it wasn't what it seemed?"

"Happenstance. Wrong place at the right time."

"Or right place at right time."

"Sure, if the end game was me losing everything that mattered to me."

"I'm sure God let it happen for a reason."

He snorted again. "What reason would that be? I didn't get to warn anyone, because they wouldn't listen. I lost my career, my wife… almost my kid."

"You didn't lose me though," I assured, squeezing his hand. "Sure, at times it was hard to believe your claims that evil beings were plotting to end the world. Despite that though, I loved you and trained with you. If you hadn't taught me the survival skills that you did, I don't know if I'd still be around. You helped Mel stay alive too."

"She's a good kid," he said with a smile in his voice. "At least I was able to help you two, or so you say."

"You did. I love you Dad."

He squeezed my hand, and I decided to let the conversation end. We were both tired, and there would probably be plenty of time to talk tomorrow. For now, all that mattered was that we were alive. Mel was out there somewhere with Mikael, so surely she was okay. I had accomplished my goal; I had found my dad.

What new horrors tomorrow would bring, I didn't know, but I did know my dad and I were together.

As I thought that, my free hand went to the necklace around my neck. I gently closed my fingers around the pendant, which felt cool on my skin. A small smile crept across my lips.

"Hey Addie?" my dad called.

"Yeah?" I asked, waking up as I rolled towards him again.

"Things are going to get a whole lot worse before they get better."

"What?" I gasped, leaning over to look at him. I recoiled slightly at the sight; he was dead asleep. I prodded him a couple times, but he didn't wake up.

Fearfully, I rolled onto my back. Try as I might, I couldn't get those words out of my mind. *Things are going to get a whole lot worse before they get better.*

EPILOGUE

Our door swung open, jolting us from our deepest sleep.

"On your feet!" soldiers thundered. Two of them pointed bright flashlights at us, dancing the beams across our sensitive eyes.

"All right, all right!" my dad griped as we staggered to our feet.

We didn't get a chance to change clothes or grab anything before they swept us from the room. They pushed us towards the front of the house, and along the way I saw that no light was coming in through the windows. It felt like it was a few hours before dawn.

"Hurry up!" they bellowed.

I moved faster, surprised by the urgency.

Just beyond the house I could hear something rumbling. As we got to the front door, I realized it was a helicopter. We were being moved.

I glanced over at my dad, making sure he was being taken the same way I was. Thankfully that was the case.

"Let's go!" another man barked. "He's almost here!"

"Who? Nick?" I asked, but of course he didn't answer me. It was almost if he had shouted that purely for his own nerves. Why would he care if Nick was almost here? Hadn't he been here earlier?

Once we were outside, it was about fifty feet to the helicopter. Although I knew I should comply, something about the situation was freaking me out. Everything inside of me wanted to fight my way out this. I looked at my dad again, willing myself to calm down. That didn't seem to work. There was something else inside me, screaming and raging. It wanted to fight.

Suddenly pain shot through my whole body. I screamed and fell to my knees, thinking I'd been shot. When I glanced down though, I saw the truth. My veins were black.

Shock made me freeze, allowing evil men to grab me and hold me in place. I screamed and thrashed, somehow throwing them aside like they were ragdolls. I bellowed out a ferocious cry and jumped to my feet, looking to my dad.

"Come on!" I yelled, thinking we could escape.

My dad wasn't moving, though. He was staring at me in horror. Why?

"Dad what's wrong?" I cried, gripping his arm to make him move.

"You!" he cried. "You're not my daughter! I knew it! They tricked me!"

"Dad it's me!" I urged, but more men were coming my way.

"You're one of them!" he shouted, leaping at one of the guards and grabbing his knife. In the next instant, he was thrashing at me.

"Dad, stop!" I pleaded, barely avoiding his swings and jabs. "It's me, Addie!"

"You're a demon!" he screamed, this time slicing a gash in my arm.

"Ahhh!" I cried, recoiling from the pain.

Then Nick was there. He landed a roundhouse kick on my dad, momentarily stunning him. In the next instant, he had recovered and was lunging at Nick. More men showed up, trying to restrain him. It took four of them to get him under control.

Nick scooped me off the ground and turned towards the helicopter. He paused by my dad, who was eyeing us.

"Sir, we need to go," one of the guards insisted.

Nick nodded, continuing to glare at my dad. The sedative had weakened him, but he was still awake. I looked down at him sadly, hoping this wouldn't permanently separate us. I stifled a sob as I saw the fear in his eyes. I clung to Nick as my strength left me; my blood was gushing all over him.

"You're one of them," my dad whispered. I couldn't hear him over the helicopter, but I could read his lips. A pang of sorrow hit my heart.

"Don't you ever attempt anything like that again," Nick's voice boomed, easily heard over the noise of the blades. "Eve is *mine*." He clutched my bruised and bleeding body closer to him, in which I found a sickening comfort.

"Sir!!!" a man bellowed, suddenly firing his gun at something out of sight.

The world dimmed around me, and I wasn't sure if it was real or if I was passing out. Judging by how the soldiers reacted, it was real.

Nick quickly moved to the helicopter as I saw a couple men hoist my dad off the ground. Suddenly the ground shook, making me weakly recoil in fear. Our helicopter took off moments later, allowing me a sigh of relief.

"He's here," Necromarthe whispered, instantly bringing back all my anxiety.

"Who?" I questioned, but he ignored me. Could he be referring to Mikael? Or even better, the one whom the archangel served? No, surely I'd be filled with exultation if his presence was nearby. Instead I felt darkness.

I gulped and looked up at Nick's grim countenance. How awful was this darkness that even Nick feared it?

"Who is he?" I repeated, hoping he would answer me.

Again he didn't seem to hear the question. He stared fearfully at something below us and whispered, "He can't have her. He can't harm her. It would bring him too much pleasure and take too much from me. He can't have Eve."

LET THERE BE

WAR

BOOK 2: FIRE AND FURY

COMING SOON

SAMANTHA EKLUND

GOLDEN MASQUERADE | BOOKS

FREE LOOT

Learn more about your five favorite (or most hated) characters by going to Samantha's site!

Download character cards to see what they look like, learn more about them, and discover their favorite things:

When you download them, you'll also be entered to WIN free merch PLUS a FREE signed copy of this book!

CAN YOU HELP?

Thank you for reading *War!*

What did you think of it? I greatly appreciate your feedback and love hearing your opinion.

Believe it or not, I use your input to make the next version of this book and my future books even better.

Please leave me an honest review on Amazon, Barnes and Noble, and Goodreads letting me know what you thought of *War*.

If you choose to leave a review on those three sites, I can't thank you enough. Thank you so much in advance!

~Samantha

ABOUT THE AUTHOR

Samantha Eklund is an author who envisions a better future for fellow creatives. She loves to understand and encourage others and happens to be unwaveringly determined in everything she does.

In college, she majored in Religious Studies. Her sporadic job choices since then have ranged from finance, marketing and graphic design, all the way to human resources (no, not the annoying kind).

To her surprise and delight, she has been described as a generous and badass dreamer (among other things). When she's not writing, she's riding. Her street bike, dirt bike, horses, boats… anything that can get the adrenaline going.

Want to get the full story on Samantha, including backstage access to little-known facts about her and what she's working on next? Visit her at SamanthaEklund.com!

If you loved this book, try the others by Samantha Eklund!

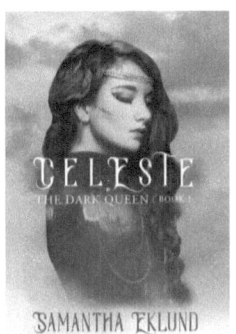

CELESTE
(THE DARK QUEEN, #1)

Celeste, the wise and beautiful queen of Vehrys, has been betrayed.

On the night of her 26th birthday, the man who had loved her since their shared childhood poisoned her, stabbed her, and then left her for dead.

Since then, the sun hasn't risen in their land. Since then, bloodthirsty and abhorrent beasts have roamed the earth and slain her innocent people.

Kiev, her traitorous husband, is the son of her neighboring kingdom's vile queen. For years the two kingdoms had been at war, until hers and his marriage. Celeste had never doubted the substance of his love, until now.

The fair queen finds herself caught in a battle between light and dark; the purest of good and most dreadful of evil.

As she battles for survival, she also fends to maintain her sanity in the terrifying and dark new world. Hope for her husband dwindles more with each passing day, but the faint spark of unexpected new love drives her to keep fighting for her kingdom.

With her recently discovered magic and the aid of an ancient deity, she must attempt to rid her land of the terrifying abominations stalking its people. Can she do so before her former love destroys her new one? More importantly, can she rid the world of this suffocating darkness before the evil causing it overtakes her soul?

Get it on online now!